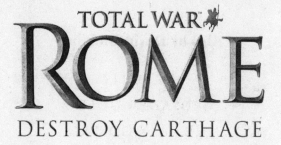

TOTAL WAR
ROME

DESTROY CARTHAGE

Also by David Gibbins

ATLANTIS

CRUSADER GOLD

THE LAST GOSPEL

THE TIGER WARRIOR

THE MASK OF TROY

THE GODS OF ATLANTIS

PHARAOH

TOTAL WAR™
ROME
DESTROY CARTHAGE

DAVID GIBBINS

THOMAS DUNNE BOOKS
St. Martin's Griffin ✹ New York

This is a work of fiction. All of the characters, organizations, and events portrayed in this novel are either products of the author's imagination or are used fictitiously.

THOMAS DUNNE BOOKS.
An imprint of St. Martin's Press.

TOTAL WAR ROME: DESTROY CARTHAGE. Copyright © 2013 by David Gibbins.
All rights reserved. Printed in the United States of America. For information, address
St. Martin's Press, 175 Fifth Avenue, New York, N.Y. 10010.

www.thomasdunnebooks.com
www.stmartins.com

The Library of Congress has cataloged the hardcover edition as follows:

Gibbins, David J. L.
    Total war Rome : destroy Carthage / David Gibbins.—1st U.S. ed.
        p. cm.
    ISBN 978-1-250-03864-7 (hardcover)
    ISBN 978-1-250-03865-4 (e-book)
1. FICTION / Historical. 2. FICTION / Action & Adventure. 3. FICTION / Media Tie-In.
I. Title.
    PR6107.I225T68 2013
    823'.92—dc23

                                                            2013020413

ISBN 978-1-250-05485-2 (trade paperback)

St. Martin's Griffin books may be purchased for educational, business, or promotional use.
For information on bulk purchases, please contact Macmillan Corporate and Premium Sales
Department at 1-800-221-7945, extension 5442, or write specialmarkets@macmillan.com.

First published in the UK by Macmillan, an imprint of Pan Macmillan,
a division of Macmillan Publishers Limited

First St. Martin's Griffin Edition: November 2014

10   9   8   7   6   5   4   3   2   1

Acknowledgements

I am very grateful to my agent, Luigi Bonomi of LBA, and to Rob Bartholomew of The Creative Assembly for having set this project in motion; to Jeremy Trevathan, Catherine Richards and the team at Macmillan for their work in getting this book into production, as well as to Peter Wolverton and Anne Brewer at St Martin's Press in New York; and to the team at The Creative Assembly and at Sega® for all of their support and input. I owe special thanks to Martin Fletcher for his excellent editorial work, to Jessica Cuthbert-Smith for her excellent copyediting and to Ann Verrinder for proofreading and scrutinizing the manuscript at every stage and giving much useful advice.

I am grateful to Brian Warmington, Emeritus Reader in Ancient History at the University of Bristol and author of *Carthage* (Penguin, 1964), for having taught me Republican Roman history in such a memorable fashion and for having encouraged my interest in the Punic Wars. My involvement with the archaeology of Carthage owes much to Henry Hurst, my doctoral supervisor at Cambridge and director of the British Mission in the UNESCO 'Save Carthage' project, who invited me to join his excavation at the harbour entrance and supported my own underwater archaeology expedition to Carthage the following year. That project was made possible by the British Academy, the Cambridge University Classics Faculty, the Canadian Social Sciences and Humanities Research Council and Dr Abdelmajid Ennabli, director of the Carthage Museum; I am also grateful to the many expedition members for their work on those projects.

I first studied the battlefield of Pydna and the sculpture from the monument of Aemilius Paullus on travels in Greece funded by the

Acknowledgements

Society of Antiquaries of London. My knowledge of ancient naval warfare was greatly expanded during my tenure of a Winston Churchill Memorial Travel Fellowship in the east Mediterranean, when I was able to spend time in Haifa, Israel, and study the Athlit Ram – the only surviving ram from an ancient warship – and then in Greece to examine the trireme *Olympias*. My interest in ancient Rome developed over many visits to explore the archaeology of the city, most memorably with my father, when we discussed the possibility of pinpointing remains from a particular date and creating a book out of it; that led me to trace the likely route of the triumphal procession of Aemilius Paullus in 167 BC, and to study structures still extant among the ruins of the Forum and elsewhere in Rome dating from that period. I am also grateful to my brother Alan for his photography and film-making, and to Jordan Webber for her help with my website www.davidgibbins.com.

This book is dedicated with much love to my daughter Molly.

Introductory Note

In the second century BC Rome was still a republic, ruled by wealthy patricians whose families traced their ancestry back to the first years of the city some six hundred years earlier. The republic had been formed when the last king of Rome was ousted in 509 BC, and it was to survive until the establishment of the empire under Augustus towards the end of the first century BC. The main administrative body was the Senate, led by two annually elected consuls. Outside the Senate were twelve elected tribunes, representatives of the common people (the *plebs*), who had power of veto over the Senate. The complex alliances and rivalries between the patrician families (the *gentes*, singular *gens*), as well as between the patricians and the plebs, are crucial to understanding the history of Rome at this period, at a time when overseas conquest gave a tempting vision of personal power to generals that eventually led to civil war in the first century BC and to Octavian proclaiming himself Augustus. Why the establishment of an empire should not have happened more than a century earlier, when Rome's armies stood supreme and its most outstanding general, Scipio Aemilianus Africanus, had the world at his feet, is one of the most fascinating questions of ancient history and the backdrop to the story in this novel.

The Roman army at this date was not yet a professional force; legions were called up from among the citizens of Rome in response to particular crises. The army would only take on a professional guise during times of protracted war, when the advantages of keeping a standing army would have become apparent. Throughout the second century BC, the period of this novel, a tension existed between those who feared that the development of a professional army could lead to military dictatorship, and those who saw it as a necessity if

Rome were to hold its own on the world stage. Eventually, the latter won out, leading to the army reforms of the consul Marius in 107 BC and the establishment of the first permanent legions.

At the time of this novel, the familiar legion titles of the imperial period, such as 'Legio XX Valeria Victrix', did not yet exist; legions raised for particular campaigns and disbanded afterwards might have a number, but would not carry forward their identity. The main formation within a legion was the *maniple*, a unit discarded by Marius in favour of the smaller *cohort*. The maniple might be equated with the 'wing' of a Victorian British regiment, a formation about half the size of a modern infantry battalion that was faster to deploy and more manoeuvrable in battle. The main unit within the maniple was the *century*, roughly equivalent to a modern infantry company. Traditionally, the men within a legion were classed by wealth and age, from the poorest *velites* (skirmishers) through the *hastati* and *principes* to the wealthiest *triarii*, with each category corresponding to increasing quality of armour and equipment, as well as to positions in the line of battle that were generally more exposed and dangerous for the poorer and more lightly equipped troops.

Centuries were commanded by *centurions* – men who had risen through the ranks based on ability and experience. They held responsibility similar to that of a modern-day infantry captain, but are best seen as non-commissioned officers. The *primipilus* ('of the first file') was the senior centurion in a legion, the equivalent of a regimental sergeant-major. Another common rank was *optio*, a subordinate rank to centurion with responsibility similar to that of a lieutenant but best seen as a sergeant or corporal. A wide social gulf existed between these men and the more senior officers in the legion, who came from patrician families for whom military appointments were part of the *cursus honorum* (the 'course of offices'), the sequence of military and civil offices that a wealthy Roman male would hope to hold through his lifetime. The middle-ranking officers of a legion were the military *tribunes*, young men at the start of their careers or older men who had volunteered in time of crisis to serve in the army but were not yet at the stage in the *cursus honorum* where they could command a legion. That role went to the *legatus*, the equivalent of a colonel or brigadier, who might command several thousand men in the field, including attached cavalry and allied forces.

There was no rank of general, because armies were commanded by a *praetor*, the second highest civil rank in Rome, or by one of the consuls. The competence of an army commander was therefore a matter of chance, as military prowess was not necessarily a prerequisite for the highest civil office; the ability of an army commander might depend on whether there had been opportunities for active service earlier during his career. However, with war in the offing, a man might be elected to the consulship on the basis of his military reputation, and the law restricting the repeat holding of office temporarily overturned to allow the re-election of a man who had proved to be an able general.

This system worked well enough to allow Rome her military successes in the second century BC, but veterans would have been acutely aware of its deficiencies, including the absence of formal schooling in war for young men before they were appointed tribune and sent into the field. Equally pressing was the lack of continuity among the legionaries, as they were discharged after campaigns and much accumulated knowledge was lost in the intervals between wars. When the call to arms came again, men might go not so much for professional pride or for the glory of war but for the chance of booty, an increasing attraction with the wars of conquest in Greece and the east bringing much visible wealth into Rome at this period.

At the time of this novel, Rome was engaged in two great wars of conquest: one against the kingdoms in Macedonia and Greece that had grown out of Alexander the Great's empire, and the other against the North African people whom the Romans called 'Punic', their term for the descendants of Phoenician seafarers from the area of modern Lebanon who had established the city of Carthage some seven hundred years before. Rome fought three wars against Carthage, in 264–261 BC, 218–201 BC and 149–146 BC, progressively taking Carthaginian overseas territories in Sardinia and Sicily and Spain until Carthage was left with little more than her hinterland in modern Tunisia, hemmed in by Rome's Numidian allies. The Second Punic War, when the Carthaginian general Hannibal marched with his elephants through Spain and over the Alps towards Rome, is perhaps the most famous of these campaigns, yet because it left Carthage intact was really only the stage-setting for one of the most devastating events in ancient history some fifty years later when Rome finally made the decision to destroy her enemy altogether.

By the time of the final assault on the city in 146 BC and on Corinth in Greece in the same year, Rome was poised for domination of the ancient world, held back only by a constitution that had been designed to manage a city-state and not an empire. For the modern war-gamer this period is one of the most fascinating in antiquity, a time when small changes could have altered the course of history, and when all of the factors of campaigning come vividly into play: the political backdrop, rivalries and alliances among the patrician *gentes* of Rome, problems of supply and maintenance of overseas armies, evolving battle tactics on land and at sea, and above all the personalities and ambitions of some of the most powerful individuals in history, in a period that is only imperfectly known from the ancient sources and therefore leaves much open to speculation and gameplay.

The story of the Punic Wars has huge resonance today, with some lessons that have been learned well, others less so. The decision to leave Carthage intact at the end of the Second Punic War can be compared with the decision by the Allies not to conquer Germany and instead accept an armistice at the end of the First World War, or the decision by the US-led coalition to stop short of the invasion of Iraq at the end of the Gulf War in 1991; in both cases the decision to hold back led to far more costly and devastating war years later. Archaeology has revealed that despite the defeat of

Hannibal, Carthage rebuilt her war harbour unhindered by Rome, just as the Allies stood by while Hitler rebuilt the German navy and air force in the 1930s. In many ways, the Punic Wars were the first true world war, the first 'total' war, encompassing more than half the ancient world and with repercussions far beyond the west Mediterranean. Just like the world wars of the last century or the present global war against terrorism, the main lesson of history is perhaps that war on that scale leaves little room for concession or appeasement. Total war means just that: total war.

Distances

The basic unit of Roman linear measurement was the foot (*pes*), divided into twelve inches (*unciae*), roughly similar to the units we use today. For longer distances they used the mile (*milliarum*), a distance of 5,000 *pedes*, so just over nine-tenths of a modern mile or about one and a half kilometres. An intermediate unit of Greek origin was the *stadium* (plural *stadiae*, derived from the Greek *stadion*, a racing track), about 600 *pedes*, so a little under an eighth of a mile or a fifth of a kilometre. In translation it is common to use the Anglicized *stade* and *stades*, as in this novel.

Dates

The Romans dated years *ab urbe condita*, 'from the founding of the city' in 753 BC, but more commonly used the 'consular year', naming the two consuls in office at any one time. Because the consuls changed annually and in theory no two men could hold the office twice, the consular date gave a unique year. It was often necessary to spell out the full names because of the dominance through the Republican period of men from a small number of *gentes* such as the Scipiones, so it might not be enough to say 'in the consulship of Scipio and Metellus'; the full names would have to be given.

Gens

The *gens* (plural *gentes*) was the family of a patrician Roman. A person might be from an established branch of a *gens*, so that, for example, Scipio Africanus was from the Scipiones branch of the *gens* Cornelii, and Sextus Julius Caesar from the Caesares branch of the *gens* Julii. The *gentes* can be compared with the aristocratic families of Europe in recent centuries, although for the Roman *gens* behaviour was even more formalized and restrictive – governing, for example, marriage as well as rights and privileges. Most of the main players of the Roman Republic came from a small number of *gentes*, so that names such as Julius Caesar and Brutus that have such historical resonance for the Civil War period crop up frequently in preceding generations, often with similar prominence and fame.

Names

Romans could be known among friends by their *praenomen* (first name), just as we are today, though they could be also known by their other names, in the case of Scipio his *cognomen* (third name), which was a common usage among aristocrats. The *cognomen* was the branch of the family (*gens*) that was revealed in the second name; thus the Scipio of this novel, Publius Cornelius Scipio, was from the Scipiones branch of the *gens* Cornelii. The Cornelii Scipiones were not the *gens* into which he had been born, as he had been adopted by the son of the famous elder Scipio, Publius Cornelius Scipio Africanus, when he was a small child: however, following custom, the younger Scipio also retained the *gens* name of his real father, Lucius Aemilius Paullus Macedonicus. Just as Aemilius Paullus had been awarded the *agnomen* Macedonicus for his triumph over the Macedonians at Pydna in 168 BC, so the younger Scipio's full name in 146 BC, Publius Cornelius Scipio Aemilianus Africanus, included the *agnomen* Africanus inherited from his adoptive grandfather after he had been awarded it following the Battle of Zama in 202 BC. The burden of expectation that this name put on Scipio as a young man, and his efforts to earn it in his own right, form an underlying theme of this novel.

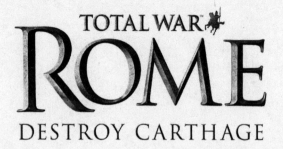

TOTAL WAR

ROME

DESTROY CARTHAGE

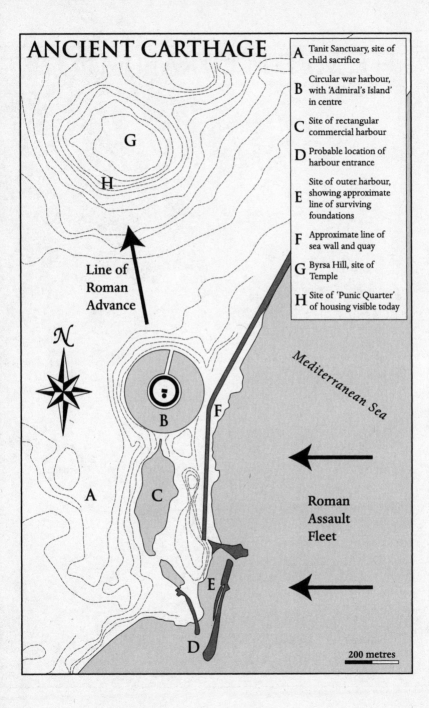

ANCIENT CARTHAGE

A — Tanit Sanctuary, site of child sacrifice

B — Circular war harbour, with 'Admiral's Island' in centre

C — Site of rectangular commercial harbour

D — Probable location of harbour entrance

E — Site of outer harbour, showing approximate line of surviving foundations

F — Approximate line of sea wall and quay

G — Byrsa Hill, site of Temple

H — Site of 'Punic Quarter' of housing visible today

Mediterranean Sea

Line of Roman Advance

Roman Assault Fleet

N

200 metres

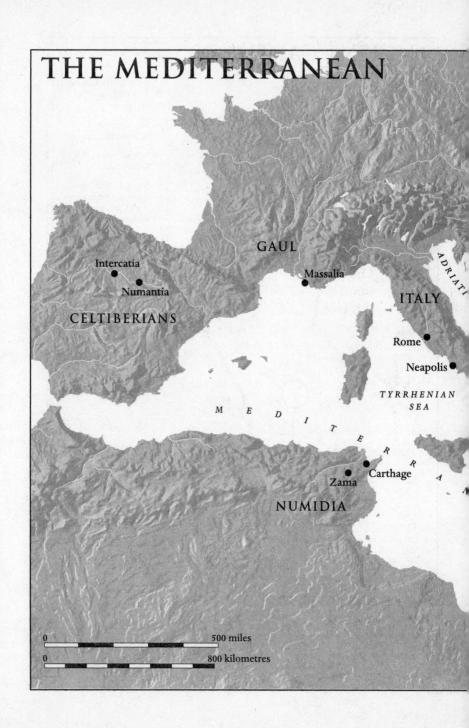

THE MEDITERRANEAN

GAUL

Intercatia

Massalia

Numantia

ITALY

CELTIBERIANS

Rome

Neapolis

ADRIATI

TYRRHENIAN
SEA

M E D I T E R R A N

Carthage

Zama

NUMIDIA

0   500 miles

0   800 kilometres

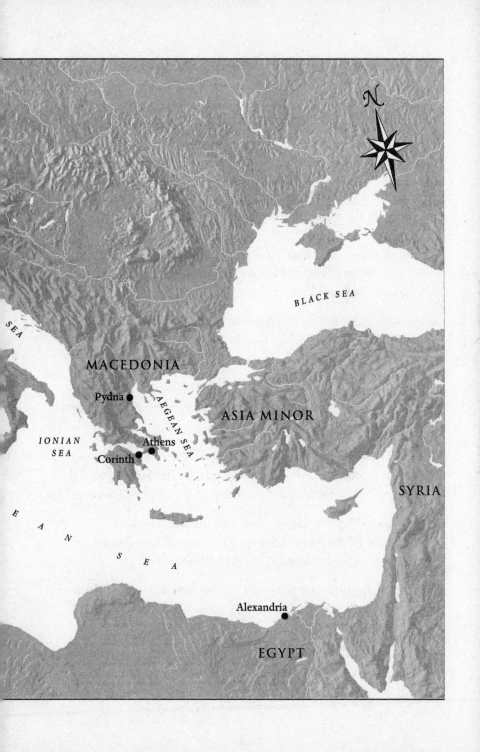

Characters

The following are historical characters unless they are noted as fictional; the biographical notes go up to 146 BC. The names are those used in the novel, followed by their full name where known.

Aemilius Paullus – Lucius Aemilius Paullus Macedonicus (c. 229–160 BC), father of Scipio and distinguished general who defeated the Macedonians at the Battle of Pydna in 168 BC.

Andriscus – Ruler of Adramyttium in Asia Minor who claimed to be the son of Perseus, was briefly self-appointed king in Macedonia and was defeated by the Romans under Metellus at the second Battle of Pydna in 148 BC.

Brasis – Fictional gladiator, a former Thracian mercenary captured in Macedonia.

Brutus – Decimus Junius Brutus, a fictional son of the historical Marcus Junius Brutus, of the *gens* Junia; a friend of Scipio and commander of the Praetorian Guard at the siege of Carthage.

Cato – Marcus Porcius Cato (c. 238–149 BC), famous elder statesman of the Roman Senate who repeatedly called for Carthage to be destroyed, '*Carthago delenda est*'.

Claudia Pulchridina – Of the *gens* Claudia, fictional wife of Scipio by arranged marriage; her name means 'beautiful'.

Demetrius – Demetrius I, later named Soter ('Saviour'); contemporary of Scipio Aemilianus, a scion of the Seleucid dynasty held hostage in Rome during his youth. He became king of Syria from 161 BC.

Ennius – Ennius Aquilius Tuscus, a fictional scion of the original Etruscan branch (the Tuscii) of the *gens* Aquilia; a close friend of Scipio and commander of the *fabri*, the army engineers.

Eudoxia – Fictional British slave girl and friend of Fabius.

Fabius – Fabius Petronius Secundus, a fictional legionary from Rome who is the bodyguard and friend of Scipio in the novel.

Gaius Paullus – Gaius Aemilius Paullus, fictional cousin of Scipio on his father's side.

Gnaeus – Gnaeus Metellus Julius Caesar, of the *gens* Metelli. Fictional son of Metellus and Julia whose true paternity is revealed in the novel; present as a tribune at the siege of Carthage.

Gulussa – Second son of Masinissa, sent by his father to Rome in 172 BC to present the Numidian case against Carthage; on Masinissa's death Scipio made him commander of the Numidian forces, which he led in the siege of Carthage.

Hasdrubal – General who defended Carthage in 146 BC; the fate of his wife and children is described by the historian Appian.

Hippolyta – Fictional Scythian princess who joins the academy in Rome and later leads the Numidian cavalry alongside Gulussa in North Africa.

Julia – Fictional daughter of the historical Sextus Julius Caesar, from the Caesares branch of the *gens* Julia; friend and lover of Scipio, but betrothed to Metellus.

Masinissa – (*c.* 240–148 BC) Long-lived first king of Numidia in North Africa, foe and then ally of Rome during the Second Punic War (218–201 BC) whose conflict with Carthage over disputed territory led to the Third Punic War (149–146 BC).

Metellus – Quintus Caecilius Metellus Macedonicus (born *c.* 210 BC), praetor in Macedonia in 148 BC who defeated the upstart Andriscus and then went on to serve under Mummius in the siege of Corinth in 146 BC; in the novel he is the rival and enemy of Scipio, and husband of Julia.

Perseus – Last king of the Antigonid dynasty in Macedonia, defeated by Aemilius Paullus at the Battle of Pydna in 148 BC.

Petraeus – Gnaeus Petraeus Atinus, fictional 'old centurion' who trains the boys in the academy at Rome.

Petronius – Fictional tavern-keeper near the Gladiator School in Rome.

Polybius – (born *c.* 200 BC) Greek cavalry commander and historian, famous for his *Histories*, who became a close friend and adviser to Scipio; present at the siege of Carthage.

Porcus – Porcus Entestius Supinus, fictional servant and adviser to Metellus.

Ptolemy – Ptolemy VI Philometor ('mother-lover'), a contemporary of Scipio Aemilianus and scion of the Ptolemy dynasty who became king in Egypt in 180 BC, marrying his sister Cleopatra II.

Quintus Appius Probus – Fictional centurion at Intercatia in Spain.

Rufius – Fabius' hunting dog, present with him and Scipio in the Macedonian Royal Forest.

Scipio – Publius Cornelius Scipio Aemilianus Africanus, the 'Younger' Scipio (born *c.* 185 BC), second son of Aemilius Paullus and adoptive grandson of Scipio Africanus; what is known of his historical career up to 146 BC forms the framework for the novel.

Scipio Africanus – Publius Cornelius Scipio Africanus, the 'Elder' Scipio (*c.* 236–183 BC), of the Scipiones branch of the *gens* Cornelia, outstanding Roman general of the Second Punic War who defeated Hannibal at the Battle of Zama in North Africa in 202 BC.

Sextius Calvinus – Gaius Sextius Calvinus, a senator who is an enemy of Scipio; of the Calvini branch of the *gens* Sextii, father of a man of the same name who was consul in 124 BC.

Terence – Publius Terentius Afer (*c.* 190–159 BC), playwright of North African origin (hence his *cognomen* Afer, from Afri), brought from Carthage to Rome as a slave by the senator Terentius Lucanus (hence his *nomen* Terentius, adopted on being given his freedom); one of Scipio's literary circle in Rome.

PROLOGUE

On the plain of Pydna, Macedonia, 168 BC

Fabius Petronius Secundus picked up his legionary standard and stared out over the wide expanse of the plain towards the sea. Behind him lay the foothills where the army had camped the night before, and behind that the slopes that led up to Mount Olympus, abode of the gods. He and Scipio had made the ascent three days previously, vying with each other to be the first to the top, flushed with excitement at the prospect of their first experience of battle. From the snow-covered summit they had looked north across the wide expanse of Macedonia, once the homeland of Alexander the Great, and below them they had seen where Alexander's successor Perseus had brought his fleet and deployed his army in readiness for a decisive confrontation with Rome. Up there, with the glare of the sun off the snow so bright that it had nearly blinded them, with the clouds racing below, they had indeed felt like gods, as if the might of Rome that had brought them so far from Italy was now unassailable, and nothing could stand in the way of further conquest.

Back down here after a damp and sleepless night the peak of Olympus seemed a world away. Arranged in front of them was the Macedonian phalanx, more than forty thousand strong, a huge line bristling with spears that seemed to extend across the entire breadth of the plain. He could see the Thracians, their tunics black under shining breastplates, their greaves flashing on their legs and their great iron swords held flat over their right shoulders. In the centre of the phalanx were the Macedonians themselves, with gilt armour and scarlet tunics, their long *sarissa*

1

spears black and shining in the sunlight, held so close together that they blocked out the view behind. Fabius glanced along their own lines: two legions in the middle, Italian and Greek allies on either side of that, and on the flanks the cavalry, with twenty-two elephants stomping and bellowing on the far right. It was a formidable force, battle-hardened after Aemilius Paullus' long campaigns in Macedonia, with only the new draft of legionaries and junior officers yet to see action. But it was smaller than the Macedonian army, and its cavalry were far fewer. They would have a tough fight ahead.

The night before, there had been an eclipse of the moon, an event that had excited the soothsayers who followed the army, signalling a good omen for Rome and a bad one for the enemy. Aemilius Paullus had been sensitive enough to the superstitions of his soldiery to order his standard-bearers to raise firebrands for the return of the moon, and to sacrifice eleven heifers to Hercules. But, while he had sat in his headquarters tent eating the meat from the sacrifice, the talk had not been of omens but of battle tactics and the day ahead. They had all been there, the junior tribunes who had been invited to share the meat of sacrifice on the eve of their first experience of battle: Scipio Aemilianus, Paullus' son and Fabius' companion and master; Ennius, a papyrus scroll with him as always, ready to jot down new ideas for siege engines and catapults; and Brutus, who had already fought wrestling matches with the best of the legionaries and was itching to lead his maniple into action. With them was Polybius, a former Greek cavalry commander who had the ear of Paullus and was close to Scipio – a friendship that had been forged in the months since Polybius had been brought as a captive to Rome and been appointed as an instructor to the young men, even teaching Fabius himself how to speak Greek and some of the wonders of science and geography.

That evening, Fabius had stood behind Scipio, listening keenly as he always did. Scipio had argued that the Macedonian phalanx was outmoded, a tactic from the past that was over-reliant on the spear and left the men vulnerable if an enemy got within them. Polybius had agreed, adding that the exposed flanks of the phalanx were its main weakness, but he had said that theory was one thing and seeing a phalanx in front of you was another: even the strongest enemy would baulk at the sight, and the phalanx had never been defeated before on level ground. Their chief hope was to shake the phalanx out of its formation, to create a weakness in its line. From his vantage point now, looking across at the reality, Fabius was inclined to side with Polybius. No Roman legionary would ever show it, but the phalanx was a terrifying sight and many of the men along the line girding themselves for battle must have felt as Fabius did, his breathing tight and a small flutter of fear in his stomach.

He looked at Scipio now, resplendent in the armour left to him by his adoptive grandfather Scipio Africanus, legendary conqueror of Hannibal the Carthaginian at the Battle of Zama thirty-four years before. He was the younger son of Aemilius Paullus, only seventeen years old, a year younger than Fabius, and this would be their first blooding in combat. The general stood among his staff officers and standard-bearers a few paces to the left, with Polybius among them. As a former *hipparchus* of the Greek cavalry, experienced in Macedonian tactics, Polybius was accorded a special place among the general's staff, and Fabius knew he would be wasting no time telling Aemilius Paullus how he should run the battle.

The pendant on top of the standard fluttered in the breeze, and Fabius looked up at the bronze boar, symbol of the first legion. He gripped his standard tightly, and remembered what he had been taught by the old centurion Petraeus, the grizzled veteran who had also trained Scipio and the other new tribunes who were preparing for battle today. *Your first responsibility is to your standard*, he had growled. As standard-bearer of the first cohort of the first legion he was the most visible legionary in his unit, the one who provided a rallying point. *Your standard must only fall if you fall.* Secondly, he was to fight as a legionary, to close with the enemy and to kill. Thirdly, he was to look after Scipio Aemilianus. The old centurion had pulled him close before he had seen them off on the ship at Brundisium for the crossing to Greece. *Scipio is the future*, the centurion had growled. *He is your future, and he is the future I have spent my life working for. He is the future of Rome. Keep him alive at all costs.* Fabius had nodded; he knew it already. He had been watching out for Scipio ever since he had entered his household as a boy servant. But out here, in front of the phalanx, his promise seemed less assured. He knew that if Scipio survived the initial clash with the Macedonians he would go far ahead, fighting on his own, and that it would be the skills in combat and swordplay taught by the centurion that would keep him alive, not Fabius running after him and watching his back.

He gazed up at the sky, squinting. It was a hot June day, and he was parched. They were facing east, and Aemilius Paullus had wanted to wait until it was late enough in the day for the sun to be over them, not in the eyes of his troops. But up here on the ridge they were away from a good water supply, with the river Leucos behind enemy lines in the valley below. Perseus would have understood this as he ordered his phalanx to advance slowly through the day, knowing that the Romans would be tormented by thirst, waiting until his own troops did not have the sun in their eyes after it had passed over the mountains to the west.

Fabius stared at the spider in the long grass that he had been watching earlier to calm his mind, to keep his nerves for the coming battle. It was large, as wide as the palm of his hand, poised on its threads between the few yellow stalks of corn stubble that had not yet been trodden down by the soldiers. It seemed inconceivable that such a large spider should hang by such delicate threads on two stalks of corn, yet he knew that the threads had great strength and the stalks were dried and hardened by the summer sun, making the stubble so rigid that it grazed the unprotected parts of their legs. Then he saw something, and knelt down, watching carefully. Something was different.

The web was shaking. *The whole ground was shaking.*

He stood up. 'Scipio,' he said urgently. 'The phalanx is moving. I can feel it.'

Scipio nodded, and went over to his father. Fabius followed, careful to keep his standard high, and stood outside the group, listening while Polybius engaged the other staff officers in a heated discussion. 'We must not engage the phalanx frontally,' he said. 'Their spears are too close together, and are designed to pierce the attackers' shields and hold them fast. Once the attackers are without shields, then the second line of the phalanx will dart out and cut them down. But the strength of the phalanx is also its weakness. The *sarissa* spears are heavy and unwieldy and difficult to swivel in unison. Get among them when they are still massed together, and they are yours. The short Greek swords are no match for the longer Roman *gladius*.'

Aemilius Paullus squinted at the phalanx, shading his eyes. 'That's why our cavalry are on either wing, with the elephants. Once the phalanx begins its final assault, I will order them to charge and outflank it.'

Polybius shook his head vehemently. 'I advise against it. The Macedonian spearmen on the flanks will be ready for that. You need to go for the middle of the line, to break it up in several places, to create gaps and exposed flanks where it's difficult for them to manoeuvre. Infantry alone can't do that by frontal assault, as they'll be stopped by the spears. You need to use your elephants, several of them together in four or five places a few hundred paces apart. The elephants have frontal armour and even if they're pierced they'll carry on for many paces with the momentum of their huge weight and smash through the line before they fall. If the legionaries follow closely behind, they will pour through the gaps and create four or five separate assaults, eating away at the exposed flanks. The phalanx will collapse.'

Aemilius Paullus shook his head. 'It's too late for that. The elephants are mustered in one squadron on the right flank, and that's where they'll attack. They have strength in numbers, and a massed elephant charge will terrorize the enemy. The cavalry will follow and sweep round the rear of the phalanx.'

'And the infantry?' Polybius persisted. 'Even if you order your infantry to follow after the cavalry at double pace they would never make it to the right flank and around the back of the phalanx in time to consolidate the gains made by the cavalry. The phalanx will have had time to form a defensive line to the rear. Our own line will have been gravely weakened.'

'There can be no change of plan, Polybius,' Aemilius Paullus said, squinting ahead. 'The phalanx is beginning to move again. And I promised the leader of the Paeligni in our front line that they would lead the assault. The die is cast.'

Polybius turned away, exasperated. Scipio went up to him and put a hand on his shoulder, pointing at the gap between the two armies. 'Look at the terrain,' he said quietly. 'The phalanx is at the head of the valley leading up from the sea, on relatively level ground where they can form a continuous line. We're in the foothills of the mountains. As the phalanx marches forward, the line will be broken up as they encounter the rough ground and gullies where the valley ends and the slope rises ahead of them. As long as we are ready to pour legionaries into those gaps, all we have to do is keep our nerve and wait for them. The terrain will do the job for us.'

Polybius pursed his lips. 'You may be right. But it will be too late to stop the Paeligni from making their charge. They are Latin allies and brave men, but they are not equipped or disciplined as legionaries and they will be cut down. And once your father sees the result, it may cause him to use restraint and keep the rest of the line from following.'

'My father is an excellent reader of terrain,' Scipio said pensively. 'Your strategy is sound, but we cannot redeploy the elephants now. By waiting here for the phalanx to come to us, the same effect of breaking up the line will be achieved. A suicidal charge by the Paeligni may be a sacrifice worth making, as it will boost the confidence of the phalanx and make them less cautious about keeping their line tight as they encounter rough terrain. And once we send legionaries into those gaps, my father can use the cavalry and elephants as he planned to outflank the phalanx and come up on their rear, at a time when they will be focused on confronting the incursions into their line from the front and will be less well organized for creating a rear defence. If the legionaries keep steady, the Macedonians will be routed.'

'The resolve of the legionaries is one thing that cannot be doubted,' Polybius said. 'This is the best army that Rome has ever fielded.'

Fabius saw a shimmer go along the spears of the phalanx as they locked together in close formation and moved slowly forward. He looked beyond the second legion to his right and saw the Paeligni, tough warriors from the mountain valleys to the east of Rome who were always given a loose rein to keep them loyal. They wore bronze skullcaps and quilted linen chest armour and carried vicious wide-bellied slashing swords, and when they charged they bellowed like bulls. A rider appeared from their midst and galloped out of the line, straight towards the phalanx, pulling left just before reaching the spears and hurling a javelin with a banner into the midst of the Macedonians, then turning and galloping back towards the Roman lines. The charge was now inevitable. The Paeligni were sworn to recover their standard whatever the cost, and before a battle to prove their intentions to their Roman commanders they always threw it into the enemy lines.

Polybius suddenly turned and took the bridle of his horse from his equerry. 'There is one thing I can do.' He turned to his sword-bearer and took his helmet, an old Corinthian type with a large nose guard and cheekpieces that concealed his face almost completely. He put it on, pulled the strap tight under his chin and then leapt expertly onto the horse, leaning forward and patting its neck as it stomped and whinnied. He pointed to his shield and his equerry handed it up to him, a circular form embossed at the centre with a thick rim of polished steel around the edge. He put his left forearm through the two leather straps at the back and held it tight to his side, keeping his right hand on the neck of the horse. There was no saddle, and he had cast off the bridle; Fabius remembered Polybius telling him how he had learned to ride bareback as a boy and always charged into battle that way. The horse reared up on its hind legs, its eyes wide open and its mouth chomping and foaming, knowing what lay ahead.

Scipio looked up at him, alarmed. 'What are you going to do? You haven't even got a weapon.'

Polybius raised his shield. 'The edge of this is as sharp as a sword blade. We trained to use our shields as weapons under the riding master at Megalopolis when I was your age. Another weakness of the phalanx is that the spears are held so rigidly together that they can be broken by riding at them along the line.'

'You'll be cut down,' Scipio exclaimed. 'You're too valuable to die like that. You're a historian. A strategist.'

'I was commanding officer of the Achaean cavalry before I was sent as a captive to Rome. I was your age, leading my first cavalry charge when you were barely able to walk. But you know where my allegiance lies now. I can't bear to see a Roman ally charge to their deaths without giving them a chance, and I'm the only one here who knows how to do this.'

'If the Macedonians unhorse you and take off your helmet and recognize you as a Greek, you'll be hacked to death.'

'The *sarissae* are not throwing spears, remember. As long as I stay just beyond their reach and my horse Skylla does her duty, I will survive. *Ave atque vale*, Scipio. Hail and farewell.' Polybius dug his shins into the horse and it thundered off, kicking up a cloud of dust that momentarily obscured the view. As it cleared, Fabius could see the reason for his abrupt departure. The Paeligni had already begun their charge, bounding forward like wild dogs, making a noise like a thousand rushing torrents. They were running at astonishing speed, and the distance between them and the phalanx had already narrowed. Fabius could see Polybius making for the gap, his shield held out diagonally to the left, charging in a swirl of dust. Another horse had followed, riderless, breaking away from the Roman lines until it overtook Polybius and disappeared into the storm of dust. For a horrifying moment it seemed as if he would not make it in time, as if the gap would close and he would hurtle among the horde of Paeligni warriors. But then he was gone, and all Fabius could see was a streak of silver along the line of Macedonian spears, as if a wave were passing along it. The spears in front of the Paeligni were broken and in disarray, leaving the phalanx vulnerable and exposed. Then the Paeligni were among them, their huge curved swords scything and slashing, their yells and screams rending the air. Fabius could see no way that Polybius could have survived to come out the other side; he closed his eyes for a moment and mouthed the brief words of prayer that his father had taught him to say at the passing of a fellow soldier in battle.

'Look to your front, legionary,' Scipio ordered, his voice hoarse with tension. He stood beside Fabius with sword drawn, staring ahead. While they had been watching Polybius the rest of the phalanx on either side had moved rapidly forward, exactly as Scipio had predicted. They were no more than two hundred paces away now, but the line directly in front of Fabius and Scipio had been broken as the Macedonians negotiated a dried-up watercourse caused by melt-water run-off from the mountain, widening into a gulley with sides about the height of a man.

'There's our chance,' Scipio said. 'We need to get at them while they're in the gully, before they close up the line again.'

Fabius glanced at Aemilius Paullus, who had put his helmet on and stood among his other staff officers with sword drawn. Behind them the maniples of the first legion stood in full battle array, the centurions marching up and down in front of them, bellowing orders to keep in position, to wait for the order, to do what legionaries do better than any others, to kill the enemy at close quarters, to thrust and slash and draw blood and show no mercy.

Scipio put his hand on Fabius' shoulder. 'Until we meet again, my friend. In this world or the next.'

As Scipio turned to him he looked young, too young for what they were about to do, and Fabius had to remember that Scipio was only seventeen years old, a year younger than he himself was; it was an age difference that had given him an edge of authority over Scipio when they had been boys, which made Scipio still listen to him even though they were divided by rank and class, but now the difference was irrelevant as they stood as one with six thousand other legionaries ready to do their worst. Fabius replied, his voice hoarse, sounding strangely disembodied, *Ave atque vale*, Scipio Aemilianus. In this world or the next.'

He grasped his standard tightly and drew his sword. He saw Scipio catch his father's eye, and Aemilius Paullus nodding. Time suddenly seemed to slow down; even the increasing crescendo of noise seemed drawn out, distant. Fabius watched Scipio run to the left, out in front of the first maniple, and then turn to the lead centurion, leaning forward and bellowing at him, then looking back to face the enemy, the sweat flicking off his face. He raised his sword and shouted again, and the legionaries behind him did the same – a deafening roar that seemed to drown out all other sensations. Fabius realized that he was doing the same, yelling at the top of his voice and shaking his blade in the air.

He tried to remember what the old centurion had told him about battle. *You will see nothing but the tunnel in front of you, and that tunnel will become your world. Clear that tunnel of the enemy, and you may survive. Try to see what goes on outside the tunnel, take your eye off those who have their eyes on you, and you will die.*

Scipio began to run. The whole ground shook as the legionaries followed. Fabius ran too, not far behind Scipio, parallel with the *primipilus* of the first legion. The gap in the phalanx was narrowing as the Macedonian soldiers divided by the gully realized their mistake and ran forward to the head of the gully to join up again; but in so doing they extended their line along the sides, some of them swinging their spears around to protect the flanks and others surging ahead to try to close the gap.

Fabius was breathing hard and could feel the dryness of his throat. Scipio was no more than a hundred paces from the phalanx now. Suddenly an elephant appeared in a swirl of dust from the right, a Macedonian spear stuck deep in its side, out of control and dragging the mangled corpse of a rider behind. It saw the gulley and veered right into the phalanx, trampling bodies that exploded with blood as it crashed through the lines and then tripped and rolled to a halt inside the gully, creating further disarray in the Macedonian ranks. Following the elephant came the first of the Paeligni warriors, screaming and waving their swords as they hurtled into the Macedonian line. The first one was skewered on a spear but kept running forward into the shaft until he reached the Macedonian soldier, beheading him with a single swipe of his sword before falling dead. The same happened all along the line, suicidal charges that opened more and more gaps in the phalanx, allowing the mass of legionaries who followed to break through and get behind the front ranks of spearmen, using their thrusting swords to bring down the Macedonians in their hundreds.

In seconds, Fabius was among them. He was conscious of passing through the line of spears and swerving to avoid the dying elephant, and then seeing Scipio stabbing and hacking ahead of him. He swept his sword down across the exposed ankles of the line of spearmen beside him, leaving them screaming and writhing on the ground for the legionaries who followed to finish off. Then he was close behind Scipio, thrusting and slashing, going for the neck and the pelvis, his arms and face drenched in blood, always keeping the standard raised. A huge Thracian came behind Scipio's back and whipped out a dagger, but Fabius leapt forward and stabbed his sword up through the back of the man's neck into his skull, causing his eyeballs to spring out and a jet of blood to arch from his mouth as he fell. All around him the din and smell was like nothing he had experienced before: men screaming and bellowing and retching, blood and vomit and gore spattering everywhere.

Then Fabius was conscious of another noise, of horns sounding – not Roman trumpets but Macedonian mountain horns. The fighting suddenly slackened, and the Macedonians around him seemed to melt away. *The horns had sounded the retreat.* Fabius staggered forward to Scipio, who was leaning over and panting hard, holding his hand against a bloody gash in his thigh. The combat had only lasted minutes, but it felt like hours. Around them the legionaries passed forward over the mound of bodies where the Macedonian line had been, slashing and thrusting to finish off the wounded, like a giant wave crashing over a reef and disappearing to shore. Scipio stood up and leaned on Fabius, and the two of them surveyed the carnage around them. As the dust settled, they could see the cavalry pouring around the flanks and pursuing the retreating Macedonians far ahead, a rolling cloud of death that pushed the enemy back into the plain and towards the sea.

Fabius remembered another thing the old centurion had told him. The tunnel that had been his world, the tunnel of death that seemed to have no end, would suddenly open up and there would be a rout, a massacre. There would seem no logic to it, but that was how it happened. This time, it had gone their way.

Aemilius Paullus came down the slope towards them, his helmet off, followed by his standard-bearers and staff officers.

He made his way over the mangled bodies and stood in front of Fabius, who did his best to come to attention and hold his standard upright. The general put his hand on his shoulder and spoke. 'Fabius Petronius Secundus, for never letting the standard of the legion drop and for staying at the head of your maniple, I commend you. And the *primipilus* said he saw you save the life of your tribune by killing one of the enemy while still holding the standard high. For that I award you the *corona civica*. You have made your mark in battle, Fabius. You will continue to be the personal bodyguard of my son, and one day you may earn promotion to centurion. I fought beside your father when I was a tribune and he was a centurion, and you have honoured his memory. You may go back to Rome proud.'

Fabius tried to control his emotions, but felt the tears streaming down his face. Aemilius Paullus turned to his son. 'And as for the tribune, he has proven himself worthy to lead Roman legionaries into battle.'

Fabius knew there could be no greater reward for Scipio, who bowed his head and then looked up, his face drawn. 'I congratulate you on your victory, Aemilius Paullus. You will be accorded the greatest triumph ever seen in Rome. You have honoured the shades of our ancestors, and of my adoptive grandfather Scipio Africanus. But I now have another task. I must prepare the funeral rites for Polybius. He was the bravest man I have known, a warrior who sacrificed himself to save Roman lives. We must find his body and send him to the afterlife like his heroes, like Ajax and Achilles and the fallen of Thermopylae.'

Aemilius Paullus cleared his throat. 'Fine, if you can persuade him to leave aside the far more interesting business of interviewing Macedonian prisoners of war for the account he intends to write of this battle for his *Histories*.'

'What? He's alive?'

'He carried on riding to the right flank of the phalanx, turned back to our lines, and charged again at the head of the cavalry, and then came back to collect his scrolls so that he could write an eyewitness account while it was still fresh in his mind. That is, before he had a sudden brainwave and galloped off by himself to find King Perseus, wherever he might be hiding, to get his take on the battle.'

'But he couldn't be bothered to stop and tell his friends that he was alive?'

'He had far more important things to do.'

Scipio shook his head, then wiped his face with his hand. He suddenly looked terribly tired.

'You need water,' Fabius said. 'And that wound needs to be tended.'

'You too are wounded, on your cheek.'

Fabius reached up with surprise and felt congealed blood from his ear to his mouth. 'I didn't feel it. We should go to the river.'

'It runs red with Macedonian blood,' Aemilius Paullus said.

'It's everywhere.' Scipio looked at the drying blood on his hands and forearms and on his sword. He squinted at his father. 'Is this an end to it?'

Aemilius Paullus looked over the battlefield towards the sea, and then nodded. 'The war with Macedonia is over. King Perseus and the Antigonid dynasty are finished. We have extinguished the last remnant of the empire of Alexander the Great.'

'What does the future hold for us?'

'For me, a triumph in Rome like no other in the past, then monuments inscribed with my name and the name of this battle of Pydna, and then retirement. This is my last war, and my last battle. But for you, for the others of your generation, for Polybius, for Fabius, for the other young tribunes, there is war ahead. The Achaean League in Greece to the south will need subduing. The Celtiberians in Spain were stirred up when Hannibal took them as allies, and will resist Rome. And, above all, Carthage remains – unfinished business even after two devastating wars. It will be a hard road ahead for you, with many challenges to overcome, with Rome herself sometimes seeming an obstacle to your ambitions. It was so for myself and for your adoptive grandfather, and will be ever thus as long as Rome fears her generals as much as she lauds their victories. If you are to succeed and stand as I am victorious on a field of battle, you must show the same strength of determination to remain true to your destiny as you have shown strength on the field of battle. And for you, the stakes are even higher. For those of your generation, for those of you who are young tribunes today, those whom we in Rome concerned for the future have nurtured and trained, your future will not be to stand on a battlefield as we are today at Pydna or as your grandfather did at Zama, to see the glory of triumph and then retirement. Your future will be to look away from Rome, to see from your battlefield a horizon that none of us has seen before, and to be tempted by it. The empire of Alexander the Great may be gone, but a new one beckons.'

'What do you mean?' said Scipio.

'I mean the empire of Rome.'

PART ONE

ROME

168 BC

Three months before the Battle of Pydna

1

Fabius Petronius Secundus strode purposefully down the Sacred Way through the old Forum of Rome, the Capitoline temple behind him and the aristocratic houses on the slope of the Palatine Hill to his right. He was carrying a bundle containing the bronze greaves that his master Scipio Aemilianus had forgotten to take that morning to the Gladiator School, where the old centurion Petraeus was due shortly to supervise training for the young men who would be appointed as military tribunes later that year. Scipio was the oldest of the pupils at the school, almost eighteen now and in charge of the others while the centurion was absent, so it would be double the humiliation, and more than double the punishment, if the centurion found that he was missing any of his equipment.

But Fabius knew the old centurion's movements exactly. Every morning with military precision he spent half an hour in the baths, an amusing indulgence for a hoary old soldier, and Fabius had seen him enter his favourite bathhouse behind the Temple of Castor and Pollux only a few minutes before. It was not the first time that Fabius had saved Scipio's skin, and Fabius knew the value of becoming indispensable. But his feelings towards Scipio were those of a friend rather than a servant: in future he might be destined to be a legionary while Scipio became a general, but they had first met on equal terms on the streets of Rome when Scipio had wanted to shed his aristocratic grandeur for a night and run with the gangs, and that was how it stayed between them, even though convention dictated that in public the one must be master and the other a servant.

An official with the rod of a lictor was waving an olive branch to signal a procession and stopped him as he was about to cross the road. Fabius stood behind the crowd of onlookers and glanced up and down to see if there was a way across, but then thought better of it. If it was a religious procession the lictors would chase him down and beat him for it, and he could not afford a transgression that might jeopardize his position in the Scipio household. His friendship with Scipio Aemilianus after Fabius had saved him from being beaten up that night had been the big break of his life, the chance to escape the slums of the Tiber bank and honour his father's memory. He remembered the last time he had seen his father in full armour, near this very spot, marching in triumph after the first Celtiberian War, a centurion of the first legion resplendent in his *corona civica* and the silver arm bands he had been awarded for valour. But that had been followed by years of peace, and when the legions were called up again he had been too old, too dissipated by his weakness for wine, and after that the hard times had only got worse. Fabius knew that his father's name was one reason why Scipio's father Aemilius Paullus had accepted him into his household as a servant, and had put his name forward for the first legion when he came of age. Had Aemilius Paullus and Scipio's adoptive grandfather, the great Scipio Africanus, been given the power by the Senate, then Rome would not have let his father down; they would have ensured that experienced soldiers remained in the ranks and were not thrown back into civilian life where their skills were wasted and they could never settle down.

Fabius peered over the heads of the people to see what was passing. It was the twelve Vestal Virgins, garlanded in laurel and wearing white, followed by a group of girls who served as their retainers, spreading incense and flower petals over the bystanders. Among the retainers he spotted Julia, her flaxen hair visible above the others. She should have been with him today, secretly joining the boys to study battle tactics while the old centurion was out. It was Fabius' job to escort her into the academy and then to spirit her out again by a back entrance as soon as they heard the clunk of the centurion's staff in the corridor. Julia's greatest dread was that she would be forced to spend so much time with the Vestals that she would become one herself, but to have missed today's procession would have been to upset the tolerance her mother showed towards the time she spent with the young men in the academy, which was the one thing that made life as an aristocratic girl in Rome with all of its conventions and restrictions tolerable for her.

Julia saw him, flashed a smile, and he waved. Once, months before, she had come to him in the servants' quarters of Scipio's house and had stroked his hair, admiring its auburn curls. He had been momentarily taken aback, his heart pounding, and had told her that his hair colour came from his mother, the daughter of a Celtic chieftain imprisoned in the Tullianum dungeon under the Capitoline Hill and guarded by Fabius' father. He had sensed Julia's breathing quicken, excited perhaps by the exotic, by a boy who was not from her own social class and not even fully Roman, who opened out the possibilities of the world for her. But he had come to his senses and had moved out of her reach. It was not as if he were innocent of the pleasures of women; on occasion he had spent the few *asses* that he made on the *prostibulae* in the bathhouse, and he had his admirers among the girls of his own neighbourhood. But he knew there could be no hope with Julia. As a servant boy, little better than a slave, he would be whipped out of the house if they were found out, or worse. And, above all, he had known that Scipio was in love with Julia, a love that had blossomed secretly in the months that followed after Julia had become aware of his feelings, despite her own betrothal since childhood to Scipio's distant cousin Metellus. If Fabius lost the patronage of Scipio he would never rise above the streets again. But it was Scipio's friendship that mattered most: a friendship that had enriched his life, that had introduced him to Polybius and a world of books and knowledge that had lit his imagination and made his dream the same dream as Scipio's, to see a world his father had seen as a soldier that he yearned to explore himself.

The procession passed, and Fabius hurried over the road towards the Gladiator School, making his way through the warren of alleyways and wooden houses until he came to the two-storey building that surrounded the practice arena. He pushed past the crippled old soldiers begging at the entranceway, past the mound of sand that was used to mop up the blood, and then the stable where they kept Hannibal, the gnarled old war elephant who was the last survivor of his namesake's march over the Alps almost fifty years before – the final Carthaginian prisoner left alive in Rome. Fabius ran along a dark passageway and up the stairway to the closed door, careful not to brush against the sputtering tallow candles that lined the walls. Officially, the academy was a private school for the instruction of sons of senators in philosophy and history, staffed by professors recruited from the hundreds of Greek captives taken to Rome since the war with Macedonia had begun. Unofficially, it was a training school established by the elder Scipio before he died to ensure that the next generation of Roman war leaders were more skilled than the last, and better able to hold their own against the agitations of the Senate. It was this last fact that made the elder Scipio keep the academy as private as possible, away from the eyes of those who were suspicious of anything he did. In theory, the old centurion Petraeus was there only to instruct the boys in swordplay, but for two mornings of the week behind closed doors they were allowed to simulate the great battles of the past, battles that the centurion or other veterans brought in for the purpose would mastermind for them based on their own experience of tactics and combat.

He pushed the door open and crept inside, shutting it quietly behind him. The room was large, windowless where it faced the street outside but with an open gallery on the other side overlooking the arena in the courtyard below. Two slaves stood in attendance against the back wall, holding trays with fruit and water pitchers, beside an open passageway coming up from the courtyard where the old centurion would make his entrance. In the centre of the room was a large table, some three arms' breadths in length, covered with the diorama of a battlefield; the terrain was represented by sand and stones and tufts of grass, and the opposing armies by coloured wooden blocks arranged in rows. Fabius knew exactly which battle was being represented. When Polybius had taught him Greek he had read him a passage on the battle from the history of the war against Hannibal that Polybius had been writing ever since he had arrived from Greece as a willing captive who had always been a great admirer of Rome. And the old centurion had told Fabius about it, an eyewitness who had fought there beside the elder Scipio himself. Fabius had gone to the tavern one evening with him and had spent hours drinking wine and listening to the stories. It was the Battle of Zama, the final confrontation with the Carthaginians in North Africa that had forced Hannibal to surrender and the city of Carthage to lay itself at Scipio's mercy, almost thirty-five years ago now.

The table was lit by four candles at each corner, and by an open skylight in the roof. In the gloom Fabius could make out a dozen or so figures standing back in the shadows, including the bearded figure of Polybius, taller than the rest and some fifteen years older, attending today as their professor in order to better his understanding of Roman tactics for a special volume in the *Histories* that he was writing.

Scipio was leaning forward with his hands on the table, staring intently. Fabius quietly passed him the bronze greaves he had been carrying, and Scipio put them on, deftly tying them behind his legs and nodding acknowledgement to Fabius before looking at the table again, concentrating. Fabius knew the protocol. They had finished reconstructing the actual battle, and now were entering the realm of speculation. Each one in turn would come up to the table and alter a series of variables, and the next would suggest possible outcomes. It was a game of tactics and strategy to show how easily the course of history could have been altered. Scipio as leader of the group was the last player, and Polybius as the previous player had set him the challenge.

'You've taken away the Celtiberians,' Scipio muttered.

'They're mercenaries, remember?' Polybius replied. 'Almost the entire Carthaginian army is mercenary. I've imagined that on the eve of battle they've demanded their pay, and Carthage has no gold left. So they've melted away into the night.'

Another voice piped in. 'Have you heard the rumour that the Carthaginians have revived the Sacred Band? An elite unit made up entirely of Carthaginian noblemen. They say it's been resurrected in secret, for the last defence of Carthage, should we attack again.'

Scipio looked up. 'My friend the playwright Terence told me that too. He was brought up in Carthage, so should know. But it's irrelevant to the game. At Zama it's the year 551 *ab urbe condita*, and the Sacred Band was annihilated years before.' He turned back to the diorama. 'So, removing the Celtiberians makes Roman victory even more assured.'

'Not necessarily,' Polybius replied. 'Look at your food supplies.'

Scipio glanced at a cluster of coloured counters behind the Roman lines, and grunted. 'You've depleted it by three quarters. What happened?'

'In the lead-up to the battle the Romans ravaged the land, taking all of the crops at once instead of foraging carefully with a view to a long campaign. For three weeks before the battle the legionaries have lived on half-rations.'

'So, morale plummets. And physical ability. An army lives on its stomach.'

'And I've made another change, the third one I'm allowed. Scipio Africanus, your grandfather, has told the legionaries that there will be no looting in Carthage if they take the city. All of the treasures stolen by the Carthaginians from the Greeks in Sicily will be returned.'

'Even worse,' Scipio muttered. 'No food, no loot.'

'But there is one saving factor,' Polybius said.

'What's that?'

Polybius came forward out of the shadows. 'Another change: my fourth and final one. Five years before, Scipio Africanus has been allowed by the Senate to create a professional army. He has set up an academy for officers, the first ever in Rome, in the old Gladiator School, identical to the academy here today. As a result, when the legionaries go to war they have the pride and solidarity of a professional army. They fight for one another, for their honour, and not for loot. And the officers have simulated past battles just as we are doing, they're always one step ahead of the enemy. So they win the battle, as we would.'

'And then they go on to destroy Carthage,' Scipio said, grinning at Polybius. 'Without the interference of the Senate.'

Polybius cocked an eye at him. 'So what do you do, then? You've won the battle, and the campaign. But have you won the war? When are wars ever over? Do you return to Rome for your triumph and rest on your laurels, or do you capitalize on your victory and seek out the next threat to Rome, the next region ripe for conquest?'

'It would depend on the will of the Senate and the people of Rome,' one of the others said.

'And on who was consul,' another added. 'Consuls are in office for only one year, and if the next consuls see little in it for themselves they may order the legions to return to Rome.'

Scipio pursed his lips. 'That's the problem,' he said. 'The constitution of Rome puts a lid on any attempt at a wider strategy.'

'Constitutions are made by men, not gods,' a figure with a deeper voice said. He stepped up beside Polybius, and Fabius saw that it was Metellus, a man closer in age to Polybius. He was already a serving tribune, at home on leave from the Macedonian war to recover from wounds; he already bore the scars of an eagle's talons from his youth, where a hunting bird had missed his wrist and landed on his face. 'Rome has already changed her constitution once, when she got rid of the kings and created the Republic,' he said. 'She could do it again.'

'Dangerous words, Metellus,' Polybius said. 'Words that smack of dictatorship and empire.'

'If that's what we need to keep Rome strong, then so be it.'

Polybius leaned his hands on the table, looking at the diorama pensively. 'It will be up to those of you here, the next generation of war leaders, to navigate the best course for Rome. All I would say is this. The course of history is not a matter of chance, nor a game in which we are pieces like these wooden blocks, moved about on a whim by the gods. In the real world, you are not the gaming piece; you are the player. You follow the rules of the game, yes, but you bend them, you press against them. The rules will not win the game for you: you must do it yourselves. History is made by people, not by gods. Scipio Africanus was not a slave to some divine will, but was his own master and his own tactician.'

'And what of empire?' Metellus asked. 'Could Rome have an empire?'

'Imperialism must be built on moral responsibility for the governed. Outrageous behaviour will bring retribution. An empire must not grow beyond the capacity of its institutions to manage it.'

'Then we have done so already,' Metellus said. 'We already have provinces, but we do not yet have the organization to administer them. We are an empire in all but name, yet Rome persists in behaving like a city-state. Something must change. Someone must rise above it all and see the future. As you have taught us, Polybius, history is made by individuals, and it is they and not institutions that cause change. That is what this academy is about. It's about creating future emperors.'

'I don't think that was exactly what my grandfather intended,' Scipio said, looking at Metellus coldly.

'Should we not look to the past?' one of the others said. 'The lessons for wars of the future are in the wars of our ancestors.'

Polybius stood back from the table. 'That is the Roman way, to feel that the busts of the ancestors you all have in the *tablinae* of your houses are constantly looking over you, guiding you,' he said. 'But sometimes we need to make our obeisances to the past and then shut that door, and look solely to the future. Studying history is about learning from the past, but not always about seeking a precedent from it. Strategy and tactics in war are built on experience of past wars, but each new one is unique. The world is not static. If you choose to look forward, and do so aggressively, and you learn all of the lessons that you have been taught in the academy, then you may change history. History is not laid out for us like some ever-rolling rug. You may weave your own thread in it, or you may twist the rug sideways, and send it tumbling down the steps into the unknown. That's my lesson for today. We end with a final thought from each of you, as usual. Ennius?'

'Keep your word. Only then will cities surrender to you.'

'Good. Scipio?'

'In a new province, define your borders,' Scipio said. 'Otherwise war is inevitable.'

Polybius nodded. 'When Carthage was allowed to keep some of her territory in Africa after the Battle of Zama, the borders were ill defined. It was a recipe for war. Lucius?'

'Exploit superstition. If your army feels they have divine guidance, then encourage them to believe it.'

'Brutus?'

'Punish savagely those you have conquered who are not yet obedient, to inspire fear and terror.'

'Zeus above,' Polybius murmured. 'That sounds like something from Sparta.'

'My father taught it to me,' Brutus said, his massive forearms folded over his chest. 'He said there would be more to the academy than swordplay, and that I should be ready with some ideas.'

'Maybe you'd better stick to your strengths,' Polybius muttered. 'Fabius?'

Fabius was discomfited. 'I'm only here as Scipio's servant, Polybius. I will never lead an army.'

'You may not lead an army, but men like you will be the backbone of the army. What do you say?'

Fabius thought for a moment. 'Cowardice must not go unpunished.'

Polybius nodded slowly, and then smiled. 'All right. That's enough *gravitas* for today. Hippolyta's offered to teach you how to use a Scythian bow. See you all in the arena in half an hour.'

Scipio said, standing up and stretching, 'Twenty minutes' rest before the centurion arrives. Drink some water and eat some fruit. You'll need it if we're going out on to the arena.'

Polybius pointed at the diorama. 'If Julia had been here, she could have told us more. Her father Sextus Julius Caesar was at Zama as a junior tribune. She knows the battle like the back of her hand.'

Scipio looked around, suddenly missing her. 'Has anyone seen Julia?'

'She's not coming today,' one of the others said. 'She's accompanying her mother to the Temple of the Vestal Virgins for some kind of ceremony.'

'Let's just hope the Virgins don't take her,' someone else sniggered. 'That would deprive us of some fun. That is, if Scipio will let us have it.'

'Shut it, Lucius,' Polybius said tiredly. 'Or Scipio will have his friend Brutus here hack off your manhood.'

Fabius saw Scipio clasp the amulet around his neck that he knew Julia had given him, an ancient Etruscan device of an eagle passed down through her *gens*, and then look down in annoyance. He knew that Scipio hated himself for showing his feelings for Julia. He saw Metellus staring at Scipio, questioningly, and he suddenly remembered. Metellus had been away in Macedonia for almost two years, so would have no idea of Scipio's affection for Julia. Scipio shook his head dismissively, as if Julia was of no consequence to him, and then stood square and folded his arms over his chest, nodding at the diorama. 'I'm expecting all of you to memorize the entire order of battle, down to the last maniple and rag-tag auxiliary unit. You can spend the next twenty minutes doing that instead. When the centurion returns, he'll test you on it. Get one thing wrong, and you know what will happen. I can assure you that the pain from his vine staff will be greater than anything Brutus might be likely to mete out. Now get on with it.'

In the silence that followed, Fabius scanned the room. Most of them were sixteen or seventeen years old, on the cusp of manhood, several a year or two younger. When the trumpets of war sounded, when the centurion deemed them ready, they would be appointed as military tribunes in the Roman army, the first rung in the ladder that might lead those who survived to command legions, to lead armies, even to the consulship, the highest office in the Republic. They were scions of the greatest patrician families of Rome: the *gens* Julii, the *gens* Junia, the *gens* Claudia, the *gens* Valeria, and Scipio's adopted branch of the *gens* Cornelia, the Scipiones. In their sprawling houses on the Palatine were shrines filled with wax busts of ancestors who had gained glory in war, some dating back to the time of Romulus and the foundation of the city almost six hundred years before, and many from the succession of devastating wars that Rome had fought in recent centuries: against the Latin tribes and the Etruscans near to Rome, against the Celts to the north, against the Greek colonies of Italy and Sicily, and above all in the titanic struggle against Carthage, a conflict that had begun almost a hundred years before and still haunted them all, a war that should have ended with the Battle of Zama if the senators had allowed the act of destruction that would have secured Rome's dominance in the west Mediterranean and allowed her to focus her whole might on Greece and the riches of the east.

And they were not all men. Fabius let his eyes linger on a dark corner of the room and saw her, taller than any of them except Polybius, watching everything intently, her eyes briefly catching his. Her red hair was woven into a long tail behind her head, and she had dark kohl rings around her eyes. In the arena she took off her gold neck torque and bracelets and fought without armour, wearing only a white tiger skin wrapped tightly around her midriff and chest. They had been astonished at the tattoo on her back, an eagle with wings outstretched from shoulder blade to shoulder blade. They knew her by her Greek name, Hippolyta, meaning 'Wild Mare', but the centurion had told them before she arrived that her name in her own language was Oiropata, meaning 'Killer of Men'. They had scoffed at it, but everyone had gone silent when she had walked through the door and they had seen her physique. She was a Scythian princess, the daughter of a client king from the steppe lands to the north of the Black Sea, and the centurion had explained that there were more of them, expert female horse riders and archers, and that one day she might lead an *ala* of Scythian cavalry alongside a Roman army. Polybius spoke her language and had questioned her at length about Scythian history, and had helped to improve her Latin. The others kept their distance, fearful of being singled out by the centurion to fight her in unarmed combat and endure the humiliation of almost certain defeat.

And then there was Julia. She was from the Caesares branch of the *gens* Julia, the daughter of Sextus Julius Caesar who had fought as a tribune at Zama. She was no warrior princess like Hippolyta, but she had a shrewd tactical mind and would have swept the floor that day with her knowledge of the battle that had made her father's name. Fabius had seen how Julia had made Scipio's pulse quicken, how when she was watching him in the arena fighting he was possessed by a force that seemed to come from the gods. Fabius himself had felt a stab of pain when he first saw Julia's affection for Scipio, casting his mind back to that night when she had come to him in the servant's quarters, but it had quickly passed. He remembered the look that Metellus had given Scipio. Fabius knew that Scipio had been dreading the arrival of Metellus, and welcoming it at the same time: dreading it because it might break the bond between him and Julia, welcoming it because it might help to suppress the feelings he had for her which could threaten his career. Metellus had been betrothed to Julia since she had been a small child, and he was Scipio's second cousin on his mother's side.

Scipio himself was enmeshed in social obligations; he was the son of Aemilius Paullus of the *gens* Aemilii but also the adoptive son of Publius Cornelius Scipio, eldest son of the great Scipio Africanus, who was also Scipio's great-uncle on his mother's side. He had been given up for adoption only because he had two elder brothers, and because the third son was never accorded the same privileges in his career; without adoption he would never have been poised to become a military tribune as he was now. It had been a huge honour to be adopted by the son of Scipio Africanus, but it had come with the burden of his own betrothal to Claudia Pulchra of the *gens* Claudia, a girl he profoundly disliked who hardly lived up to her cognomen, yet whom he knew was counting down every day with bated breath until his eighteenth birthday and the formal beginning of the marriage rites. Every time that he and Fabius had to go near her house on the Esquiline Hill they made elaborate detours to avoid being spotted from the bower where she sat with her slave girls overlooking the city, looking forward to the kind of future doing the social rounds and scheming with the matrons of the other *gentes* that Scipio dreaded far more than the worst enemy on the battlefield.

But to go against these obligations, to pursue his feelings for Julia, would be to betray the memory of Scipio Africanus and the trust of his own birth father, to risk being outcast and losing everything. Once, when he and Fabius had been lying side by side at night on the slopes of the Circus Maximus, staring at the stars and sharing a flagon of wine, Scipio had confided his feelings for Julia to him, had shown him the amulet and had talked of his frustration. He had told him how he imagined a time when as a victorious general he would throw off the shackles of Rome and take her with him, but they both knew that in the cold light of morning it could be little more than a dream; even if it came about it could only be many years ahead when Scipio would be a battle-hardened soldier and his love for her might be a distant memory. Fabius knew only too well what was at stake for Scipio, how the career he was watching unfold would be driven by knowledge of the sacrifice he was making to honour his father and the elder Scipio, and to satisfy his own burning ambition to lead the greatest army Rome had ever seen back to Carthage to finish a conflict that could still threaten to destroy their world.

Fabius had stopped earlier that morning in the Forum and looked at the consular *fasti*, the list of the names of past consuls who represented all of the great patrician *gentes* of Rome, the forefathers of the boys in the academy. He remembered the first time he had overheard the Greek professors in the academy lecture the boys about morality: they must have courage, and they must have *fides*, be true to their word, and be temperate in their personal lives. He had smiled to himself when he heard that; he had seen what the boys got up to at night in the taverns and the brothels around the Forum. But that was before he had met Scipio. He was able to fight and brawl like any of them, and relish it; Fabius knew that only too well from his first encounter with him years before in the back alleys by the Tiber. But Scipio did not indulge in the vices like the other boys. It was as if something were restraining him, holding him back. Fabius knew from studying the *fastes* that Scipio was the noblest of them all, a boy whose birth *gens* was elevated enough but whose stakes were stacked even higher by being adopted into the family of Scipio Africanus, a name that still sent tremors through Rome more than thirty years after his victory in the war against Hannibal. Fabius had wondered whether history weighed too heavily on the younger Scipio, and whether he took that burden too seriously. A boy who could only excel in his own eyes if he equalled the achievements of his father and his adoptive grandfather, both of them illustrious generals, could not afford to indulge his base desires in the taverns and whorehouses of the city, if one day he might need to exert his moral authority to lead Rome to victory.

But Fabius knew there was more to it than that. Scipio was shy and could seem aloof; that had already earned him the scorn of those without the imagination to see the strength within but with the power to humiliate and torment him while he still had the vulnerabilities of adolescence. Scipio was Roman to the core, a true exemplar of Roman morality rather than one who simply paid lip service to it as so many of the others did, but he had also benefited from the intellectual rigour of a Greek education and could see where Rome had become self-absorbed, where the lives that aristocrats were expected to lead no longer had the hard edge of the old ways. He hated the oratory and sophistry that they were expected to learn in the law courts, the skills that would see the sons of patricians climb steadily through the *cursus honorum*, the step-by-step sequence of magistracies that were essential to rise to the highest office, to the consulship. Above all, he hated the fact that the *cursus honorum* was also the route to army command, rather than military experience itself. Scipio had to endure the critical eye of those who questioned the ability of a young man to rise to high office and honour his *gens* – a young man who, instead of being in the law courts, spent his days studying military strategy and learning swordplay, and his leisure time hunting in the mountains as far away from Rome as he could get.

But Fabius had overheard Scipio's father Aemilius Paullus talk to his mother about him one day in their house, about how Scipio was living up to the hopes that Africanus had expressed for his successors, for the next generation of Roman war leaders. He had said that morality was the key, a personal code of honour. Aemilius Paullus had known that his son would suffer for it, but that his sensitivity to the criticism of others would be the seedbed of his strength. Scipio already had a reputation for keeping his word, for *fides*, and his abstinence from debauchery was also a good sign. It was then that Fabius had made it his own mission to watch out for Scipio, not only protecting him physically but also keeping him from being ruined by his own sensitivities, and from developing a resentment of Rome that would be self-destructive. Seeing him here at the head of the boys in the academy was an important step in the right direction, although there were many challenges ahead.

He glanced at the sand-timer on the table, seeing that the twenty minutes of study were nearly up and the boys were becoming restless. Ennius had been working on something in the corner that Fabius hoped would keep them preoccupied until Petraeus arrived. What happened then would depend on the old centurion's temperament that day, on whether the baths had soothed the fire that raged within. Fabius had smiled wryly to himself when he had seen the newest arrival in the academy, Scipio's cousin Gaius Paullus, go white at the mention of the centurion's imminent arrival, his fearsome reputation having preceded him. Whether or not Petraeus was in an indulgent mood, there could be no doubt that the next big challenge confronting the boys was not some distant enemy on a Macedonian battlefield but the very embodiment of all that was strong about Rome herself. The old centurion Petraeus was about to bear down on them and mete out wisdom and toughness that one day might make some of them the equal of such a man on the battlefield.

2

'Scipio! It's ready!' The voice came from the corner of the room opposite Hippolyta, from a wide recess containing a fireplace. Fabius could just make out a figure in the gloom squatting over the brazier, a lighted tallow candle in one hand. He saw Scipio glance anxiously at the door where the centurion would arrive, and then look at the others. 'All right. Ennius has something to show us. But at the first sound of the centurion coming down the corridor, everyone rushes back to their places around the table. You know what old Petraeus thinks of Ennius' inventions. We'll all be for it.'

They crowded around the recess, Hippolyta included. Polybius stood alongside Scipio, his hands behind his back, peering with interest over the others, looking much more a scholar than a soldier. Ennius' experiments of the last few months owed much to Polybius, who had introduced him to the wonders of Greek science and fuelled his fascination with military engineering. Scipio nudged Polybius. 'So what ancient magic have you revealed to him this time, my friend?'

Polybius shrugged. 'We talked yesterday about Thucydides' account of the siege of Delium.'

Gulussa was standing beside them, and looked keenly at Polybius. 'In the year of the three hundred and fiftieth Olympiad, that is, a hundred and fifty-six years ago,' he said, his Latin accented with the soft guttural sound of Numidian. 'The action where the philosopher Socrates fought as a hoplite, when the Athenians were routed by the Boeotians. The first major battle in history to involve full-scale tactical planning, including the detailed coordination of cavalry and infantry.'

Polybius cocked an eye at him. 'You listen to my lectures well, Gulussa. Full marks.'

Scipio peered into the recess. 'So what is it? Some kind of engine of war?'

'All I know is that after I told him about the siege he disappeared off to Ostia, where he has a friend in a back alley behind the harbour who supplies him with all manner of exotic substances, brought from all corners of the earth,' Polybius replied.

'That would be Polyarchos the Alexandrian,' Scipio said resignedly. 'Usually that means pyrotechnics, and usually you can't get the smell out of your clothes for days.'

Ennius had his back towards them and was shaping something with his hands on the brazier, moulding it. 'Just give me a moment,' he said, his voice muffled in the recess. Fabius listened out for the centurion's distinctive step, but only heard the swish of blades and the sound of scuffled feet in the arena below, and the occasional grunt. Brutus had left them during the study period, and was practising his swordplay again. Fabius turned back to the squatting figure in the gloom. Since Fabius had first met him as a boy, playing on the Palatine Hill with Scipio, Ennius had been intrigued by all manner of contraptions: bridges, boats, cranes for bringing stone columns and blocks into the city, the principles of architecture. The old centurion approved of that: when a legionary was not fighting, his proper job was to dig fortifications and build forts, presided over by centurions who prided themselves on their building skills almost as much as their fighting prowess.

But Ennius' latest craze was a different matter altogether. With Polybius' introduction to Greek science had come a fascination with fire. Ennius had even accompanied Ptolemy when he had sailed back to Egypt three months ago, after Ptolemy had been recalled from the academy to assume the throne of Egypt. Ostensibly Ennius had accompanied him for Ptolemy's marriage ritual and to go crocodile-hunting, but mainly he had wanted to visit the university at Alexandria to see the work of Greek scientists at first hand, and he had returned only the week before, overflowing with enthusiasm. He had even suggested to Petraeus that the Roman army needed a specialised cohort of *fabri*, engineers, with himself as tribune, tasked to supervise and improve fortifications and also to develop new weapons of war. Scipio had never seen such a black cloud descend over the old centurion's face. To suggest that specialists should do the traditional work of legionaries was an affront to their honour. To suggest that new weapons of war were needed was not only an affront to the legionaries, but also an insult to the centurion himself; Ennius was questioning his ability to kill with the time-honoured weapons of thrusting sword and javelin and bare hands. But even the week of punishment Ennius had endured mucking out the dung of the elephant stable had failed to diminish his ardour, and here he was again risking the wrath of the centurion to show them yet another miracle of science.

'All right.' Ennius shuffled back from the fireplace and swivelled round to face them, the object he had been shaping lying in his hands. It looked like a sphere of wet clay, only it glistened black. In front of the fireplace were pots filled with powders – one bright yellow, others red and brown. Ennius coughed, then stared at them, his expression brimming with excitement.

'Well?' Scipio said. 'We haven't got all day.'

Ennius picked up a waxed writing tablet and a metal stylus. 'First, you need to understand the science.'

'No.' Scipio held up his hand. 'No, we don't. Just show us.'

Ennius looked briefly disappointed. He put down the tablet, and picked up the lit candle again. 'What do you know about Greek fire?'

Scipio thought for a moment. 'The Assyrians used it. They made it from black tar that boils up in the desert.'

'I myself have seen the tar, when I visited the land of the

Israelites, beside the briny inland sea,' Metellus added. 'The Greeks call it *naphtha*.'

'They also call it water fire,' Polybius murmured. 'It's not extinguished by water, and will even continue to burn if you throw it on the surface of the sea.'

'Right,' Ennius said, twitching with excitement. 'Now watch this.' He put the ball into a bed of kindling below the brazier and thrust the candle into it. The chips of wood ignited and flames enveloped the ball, the flames rising towards the chimney. Suddenly the ball crackled and erupted in a violent flame that roared up the chimney and disappeared, followed by a suck of wind and leaving nothing but embers in the brazier and an acrid smell in the air. Ennius tossed a pot of water on the flames, watched the smoke disappear up the chimney and turned to them again, a broad smile on his face. 'Well?' he said. 'Impressed?'

Metellus was closest to the fire, and held his nose. 'What did you put in that, Ennius? Elephant dung?'

'Not far off.' Ennius wiped his forehead, leaving a black smudge. 'Nitre, made from ground-up bird droppings. An Egyptian priest showed me how to do it. But the smell is sulphur.'

'What's your point, Ennius?' Scipio said, his ear cocked for any sound from the corridor.

'Did you see how the rising heat from the fire drew the flames from the naphtha up the chimney? By the time it reached the roof, it would have erupted out in a jet of flame far higher even than the Capitoline Temple.'

'Jupiter above, I hope the old centurion didn't see that,' Scipio muttered.

'So you think this might be a weapon?' Metellus said doubtfully.

Ennius looked up. 'Polybius, tell them.'

Polybius cleared his throat. 'At the siege of the Boeotian fortress of Delium, the Athenians set up metal tubes to throw fire at the enemy. Thucydides called them flamethrowers.'

'You see?' Ennius said. 'Somebody had the idea almost three hundred years ago, but then it's forgotten. It's typical of our attitude to technology. Why? Look at our beloved centurion. Total inflexibility.' He shook his head in frustration but then became animated again, gesticulating as he spoke. 'You would need a tube of bronze about six feet high and a hand's breadth in width, set at an angle facing the enemy. At the base would be a brazier with a fire to create the necessary draught up the tube. You drop a ball of naphtha down the tube, and then you have an arc of flame a hundred or more feet high.'

Scipio looked sceptical. 'To operate such machines would take valuable men away from the front line, men who could kill more of the enemy with their bare hands than with this contraption.'

'They wouldn't be legionaries. They'd be recruits of the third or fourth class, unsuited to front-line action. They'd be a special-ised maniple of fire-throwers.'

Scipio pursed his lips. 'You might use it against the wooden palisades of the Celts, but it wouldn't be much use against a stone wall. You'd have to get close enough to project the fire over the ramparts, and then you'd be within easy range of the defenders' arrows and javelins. As a battlefield weapon the burning naphtha falling on men would cause terrible injury, I'd grant you that, but assault under interlocked shields, the *testudo*, would provide a barrier, and by advancing rapidly the attacking force would soon be in relative safety, under the arc of fire.' Scipio put his hands on his hips, thinking. 'I can see its use in naval warfare, providing the wind was in the right direction and you didn't burn your own ships. But for land warfare, I'd be on the centurion's side with this one. It would be little more than a spectacle. Come on, let's get back to the table before he arrives.'

'Wait a moment,' Ennius said, agitated. 'We've only been thinking about a crude version, and I'd agree with you. That's precisely why it didn't go anywhere three hundred years ago. But my idea is different. Suppose you seal up one end of the tube, leaving only a small hole at the base to introduce the flame. And supposing you then pack the naphtha down the tube, and drop a stone or lead ball down on top of it, of a width to fit snugly in the tube and keep the gases from blowing out around it. The Greek scientists in Alexandria showed me that volatile substances can burn more violently when they are compressed into a small space. With this tube, it would not be the fire that was the weapon, but the missile. A heavy ball projected out of the tube at sufficient velocity could damage wooden walls, even stone ones. Smaller projectiles could be used on the battlefield: spheres of lead or iron, weighing less than a pound each. Thrown at high speed such a ball could decapitate a man, or tear him in half. As individual weapons, the fire tubes might not make much difference to the outcome of a battle. But massed together, fired in volleys like arrows or javelins, they could unleash hell. Even armoured men could be knocked down and killed by the shock of impact.'

Scipio stared at him. 'Well, have you tried it?'

Ennius looked down, suddenly dejected. 'The ball only goes part-way up the tube. The force of the naphtha isn't powerful enough. I need a mixture that would really explode.'

Fabius cocked his ear. Over the months he had become attuned to the distinctive step of the centurion and the bang of his staff. And there it was. Thump thump *bang*. Thump thump *bang*. Soon there would be the clank of armour, the rattle of decorations on the breastplate. 'Quick,' he whispered to Scipio. 'The centurion!'

Scipio clapped his hands and everyone hurried back to assemble around the table, all of them peering intently at the battle diorama. Ennius brushed the soot off himself as best he could and threw a cloth over the pots by the fireplace, then joined them. Scipio touched the small bronze gorget hanging from his neck that was the insignia of authority over the others given to him by the centurion, and straightened his sword. Fabius sniffed the air cautiously, and his heart sank. The smell of rotten eggs from the sulphur was unmistakable. The centurion was bound to notice it, and Ennius would be down doing duty with Hannibal the elephant for the next month.

He thought about Ennius' concoction. Suddenly he remembered Julia, the ceremony she was attending today with her mother. The lictors who led the Vestal Virgins to the temple would throw clouds of coal dust into the air, and then thrust burning tapers into it. The dust would ignite, crackling and sparkling in a rainbow of colours. He glanced at Ennius, but then thought again. The last thing he wanted was for Ennius to blow up the Gladiator School. And Ennius needed to learn his place; there was a reason why the centurion came down harshly on him. Before he carried his experiments further, Ennius would need to earn his credentials in blood on the battlefield like the rest of them. Then, and only then, would men like the centurion listen to him. Fabius put the thought from his mind, and turned back to the door, tensing and coming to attention as he saw the figure who was standing there. Now the day's training would really begin.

Marcus Cornelius Petraeus, *primipilus* of the first legion on three campaigns, was the most decorated soldier in the Roman army. Standing in the doorway, he looked as old and hard as an ancient olive tree, his legs and arms knotted masses of muscles and veins, his face creased and bronzed. In his left hand he carried a gilded bronze helmet capped with the *crista transversa*, the crest of the centurion made up of eagle feathers, and in his right hand he bore the other insignia of a centurion, the vine staff. Over his short-cropped white hair he wore the grass wreath of the *corona obsidionalis*, the highest Roman military decoration, awarded to him in Macedonia for killing his own tribune after the man had faltered, and for then taking over his maniple to lead it to victory. On his muscled breastplate were other decorations, the embellishments of more than forty years of war. Every time Fabius saw him at that doorway it was as if he were confronting an apparition from their hallowed past, as if the war god Mars himself had walked into the classroom. His battle credentials were second to none: the centurion had fought alongside Fabius' own father and Scipio's adoptive grandfather against Hannibal at Zama in North Africa, the very battle they had been war-gaming on the table in front of them.

They all knew that the centurion had intended to question them on the order of battle. From the corner of his eye Fabius could see the young arrival Gaius Paullus nervously mouthing the formation names to himself, knowing that Scipio had briefed him to answer the first questions. But then Petraeus curled his lip, sniffing. 'What's that reek?' he growled. His voice was hoarse, and his accent was the rough country dialect of the Alban Hills. He smelled the air again, crinkling his nose. Ennius coughed, and looked down. Fabius closed his eyes, expecting the worst. The centurion grunted, sniffing loudly again. 'Did someone break wind?' His eyes alighted on Gulussa. 'You haven't been eating raw camel again, have you, Gulussa? I well remember your father Masinissa feeding it to us the evening before the battle of Zama. Later that night our tent stank like a sulphur mine. If someone had lit a fire, the tent would have ignited and risen into the air like a Greek firework.' He guffawed, and waved his arm at the diorama. 'That's what you don't learn here. The blood and guts of war. The smell of victory.'

Fabius let his breath out slowly. Ennius was off the hook, but they all knew that the new arrival Gaius Paullus was about to have his day of reckoning. He had been standing rigidly to attention, staring at the centurion. When Petraeus was like this, nostalgic about past battles, his hand clenching his staff, he was like a man stoking himself up for an evening in the taverns; only it was not the prospect of wine that was making his eyes gleam, but the prospect of blood. Today was the day of the month when criminals due for capital punishment were paraded into the arena, and the boys were allowed to use weapons on live victims. Today, Gaius Paullus would become a killer, if he had the stomach for it. Scipio knew the centurion would be as ruthless with Gaius Paullus as he had been with each of the others when he had first made them push cold iron into the chest of a living man.

The centurion slammed his staff down, put his helmet on and grasped the pommel of his sword. He scanned the room, his breathing harsh and quick. 'Now then,' he snarled. 'Are we ready to play?'

He snapped his fingers and pointed at the nearest of three slaves standing against the wall holding trays, a tautly muscled, brown-skinned young man who looked Assyrian, his hair dark and curly and the wispy beginnings of a beard on his chin. The slave paused for a moment, uncertain what to do, and the centurion beckoned him forward. 'Put down the tray,' he growled. 'Come over here.' The slave did as he was told, and then the centurion fingered Scipio and Fabius. 'Hold his arms,' he said. Fabius took the slave's left wrist, feeling the sinewy muscle in the forearm, and twisted it behind his back as he had been taught to do with prisoners in the arena; Scipio did the same on the other side. He could feel the slave tensing, expecting a beating. It would not be the first time the old centurion had used slaves to demonstrate a wrestling hold or knockout blow, an occupational hazard for slaves who had the unlucky lot of working in the Gladiator School.

The centurion drew his sword. It was a *gladius*, but with a more elongated leaf-shaped end than the usual Roman form, a shape they knew the centurion had ordered copied from the Iberian blades he had encountered in campaigns against the Carthaginians in Spain, before Hannibal had crossed the Alps into Italy. He held it up and put his forefinger on the tip, drawing blood, and then held the flat of the blade down on the palm of his hand, aiming the point at the slave's upper abdomen. 'Not to the heart,' he said. 'I want him to live long enough for you to see how the muscles of the body react to a blade pushed deep into it. This is how you learn.'

The slave had gone wide-eyed with terror, his mouth open and drooling. He cried something Fabius did not understand, words in his native tongue, and gazed imploringly at them. The centurion grunted, looked around and then snatched a scroll Polybius had been holding and ripped off the papyrus, thrusting the wooden spool sideways into the slave's mouth to act as a gag. The man made a terrible noise and then retched, bringing up a dribble of vomit that sent a distasteful odour through the room. His head lolled forward, and the centurion gestured for Fabius and Scipio to grasp each end of the spool with their other hands to hold the slave's head up. His knees were shaking and buckling, and Fabius felt the weight of his body. He saw a streak of brown drip down the man's inner leg and smelt it, turning away and swallowing hard.

Gaius Paullus stood at the front, shorter and slighter than the others, looking barely old enough to be there, rooted to the floor and staring at the slave. The centurion pointed at him. 'You. New boy,' he snarled. 'Don't think I don't know who you are: Gaius Aemilius Paullus, nephew of Lucius Aemilius Paullus, father of Scipio and the greatest living Roman general. I served under your father when he was a tribune. He began as a scrawny little wimp just like you, but we soon toughened him up. Let's see if you've got the same mettle.'

He walked over, grasped Gaius Paullus' right hand and put the sword hilt in it. He stood back, and the boy held the blade forward, the tip wobbling. For a moment he stood still, and all Fabius could hear was the rasping breathing of the slave, then coughing as he retched again. Gaius Paullus looked away from the slave's terrified eyes, and then the centurion strode over and ripped open the man's tunic, revealing the tensed muscles of his abdomen. He turned back to Gaius Paullus, leaning close to him, his face red and contorted. 'Come on, man,' he bellowed. 'What are you waiting for? Drive it right through to the spine. That'll kill him in a few seconds, but not as quickly as the heart.'

Gaius Paullus aimed the blade, and stepped forward. The slave struggled, his breathing coming hoarse and fast, and Fabius and Scipio held him upright. The tip of the blade touched the abdomen just above the navel, but the boy's arm was extended too far forward to give the blade a good thrust; he needed to step closer, but seemed unable to do so. Gaius Paullus looked at Fabius, and in that split second he saw everything: the boy and the man, the fear and the resolve. The centurion snorted with impatience, clasped his right hand over the boy's hand and pushed him forward, and together they thrust the blade deep into the slave's body. The man gave a terrible groan and retched again, spattering blood and bile over the spool in his mouth. Gaius Paullus kept his nerve, thrusting harder until the bloody tip emerged from the slave's back below the ribcage. The man's legs slumped but his torso and arms remained rigid, as if his body were making a last attempt to resist, a final hold on life that Fabius knew would give way in moments to the throes of death.

The centurion looked at the others. 'You see there is no blood yet from the entry wound?' He turned to the boy. 'Try to get the sword out.' Gaius Paullus pulled hard, but was barely able to budge it. The centurion grunted. 'So far this month I have taught you killer blows, thrusts to the throat and heart that bring instant death. But a thrust to the abdomen where there are walls of muscle is different. The muscles contract around the blade. If you are in battle, you need to be able to get the blade out quickly or you will be killed. You need to twist it, to use your foot. Watch me closely.'

He pushed Gaius Paullus aside, raised his right foot against the man's abdomen, grasped the hilt of the sword and twisted it hard, then pulled it out in one clean stroke. Blood gushed from the wound and the slave's body went limp, his jaws releasing the spool and his head arching backwards, his mouth and eyes wide open. Fabius and Scipio let go and the body fell into the slick of blood and bile that had pooled on the floor, the head hitting the stone hard and cracking open. The centurion clicked his fingers at the two remaining slaves, indicating the body, then pointed at Ennius and Gulussa. 'You two clean up the mess here. I want this floor spotless when I return. That one wasn't just a slave. He was a prisoner of war, a former mercenary, and his life was forfeit. All of the new batch of slaves working in the Gladiator School are like that. If any of the rest of you want to practise on one before having a go with the condemned criminals, you don't need to ask me.' He wiped his sword blade on the torn piece of the man's tunic, sheathed it and looked at them. 'We meet here again an hour before sundown. The prisoners due for execution this month include two young initiates for the Vestal Virgins caught *in flagrante delicto* with a slave. Gaius Paullus can bring his own sword and show us that he's learned today's lesson.' He stomped off out of the room and down the corridor, the bang of his centurion's staff receding into the gloom as he headed off towards the arena.

Gaius Paullus stood stock-still, his face and tunic spattered with the man's blood, staring at what he had done. Scipio brought a bucket of water from by the door and a wet towel, which he tossed to him. 'Clean yourself up. You and I need to be presentable for a temple dedication by the *gens* Aemilii in the Forum in an hour. And, by the way, welcome to the academy.'

3

At the appointed hour they stood waiting for the centurion to enter the room and lead them out into the arena, where Brutus had been training hard all afternoon. Scipio and Gaius Paullus were wearing the purple-hemmed tunics they had donned for the ceremony in the temple, but had removed the laurel garlands that marked them out as *viris principes*, young men within their *gens* who were nearly of age to lead the rituals themselves. Fabius looked over the balustrade and into the arena, a smaller, practice version of the oval arenas surrounded by raised wooden stands that were erected for gladiatorial contests in the Field of Mars. In the early days of Rome, fights had taken place on the Sacred Way in the Forum, even within the temple precincts – in any open space where spectators could assemble on surrounding walls and balconies. But as space in the Forum became constricted and the crowds grew larger, the contests had been held in the Circus Maximus and then in the temporary arenas on the Field of Mars, next to the military training ground. Neither venue was satisfactory, and there was even talk of building a permanent stone structure with tiered seating and underground holding pens, so the animals would no longer have to be dragged snarling though the streets and threaten the lives of spectators as much as the gladiators who fought them. But the idea had been scoffed at by the more conservative senators who controlled public works, those who thought that building a structure on that scale solely for the purpose of entertainment was a frivolous use of money and smacked of Greek effeminacy: they harked back to the time when their Etruscan and Latin ancestors had created the boundary of the arenas with their own bodies, and revelled in the sweat and blood of the contest. They said that a structure large enough to accommodate all of those who would attend the contests would destroy the majesty of Rome, dwarfing the temples of the Forum and making a mockery of the gods and the *pietas* and *dignitas* on which the city had been built.

In the academy the gladiators were used as sparring partners for the boys, all of whom bore scars from the hours they had spent in the afternoons moving from one opponent to another, testing their skills and weapons against enemies of Rome who had been taken prisoner in wars of conquest: Iberians and Celtiberians, Gauls and Germans from the north, Balearic slingers and Cretan bowmen, and swordsmen from all of the regions of the east encompassed by the former empire of Alexander the Great. Brutus' opponent today was a giant Thracian named Brasis who had been captured as a mercenary in Macedonia some ten years before, but his fighting skills had meant that he was spared by a Roman commander with an eye to bringing back a prisoner who could excel as a gladiator to increase his popularity among the *plebs*. Brasis had won enough contests to secure his freedom but had remained in the Gladiator School, and still fought lions with his bare hands and his vicious Thracian knife when he was sober enough to do so. Fabius had seen slyness behind the glazed-over eyes, and wondered whether Brasis was truly still here because he had nowhere else to go, as he claimed, or whether he was in the pay of the faction in the Senate who opposed the academy and wanted an insider strongman for when the time came to clear it out. All that was certain was that the man was an extraordinary sword fighter who had honed Brutus' skills to the point where they were evenly matched, evidenced by the clashing blades and shuffling movements that could go on for hours, with neither man giving quarter, only to be broken up when the ringmaster called the contest to a halt and sent Brutus reluctantly on to his next class.

Fabius turned back to the room. That lunchtime he had heard

rumours in the Scipio household about events in Macedonia, and everyone was tense with excitement. They all prayed that Aemilius Paullus had not defeated the army of King Perseus, a triumph for Rome but the death-knell for their chances of seeing active service any time soon. The rumours were that a final battle was imminent, but that Aemilius Paullus was stalling until he had a fresh draft of legionaries as well as the tribunes needed to lead them. Metellus had already left that afternoon on horseback to rejoin his legion, and would be followed by the other young officers who had been on leave in Rome during the lull in the fighting over the past months. But to put those men in charge of newly raised troops would be to spread them too thinly, and Fabius knew that Scipio and the other boys would be crossing their fingers that they were next in line; apart from Metellus, who was ten years older and only visiting the academy, none of them had yet reached the age of eighteen, so they could not be given official appointments as tribunes within a legion, but a general could make temporary appointments on his staff and attach them to the maniples on an emergency basis.

Their numbers in the academy were already depleted, Ptolemy and Demetrius having left for Egypt and Syria in the last month, with Gulussa and Hippolyta due to return to their homelands as well. Everyone left would therefore stand a good chance of an appointment if the call to arms came. Fabius was already eighteen, a year older than Scipio and old enough to be recruited as a legionary, and had undertaken basic training on the Field of Mars; if the call to arms came, he was sworn to protect Scipio and would remain his bodyguard, but he knew that Scipio himself would not countenance him going simply as an officer's servant and would insist on his appointment as a legionary in the front line, a demand that Petraeus would also support.

For now, the talk was just rumours and his main focus was on the academy and the needs of the day. He had heard Scipio warning Gaius Paullus that as the newest of the boys he still must not put a foot wrong, despite passing the test with the *gladius* that morning. But Fabius had a sinking feeling as he saw Gaius Paullus detach himself from the group and come to attention, evidently aiming to please. '*Strategos*,' he said loudly, saluting as he did so.

Fabius groaned inwardly, and the centurion glared at Gaius Paullus. Scipio leaned forward and nudged his cousin. 'For Jupiter's sake, call him centurion,' he whispered.

'But they call him *strategos* here, the slaves who led me in,' the boy whispered back. 'And so do the Greek professors.'

'That's exactly why he hates it,' Scipio whispered back. 'They're *Greek*. Don't you know what the vine staff he's carrying means – the *vitis*, the centurion's badge of rank? Well, you'll know soon enough, because you're in for it now.'

'Silence!' The centurion stepped forward, slamming his staff down on the floor in front of Gaius Paullus. The colour drained from the boy's face, but he stood his ground. In one deft movement the centurion twirled the staff and brought it down hard against the boy's shins. Gaius Paullus buckled forward, only just retaining his balance, then came to attention again, inches from the centurion's face. Fabius watched him trying to stay emotionless, to show no pain, holding back the tears. The centurion stared at him mercilessly, watching for any sign of weakness. After what seemed an eternity, he grunted, stamped his stick down and walked past Gaius Paullus towards the table. The boy's face crumpled in pain, and Scipio nudged him again, shaking his head violently. The centurion banged his stick, and they turned to follow his gaze as he pointed at the battle diorama.

'I was there, in the front rank of the first legion,' Petraeus said gruffly, pointing at the wooden blocks representing the Roman infantry. He narrowed his eyes at Gaius Paullus, and then glanced at Scipio. 'I was your adoptive grandfather's standard-bearer then. After ten more years in the ranks I became a centurion, and then *primipilus*, senior centurion of my legion. Three times I held that rank, three times as new legions were raised for new wars. And then I could rise no further, because my father was a mere peasant, an honest Roman who toiled with his oxen on the slopes of the Alban Hills all his life: the type of Roman the consuls love to praise, the backbone of the army, yet unable to command units larger than a century. Except that your grandfather saw otherwise. A few of us senior centurions he promoted to command auxiliary cohorts. My lot was the elephants. He glared at Ennius, who again had the job of mucking out old Hannibal that day. 'The elephants, mark you.'

'Centurion,' Ennius said, his voice quavering.

'And then when he became *praetor*, general of the army, he put me in command of his personal troops, the Praetorian Guard. And then before he departed to the afterlife he chose me to look after you boys. There were so many Greeks teaching here that they started to call me *strategos*. The name stuck.'

Polybius cleared his throat. 'It has an honourable pedigree. Think of the heroes of Thermopylae, of Marathon, of Alexander the Great and his generals, of Perseus and his Macedonian phalanx.'

The old man snorted. 'When I am back in the village of my forefathers I am called centurion. That is what I will be called when I retire.'

'You will only retire when the gods call you to Elysium, centurion. You were born a soldier, and you will die a soldier.'

Petraeus snorted again, but looked pleased. Polybius knew how to flatter him. And the centurion had not got where he was solely by brawn: he was a skilled tactician who could see Polybius' unusual ability as a strategist, despite the posturing that always came before they entered the arena. 'Enough of this,' he said gruffly, as if on cue. 'There is only one way to win a war, and that is to do what we Romans do best: killing at close quarters, with the spear, with the sword, with our bare hands. All this talk of strategy is making you soft. It is time we went below to help Brutus execute criminals.'

'*Ave*, centurion.' They all stood loosely to attention, waiting for him to bang his staff and lead the way. But before he could do so, Scipio advanced a few steps and stood in front of him, addressing him formally. 'Gnaeus Petraeus Atinus, tomorrow I must go to the family tomb of the Scipiones on the Appian Way to honour my ancestors. From there I march three days down the coast to Liternum, to the tomb of my adoptive grandfather Publius Cornelius Scipio Africanus. You know that he chose to end his days and be buried away from Rome because he felt forsaken by the Senate, by those who were envious of his fame and refused to heed his advice. Now, fifteen years after his death, the consuls have finally allowed the full *lustratio* to be carried out at his tomb, to accord him the highest honour as a Roman.'

Petraeus snorted. 'So they say. I do not trust the Senate. And Scipio Africanus will only rest easy once Carthage has been destroyed.'

Scipio reached into a bag he was carrying and took out a folded white garment with purple borders. 'When my father Aemilius Paullus stood before my adoptive grandfather's death-bed, Scipio Africanus told him that there was a place for you in his tomb, that you would hold the standard for him in the after-life just as you did in this world. My family would be honoured if you would wear this *toga praetexta* and perform the *lustratio* at his tomb, the sacrifice of purification. As a *centurio primipilus* who has won the *corona obsidionalis*, you are allowed by law to perform the rite.'

The centurion stood stock-still, but Fabius could see that his lips were quivering with emotion. He gripped his staff hard, then held out his right hand stiffly, taking the toga. He cleared his throat. 'Publius Cornelius Scipio Aemilianus, I accept this honour. I served your grandfather, in this world, and will do so in the next.' He held the toga against his breastplate, then eyed Scipio. 'Liternum is only an hour's march from the Phlegraean Fields, where Aeneas visited the underworld. You know who lives there.'

There was silence, a sudden uneasy tension. The centurion banged his staff. 'Come on, out with it, one of you. She's just an old hag in a cave.'

'The Sibyl,' Polybius said quietly.

The centurion grunted. 'Old hag she may be, but she speaks the words of Apollo in her riddles. Fifty years ago I went there with Scipio Africanus, when he was a boy like you and I was his bodyguard. The Sibyl foretold of a day when the god would reveal himself to another Scipio, on the Ides of March, 585 years *ab urbe condita*. That is four days from now, and on that day Scipio must await her in the cave.'

It was Scipio's turn to stare. 'You mean me?'

'It was foretold.' He paused. 'One other will have been there before you, stopping off on his ride south towards Brundisium, he who bears the mark of the eagle.'

Scipio stared at him. 'You mean Metellus?'

'The Sibyl foretold it, of the one who would bear the mark of the sun, the symbol of the Scipiones, and the other the eagle. She said that you were to be two young warriors of Rome, and Metellus is the only one among you who bears such a mark.'

'And what else did she foretell?'

'In some way your future is bound up together, but in a way that only the Sibyl will tell.'

Scipio looked away pensively. His future was already bound up with Metellus through Julia, and he knew too well that he was the one who was going to lose out. Fabius knew that he would not want to travel all the way to the Phlegraean Fields to hear an old hag speak an obscure riddle that would be interpreted by some as evidence that he had no future with Julia, a fact that the Sibyl could easily have surmised from her network of spies in Rome, feeding her with information that she used to convince the gullible that she had some kind of clairvoyance. But then Fabius looked at the old centurion and remembered Polybius that morning, telling them that soldiers should be allowed their superstitions. Petraeus knew better than any of them that wars were won by strategy and tactics, not by divine oracles, but like many who had survived battle, he had come to believe that there was more to it than chance and skill, that luck was divinely bestowed. And for Scipio to visit the Sibyl would mean more than that to Petraeus; it would be part of a pilgrimage to honour the memory of the revered Africanus. It was Scipio who had invited Petraeus to Liternum, and now he was going to have to indulge him.

Ennius spoke up. 'Can the rest of us come? To the tomb of Scipio Africanus, to the rite of purification?'

The centurion glared at him, and then sniffed exaggeratedly. The distinctive odour of elephant dung had been wafting over them from the window for some time now. 'After what you're about to do this evening for old Hannibal, there'll be no chance of purification for you, Ennius, in this world or the next.' His face cracked into a rare grin, and the others laughed, the tension eased. He put a hand on Ennius' shoulder. 'Your time will come. It will come for all of you. You will know your destiny soon enough. There is war in the air.'

A clanking sound of chains came up from the arena, the swoosh of whips and cries of pain as the prisoners were brought in. The centurion leaned his staff against his chest, held up his hands and examined them theatrically, his eyes gleaming. 'But meanwhile there is work to do. Look, the blood on my hands from that slave this morning has dried. It's time I got them wet again.' He slapped Polybius on the shoulder, clasped the pommel of his sword and took up his staff again, banging it down. 'Are we ready?' he bellowed.

They all answered as one. '*Parati sumus*, centurion. We are ready.'

Four days later Fabius stood among the steaming fumeroles of the Phlegraean Fields near Neapolis, tasting the tang of sulphur and wishing he were in the fresh air a few miles away below

Mount Vesuvius in the town of Pompeii, where he had cousins. He and Scipio had been accompanied from Rome by Gaius Paullus, who as a distant scion of the *gens* Cornelia had been sent to represent his family at the *lustratio* for Scipio Africanus; he was with them now, looking pale and exhausted. It had been rough going for him from the outset. The old centurion had made up for his show of sentiment on being invited by Scipio to Liternum by treating the trip south as an army route march, making them each carry a sack of rocks on their backs equivalent to a legionary's pack. Gaius Paullus was only sixteen and small for his age and had suffered the most, with Petraeus hounding him mercilessly and frequently flicking his whip across the back of the boy's legs. By the time they reached Liternum after three days and nights on the road, stopping only for the odd hour of sleep before Petraeus roused them again, the boy could barely stand. During the ceremony at the tomb Fabius and Scipio had wedged him between them to stop him from collapsing and dishonouring both his family and Petraeus, who had been resplendent in *toga praetexta* as officiating priest in a ceremony to perpetuate the memory of a man he regarded as something akin to a god.

The route march had been bad enough, but it had been punctuated by an experience that was etched in Fabius' memory. On the Appian Way a few miles outside Rome, beyond the family tomb of the Scipiones, they had come across a line of wooden crucifixes being set up on the edge of the road. There had been a slave revolt in a travertine quarry to the east of the city, and the culprits were paying the penalty. They had seen the progression of death by crucifixion as they marched alongside, from those nearest the city who had been hoisted up first to the ones being set up that day: from the grey dangling corpses to the men still struggling for breath, their eyes wide open with fear, no longer with the strength in their arms to hold their chests up and prevent themselves from drowning in their own fluids, their legs and the post below streaked with faeces and urine and blood.

Gaius Paullus had turned away and retched, and the old centurion had pounced on him, pulling him up by the collar of his tunic and snarling into his face. 'You can fight all the wars you want in the dioramas and sandpits of the academy. But you will never fight a real war unless you learn to love the sight of death. Breathe it all in. Learn to relish it. Otherwise you may as well go back and join the spotty youths in the Forum learning oratory and social niceties. Give me a girl like Julia in my legion any day over any of them.' He had dragged Gaius Paullus along to the front of the line of crucifixes, stripped him of his load and spoken with the centurion commanding the execution party, who had gladly handed over the hammer and nails and ropes to the boys to carry on with the job. They had spent the next several hours hoisting and nailing prisoners to the crosses, enduring their writhing attempts to break free and the screams of pain as they knocked the foot-long spikes through their wrists and feet. Fabius had been sickened and knew that Scipio felt the same too, but there was nothing they could do to ease the agony for the prisoners; many were muscular giants captured in the Macedonian wars who should have been recruited as mercenaries to fight for Rome instead of being wasted in the quarries – another failing of Roman policy that Scipio Africanus had railed against but which for now they could do nothing to change.

At the end, Scipio and Gaius Paullus had stood in front of Petraeus while he addressed them. 'I want you to become tribunes whom I would serve under,' he had said. 'That's what Scipio Africanus told me to make of the students in the academy. Make them or break them, he said. And if I break you, you'll feel the pain and the shame for all your lives. So you'd better learn what I'm telling you now. One day you are going to have to order men to be executed, some of them superb warriors like these slaves, some of them men you have fought alongside and loved like brothers. You will have to be able to do it in front of their comrades, without flinching, and without mercy. Now get back to the road, pick up those sacks of rocks and march. You've got thirty seconds or you'll feel the lick of my whip.'

Fabius followed Scipio and Gaius Paullus down the rocky path into the crater, followed by Petraeus. Somewhere ahead of them in the smoke lay the Sibyl's cave, and near that the crack in the earth that was said to lead to the underworld. As they reached the bottom of the slope they passed fissures stained yellow that reeked of sulphur, just like Ennius' concoction in the academy. The base of the crater was an expanse of glassy rock as flat as a lake, wreathed in smoke that swirled up and obscured the sun, making the way ahead seem dark and forbidding. At the edge of the crater the rock bulged up in forms that looked like half-finished giants, borne of the earth but trapped in the rock before they could fully emerge. Polybius had told Fabius how he had been high up the volcano in Sicily and seen bulbous shapes like these as they were being formed, solidified from rivers of molten rock. He had said that the Phlegraean Fields truly were an entrance to the underworld, a place where the rock they stood on was a mere crust over the fiery chaos within, but that it was an entrance to Hades only inasmuch as those who lingered too long near the smoke or slipped into the molten streams were certain to die. Out of earshot of Petraeus he had said that those who came here were deluded, people whose desperation to know the future or to meet the shade of a loved one had tricked them into seeing visions, their minds fogged by the fumes and by the intoxicating leaf that the servants of the Sibyl burned on her fire; it was a leaf that Polybius himself knew was not some special gift of the gods but had been shipped from India by way of Alexandria, along with the drug known as *lachryma papaveris*, poppy tears. It was said that the priests of the Sibyl gave out these drugs freely to any of those who came to see her, and that those who brought gold were given especially large doses and were the ones who kept coming back for more, some of them wealthy aristocrats who had moved their homes from Rome to Neapolis and nearby Cumae just to be close to the source of the drugs that had begun to consume their minds.

Fabius caught sight of human forms huddled behind the rocks, staring at them. These were not aristocrats but were people who had fallen away from society, emaciated forms with faces and hands blackened by the smoke. It was said that they included a sect of Jews who believed that one day their god would come to them in this place; most, though, were escaped slaves and other fugitives from the law, those at the end of their tether who had come to spend their final days here before the fumes overcame them, hoping for some kind of salvation. One of them scurried up now, a filthy wretch clothed only in a loincloth, his eyes glazed over as if drunk, gesticulating wildly and pointing down a line of rocks laid across the floor of the crater. Scipio tossed him a coin and he scurried away, and then stopped and looked back at Petraeus for confirmation. He nodded, pointing forward, and they turned and made their way along the line of rocks, their feet crunching on the glassy surface of the crater. Fabius could feel the heat underneath and was glad for the thickness of his sandals, but Gaius Paullus was hopping and grimacing, the leather of his sandals smouldering. After what seemed an age they came to the other side of the crater and a tumble of rock that had fallen from the rim, in the middle of which was a jagged black hole the size of a temple entrance; in front was a hearth, tended by two black-robed forms who disappeared among the rocks as soon as they came close.

They had reached the cave of the Sibyl. They made their way up a well-worn path towards the hearth, the rocks smoothed by the countless supplicants who had clambered this way before. A few paces from the hearth they stopped, smelling the sweet odour that rose from the embers, and stared into the yawning blackness beyond. 'They say she's three hundred generations old,' Gaius Paullus whispered, staring in awe. 'They say she was old before

Aeneas stood here, and is now so shrunken and wizened that she hangs in a little cage in the darkness, fed and tended by her priests like a pet monkey.'

'Be careful what you say,' Petraeus growled. 'The god Apollo himself will hear you, and mete out his punishment.' He turned to Scipio. 'Her attendants have seen you, and she knows you are here. You must go forward alone into the cave.'

Scipio gave Fabius a wry look, took a deep breath and strode forward, walking around the hearth and disappearing out of sight into the blackness beyond. For a few minutes there was silence, and Fabius tensed, hating to see Scipio go out of his sight. And then a strange noise issued from the cave, indiscernible, like the muffled sound of a priest's incantation in the back *cella* of a temple. A few moments later Scipio reappeared, stumbling towards them, his face flushed and running with sweat. He passed the hearth and then turned back to peer at the cave, breathing heavily.

'Did you see her?' Gaius Paullus whispered, his voice tremulous.

'I don't know.' Scipio's voice was hoarse with the smoke, and he passed his hand over his face, leaning with the other on Fabius for support. 'The fumes from the hearth were very strong, a sweetness that made me feel light-headed. It must be the weed that Polybius warned of. I'm not sure what I saw, but there might have been something in the darkness, hanging there, and I felt an exhalation that wafted the leaves over the fire, making them crackle and burn. When that happened there was a voice, a deep voice but that of a woman, ancient and cackling. I nearly fainted when I heard it.'

'Well,' Gaius Paullus asked, his voice hushed, 'what did she say?'

Scipio shook his head. 'I'm not sure. It was a verse, a riddle. All that I heard was this: *The eagle and the sun shall unite, and in their union shall lie the future of Rome.*'

'What on earth can that mean?'

Fabius led Scipio back down a few steps to where Petraeus had been waiting for them, and thought hard. 'If the eagle means Metellus and the sun represents the Scipiones, then your joint destiny is to take Rome forward.'

'Metellus in the east, Scipio in the west,' Petraeus growled. 'That's what the Sibyl foretold when Scipio Africanus and I came here all those years ago. She said that one with the name Scipio would conquer Carthage and have the world at his feet.'

'It cannot be me, then,' Scipio said, pushing Fabius away, stumbling against the rocks and then standing without assistance, blinking in a shaft of sunlight that came through the smoke. 'The Senate is too cautious to declare war, and Carthage will remain unfinished business.'

'Maybe for now, but war with Carthage is possible within our lifetimes,' Gaius Paullus said cautiously.

Scipio took a swig of water from the skin that Fabius had offered him. 'How can you know this?'

'The day that we left Rome I spent the morning in the Forum. It began as a rumour among the people, and then became a murmur in the Senate, and then a clamour that drowned out all debate, until the consuls ordered the guard to unsheathe their swords to shut everybody up. And then Cato stood up to the rostrum and said the words that had been on everyone's lips.'

The centurion stared at him. 'Out with it, man.'

Gaius Paullus swallowed hard. '*Carthago delenda est.*'

In the silence that followed, Fabius looked up and saw a crow flying high across the sky, just as his father had told him he had twice seen before sailing to war. Scipio turned to Gaius Paullus and repeated the words, his voice hoarse now with emotion. '*Carthago delenda est.* Carthage must be destroyed.'

The centurion fixed Scipio in his gaze, his eyes gleaming with a fire that Fabius had not seen in them before. 'Almost fifty years ago I stood with your adoptive grandfather at this very spot, when war was in the offing. Eighteen years later we stood before the walls of Carthage, battle-hardened, watching Hannibal crawl before us, pleading for peace. Then, the Senate baulked at issuing the final order. Now, you are a new breed of men, and when those of you who live to see the day stand in front of those walls yourselves, there will be no appeasement, no mercy to the vanquished. That much I have taught you in the academy. There will be much preparation, and much hardship, and I myself will not live to see it. But I will die happy, knowing that the job will at last be finished.'

Gaius Paullus stood at attention, staring straight ahead, the toll of the last few days showing on his face. Scipio straightened and slapped his right hand on his chest, his voice still clenched with emotion. 'You can depend on us, centurion.'

Just as they were about to turn and leave, the sound of a horse's hooves came clattering from the crater, and a rider wearing an official messenger's gold-rimmed tunic and neck gorget came into view. He dismounted, holding the horse's bridle as it stomped and snorted in the fumes, and came up to them. 'Gnaeus Petraeus Atinus, holder of the *corona obsidionalis*, I have news from the Senate. The war against King Perseus of Macedon is heading for a decisive battle. Lucius Aemilius Paullus has requested a further call to arms. The Senate has authorized the raising of another legion.'

Fabius' heart began to pound. He looked towards Scipio, seeing his eyes suddenly gleam. The messenger turned to Scipio. 'Publius Cornelius Scipio Aemilianus, your father requests that you be appointed a temporary military tribune on his staff. Gaius Aemilius Paullus, you are appointed temporary tribune to be second in command of the third maniple of the new legion. And Fabius Petronius Secundus, as your eighteenth birthday has passed, you are to be a legionary and standard-bearer of the first cohort of the first legion, on the special recommendation of *primipilus* Gnaeus Petraeus Atinus.'

Fabius felt a surge of excitement and glanced at the centurion, who nodded curtly. Petraeus must have put in a word for him in Rome before they left. He must have known that the call to arms would come before their journey was over. That was what this trip had really been about, preparing them for this moment. Scipio stood up and spoke. 'So this is it. Our time in the academy is finished.'

The centurion placed his hand on the hilt of his sword. 'Now you must prove yourselves in blood. You must learn to kill like legionaries, winning the respect of the toughest soldiers the world has ever known. I do not know what the words of the Sibyl mean. But I do know this. Your right to order legionaries into battle must be earned. Then, you can heed the call of Cato and lead a Roman army back to Carthage.'

'And today, centurion?'

'Today, you march to war.'

PART TWO

ROME

167 BC

The Triumph of Aemilius Paullus

4

Fabius shut his eyes and took a deep breath, feeling his chest swell against his breastplate and smelling the heady aroma of incense that filled the air. He opened his eyes, and was dazzled by the view. All of Rome seemed to be on fire that night, not a fire of destruction but of celebration: a thousand basins of burning oil lining the processional route from the Ostia gate through the Forum to the Field of Mars. Here on the podium below the Capitoline Temple they were at the apex of the procession, at the end of the Sacred Way where the legionaries marching towards them veered west towards the open ground of the Field of Mars for the games and spectacles that would carry on through the night.

He and Scipio had left the head of the first legion a few minutes before to bound up the steps so that Scipio could stand beside his father Aemilius Paullus as the procession reached its climax. Polybius was there too, standing behind Aemilius Paullus, and beside them was Marcus Porcius Cato, in his rightful position on the podium as elder statesman of the Senate, a former consul and censor who was one of Aemilius Paullus' oldest friends and supporters. Fabius glanced at the general, who raised his right hand in salute and held it steady as each legion marched by. Beneath the burnished armour he was now an old man, gnarled and leathery skinned like Cato, both of them veterans who had stood here as young tribunes watching triumphal processions long before Fabius and Scipio had even been born. This day would be the last dose of glory for the generation who had fought Hannibal, for those who knew they would soon follow Scipio Africanus to Elysium but only truly rest once Carthage had finally been vanquished.

Fabius cast his eye over the young men in armour and the older men in togas crowding the steps of the podium below. The patrician women were absent, waiting in the stands that each *gens* had erected at the end of the processional way to watch the execution of deserters, but Metellus and the young bloods among the tribunes were all thronged below, joined every few minutes by others who left the head of their legions and maniples as Fabius and Scipio had done to mount the steps and view the spectacle. The most conspicuous absence was the old centurion Petraeus, who had hung up his armour for good once Scipio and the others had gone off to war in Macedonia and the academy had closed. For him, war was in the past, and his pasturage in the Alban Hills had beckoned; it was November and he had needed to reap his corn and sow his winter wheat before the frost. He was a true Roman, farmer first and soldier second, more true to the roots of Rome than any of the patricians who vied with each other to claim the oldest *gens* and the strongest lineage from Romulus or some other semi-mythical warrior in Rome's past.

But there were others missing too. As he had marched past the consular *fasti* at the head of the Forum, Fabius had seen the marble plaque inscribed with the names of officers of the patrician *gentes* who had fallen at Pydna. Among them was Gaius Aemilius Paullus, temporary tribune in the fourth legion, still only sixteen when he had died. Fabius remembered the last time he had been with Gaius Paullus in Italy, seeing his exhausted face at the end of their march south to the Bay of Naples, and then the mangled body that he and Scipio had helped to carry to the funeral pyre after the battle. The boy's maniple had been the first Roman infantry unit to charge after the Paeligni had hurtled themselves into the phalanx, but after the shock of the Paeligni the Macedonians had been ready for what came next; those first legionaries did not have a chance. There were some who said that Gaius Paullus had been screaming in terror and had turned in front of the phalanx, others that he was bellowing like a bull and had turned only to fall on the body of a wounded legionary and take the thrusts of the Macedonian spears himself, an act that would have won him the *corona obsidionalis* had enough survived to vouch for it. The entire front row of the maniple had sacrificed themselves on the spears of the phalanx so that the following ranks could charge through. Fabius remembered Petraeus' brutality towards the boy, no worse than the brutality they had all experienced from him, but different because of Gaius Paullus' youth. He wondered whether in those final moments it had strengthened him, or whether he had been broken by it. The truth might never be known, but he hoped that Gaius Paullus' shade was able to stand easy in Elysium and hold his head high alongside those who had died with him.

The last of the legionaries passed by, leaving the Sacred Way empty as they waited for the next stage in the procession. Fabius looked along it now, at the monuments and temples swirling with smoke and bedecked with wreaths, and remembered racing Scipio along it when they had been young boys, and then accompanying him every day from Scipio's house on the Palatine towards the academy in the Gladiator School. Never in their dreams could they have imagined that only a few years later they would be standing here watching the greatest triumphal procession ever seen, not as gawping boys envious of the young tribunes and legionaries in the procession but as returning soldiers who had fought and killed for the glory of Rome.

He felt his cheek throb, and brushed his finger over the livid scar where his wound was finally beginning to heal. It had been over a year since the Battle of Pydna, a year during which he and Scipio had served with the occupying force in Macedonia as Aemilius Paullus had tried to establish a client republic, a province of Rome in all but name. At first their job had been to hunt down those who had refused to surrender after the battle, mainly Thracian mercenaries who knew that they faced almost certain death if captured. It had been exhilarating work, with Scipio in command of a unit of fifty light cavalry and Fabius as his companion-in-arms, ranging far and wide across Macedonia as they chased men down like wild beasts, cornering them and showing no mercy. Occasionally the enemy had banded together and their clashes had been proper skirmishes, brief and bloody encounters of several dozen men fighting to the death, but more often than not it had been single combat, ferocious duels fought by Scipio himself and sometimes Fabius with only one possible outcome, as the rest of the *ala* encircled the killing ground and prepared to spear the enemy if he should gain the upper hand. Scipio and Fabius had each accounted for more than a dozen men that way, and after six months of it they had felt more like proper veterans of a campaign than simply the survivors of one battle.

After the mopping up was over, Aemilius Paullus had recalled Scipio to the Macedonian capital Pella to gain experience acting as an arbiter in local disputes, a role he had found difficult to settle into after the excitement of the previous months but had excelled at, his reputation for *fides* and fair play putting him in great demand throughout the region under his control. They had arrived back in Italy only three weeks before, after settling a spurious claim by a man to be the vanquished Macedonian king Peleus' son and therefore the rightful head of the new republic, a misapprehension about how a republic worked that Scipio had resolved admirably by explaining how Rome had rejected its kings more than three hundred years earlier and broken the line of succession, building the Republic from new men who were elected to office. They were due to return to Macedonia after the triumph, not to more administrative work, but for some well-earned leave, hunting in the vast expanse of the Macedonian Royal Forest that bordered the towering mountain range to the north.

Suddenly a horn sounded – a shrill, strident note from somewhere behind them – and the crowd that lined the Sacred Way became silent, watching with bated breath for what might come next. From a pedestal part-way up the Palatine Hill a giant Nubian slave hurled a burning taper high into the air, aiming it towards a metal cauldron on the rostrum below the podium. The taper cartwheeled lazily, the flame whooshing as it tumbled down, and then disappeared into the cauldron and was seemingly extinguished, the taper barely hitting the sides. The crowd erupted in applause, astonished at such a prodigious feat of marksmanship. But Fabius knew it was not over. The noise of the crowd died down, and all eyes turned to the far end of the Sacred Way, where the procession would resume. Without warning, an enormous explosion erupted from the cauldron, sending a ball of fire high into the air until it too exploded, showering the crowd with sparks and leaving a billowing black cloud that darkened the sky above the Forum, making the fires along the road seem even more brilliant. This time the crowd were too stunned to applaud, staring with open mouths at something they had never seen before, a presage of the sights to come that Fabius knew would soon have them baying for more.

Scipio turned and nudged him. 'Ennius will be pleased. I told him that if he couldn't yet make his naphtha mixture into an explosive weapon, at least he could make a spectacle out of it for the triumph. He's been working on it for months.'

Aemilius Paullus turned to Scipio, and put a hand on his shoulder. 'Enjoy this spectacle, but do not be seduced by it,' he said gruffly. 'Remember this: there are true triumphs, and there are false triumphs. A victorious general may be treated like a god on a day such as this and then be the scourge of the tribunes on the next, beaten out of the city like a dog. Even today the tribunes of the people tried to prevent my triumph, by stirring up the plebs and trying to make then believe that my legionaries were immoral and out of control, that they would return to loot Rome as they looted Macedonia. And there are triumphs ordered by consuls who have exaggerated their victories, intent on creating glory for themselves when there is none, desperate to claim a military success during their year in office.'

'The defeat of Perseus is the greatest triumph ever celebrated in Rome,' Scipio replied, raising his voice against the din. 'With victory at Pydna you passed to Rome the legacy of Alexander the Great, and laid open the east to Roman conquest.'

'Such may be the judgement of history, of men like Polybius,' Aemilius Paullus said. 'But the judgement of Rome on a man's achievements in his lifetime is a fickle thing, swaying this way and that like the wind that twists through these seven hills. Heed my words today. Cato and I have discussed it, and we see dark times ahead. Until Rome truly reawakens to the threat of Carthage, there will be years in which war may seem a distant memory, in which your own destiny may seem clouded and uncertain. You must hold true to yourself, and always remember what Homer said: Those fare best in life whose fortunes swing one way and then the other. When fortune is in your favour, your ability to excel will be boosted by the strength that you will have gained in times of adversity.'

Aemilius Paullus turned back towards the Sacred Way, and Fabius caught Polybius' eye, seeing the hint of a smile on his lips. The evening before, they had walked together along the bank of the Tiber and Polybius had predicted it: that at the moment of greatest spectacle there would be a solemn moral message from father to son. He had said it was the thing he admired most about the Romans, their moral rectitude, something that had made him turn his back on Greece and make his home with those who had been his captors. He believed that it was what made the Romans such good generals and so different from Alexander the Great, his brilliance as a war leader weighed down by excess and immorality that fortunately seemed so far from the Roman character.

Fabius followed the general's gaze and watched the legionary standards shimmering in the distance, where they rose above the height of the surrounding buildings on the route to the Field of

Mars. Aemilius Paullus had been right about the disaffection of the people. After parting with Polybius the evening before, Fabius had spent much of the night in the taverns with comrades from the first maniple of the second legion, the unit he had trained with before leaving for Macedonia, and he had seen their anger. Men returning to Rome from glorious battle had been turned away from their homes by their wives and shunned by their children. He knew from Polybius what had caused it, not the tribunes of the people but those who had bribed them to spread disaffection, the same group of senators who had opposed the formation of a professional army and the foundation of the academy. It was the first time that Fabius had recognized the power that those men wielded, and how they could bring the plebs to their side. He had also realized that Metellus and his followers could use the enmity of that faction in the Senate towards the Scipiones and the Aemilii Paulli to their advantage, poisoning opinion against Scipio. That was part of the message from his father, about dark times ahead, caused not by an enemy abroad but by an enemy within. Half of those men who were standing around the podium now in togas enjoying the esteem of the people would as soon see Aemilius Paullus cast out of Rome and his triumph discredited. The general had been right about that too. The wind had blown in their favour this day, but it might not the next.

Scipio turned to Fabius and spoke close to his ear, against the noise. 'Ennius' pyrotechnical display was the signal. Take a look down the Sacred Way.' He could hear the drums now, a slow, insistent beat, hollow in the distance, that marked the second part of the procession, the parade of treasures from Macedonia that would be brought by the cartload to the foot of the podium and dedicated in the temples that lined the Sacred Way. For Fabius the greatest sight was not the spoils of war but Scipio himself, flushed with excitement and resplendent in the cuirass and plumed helmet inherited from his adoptive grandfather Scipio

Africanus, the man in whose memory Fabius had sworn that he would protect the young Scipio unswervingly, staying by his side wherever fortune should take him. Today was the crowning point of Scipio's life so far; it was the first time he had stood shoulder to shoulder with Rome's greatest living warrior and statesmen and could grasp his own destiny. Fabius tried to forget the dark side, that this was also the last day that Scipio could have with Julia, the day that marked the beginning of her formal purification rites with the Vestal Virgins before her marriage to Metellus. War may have toughened Scipio up, but not for that. Fabius peered ahead, seeing the first cartload of treasure trundle out of the smoke, drawn by a team of oxen. For now, though, for a few hours at least, he hoped that Scipio could put the future on hold, as they revelled in the greatest spectacle that Rome had ever seen.

Three hours later, the space in front of the podium was piled high with dazzling treasure and works of art, carried there by more than two hundred and fifty wagons and chariots; prominent among them was a huge heap of the silverwork for which the Macedonians were famous, including magnificent drinking cups in the shape of horns, decorated with gold leaf and precious stones, mounded over a vast libation bowl that Aemilius Paullus had ordered made from more than twenty talents of the purest Macedonian mountain gold. Fabius had been more interested in the wagonloads of arms and armour, thousands of helmets, shields, breastplates and greaves, all jumbled together and smeared with mud and dried blood as they had been when they were collected from the battlefield; among them he could identify Cretan round shields, Thracian wicker shields, Macedonian spears and Scythian arrow quivers, a residue of the mercenary force that had been arrayed against them at Pydna alongside the Macedonian phalanx. Next had come over a hundred oxen with gilded horns, destined for sacrifice that evening on the Field of Mars, and then the family and household slaves of Perseus and the deposed king himself, stripped of his armour and shambling along in a black robe, looking confused and sullen in defeat. After he had passed, there was a lull while a final spectacle was prepared; wine and fruit was passed among the spectators by slaves who had been instructed to provide the people with drink in moderation, but not so much that they would become rowdy before the procession was over and the sacrifices had taken place on the Field of Mars that evening.

Polybius had lamented the pillaging of Macedonia; he had told Fabius how so many of these treasures, ripped from the temples and sanctuaries, had lost their significance, and become mere ornaments in the houses of the wealthy in Rome. But now Fabius could see how the greatest of those works, brought here in triumph and dedicated in the temples, had attained a new meaning, been given a new stamp of ownership as they were absorbed into Rome as symbols of conquest and power. From now on, the art and the artisans themselves would work to Roman taste, shaping a new Rome just as Polybius and the other Greek professors at the academy had influenced the thinking of the next generation of Roman war leaders. It was making Rome less narrow, drawing her away from her long-established traditions: a dangerous development in the view of those in the Senate who worried about the solidity of their own power base in Rome, built as it was on maintaining the old established order. He thought of the irony of the old centurion Petraeus, conservative to the core, presiding over part of this change, chosen by Scipio Africanus to usher this generation of boys into a new way of war, one in which conquest and domination would only be possible if they were unshackled from the constitution that had anchored and curtailed personal military ambition in Rome since the early days of the Republic.

While they waited, Cato moved behind Scipio, his face craggy and lined, dressed austerely in the old-style toga of his ancestors, looking disapprovingly at the cluster of bearded Greek teachers below the rostrum who were trying to keep a class of unruly young boys in order. As far as Fabius could tell, the only Greek whom Cato had ever really approved of was Polybius, and only then because Polybius was the foremost military historian of the day and one of Rome's most vocal proponents, so much so that Cato himself had called for him formally to be released from his status as a captive and made a Roman citizen. Cato spoke close to Scipio's ear, but Fabius overhead. 'When I was your age I stood at this very spot, over fifty years ago when Hannibal had crossed the Alps with his elephants and was threatening Rome. Your father who stands beside us now was like one of those boys below, though back then we used battle-hardened centurions to show our boys how to be men, not these effeminate Greeks.'

'You did well to support the academy, Cato,' Scipio replied, cupping his hand towards the old man's ear to make himself heard. 'Those of us who attended will always be grateful. The centurion Petraeus taught us the *mos maiorum*, the ancestral ways.'

'The academy was the idea of your adoptive grandfather, Scipio Africanus,' Cato replied. 'All I did was ensure that the boys of families who support our cause against Carthage were offered a place, and that the treasure from Scipio's triumphs that he willed for the purpose was used to employ the best teachers in the art of war. But the academy is closed, and I fear will not reopen. All I see around me are senators who would appease and negotiate rather than prepare for war. Even some who support us have come to believe that with Macedonia now vanquished, Rome's wars of conquest are at an end, that their future lies not in military glory but in the law courts and the Senate. We both know how wrong they are. Peace may lie ahead of us, but it will only be a transitory peace, a lull before the storm. Mark my words, Scipio.'

'Those of us who have been through the academy will ensure that its ethos survives,' Scipio replied earnestly. 'You need have no fear.'

Cato looked towards Metellus and the other young officers strutting on the podium below. 'I can remember what it was like to be your age with my first taste of battle, and to be itching to go again. For me there were fifteen years of hard campaigning ahead before Hannibal was finally defeated at Zama – all of the blood and glory that a young man could want. But for you the path to the next war is less certain, and you are burdened with expectations. You must not let that armour of Scipio Africanus weigh you down. One day you will earn it in your own right and stand where your father is standing now.'

'If the gods will it, and the people of Rome.'

Cato pursed his lips. 'The time will come when men will not just play out their ambitions against each other in the debating chamber but will seek recourse in intimidation and assassination. When that happens, the struggle for power will be long and bitter. Armies will be raised against each other, and there will be civil war. And when Rome rises again – *if* Rome rises again – she will no longer be a republic. The man who stands astride the new Rome will be the one who can cast aside the shackles of the past and see Rome for what she is: the core of a mighty empire, not some theatre play of intrigue and squabbling and lofty speeches in the Senate full of clever rhetoric that signifies nothing.'

Scipio turned to him. 'But these shackles are the *mos maiorum*, the ancestral ways.'

'The *mos maiorum* are honour and duty, not patronage and privilege bought with bribes and intrigue and dynastic marriages,' Cato growled. 'I am the staunchest Republican that Rome has ever known, but if she loses sight of the old ways I would rather she were ruled by one man who knows the *mos maiorum* than by the many who do not. That was the other reason why we set up the academy; it was not just about military training. It was about restoring honour and duty to those who would lead Rome, not just in war but also in peace.' He looked towards Metellus and the other tribunes, his cheeks creased and his brow furrowed. 'With some, with you and Ennius and Brutus, with the foreign allies Gulussa and Hippolyta, we have succeeded; with others I fear not. They are the dangerous ones, as dangerous to you as any foreign enemy, and you must watch them. I must leave now. I have one last role to play, in the last great triumph I shall witness in my lifetime.'

Scipio bowed towards him. '*Ave atque vale*, Marcus Porcius Cato. Until we meet again. I will remember your words.'

He turned towards his father, resplendent in his golden cuirass and plumed helmet, knowing that at this point in the triumph the son gave formal congratulations to his father. 'Salutations, Lucius Aemilius Paullus Macedonicus,' Scipio said, for the first time using the *agnomen* awarded to him that day for his defeat of the Macedonians. 'No more glorious a triumph has ever been celebrated in Rome. Mars Ultor shines on you.'

By tradition the *triumphator* remained dignified and silent, presiding over the triumph like a god himself, but Aemilius Paullus allowed himself to turn and smile. 'Mars Ultor shines over my son too for prowess in battle, and over all Rome this day. I will give thanks in the shrine of our ancestors in my house this evening when the games are over. Will you join me?'

Scipio raised his arm in salute so that all those around could see him honour his father, and he bowed his head. 'I shall attend, Father. And then I will sacrifice at the *lararium* of my adoptive grandfather Publius Cornelius Scipio Africanus, who watches your glory from Elysium.'

Aemilius Paullus bowed in turn, showing due respect to the revered memory of Scipio Africanus, and then turned back to stare at the Sacred Way through the Forum. Outside the Temple of Fortuna the priests were dedicating a statue of Athena by the venerated Greek sculptor Pheidias, raising it up in the temple precinct and then following it between the columns. Fabius watched the statue totter through, carried on a bier by captured Greek slaves, its golden helmet and vermilion *chiton* more vivid than the sombre colours of Roman sculpture. In all the temples of the Forum the gods and goddesses of Greece were being made subordinate to Rome, just as the houses of the wealthy had been filled with looted bronzes and paintings brought back by the officers of the legions who had fought in Macedonia, spoils of war that had been the right of victors since time immemorial.

But there was more to it than just loot. Aemilius Paullus had also commissioned the Greek artist Metrodorus to make paintings of the main events of the campaign, and had ordered them attached to the sides of the bullock carts full of treasure that had trundled through the Forum. Fabius knew from Polybius that Metrodorus had saved his crowning achievement to last, and it was coming towards them now, a towering structure covered in a shroud and carried on poles by Macedonian spearmen of the phalanx captured at Pydna. They set it down in the last remaining space beside the rostrum and then marched off towards the Field of Mars, the whips of the slave-masters cracking against their taut muscles and sending sharp reports through the still air of the Forum. Metrodoros himself appeared last in the procession, tall and bearded, bowing towards Aemilius Paullus and picking up a cord attached to the shroud that covered the structure. Trumpets suddenly blared from the steps of the Capitoline Temple behind them, a shrill blast that must have been audible all over the city. The crowd waited with bated breath, watching for Aemilius Paullus to give the signal. Scipio turned and whispered to Fabius. 'It's made of wood, but it's the model for a stone monument that's being set up at Delphi in Greece outside the Temple of Apollo. When my father travelled there after Pydna he found a half-finished monument like this that had been commissioned by King Perseus before his defeat, and it seemed only fitting that the victor should complete it with his own embellishments on top.'

Aemilius Paullus raised an arm, and let it drop. With a swirl, Metrodorus pulled off the shroud, and the crowd gasped. It was a rectilinear pillar, at least five times the height of a man, tapering towards the top and built from blocks of wood painted white. At the base was an inscription in gold lettering, and at the top a sculpted frieze beneath a magnificent gilded statue of a general on a rearing horse. The frieze was at eye-level to their place on the podium, cleverly positioned at that height so that Aemilius Paullus could see it clearly, and they all stared. It showed a battle-scene, with life-sized men pressing and lunging, hacking and stabbing. It was so realistic that Fabius felt he could walk right into it. Dying soldiers were shown on the ground with wounds laid bare, dripping with blood that must have been applied by Metrodorus just before the procession. In the centre of the melee was a riderless horse that Fabius remembered from Pydna, one that had broken free from the Roman ranks and galloped between the lines, stirring them to battle. He glanced at Polybius, knowing that Metrodoros could as easily have shown Polybius himself, riding heroically along the line of the phalanx to break their spears; but Polybius had worked closely with Metrodoros on getting the depiction right and must had advised him against it, rightly judging that the Romans may have taken him into their fold but would rebel against a depiction showing the battle hinging on the action of a Greek captive who was officially not present in the Roman lines anyway.

The horse reminded Fabius of one that he and Scipio had seen on the pediment sculpture of the Parthenon in Athens, twisting and rearing upwards, as if straining to break free from the rock; only, unlike those Greek sculptures, this was not a mythological battle but a real one. He could recognize the armour and weapons of the Macedonians and their Gallic and Thracian allies, as well as that of the legionaries. And the larger-than-life equestrian statue was not a god but a man, clearly Aemilius Paullus himself, his lined face and receding hair instantly recognizable even from this distance.

He read the inscription in gold along the base:

DESTROY CARTHAGE

L.AEMILIUS L.F. IMPERATOR DE REGE PERSE MACEDONIBUSQUE CEPET

Lucius Aemilius, son of Lucius, Imperator, set this up from the spoils which he took from King Perseus and the Macedonians. That would be the message Greek emissaries saw when they went to Delphi to make their obeisances to Apollo. To Fabius the monument seemed the crowning symbol of triumph, not some work of art looted and locked inside a temple in Rome, but a sculpture made in the Greek fashion and set up in the most sacred sanctuary of the vanquished, with a distinct new message: men, not gods, would conquer all, and those were not just any men, but Romans. Fabius felt uplifted. The future might be uncertain; fortune might smile on them tomorrow, or it might not. But after this day, anything seemed possible.

One of the attendants threw a burning taper into Ennius' cauldron and another jet of fire erupted above the Forum, lighting up the equestrian statue of Aemilius Paullus as if he were riding across the heavens. Even after the flash of light had ended, the image remained imprinted in Fabius' vision, and then the statue appeared wreathed in smoke with the evening light silhouetting its form against the darkening sky, an equally awesome sight that had the crowd silent and gaping.

After a few minutes of reverence the people began to stir, eager to move on to the next stage in the entertainment. Scipio picked up a leather tube containing a scroll he had been carrying, and turned to Fabius. 'I promised Julia that I'd meet her outside the Field of Mars. Her father has a stand for his family and clients overlooking the end of the processional way, and I want to make sure I see the legionaries of my own maniple march through as they make their way towards the games. If we don't go now, we'll miss them. Come on.'

'Wait a moment,' Fabius said, pointing down the Sacred Way. 'There's something else coming.'

The crowd had seen it too and become hushed again, and they both stared. Out of the smoke came a solitary beast, its back bowed with age and its legs swollen, its trunk swaying from side to side, its eyes red and sullen as it lumbered forward.

'Jupiter above,' Scipio murmured. 'Unless my eyes deceive me, that's old Hannibal.'

Fabius peered closely. He was right. It was the elephant that Scipio Africanus had captured from Hannibal's army, the one that the boys had fed and mucked out in its stall in the Gladiator School. As it came closer they could see the white streaks on its sides where Roman swords had slashed it more than fifty years before, the bumps and dents in its trunk where chunks of flesh had been hacked away, but still it came on, a lumbering testament to the scars of war. The closer it came, the stronger it seemed, the eyes no longer sullen but glowering red, the legs no longer leaden but poised to charge, as if the strength that had kept it alive for all these years had suddenly revived the beast of war within, here in the most sacred place of an enemy that had never truly vanquished it.

And then as it turned in front of the podium they saw an even more extraordinary sight. A few paces behind, holding a rope attached to the elephant as if he were chained to it, came a single figure, his head bowed. Fabius could hardly believe his eyes: it was Cato. Together man and beast passed the podium, neither of them looking up, both of them plodding resolutely forward and then disappearing from view, the elephant swishing its tail and Cato remaining bowed. For a few moments the crowd remained in stunned silence, as if unnerved, uncertain what to think or do.

Fabius glanced at Aemilius Paullus. He was impassive, staring ahead. Fabius suddenly realized what had happened. They had planned this together, Aemilius Paullus and Cato, two old men who looked back to the past but also shared a sense of responsibility to the future. It would enrage the faction in the Senate who were opposed to them; Fabius could already see impatient movement and hear snorts of derision from among the toga-clad men below them. At his moment of greatest triumph, Aemilius Paullus had chosen to leave a warning to the people of Rome: Carthage was still there, battle-scarred but strong, leading Rome on as the elephant led Cato, gaining renewed strength even as Rome watched and did nothing. Conquest in the east was a shallow victory as long as Carthage remained defiant. Perseus and the Macedonians were never going to threaten Rome; Hannibal's elephants had stomped and snorted on the edge of the city itself.

Something else had happened. It was as if the light that had shone on Aemilius Paullus had shifted to Scipio. Everyone knew the legacy of his adoptive grandfather, and the burden that had become Scipio's when he had adopted that name. What had begun as a celebration of victory in which he had played a part had become a portent of uncertainty and expectation; and the loyalty of the legionaries who had seen his valour in battle would be no guarantee of the affections of the people of Rome, who could be persuaded to shift their loyalties at a whim. Fabius knew that the armour of his adoptive grandfather would be weighing especially heavily on Scipio now, and that what was to come in the years ahead would be a greater test of his resolve than anything they had experienced on the battlefields of Macedonia.

Scipio turned and put a hand on his shoulder, a wry look on his face. 'What is it that the Epicureans say? *Carpe diem*. Seize the day. For once, I will try to forget the future. Julia is waiting for us beside the Field of Mars to watch the execution of deserters, and it's my duty as an army officer to be there. Let's move.'

5

Half an hour later, Fabius and Scipio made their way up the
wooden stand built for the Caesares branch of the *gens* Julii just
outside the Field of Mars, where the street that had been embel-
lished for the triumphal procession opened out on to the army
training and marshalling ground. The *gentes* vied with each other
for the best position for their stands, securing preference from the
tribunes of the people according to the extent of their benefac-
tions to the city since the previous triumph – one of the small
ways in which the plebs were able to influence the privileges of
the wealthy. The Caesares had done exceptionally well that year,
having funded a free corn handout and the building of a public
bathhouse on the Esquiline Hill, and had been allocated a position
where they could see both the execution of deserters on the
roadside and the spectacles on the Field of Mars planned for that
evening. The events included bear-baiting, fights to the death
between Macedonian prisoners and gladiators, and the mass sacrifice of hundreds of head of cattle that would provide meat in
plenty for all who wanted it, roasted on spits and braziers over the
numerous bonfires that dotted the field, their flames already
roaring high into the evening sky.

First up was the execution of deserters, an event that Scipio
was obliged to witness as an army officer; he and Fabius had
arrived only a few minutes ahead of the first bullock cart, so there
was little time to lose. They picked their way up the tiers of seats
past the elegantly coiffeured matrons and their children and
the men in togas, some of them wearing the purple-rimmed
senatorial toga and bearing laurel wreaths on their heads, awards
for civic accomplishment. Among them was a scattering of men

in uniform, including Julia's brother Sextus Julius Caesar, a fellow tribune who had also served in Macedonia, and their distinguished father of the same name, a decorated veteran of the Battle of Zama who nodded gravely at Scipio and returned their salute as he and Fabius passed.

Julia was standing apart from the other women of her *gens* in the upper tier with her two slave girls in attendance, and waved to Scipio and Fabius as they approached. She was not arrayed like the others and looked as if she had just returned from one of her secret sessions in the academy, her wavy hair loosely tied back and falling over her shoulders, her robe belted around her waist to reveal the firm curves of her hips and breasts. She was not allowed to wear any military ornamentation but carried an ancient family heirloom, a winged helmet of Attic Greek design with the eagle emblem of the Caesares embossed on the front. It was a small act of defiance that Fabius knew her father had allowed her, against the wishes of her mother and the other Vestals. Standing there with the helmet she looked as if she had been cut from the same mould as the caryatid sculptures that Fabius had seen on the Acropolis in Athens, yet finished in a manner that was wholly Roman; she had the straight nose and high cheekbones of the Caesares family, and the auburn hair and large eyes of her mother. As she turned to greet them she looked radiant, with none of the sadness that Fabius had seen in her since Metellus had returned, and he hoped that, like Scipio, she would be able to enjoy this evening and forget the future, the life that she would have to lead as a matron of the *gens* Metelli in the years ahead.

The crowd had already begun shouting and jeering, and Fabius saw the first in a line of wagons drawn by oxen trundle into view from the direction of the Forum. Each wagon bore a large iron cage, and as the first one came closer he could see a female African lion pacing to and fro inside, its eyes bloodshot and its tongue hanging out. He knew it would be half-crazed with hunger, its body lean from days of starvation in advance of the spectacle. Behind each wagon a man staggered with his hands bound behind his back and his ankles loosely shackled, a long rope extending from his wrists to the cage and another from a halter around his neck to a muscle-bound gladiator behind, dressed in the full armour of a *bestiarius* and cracking a whip every few moments against the prisoner's back.

From a wagon somewhere behind, a lion roared, the sound rumbling through the stand like an earthquake, and the crowd hollered and bayed. They all knew what was coming next; the prisoners had been condemned *damnatio ad bestias*. Aemilius Paullus had shown mercy to many of those captured at Pydna, to the Macedonians themselves and to a few of the Thracian mercenaries suited to gladiator training, but any prisoner who was marched through a triumph in chains had only been temporarily spared. The plebs knew it, and would howl at any show of clemency. And these prisoners were the worst, not enemies but deserters, men whose former comrades and families were among those baying for their blood in the crowd today. Rome might send her men out garlanded and feted for war, but those who failed in courage or fortitude must know that they would be treated more harshly than any enemy, returned to Rome shackled and humiliated, brought to justice before those same crowds whose trust and expectations they had so grossly betrayed.

At intervals along the road thick wooden poles like crucifixion posts had been sunk into the ground, but instead of a crossbeam an iron loop had been attached to the upper ends. As each wagon drew up at a post, the crowd retreated to form a circular space, those in the front row holding hands and pressing back to make enough room. At the post nearest to them Fabius watched the beast-master alight from beside the wagon driver, go to the back of the cage and untie the rope that led to the prisoner's wrists, and pass the end through the loop on the post before handing it to the *bestiarius*. He then reached into the cage and hauled out a coil of chain that was attached to an iron collar around the lion's neck, hooking the other end to the loop on the pole. At a signal from the *bestiarius* the driver whipped the bullocks and the wagon lurched forward, causing the rear of the cage to open and the lion to leap out, its neck caught violently on the chain as it pulled taut. Enraged, the beast tossed its head and roared, then charged headlong at the crowd until the chain brought it short again, causing it to sprawl on the ground and snarl and chafe against the collar. It tried again, hurtling itself in the other direction, and then got up and paced around the edge of the clearing, slavering and pawing at the crowd, its claws sweeping within inches of the boys who dared each other to leap out in front. Fabius remembered when he had done it himself, dicing with death many times, goading the lion with severed bull's legs they had taken from carcasses beside the sacrificial altars in the Field of Mars; the priests always left cuts of meat for this very purpose, remembering their own fun as boys when baiting the lions and acquiring scars was the quickest way to earn esteem as a street warrior.

The crowd went silent, watching the lion as it paced round and round. The *bestiarius* kept the rope to the prisoner's hands taut, releasing enough slack through the loop so that the man could strain back and keep close to the edge of the crowd, just beyond the lion's reach. Each time the lion came close, the boys tried to push the man forward, and on the third occasion he stumbled and the lion swiped at him before he could lurch back, ripping the side of his face off and pulling out one eye. The man screamed, falling to his knees, a bloody flap of skin hanging below his chin. Sometimes the *bestiarius* would allow more baiting, until the victim was nearly flayed alive, but this time he knew that the crowd had been stoked up and wanted gratification. He suddenly heaved on the rope and the prisoner lurched forward, tripping and twisting as the rope pulled his wrists up the pole until he was dangling from it, his feet kicking and shaking uncontrollably, his one remaining eye following the lion as it paced around him. The moment the lion stopped and looked at him, realizing that he was now within reach, the *bestiarius* released his hold on the rope and heaved on the one from the prisoner's neck, hauling him back to safety just in time. The crowd roared, and Fabius could see the prisoner more clearly now, grey with terror, his legs brown with faeces.

The *bestiarius* stood with his feet planted apart and his chest puffed out, and bellowed at the crowd. 'Is the lion hungry?'

The crowd roared again.

'Shall we feed him?'

Another roar, and the *bestiarius* dropped the neck rope and pulled on the other as hard as he could, his muscles rippling and taut, heaving the man up the pole again until he was dangling off the ground, his feet kicking frantically and his head twisting from side to side in terror as the lion continued to pace the perimeter, eyeing him now, flexing its shoulders and then coming to a halt and pawing the ground.

In a flash it leapt, and the crowd gasped. It happened so quickly that the man had no time to scream. The lion sank its jaws into his back and wrenched him from the pole, shaking him violently to and fro, breaking his bones just as if he were a beast caught on the plains of Africa. The *bestiarius* released the rope entirely and stood back with the crowd. A fountain of blood erupted from the man's neck, spraying the boys in the front row. The lion dropped his body, sat down on his haunches and began to eat. It took a huge bite from the man's chest, crunching through the ribs and leaving a gaping hole in his side, ripping out one lung and swallowing it, the windpipe and arteries hanging down from its jaw. It slurped them up and took another mouthful, this time from the abdomen, gorging itself on the man's stomach and intestines, its face dripping with blood and bile.

Scipio turned to Julia, who had been watching with rapt attention. 'That's the end of the entertainment here,' he said. 'It will carry on all night in the Field of Mars, but I promised my friend Terence that I'd look in at the play he's put on specially for the games, in the peristyle garden of his patron Terentius' house on the Palatine. Before then, Polybius and I have arranged to meet. I want to tell him something that Terence told me, and Polybius apparently has something to tell me. Will you come along?'

'My mother will find I'm missing, and send out the Vestals to hunt me down,' Julia said, smiling. 'But that'll make it more fun. She's not watching now, so we can go.'

They stood up, making their way through the others seated on the stand, Fabius following them. Already the crowd around the lion had begun to disperse, some moving to the other wagons where the executions had yet to happen, others heading off towards the Field of Mars. Fabius glanced at the lion as they passed by, its stomach visibly bloated, the man's dismembered body reduced to a mess of blood and bone. The lion had taken the man's head in its jaws and crushed it as they passed. He remembered the feast that would follow the sacrifice of the bulls in the Forum, and the slabs of meat that the priests would hand out to be roasted on a fire below the rostrum. Fabius had promised to meet Hippolyta's slave girl Eudoxia there later on, so he hoped that Scipio and Julia would not stay too long at the play. He was already beginning to feel hungry.

Back in the Forum they met Polybius inside the Basilica Aemilia, the great law court where he had been addressing a gathering of Greek scholars and teachers who had been brought by Aemilius Paullus to Rome for the triumph. As they arrived, he was seeing off a cluster of white-robed men with flowing grey beards and unshorn hair, holding wound-up scrolls and staring haughtily ahead. Scipio turned to Polybius, grinning. 'Unless I'm mistaken, my father has captured Greek philosophy and brought it to Rome.'

'They are not captives, but a delegation from Athens,'

Polybius muttered. 'Come at your father's invitation to teach the miscreant youths of Rome how to think.'

'You sound sceptical, Polybius.'

'I've seen what it's like in Athens. The wisdom of the true philosophers, of Socrates and Plato and Aristotle, has been diluted and debased, by men who think that wearing the robe of a teacher and sporting a flowing white beard qualifies them for our esteem. Most are men like those ones: constitutionally incapable of original thought, yet trying to peddle their muddled ideas to the weak and the gullible. Rome is like a bright but uneducated youth, eager for learning, but with no critical facility. These men do not teach philosophy, but mere sophistry, wordplay, and will only speak in riddles as the Sibyl does, but without the benefit of Apollo to guide them.'

'You underestimate us, Polybius,' Scipio said, looking at him with mock seriousness. 'To most of us these men are mere ornaments, like those bronzes and paintings we took from Macedonia. They will provide after-dinner entertainment in the villas of Rome and Neapolis, at Herculaneum and Stabiae. It will doubtless become imperative to have a Greek philosopher among one's slaves, just as it has become the fashion to have a Greek doctor and Greek musicians. But they'd better have some good tricks up their sleeves. Nobody at those dinner parties will actually listen to what they say. They will be mere performers.'

'Even so, Scipio, I know you will attend their lectures. You are too inquisitive to stay away. Beware of Greeks speaking in forked tongues.'

Julia nudged him. 'Does that include you, Polybius?'

Scipio laughed, and slapped Polybius on the back. 'Not a chance. What Polybius really loves is the war horse and the boar spear. Isn't that right, Polybius? That's why you're so fascinated by us Romans. You love our practicality. For you, to study history is not to muse about the human condition like a philosopher, but to understand past battles and find out the best way to use a skirmishing line or deploy light cavalry. Am I right?'

Polybius eyed him keenly. 'Speaking of hunting, I hear that your father has given you the Macedonian Royal Forest as a coming-of-age present. Did you know that I learned to hunt there as a boy? It has the best boar in any forest south of the Alps.'

Scipio glanced at Julia. 'See what I mean? Mention boar spear, and he's yours.' He turned back to Polybius, grinning. 'You're right. I can't wait to get there. But it's really only a temporary present while Macedonia is my father's personal fiefdom, in the afterglow of Pydna. In a few years' time he reckons that Rome will try to annex Macedonia as a province, and they'll send out a praetor. The forest will no longer be mine to hunt in, so now's my chance.'

'You said you wanted to see me,' Polybius said.

Scipio nodded, suddenly serious. 'Since we last saw you, Publius Terentius Afer has been telling Fabius and me about Carthage.'

'Terence the playwright? You keep interesting friends.'

Scipio nodded. 'Terence was a slave in Carthage, and his mother was an Afri from the Berber tribes of Libya, related to Gulussa's Numidians. Do you remember the model of Carthage I made in the academy?'

'The one you used to plan a possible assault on the city? I remember wondering how you'd got the details. I'd been meaning to ask you, but then the call to arms got in the way. Rome hasn't bothered having spies in Carthage since the end of the war against Hannibal, and now Romans who try to enter the city are turned away. It is said that great construction works are afoot, but all of it behind the high sea walls and so invisible to ships sailing by.'

Scipio glanced behind. 'Tell him, Fabius.'

Fabius cleared his throat. 'My mother worked in the household of the senator Publius Terentius Lucanus, who kept Terence as a slave and freed him after educating him and seeing his talents as a playwright. Terence and I became friends while he was still a slave. He told me that Carthage was far better for hide-and-seek than Rome, because of the tightly clustered houses around the foot of the Byrsa, the acropolis hill. When Scipio years later said that he was planning to build a model of Carthage, I brought Terence along and he advised on the construction.'

'Do you remember how I war-gamed the assault?' Scipio said, turning back to Polybius. 'I said that too often we just focus on the obviously defensible features: the walls, the temples, the arsenals. Those features were all that the veterans of the last war against Carthage were able to tell me about, but that was before I met Terence. He told me about the ring of ancient houses that surround the Byrsa, to a depth equivalent of two or three of our tenement blocks. Think of the houses of the plebs that surround us now in Rome, pressing up against the edge of the Forum. A general planning an assault on Rome would hardly concern himself with them, because they're in city blocks and you could march straight past them down the streets towards the Forum. If there was any resistance, you'd simply torch them because they're mostly wood and plaster. No defender worth his salt would set up a position there, but would instead fall back on the stone buildings of the Forum.'

'But Carthage must be different,' Polybius said pensively. 'There's less timber available in Africa, so more use of stone for even the rudest of dwellings.'

Scipio nodded enthusiastically. '*Precisely.* Those houses seen by Terence are made of stone: the walls from upright pillars, the spaces in between filled with masonry. Terence says they've inset wooden beams as joists for the floors, but you wouldn't be able to burn them easily unless you could rain fire through the roof. For that, you'd need siege engines, or catapults on ships anchored close up to the sea wall. And the houses themselves are like a rabbit warren, not laid out in regular blocks but with narrow alleyways and rooftop walkways, as well as underground cisterns in each house where defenders could lurk. That's what Terence meant about hide-and-seek. An assaulting force within a stone's throw of the Byrsa might think they'd won the day, but they'd be sorely mistaken. The elite forces of mercenaries and special guards who are usually the last to hold out in a siege – the ones who know they'd be shown no mercy if they were to surrender – could organize a defence in depth and make the assault force pay dearly for it, at precisely the time when the legionaries would have begun to turn their thoughts to victory and booty. The assault commander would have to ensure that they kept up the momentum and rolled forward into those houses with the blood-lust still high. It's a tactical insight I wanted to share with you. I've been thinking of Carthage again, Polybius. I've got Terence to thank for that.'

Polybius gave him a wry smile. 'Well, I've always been scep-tical about playwrights. But now I can see they have their uses.' He stood up and looked through the columns of the entrance at the massed ranks of Latin troops who had begun to march past them along the Sacred Way, the beginning of a long procession of victorious allies who followed on behind the legionaries and the spoils of war. 'You'd better get going and get your dose of drama before the evening festivities really take off. I've just spotted Demetrius of Syria with his bodyguards, and I want to catch him for any intelligence about another upstart who's claiming the succession from Perseus in Macedonia. It's not often that you get so many of Rome's allies in the city at one time, and I need to use the opportunity.'

'We have a little over an hour until the play begins,' Scipio replied. 'You wanted to tell me something too?'

Polybius turned to gaze at Julia and Scipio, and Fabius saw something else in his eyes, a faltering look, even a sadness. 'This day is a chance for you to be together without others watching you, or knowing where you are. I wanted to tell you that the doors of my little house below the Palatine are open, and my slave girl Fabina knows you may be coming. You do not know when you may have the chance again. As for me, I'm off. *Ave atque vale*. And remember what I said. Seize the day.'

6

The courtyard of the house of Terentius Lucanus on the Esquiline Hill had been designed in the Greek fashion, with a colonnaded peristyle surrounding a garden and a pool in the centre. One end had been built up into a stage for performances and the garden had been partly boarded over to provide seating for a small audience. Fabius had followed Scipio and Julia in from the atrium of the house, and sat down with them among the two dozen or so others who had come to see the play. An hour earlier he had left Scipio and Julia at the entrance to Polybius' house below the Palatine, and had quickly made his way back through the Forum to find Eudoxia, leading her to a hidden garden he knew on the far side of the Circus Maximus. They had met up again in time for Julia to walk visibly through the Forum on their way to the Esquiline, ensuring that word would pass back to her mother and the Vestals that she had not somehow absconded. On the way they had passed Metellus and a group of his friends, all of them the worse for wear, staggering between the temporary stalls along the Sacred Way that were serving wine without restriction now that the procession was over. Metellus had looked darkly at Scipio, swaying slightly with a wine pitcher in his hand, and had followed them with his friends, shouting and jeering, until he was diverted by a favourite tavern near the Mamertine Prison. Fabius knew that the more drunk Metellus got, the more he would want to claim Julia, as his wife to be, and that there would be nothing Scipio could do to stop him without causing a furore within the *gentes*. Fabius could only hope that the house of Terentius Lucanus was sufficiently far from the taverns to deter Metellus from making an entrance here, and that he and Scipio could spirit Julia away after the play and return her to the house of the Caesares before Metellus could get his hands on her.

As they sat down, a lithe man with the dark skin of an African saw them from the stage and came bounding over, smiling broadly. 'Julia, Scipio Aemilianus, Fabius. Welcome, my friends. I'm glad you've come. We're waiting for the arrival of my patron and the owner of this house, Terentius Lucanus, who is making a sacrifice in the Temple of Castor and Pollux, praying, I trust, for the success of my play.'

Scipio looked around. 'A delightful venue, though small and a good way off the beaten track tonight, I fear.'

Terence sighed. 'I sent plans to the Senate for the construction of a Greek-style theatre in Rome, but they were rejected by the aedile in charge of public works on the grounds that a theatre with seating would turn Romans into effeminate Greeks.'

Scipio grinned. 'What did you say?'

'I said he was right, Roman backsides weren't yet tough enough for stone seats.'

'You really know how to please them, Terence. I'm amazed you haven't been hounded out of Rome by now.'

Terence shook his head glumly. 'As a playwright, you can't win. I'd wanted to present works of my own, plays in a gritty, realistic style, suited to Roman taste. But no, those who finance my productions insist on pastiches of well-known Greek plays, because they say that's what the people want. In fact, it's what my backers want, not what my fans want. My backers want the old, but my fans want the new. My backers want repeats of the same tired old plays that have brought in pots of denarii in the past, and so, they surmise, will do so again. These people are here today only because they are clients of Terentius and are obliged to him. They'll be talking to themselves all the way through the play, hardly noticing it. The theatre's been reduced to a place for meeting friends and exchanging gossip, before going off to the real fun in the taverns.'

Scipio was still carrying the scroll he had had with him on the podium while they watched the procession, and Terence pointed to it. 'It looks as if you've brought something else to entertain you as well. What's the book?'

'My father allowed me to take what I liked from the Macedonian Royal Library. It's a copy of Xenophon's *Cyropaedia*, the life of Cyrus the Great of Persia. I thought I might have a chance to discuss it with Polybius during a lull in the proceedings, but that was before I knew I'd be able to spend so much time this evening with Julia.'

'You read for education, not for pleasure?'

Scipio looked serious. 'I want to know how to live a good life, Terence. Xenophon was a student of Socrates. But it's true that my interest in learning lies in its practical application, something Polybius has taught me. Xenophon has a practical take on the problems of war. And Cyrus the Great is someone who intrigues me; in some ways he was the ideal ruler, a benign despot. I want to know what it is that makes people willingly follow some rulers, but not others.'

Julia nudged him, grinning. 'If you're planning to become the next Alexander the Great, you can't learn it; either you have it in you, or you don't.'

'That's true enough. But Alexander could have learned a thing or two about the management of empire. We're still clearing up his mess.'

'He had no precedent,' Terence said. 'But you do, in him. You must take care that the memory of your achievements does not survive only in fragments, like the falling leaves of autumn, dry and brittle and in danger of crumbling into dust.'

'You assume there will be a life worthy of recording.'

'Oh, there will be, Scipio. It doesn't take the words of an oracle to know that.'

'Well, Polybius will see to my memory. He's already completed his *Histories* of the First and Second Punic Wars, though he's stalling publication of the second volume until he can visit Zama in North Africa and see the battlefield for himself. It's not often that a soldier has a close friend who is the greatest historian of the day, a man who shares not only my fascination with military organization but also a practical take on strategy and tactics.'

'Then let's hope that when he comes to complete his biography of Scipio Aemilianus he doesn't stall it like that other volume. Histories left unpublished on the death of an author have a nasty habit of being fiddled by the subject's enemies, or of disappearing entirely.'

Julia spoke up. 'I will write a history of Scipio Aemilianus, if Polybius does not. I will follow his life as if I were with him every moment of it, even if from afar.'

Fabius looked at Scipio, and saw a shadow flicker over his face. They all knew that time for him and Julia was running short. Terence leaned over and tapped the scroll. 'I have heard Polybius speak, in this very house after dinner. Beware of monarchical government, he said. Rome has become great because it threw out its kings three centuries ago.'

'Are not the consuls kings?' Scipio exclaimed, his unhappiness fuelling his passion, throwing caution to the wind and not caring who overheard him. 'And the Pontifex Maximus, and the princeps of the Senate, and the tribunes of the people? Are we not ruled by a committee of kings?'

'If so, they are elected kings.'

Scipio snorted. 'Kings elected for only one year, who have no time for great deeds, no time for reform, no time to develop proper administration for the provinces, whose tenure of office is dominated by legal pleading and social obligations, the life I spurned when I went to the academy.'

'A course that your adoptive grandfather Scipio Africanus chose for you.'

'I wish I had been old enough to talk to him. I wish he had

told me that he saw something in me. I grew up feeling an outsider, looked down upon even by the Scipiones for having no interest in playing the political game, as if I were not up to it.'

'Perhaps that was his design,' Terence said. 'He knew it would do a small boy no good to be told that his destiny was greater than those around him. He knew that to achieve greatness you had to be an outsider. He knew that by struggling against adverse opinion, by sometimes feeling inadequate, you would become a stronger person, and that once you recognized your strengths you would develop a burning ambition to compensate for those feelings you had as a child, an ambition that would allow you to rise above them all.'

Julia turned to Scipio. 'And yet he knew that your ambition would need to be curbed, to be controlled. So your father appointed Polybius to be your mentor. My father Sextus Julius Caesar says there's no greater check on a man's ego than to be taught by a good historian who can show how men risen to greatness can so easily fall into obscurity.'

There was a commotion at the door, and Fabius' heart sank. Metellus came staggering into the peristyle, followed by a cluster of his friends. He looked around, and then spied them, waving a flagon in their direction. 'Why don't you come carousing with us, Scipio? Afraid of the *prostibulae* in the brothels? Maybe you've forgotten what to do, spending too long in the company of those Greek eunuchs.'

Fabius saw Scipio's knuckles whiten as he clutched the edge of the seat, and he gripped Scipio's wrist. 'Keep your cool,' he whispered to him. 'He's goading you, but these are just words. If he draws a blade, then that's another matter.'

'If he mentions Polybius, I'll rip his throat out,' Scipio growled.

'He's too clever to do that,' Julia murmured. 'He may deride the Greeks, but he knows how much Polybius is respected for his military expertise in the Senate. He knows how to play the game, and he's not as drunk as he looks.'

Metellus had swayed onto the stage, and took another flagon from one of his companions. 'Or maybe you can't afford it,' Metellus jeered, raising the flagon to the audience and then taking a deep swig. 'Maybe Scipio Aemilianus has given away all of his money to women, because he's incapable of giving them any other favours.'

'That's my mother he's talking about, and my sisters, whom I've helped to support with my inheritance from Africanus,' Scipio muttered, his teeth clenched with anger. 'I'm still a richer man than he is, even so. And he'd better not mention my father's generosity.'

Julia shook her head. 'He won't do it today, at your father's triumph. He'll do it when the name of Paullus has faded from memory and he can deride him among his friends for returning from Pydna without a thought for his own pocket. He will use that against you, to show a weakness of character within your *gens.*'

'It's not a weakness, it's a strength,' Scipio growled.

Julia turned to him. 'You gave your adoptive grandmother Aemilia's fortune to your mother Papira. You paid off the dowries of your adoptive sisters. And when we were together this evening you told me that when the time comes you will give your share of your father's estate to your brother, and pay half the cost of the funeral games that by rights as eldest son should be his alone to bear; and then when your mother Papira dies you will pass on the fortune that you gave her from Aemilia to your own blood sisters.'

'I will do those things,' Scipio said quietly, watching Metellus as he pushed the actors aside and danced around the stage himself, parodying their performance, and then smashed his flagon on the floor and guffawed at his companions, turning back and bowing low to the audience in derision.

'You've been generous to others, Scipio,' Julia said quickly, as if knowing that her time was nearly up. 'You've made a virtue of being magnanimous, and Polybius and others can hold you up as an example. But be careful. Rome is suspicious of too much generosity, and it will work against you. Metellus will say that you have used your wealth to compensate for the criticisms that others have made against your character, and that it just shows more clearly the weaknesses that he wants to find in you. It's time you were generous to yourself, Scipio. You must forget the opinion of others and look to your own future.'

'Julia!' Metellus' thick voice bawled from the stage, and he waved a hand in their direction. 'It's you I've come here for. It's time I had a taste of my marriage rights. I've denied myself the *prostibulae* this evening so I can show you what I'm worth. This theatre can go to the dogs. We're leaving now.'

Scipio suddenly leapt out of his seat, bounded across the peristyle and pounced on Metellus, pushing him hard against the wall of the stage and pinning him by his chest. He whipped out the knife he carried on his belt and pressed it against Metellus' neck, forcing his head upwards. For a few moments Scipio held the position, his face snarling, while everyone watched in stunned silence. Metellus strained his head sideways, staring down at the blade. 'Go on, Scipio,' he said between clenched teeth. 'Too squeamish for the sight of blood? It's all that hunting you do. It's softened you. You should try killing men one day.'

Fabius came up behind Scipio and grasped his wrist with an iron grip, pulling the hand with the knife away and dragging him back, while several of Metellus' companions did the same for him. He shook them away, straightening himself up, and then marched across to Julia, grabbing her by the arm and pulling her into his group. 'I'll remember this, Scipio Aemilianus. You should watch your back.'

Fabius continued to hold Scipio as the group staggered off. Terence sat slumped in the corner with his head in his hands, and the audience began to get up and leave. Scipio seemed stunned by what had happened, unaccustomed to losing control, as if his rage against Metellus had been triggered to displace his feelings of impotence over Julia's departure. Now that she was gone he seemed paralysed by disbelief. Fabius could feel him shaking, and the blood pounding through his veins. Julia glanced back one last time as they rounded the corner, and then they were gone. Fabius released Scipio, took the knife from him and resheathed it, and then led him by the shoulder out of the house and on to the street, facing back in the direction of the Forum. 'Where to now?' he said.

Scipio stared grimly ahead, to where the stragglers from Metellus' group could still be seen, one of them throwing up in a doorway. 'To the shrine in my house on the Palatine, to honour the memory of my adoptive grandfather Scipio Africanus. And then we go to Macedonia, to hunt. I need to be far from men, and far from Rome. We leave tonight.'

Fabius watched Scipio reach up and touch the silver *phalera* disc on his breastplate that he had been awarded for valour at Pydna. He could guess what Scipio was thinking. The disc was the gift of a father to a son who by rights should not have been there, a year too young to have been appointed to the rank of military tribune. Only Fabius knew that he had truly earned the decoration, that the *phalera* was not a sign of favouritism, that Scipio had run alone at the phalanx and cleaved his way through the ranks of the enemy until he was dripping with Macedonian blood. But Scipio knew perfectly well that there were others who would not see it that way: detractors and enemies of his father and grandfather, those who would scorn his achievements at Pydna as exaggeration and even use the award of the *phalera* against him. In the fickle world of Rome, the patronage of his father that had got him to Pydna and put him on the first rung of the military ladder could also be his undoing, allowing his detractors to claim that he had always had an easy ride of it and had hung on the togas of a father and a grandfather he could never hope to emulate.

Fabius knew him well enough to read his thoughts. Scipio loved Rome, and he hated Rome. He loved Rome for giving him the path to military glory, but he hated Rome for taking Julia from him. He remembered what Scipio had said that night when they had shared a flagon of wine staring at the stars from the Circus Maximus. One day he would return here wearing a breastplate of his own, more magnificent than this one, made of gold and silver taken in his own conquests, decorated not with images of past wars but with those of his own greatest victory, a burning citadel with a general standing astride the vanquished leader of Rome's greatest enemy. He would return to celebrate the greatest triumph that Rome had ever seen. He would wait until he had received the adulation of the Senate, but then would turn his back on it and discard the ways that had been destined to bring him such unhappiness today, the day of his father's triumph, also the appointed day of Julia's betrothal. He would leave the Senate impotent, powerless, because he would take with him the people, the legionaries and the centurions, and together they would forge the greatest army the world had ever seen – one that would break free from the shackles of Rome and sweep all before it, led by a general whose conquests would make those of Alexander the Great seem paltry by comparison.

The last of the men ahead of them staggered away, shouting slurred words of contempt, one of them hurtling a half-full flagon of wine that smashed and left a red smear across the road. Already the glow from the huge fires on the Field of Mars could be seen, the signal that the evening's bloodletting was well underway.

Fabius turned to Scipio, who was still staring ahead. He remembered when they had fought alongside each other in the backstreets of Rome almost ten years before, beating off the gang that had been pursing them, and afterwards Fabius had lifted him up and dusted him off. Scipio had laughed with pleasure at finding a new friend and sparring partner, at the freedom he had discovered on the streets outside the stifling conventions of his aristocratic background, conventions that had now taken Julia from him. But Fabius also remembered the hardness he had seen in those eyes, a hardness that others around him saw and feared, a fear that led the boys who were now those drunken young men to deride him for not being one of them. Fabius would have to see to it that the hardness remained, that Scipio would ride out this storm as he had ridden out the derision of others, that he did not fall into bitterness and self-destruction. He knew what they had to do.

He turned to Scipio. 'Do you remember that stag you took above Falernium last summer?'

Scipio was silent, still staring. After a few moments he dropped his head, and nodded. 'It was early summer; I remember it well,' he replied quietly. 'The snow still lay in patches on the upper reaches of the mountains.' He squinted up at Fabius. 'Don't try to console me, Fabius. I don't need it.'

'I'm just thinking of the hunting equipment we'll need for Macedonia. It'll not just be stags we're after there, but boar. Polybius said the place offers the best boar hunting he's ever experienced. We'll need spears, as well as bows. And I have a new puppy to train as a hunting dog. It's always best to train a dog in the place where you want to use it, and the Macedonian Royal Forest can be his home. I'll train him to stalk boar.'

Scipio gave a tired smile. 'A dog. What's his name?'

'Rufius. It's after the sound he makes. I can't stop him barking. Eudoxia gave him to me.'

Scipio took a deep breath. 'Then Rufius shall be our companion. We'll need to collect our things tonight. And don't get too close to that slave girl. We might be gone for a long time.'

There was a sudden commotion in the street ahead, and someone burst through the throng and ran up to them. It was

Ennius, holding his helmet and drenched in sweat. 'It's the old centurion Petraeus,' he panted. 'We've got to get to him, now. They're going to try to kill him.'

Scipio held him by the shoulders. 'Calm yourself, man. What's happened?'

Ennius bowed his head, took a few deep breaths, and then looked at Scipio, the sweat dripping off his face. 'After the pyrotechnics display in the Forum I sent my *fabri* off for a well-earned drink. The nearest tavern to the Sacred Way is that one beside the Gladiator School, you remember, run by that rogue Petronius? Some of us used to sneak in there between classes. One of my centurions came running back to say they'd had an altercation with Brasis, the former gladiator from Thrace who used to fight with Brutus. I never did trust him, even though he was the best sword fighter in the school. He was drunk and slashed one of my *fabri* across the legs with his Thracian *sica* dagger, and then smashed his way out, bellowing that he was going to kill someone that night. Earlier on he'd been seen huddled in a corner of the tavern with a man in a hooded cloak that Petronius told my men he recognized as a senator, Gaius Sextius Calvinus. He gave Brasis a few denarii from a money pouch. It was after Sextius Calvinus left that Brasis began drinking heavily and brawling.'

'Sextius Calvinus,' Scipio said grimly. 'One of my adoptive grandfather Scipio Africanus' worst enemies. He tried to bring him to trial on false charges of misappropriating public funds, and he violently opposed the formation of the academy.'

'My *fabri* saw Sextius Calvinus pass someone in the street on the way out and hand him the money pouch, and then that person went into the tavern. All of my men recognized him. It was Porcus Entestius Supinus.'

Fabius let out a low whistle. 'Why does that not surprise me.'

'He runs errands for Metellus, doesn't he?' Scipio said.

'More than that,' Fabius said grimly. 'He's become Metellus' right-hand man. It's sometimes hard to tell who pulls the strings.'

'You have a history with him?'

'We both do. Remember that night when you and I first met years ago, when you thought you'd see what it was like in the streets at night by the Tiber? Porcus and his gang were chasing me, and you got caught up in it.'

'So *that* was Porcus,' Scipio exclaimed. 'You've never mentioned him by name.'

'He was a few years older than me, and bullied me relentlessly. He drove my mother to the illness that killed her. He and his gang picked on my father when he was at his lowest ebb, I was too young to defend him, and the bullying led him to an early grave too. One day I will get my vengeance, but I will do it alone.'

'Why should he want Petraeus dead?' Scipio said.

'Because Metellus is under the influence of Sextius Calvinus and their faction in the Senate. Metellus sees his future glory in Greece, not in Carthage, and sees Petraeus as a malign influence. The riches of Greece and power in the east are the future that Porcus sees for himself, too. But there's also a personal reason. Porcus tried to join the legions for the war in Macedonia, after we'd gone to Pydna, but Petraeus had been dragged out of retirement and put in charge of recruitment as his last job after the academy, and he rejected Porcus. He said that his reputation preceded him, and that he was a coward.'

'But Porcus was a street boy from the Tiber districts, your own home,' Scipio said. 'The breeding ground of the best legionaries.'

Fabius shook his head. 'Not always. Do you remember how he stood back gloating while his gang laid into us? He gets others to do his dirty work for him. That's what he'll be doing now, getting Brasis drunk and then paying him to go after Petraeus.'

'Well, he stoked up Brasis, well and truly,' Ennius said. 'My *fabri* overheard everything. Porcus told Brasis that the Thracian mercenaries captured at Pydna have been scheduled for execution tomorrow afternoon, which is true enough. But it turns out that one of them is his brother. Porcus also reminded Brasis of a story that the old centurion Petraeus used to tell us, of how when he was a young legionary an inexperienced tribune surrendered his cohort to a group of Thracian mercenaries and the Romans were promptly put to the sword, including Petraeus' own brother. Petraeus never told it out of any antagonism towards Thracians, but just to show us that we should never surrender to mercenaries. But Porcus let Brasis get it into his head that Petraeus put in a word to Aemilianus to have the Thracians singled out for special attention tomorrow, as revenge for what the Thracians did to his brother all those years ago.'

Scipio stared at him. 'That's exactly what Sextius Calvinus and his faction would wish him to think. It's a set-up. They've been trying to find a way of getting rid of Petraeus ever since Scipio Africanus appointed him to the academy. He's never moderated his opinions about the need for a professional army or his scorn of the Senate, and the plebs respect him. Where is he now?'

'At his farm in the Alban Hills. My *fabri* helped him to build a new stone barn there only a few months ago. His wife is long dead and his children are grown up, so he lives alone.'

'I was there too, only last week,' Fabius said. 'I'd promised to spend time with Petraeus when we came back from Macedonia, to tell him about Pydna and help him dig a terrace for some olive saplings. They won't come to fruit in his lifetime, but he's bequeathed the land to me on his death.'

'And Brasis?'

'Last seen heading for the Ostian Gate. Not before he drunkenly ransacked the Gladiator School for a sword.'

Fabius stood up. 'We need to warn Petraeus.'

Scipio put his hand on Ennius' shoulder. 'I'm going to find Brutus, who was with my father's Praetorian Guard but can be spared now that the main ceremony is over. Fabius and I will strip off our ceremonial armour and be at the gate in an hour's time. If we run, we can be in the Alban Hills before midnight. After all the battles he has fought and all he has done for Rome I will not allow Petraeus to die in his bed at the hands of a drunken Thracian gladiator. Nor will I forget what our enemies have been prepared to do to bring us down. We move now.'

Four hours later, Fabius clambered up a gorse-infested slope on the lower reaches of the Alban Hills, followed close behind by Scipio and Brutus. He had led them off the road on a short cut over rough ground where he had scrambled with his puppy Rufius only a few days before when he had stayed with Petraeus. His legs were criss-crossed with scratches from the spiny under-growth, but he did not care. He could smell burning, and he had a dread sense of foreboding. Brasis was at least half an hour ahead of them, and must have made it to the farm by now.

He reached the crest of the hill, the other two alongside him. Ahead of them lay a shallow ravine he had scrambled down with Rufius, and on the other side the farmstead, perhaps half a *stade* distant. It was a moonlit night, and they could see the buildings clearly. Beyond the main building he saw a lick of flame from a fire in the yard, evidently the source of the smell. For a few moments Fabius felt an overwhelming sense of relief. Perhaps Petraeus had relented and lit his own private bonfire in celebration of the triumph. Perhaps Brasis had never made it here after all, and had passed out drunk in a ditch somewhere outside Rome. Perhaps they would not have to embarrass and anger Petraeus by coming to his rescue, when there was no good cause.

But then he saw something that made him freeze. The flame leapt from behind the building over the roof, and then to the wooden byre where Fabius had slept with Rufius. And then Petraeus appeared from behind the byre, his bow-legged gait unmistakable, carrying a firebrand in one hand and a sword in the other, pursued by the lurching form of Brasis. He swept the brand over his wood pile, the kindling instantly igniting in the dry air, and then tossed it into the shed where he kept his olive press and oil supply. In seconds the entire farm was alight, a mass of flame crackling and erupting high into the sky. And then Petraeus stopped in the yard in front – the place where he and Fabius had sat together only a few days before, watching the sunset over distant Rome – and he staggered, falling heavily on one arm, and then struggled up again. In the light of the fire they could see that his tunic was soaked with blood, and that it was pouring in a trail behind him. Fabius realized what he had been doing with the fire-brand, why he had been burning his farm. *He had been lighting his own funeral pyre.*

There was no chance of getting there in time to help him. They watched helplessly as he staggered backwards, clearly grievously wounded, and faced his attacker. He lunged, his blade burying itself somewhere deep in Brasis' midriff. Then he slipped and was down, and Brasis was on him, slashing and thrusting, driving his blade deep into the centurion's body, over and over again, until he was still. Brasis got up, staggered backwards, leaned forward again and picked up the corpse by the hair, lopping the head off with one stroke and holding it up for a moment while it bled out. Then he sheathed his sword, put the head into a bag on his belt and turned in the direction of Rome, putting his hands on his knees and trying to marshal his strength. Petraeus' sword was still stuck in him, and he had gaping slash wounds on his arms and legs. Petraeus had not gone down without exacting his price. He had fought like a legionary to the end.

Fabius felt numb. *The old centurion was dead.*

Brutus suddenly bellowed, his fists held out and his muscles tensed, his eyes wild, staring at the scene. Scipio stood in front of him and took his head in his hands, leaning against his forehead. 'Do your worst, Brutus. And when it is over, put the centurion's body in the flames of his beloved home. That shall be his funeral pyre. I must go far away, but you need not worry. Fabius will look after me. *Ave atque vale*. We will meet again, in this world or the next.'

He held him for a few moments longer, then released him and turned back towards the fire. Brutus drew his sword and bounded forward, crashing through the spiny undergrowth like a bull as he hurtled down the ravine and up the other side, his sword held high, howling with rage.

Scipio turned to Fabius. 'Return to Rome under cover of darkness and get what we need for the forest. I'll await you here.'

'Your father will have missed you at the rite of dedication to Scipio Africanus.'

'Find him before you leave and tell him what's happened. He should at least be able to silence Sextius Calvinus, if Brutus doesn't get to him first. We will continue to have enemies in the Senate, but those who would take this step should know who they are dealing with. I'll send word to my father once we have arrived in Macedonia.'

His voice was hoarse, no longer with emotion but with cold determination. Fabius saw beyond the young man's anguish to the hardness in those eyes that he had first seen all those years ago. He would see that Scipio rode out this storm, and took strength from it, a soldier's strength.

There was a bellow from the slope opposite, reverberating down the ravine. They turned towards the fire and saw the figure of Brutus silhouetted by the flames, his sword raised, holding something up with his other hand. It was Brasis' severed head.

Scipio grasped Fabius by the shoulders, and turned him towards Rome. 'Go now.'

Fabius began to run.

PART THREE

MACEDONIA

157 BC

7

Fabius pulled hard on the reins of his horse, guiding it around the mud that oozed up where an underground spring had broken through the forest path. His hunting dog Rufius leapt over the mud and loped ahead, towards the two riders who had begun to pick their way around the rocks that had been exposed where a mountain stream had cut into the slope. The depth of the stream bed showed that in spring it was a raging torrent, bringing down melt water from the mountains that rose beyond the northern fringe of the forest. They had been told by the foresters that the path had been used years before to bring out mighty oak timbers to build the tomb of King Philip, father of Alexander the Great, many *stades* away to the south on the plain of Macedon beside the sea. The foresters had come this far north to choose the hardiest trees, here on the lower mountain slopes where the oak gave way to pine and fir and cedar, before that too petered out and all that lay beyond the treeline was snow and jagged rock, a place where only a hardy few among the foresters had ever dared to venture.

Fabius and Scipio had come up here not to marvel at the oak trees, but to hunt the elusive Macedonian royal boar, a semi-mythical creature that was said to lurk in the furthest reaches of the woods on the mountain slopes. The foresters spoke of it in hushed tones, a beast as large as a bullock that could run faster than any steed, with tusks that could toss a horse and rider high into the air and a hide so thick that it would deflect all but the strongest spears. The boar had become Scipio's obsession, his ultimate prize, a chase that seemed about to take them beyond the world of men to a place where only a Hercules or a Theseus could hope to win.

They had been searching for signs of digging, for a rooting in the ground that would give Rufius a scent to follow. Rufius had grown into a beautiful dog, sleek and agile, as fast as a hare and he had become a close companion to both of them through the cold days and nights they had spent together in the forest, his black-and-white coat growing thick and shaggy as winter came on. In the three years since they had left Rome to live in the forest he had become as skilled a hunting dog as they had ever seen, adept at following the deer and bear that they had tracked through the dense undergrowth of the lower slopes, and at retrieving the pheasant and grouse that they had sometimes been lucky enough to bring down with an arrow. But up here, where the air seemed thinner and they were oppressed by a constant cold mist, Rufius seemed cowed, rarely straying out of sight even when a scent was strong. Fabius had come to rely on Rufius as his sixth sense, and he shared the dog's apprehension.

The night before, they had fortified their camp with sharpened stakes against the ravenous pack of wolves that had been trailing them for days now, keeping Rufius jittery and alert. The wolves were after the carcasses left after each successful hunt, meaning that he and Scipio and Rufius always moved on swiftly after butchering their prey, but it had been several days now since they had made a kill; the wolves were beginning to eye them more malevolently, making the hunters their quarry. Fabius had made the fire unusually large and had stayed awake for most of the night, spear in hand, Rufius by his side, watching the eyes on the edge of their clearing as they reflected the firelight. The yipping and howling had carried on intermittently through the forest since then, an unnerving sound in daylight. Perhaps the wolves too were beginning to sense that they had strayed beyond their rightful place, following Scipio as Fabius had done, on a quest that was taking them dangerously close to the realm of the gods. He looked again at the two riders ahead, at Scipio's companion. He was glad that Polybius had come. He would talk sense into Scipio, bring him back down to earth. It was time they returned to Rome.

A snowsquall swept over the trail, obscuring the riders from view. Fabius pressed his heels into his horse and it lurched forward, slipping and sliding on the wet rocks. The riders came in sight again, and he drew closer. Polybius had reached them an hour before, blowing his horn to give them warning, having come up from the foresters' camp a day's ride away after arriving in Macedonia from Rome. Polybius knew the forest like the back of his hand, having learned to hunt here as a boy more than thirty years before, but when he arrived he had seemed out of place, with his trimmed beard and expensive cloak; his years in Rome had made him appear more of a teacher and a man of letters than a warrior and a hunter. Fabius knew that Polybius would hate to hear it, remembering how much he prided himself on his tough-ness and military experience. Scipio, by contrast, was shaggy bearded, his shoulder-length hair tied behind his neck like a barbarian, his skin bronzed and ingrained with the dirt of the forest. He looked older than his twenty-eight years, like a gnarled war veteran, yet it was precisely because there had been no wars to fight since Pydna almost twelve years before that they were here now, fighting a proxy war against the beasts of the forest rather than against men.

Fabius hoped against hope that Polybius had brought tidings of a new conflict, of a summons to arms in Rome that would draw Scipio back. He rode up to the two men, keeping a horse's distance behind but close enough to hear them talk. Polybius had been examining Scipio's bow, and handed it back to him. He had clearly been casting a critical eye over their hunting equipment, and he gestured towards the quiver of boar spears that Scipio carried in a leather pouch ahead of his saddle, angled backwards along the shoulder of the horse so that they were out of his way when he rode yet accessible for quick deployment. 'Have you ever killed a man with a boar spear, Scipio?'

'I've never had the opportunity. And perhaps never will. War seems a thing of the past.'

'Don't be too sure of it. And as for the boar spear, one day after a battle when we have deserters to punish I'll show you how it's done. The flat iron head of the spear is too wide to twist within the body, so you force it all the way through, twist it outside the body, and then pull it back and out. It's a weapon ideally suited for cavalry in a melee, when the horse is nearly stationary and the rider has the chance to lunge forward and then twist and withdraw forcibly. The key to the blade is its symmetrical shape, like a willow leaf, with a razor-sharp edge at the back as well as the front of the leaf.'

Scipio grinned. 'You've always been a mine of wisdom, Polybius. A true mentor for a young Roman aristocrat. You taught me about ethics in war, about strategy and about how to kill. And most importantly for me right now, you taught me to hunt. There could have been no better education.'

'That's what I've come to talk to you about, Scipio. About what you're doing with your life. But first, I have a question.' He peered closely at the spears. 'What on earth is that wood? It's segmented, like the stem of a Nile reed. I've never seen anything like it.'

Scipio pulled out one of the spears and passed it to Polybius, who hefted it and stared at it keenly. 'Extraordinary,' Polybius murmured. 'So lightweight, and yet so strong. And it is columnar, with each segment the same width as the last, not tapering like a normal tree branch. Am I correct in thinking it's hollow?'

Scipio nodded enthusiastically. 'Do you remember at the academy how Ptolemy and I used to ride out from Rome along the Appian Way in the evenings and hunt wild pig in the Pomptine marshes?'

'I remember Ptolemy all too well,' Polybius replied pensively. 'Do you know, in Egypt they now call him *philometor*, "lover of his mother"? But it's not his affection for his mother that's his biggest problem, it's his marriage to his scheming sister Cleopatra. I told him when he was a boy always to remember that he was a Macedonian by lineage, that just because his family had ruled Egypt since Alexander's time it didn't mean they had to behave like pharaohs and marry their own siblings. He's come running to Rome with his tail between his legs twice since taking over Egypt, first when his erstwhile friend Demetrius of Syria invaded him, and then when his own brother usurped him. That's *twice* Rome has had to bail him out. And Demetrius hasn't fared much better in Syria. The problems of those kingdoms are a lesson in how *not* to leave an empire: no structure, no administration. Alexander's legacy was as if the wealthiest man in the world had died but left no will. Ptolemy and Demetrius are only there still because they're allies of Rome and it's more convenient to keep it that way than to annex Egypt and Syria as provinces, yet propping them up will soon prove more of a headache than invading them. A Roman general – a conqueror of Carthage, let's say – could look east and see a succession of kingdoms that could fall before him like the columns of a temple in an earthquake.'

'Carthage still seems an impossible dream. The Senate is too self-absorbed to order an assault, or to sanction a standing army that would deal with the threat. Rome is becoming weak.'

'It is not the older generation that would fight Carthage, but your generation, a generation who must play the game and become legates and consuls. The best of that generation have forsaken Rome, and if they stay away too long they will never be allowed back.'

'What happened to the senator Sextius Calvinus, by the way? I know he died soon after we left Rome. My father sent word.'

'A terrible accident. Brutus saw it, by chance. He was run over by a bullock cart, and then gored by the bulls. His body was mangled beyond recognition.'

'That sounds like Brutus.'

'Those who were against you, Sextius Calvinus among them,

were fired up that night of the triumph by the ascendency of your father Aemilius Paullus, by the sudden popularity of your *gens* among the plebs and the threat those senators saw of an imminent takeover, perhaps of dictatorship. Some of them may genuinely have been moved by constitutional fears, but most of them were simply protecting their own vested interests in the established order. Petraeus was seen as the rock that held you and the other young tribunes loyal to your cause together, and getting rid of him was a way of loosening those bonds and reducing the threat without going to the extreme of political assassination, of murdering a fellow patrician. Your departure may have persuaded them that they have won, but there are others, rivals of yours, who will still see you as a threat. That will never go away, and you must always be on your guard, even out here.'

'Rome when I left was enervated by lack of direction, only able to look ahead to the next consular elections, to which marriage will tie which *gens* to another.'

Polybius cast a penetrating eye on Scipio, and then looked ahead. 'I'd love to know more about those spears. You were going to tell me about Ptolemy.'

Fabius knew what Polybius was doing. He was drawing Scipio out, talking passionately about topics that he knew were close to Scipio's heart, yet which Scipio had professed to disdain when he went into self-imposed exile in the forest. Polybius might be the only one who could snap him out of his melancholy, but he was going to have to play him carefully if he wanted them to ride out of this forest together for Rome.

Scipio pulled out another of the boar spears from his quiver, showing its flexibility as it bounced in his hand. 'Ptolemy was passionate about hunting too, and perhaps that was his undoing.'

Polybius eyed Scipio keenly. 'It has been the undoing of many men, some because success in the hunt gave them delusions of grandeur, others because they were destined for greatness but frittered away all of their energy in the hunt.'

'You always said it was ability, and not destiny, that made a man great. The joy of the hunt is that it is entirely about ability, and there is nobody burdening you with expectations of destiny, of forefathers held proud or betrayed by your course of action. Here, in the forest, the hunt is like a battle, where you live for the moment, where all depends on your courage and individual prowess, not on destiny.'

'Tell me about Ptolemy. About the spears.'

'He sought me out at my father's funeral games three years ago. He invited me to join an expedition to the upper reaches of the Nile at the cataracts, where crocodiles of huge size are said to live, beasts shrouded in myth like the royal boar we seek today. I told him that after I'd succeeded here and sent him a pickled boar's head to prove it, I'd take ship to Alexandria and join him. Meanwhile, he sent me some of his spears, and I replaced the thin iron spike they use to penetrate a crocodile's hide with the leaf-shaped head of our boar spears. As for the curious wood, he says it comes from an island called Taprobane, far out in the Erythraean Sea.'

'Taprobane,' Polybius said, astonished. 'That's to the south of India, a prodigious distance away.'

'Ptolemy said that the Egyptians have been receiving goods from there since the time of the pharaohs, shipped in native craft across the Erythraean Sea to the coast of Egypt and then taken across the desert to the Nile. They even bring goods from a distant empire called Thina, including *serikon*, a fine fabric woven from moth cocoons. This wood they call *mambu*. It has incredible strength for its weight, so that lengths of twelve or fifteen feet are as light as our throwing javelins. If the iron tip breaks off, the wood shatters into razor-sharp shards that are held in place by the strength of the next segment below it, meaning that the shaft can still be used as a spear in its own right. And finally, because the air in each segment is closed off from the adjoining segments, lengths of *mambu* thrown into a fire will explode as the air inside heats up and expands, sending lethal shards everywhere. The native warriors in those parts use them when they clear villages and towns, throwing *mambu* into burning buildings to kill and maim any occupants still left inside.'

'Fascinating,' Polybius murmured. 'The wood is perfect for long thrusting spears, to be deployed in a charge on horseback. The Sarmatians and the Parthians have used lances of this length, and Alexander tried it with his cavalry. But they were inhibited by the thickness and weight of the wood needed for a lance. If it could be acquired in sufficient quantities, this *mambu* could arm a whole new branch of the cavalry and greatly boost the effectiveness of a charge on an infantry line.'

'For now, we have it to hunt boar, and that's all that matters out here,' Scipio said, spurring his horse forward. 'We've only got a couple of hours of daylight left, and I don't want to have to camp beyond the treeline. It's cold enough as it is, and the wind up there will make it worse.' They had come up several hundred feet in elevation while they had been talking, scanning the ground for signs of boar. Polybius dropped back beside Fabius, and pointed up at the grey mist over the treetops ahead. 'Do you remember when you and Hippolyta's Celtic slave girl Eudoxia, the one from the Albion Isles, came to me to learn Greek, and I showed you Eratosthenes' map of the world to point out where she came from? That's another edge of the world up there, somewhere ahead of us.'

'I don't remember the map, but I do remember Eudoxia *very* well, Polybius. I was fourteen years old, and she had just become a woman.'

'Tell me, Fabius. Do you have a girl now, in Rome perhaps?'

Fabius cleared his throat. 'It's Eudoxia. I should say, I would *like* it to be her, above all things. But we haven't set eyes on each other for three years, since Scipio and I came out here. Hardly any word of the outside world reaches us, except through the foresters.'

'Then I have happy tidings for you. Eudoxia is well, and grown to a beautiful young woman. She has many suitors, but keeps them at arm's length. It has surprised me, but now I know why. You see, I know her well, as I took her into my household when Hippolyta left to join Gulussa in North Africa.'

Scipio had dropped back alongside them, and turned to Polybius, astonishment in his voice. 'Hippolyta and Gulussa?'

'It's not what it seems. The Numidian tradition is for a prince to have many wives, and I doubt whether she would go along with that. Zeus knows, in her homeland in Scythia the woman probably has to kill off all other female contenders for the man she desires, something I can well envisage her doing. The truth is, Gulussa's father Masinissa was so impressed by her in his visit to the academy that he invited her to lead a cohort of cavalry archers in his army, so she has gone out to train them alongside Gulussa. If Rome goes to war against Carthage again, they will be our allies. Their allegiance to us was secured in the academy. That was your grandfather Africanus' vision, and his wisdom has been borne out.'

Scipio looked at Polybius grimly. 'If Rome does *not* go to war with Carthage, then Carthage will eclipse Rome by the success of her trade, and Rome will go the way of the Etruscan cities and be forgotten to history, remembered only for the inward-looking obstinacy of its senators and their inability to field a professional army.'

'Brave words, Scipio, spoken by one who has walked away from the other vision of Africanus, that you should be the one to take up his torch against Carthage and finish the job.'

Scipio did not reply, and Polybius turned again to Fabius. 'As for Eudoxia, I will pass word that you are thinking of her. With any luck, you will be there to tell her yourself.'

'It was she who gave me the dog, Rufius,' Fabius said. 'He's from a special breed they use in the forest clearings in Albion to protect their animals against wolves, and in the uplands of that country to herd sheep. The old centurion Petraeus left me a plot of land in the Alban Hills to the east of Rome, hilly open country good for sheep. One day I will take Rufius there and we will tend my flock together.'

'With your brood of future legionaries, and their mother Eudoxia by your side?'

'If the gods will it.'

Scipio turned back to him. 'Unless you wish to fight as a mercenary for some other power, Fabius, you may be tending your flock sooner than you think. Rome, it seems, no longer has the appetite for war.'

Polybius looked at Scipio. 'If you return to Rome, you may be able to persuade the Senate of the threat of Carthage. Only then will you be able to take up the legacy of Scipio Africanus.'

'My father Aemilius Paullus gave me the Macedonian Royal Forest to tend after the Battle of Pydna,' Scipio replied. 'It is my duty to honour his legacy, too.'

'Pydna was nearly twelve years ago, and your father has been dead for three years now,' Polybius replied. 'After Pydna he knew that there would be no war in Greece for some time, and he gave you the forest to hone your hunting skills and keep your eye keen. But perhaps you have become addicted to the chase.'

'Look at this place,' Scipio said, gesturing around at the trees and the dark tunnels through the undergrowth around them. 'A man can become lost in here, and still find plenty to live on. And I know you share my passion. It was you who taught me to shoot deer from horseback.'

'Indeed. But you are twenty-eight years old now, and you have not yet held a magistracy in Rome. If you let further appointments slip by and remain out of the public eye, you will never be elected quaestor. You are old enough now, and if you are not elected at the youngest possible age it will be a mark against you in the future.'

'Quaestor, aedile, praetor, consul,' Scipio grumbled. 'The

cursus honorum maps out a man's life, and makes it hardly worth living. If there is to be no war, I would far rather be out here hunting than dying of boredom in the law courts.'

'If you do not hold those offices, you will never hold high command. Only praetors and consuls can lead a Roman army to war.'

'That's the stupidity of it,' Scipio railed. 'If we only had a professional army, I could at least be training legionaries in the Field of Mars. As it is, the generals are chosen on the basis of their ability to remember obscure details of the Roman constitution, and to arbitrate in the law courts over who owns which bit of adjoining wall between two houses next to the Cattle Forum. That was not the future my grandfather Scipio Africanus envisaged for us as boys when he set up the academy and appointed you as my teacher.'

'Perhaps not,' Polybius said, eyeing Scipio. 'But he knew the virtue of a balanced career, and the need to keep those who would be generals well-grounded in the politics of the city. The needs of Rome must outweigh the ambitions of those who would lead her citizens to war.'

'Well, then, the balance is wrong,' Scipio said. 'And there will be no more brilliant generals, because those who might have become so instead become indolent and lazy in the law courts, and any spark of military genius they might have had as young men will be extinguished by the time they are given armies to command. And, meanwhile, the legionaries of past wars have no royal forests to keep their skills honed as I have, and they grow bent and cynical in the taverns of Rome.' He craned his neck around. 'Isn't that so, Fabius?'

Fabius spurred his horse and came between the two men. 'If there is to be no chance of a professional army, all that the veterans ask for is a few weeks' training every year with the *gladius* and the *pilum*, even if it means enduring the bellowing of the centurions. The old men say that during the many years of war against Hannibal, the boys would see their fathers return with wounds and tales of bloody battle, and would yearn for the day when they too were old enough to join. Now with war a distant memory, all the boys know about is the haul of booty that came from Greece after Pydna, gold and silver that allowed their fathers to drink their lives away in taverns telling tales of war that nobody listens to any longer, that they themselves scarcely remember. The next time Rome needs to raise the legions, the recruits will be soft, with an eye only to booty. All that was learned in past wars will be lost. The old soldiers drink to drown the shame of knowing that the next Roman army in the field will stand no chance against the professionals and mercenaries of our enemies. I know this too well because my father was one of them, a veteran of Cannae, and he died in a brawl as I watched, defending the honour of the Roman army he remembered against those who would laugh him down.'

'There it is,' Scipio said, looking at Polybius. 'It's not only aspiring generals who have become cynical, but legionaries like Fabius who should not be riding here as a huntsman's attendant seeking boar and deer, but be a centurion in a crack Roman legion training every day on the Field of Mars, practising battle manoeuvres and storming mock fortifications built by Ennius and his engineers.'

'Under your command, Scipio,' Fabius said.

Polybius looked at Scipio. 'The only way for you to make that happen is in Rome.'

'There is another reason for me to be here. The people of Macedonia specifically request me to arbitrate in their disputes, and between them and Rome. I have a reputation for keeping my word, for *fides*. It's what you taught me in the academy.'

'That reputation will stand you in good stead,' Polybius said carefully. 'But you do not hold an official post out here. Do not stray into the territory of others.'

'What do you mean?'

Polybius reined in his horse, and the other two came to a halt as well, Fabius keeping a short distance behind. Polybius turned in his saddle and eyed Scipio. 'It's what I really came out here to tell you. I am no longer advising you to return to Rome just for the sake of your career. I am telling you to do so for your own well-being. There is a threat to you, and this forest is no longer a safe place to be. Metellus has been appointed proconsul of Macedonia.'

8

They rode on in silence for a few minutes, picking their way up the forest path. The air was sharper now with the cold mist that came from nearby snow, and the dense stands of oak and birch of the forest below had given way to mixed growth of fir and scrub as they climbed closer to the treeline. Scipio had ridden a short way ahead, and Fabius knew that he would have been unsettled by Polybius' news. His rivalry with Metellus had gone far beyond boyhood jostling that final night in Rome when Scipio had pinned him against the theatre wall; Fabius knew that Metellus' threat of revenge had been real. But there had been more to it than that. Julia's arranged marriage with Metellus had been the main reason why Scipio had left Rome, as well as his dislike of the *gentes* and the social requirements that constrained their lives and tied him to the *cursus honorum*. Fabius was pleased with any news that might help to persuade Scipio to return to Rome, but he knew that for Scipio to do so because of Metellus' arrival would only fuel his resentment of the man and of the world of Rome that had created his unhappiness. Not for the first time, Fabius prayed for war, to put Scipio back on track. He peered up into the mist, spurring his horse closer to the other two. It was going to be a rocky road ahead, in more ways than one.

Polybius rode up alongside Scipio. 'Do you know of Andriscus?'

Scipio shrugged. 'An insignificant ruler in Aeolis in Asia Minor with delusions of grandeur, who fancies himself the next king of Macedonia. Living in the shadow of Alexander the Great seems to do that to men. He's not the only one.'

'He's more than that now. He's landed in Macedonia with a bodyguard all dressed up in antique armour so they look like

Alexander's companions in the famous sculpture by Lykippos celebrating the Battle of Graviscus, something every Macedonian boy is taken to see as part of his education. Andriscus may be an upstart, but he knows how to play the people. He arrived shortly after he heard of Metellus' appointment, because Metellus had offered to recognize his claim by giving him the royal forests.'

'Knowing that Aemilius Paullus had given them to me, and knowing that I was here,' Scipio said grimly.

'Despite your reputation among the Macedonians for fairness, Andriscus with Metellus behind him could easily drum up support among dissident Macedonians against you. There will be many who feel bitter about the Roman takeover, and towards those who defeated them. Your deeds at Pydna could be turned against you, so that your valour in cutting through the phalanx and chasing the fleeing Macedonians could be seen as mere slaughter of men who wished to lay down their arms.'

'Metellus also fought at Pydna. And at Callicinus, three years before that. He has more Macedonian blood on his hands than I do.'

'But he is not the son of Aemilius Paullus, the man who brought Macedonia to heel, who captured Perseus and humiliated him by parading him in triumph through Rome, and who condemned thousands of Macedonian nobles to permanent exile.'

'You sound regretful, Polybius.'

'How could I not be? I am sworn to Rome now, but I am also an Achaean Greek, and the Macedonians are my kin. And it is always a loss when a once-proud warrior race is brought to its knees, even if you are on the side of the victor.'

'And what of Andriscus?'

'Before arriving here he sent a delegation to Rome, with an offer of alliance with his kingdom of Aeolis. He wouldn't go himself, because he knew that word had spread of his claim to be the son of Perseus, and he feared arrest.'

'And is he?'

Polybius paused. 'I believe that he is an illegitimate son of Perseus and a harlot of Ilium, the site of ancient Troy across the Hellespont in Asia Minor. Perseus went there as a young man seeking inspiration from the shade of Achilles, just as Alexander the Great had done. Other Greek warriors have gone there, and the local women have built up quite a trade around it. My informants tell me that she took her son to her home in nearby Adramyttium in Aeolis, and he lived there in obscurity until she told him his father's identity. People readily believed it as he shares Perseus' looks, though not his charm or his intelligence. By all accounts he is a cruel and spiteful young man, and like all bullies he has his retinue of like-minded sycophants eager to do his bidding.'

'How did they receive his embassy in Rome?'

'There are important alliances still to be had in Asia Minor, with Pergamon, for example, but hardly anyone had heard of Aeolis, let alone Adramyttium. The embassy was pretty well laughed away.'

'Except, it seems, by Metellus,' Scipio said.

Polybius nodded. 'Metellus had just been told of his Macedonian posting and evidently thought that Andriscus might have his uses. There are rumours that as well as the forests he offered Andriscus some kind of administrative position, as a mediator between the Macedonians and himself. Andriscus has agreed to lead an irregular force of Thracian mercenaries to keep the Macedonian people in check.'

'To do Metellus' dirty work for him, you mean,' Scipio said testily. 'It sounds like a set-up to me, for the benefit of Metellus and of Andriscus but not the people of Macedonia. In the end it will not work out in Metellus' favour. He does not know the Macedonian people as I do. I have given them my word of honour in my negotiations with them, and they have been satisfied. With

Andriscus in my place as chief mediator with Rome, some will feel betrayed.'

'That may be,' Polybius said. 'They may begin by resenting him as a Roman subordinate. But we should not underestimate the man. He and his followers will play on past Macedonian glory, and on his claim to be the son of Perseus. His subservience to Metellus could be seen as cunning exploitation of the Romans to gain a foothold back in Macedonia. Before you know it, Andriscus will be the pretender to the Macedonian throne.'

'Metellus may have more on his hands than he bargained for,' Scipio said.

'Or the basis for an easy victory and a spectacular triumph. We shouldn't underestimate Metellus either. He is a man who can engineer a war for his own ends.'

'He was the most cunning strategist in the academy.'

'If Andriscus is allowed to develop a power base, then we should take more seriously the other embassies I know that he sent. One went to your old friend Demetrius in Syria, soliciting military assistance from the Seleucid kingdom to expand his area of influence in Asia Minor.'

Scipio grunted. 'Demetrius has enough on his hands. Do you remember him at the academy? He'd spent his whole boyhood as a captive in Rome, and then my grandfather Africanus decided to send him to the academy to make a good ally of him, like Gulussa and Hippolyta. It never really worked, though. He was always receiving shifty delegates from the east, trying to sway him this way or that. When the authorities did eventually turn a blind eye and let him escape Rome, none of us held out any hope for him sorting out the Seleucid kingdom. It was another mess left in the wake of Alexander. The court at Damascus is a rats' nest, with everyone always murdering each other.'

'Then you'll be more concerned about Andriscus' other embassy. This time, he went himself. To Carthage.'

Scipio reined in his horse and stared at Polybius. '*To Carthage.*

Whatever for? The Carthaginians barely have the military strength to hold their borders against the Numidians, let alone entertain an alliance with an obscure city-state in Asia Minor. I hardly think the Carthaginian navy is going to sally forth and go to his rescue when he decides to march against Rome, or whoever he intends to confront. At last count, they had about ten ships, and none of them had gone to sea for years.'

'Don't be so sure of it, Scipio. Many in Rome saw the war against Hannibal as the war to end all wars and, when Carthage finally capitulated, Rome was too exhausted by decades of blood-shed to take the war to its conclusion and destroy Carthage once and for all. As a result, many in Carthage felt that the end was an armistice, not a defeat. Despite the war reparations, the confis-cation of their territory and the reduction of their army and navy, the Carthaginians were still able to hold their heads high, and look to a resurgent future. Your adoptive grandfather Scipio Africanus saw the danger, but he was hamstrung by the Senate. They were too concerned about his own power, about how presiding over the destruction of Carthage might have made him a figure too big to be contained by the constitution of Rome, a king in the making. After his death, when you were a small boy, Rome took her eye off Carthage, and the old enemy has grown powerful again. Under the guise of rebuilding their com-mercial harbour, the Carthaginians have also rebuilt their circular war harbour, surrounding it with shipsheds.'

'You are certain of this?'

'Of the rebuilding programme, yes. Of the details, only through second-hand accounts from merchants. To provide certainty, to truly persuade the Senate of the threat and to allow planning for an assault, we would need someone to infiltrate Carthage who could assess her strengths and the tactical chal-lenges posed to a Roman assault force, someone who himself might hope to be intimately involved in planning an attack.'

'Are you trying to tempt me, Polybius?'

'It is a mission for a time when Cato has drummed up enough support by his persistent call to finish Carthage, and when you yourself have attained the status in Rome needed for people to listen to you, to tip the balance in favour of war.'

Scipio stared pensively ahead, and then turned to Polybius. 'Tell me, when Metellus comes to Macedonia, will Julia come with him too?'

'She will remain in Rome.'

'Have you seen her?'

Polybius eyed him shrewdly. 'At a dinner in the house of Cato. She asked after you. She said that she had not heard from you since your father's triumph almost ten years ago.'

Scipio was silent for a moment, and then spoke quietly. 'How is she?'

'The *gens* Metelli is at the centre of the social scene in Rome. The matriarchs are known for controlling the younger women marrying into their *gens* with an iron fist, and Julia will be fully occupied with visitations and matchmaking. There are lavish feasts in her household almost daily.'

'She will be bored,' Scipio said. 'That is not the life for which she was intended.'

'She has a son,' Polybius said, cocking his eye at Scipio. 'Born the year after the triumph of your father. And a daughter, born last year.'

'Metellus will be pleased to have a son.'

'Metellus is rarely in Rome and has changed little in his ways, except that he now carouses his way through the wives and daughters of the aspiring *novi homines*, while not forgetting the *meretrices* of Ostia and the dockside taverns.'

'Julia has done her duty. She has borne his children.'

'And by turning from you, she has saved your reputation. Your wife Claudia Pulchridina is unblemished by scandal, keeping the matriarchs of her *gens* satisfied with her union with the *gens* Cornelii Scipiones and the *gens* Aemilii Paulli.'

'Except that the union has produced no offspring,' Scipio said darkly.

'Hardly surprising when you haven't shared a bedchamber with her in the entire ten years since your marriage, and haven't even seen her since your father's funeral games four years ago when you were obliged to appear alongside her with your *gens* at the public sacrifices in his honour.'

'You disapprove, Polybius?'

'Questions will be asked. You must obey the conventions of Rome if you are ever to reach a rank where you can break free of them.'

Scipio snorted. 'Well, this is one convention that I'll flaunt. Everyone in Rome knows that I loved Julia, but that I am a man of *fides* and will not behave as Metellus does. If Pulchridina had lived up to her name then I might at least have satisfied my loins with her, but that will never happen. I'd rather live as a celibate priest in the Phlegraean Fields halfway to Hades.'

Polybius gestured around them. 'To some, that's what your sojourn in Macedonia looks like. An escape from reality.'

Scipio urged his horse forward. 'Nothing will induce me back into my wife's bedchamber in Rome.'

Polybius was silent for a few minutes, steering his horse up a difficult section of track. Fabius knew that he would not have exhausted his attempts to persuade Scipio to leave, that like all good orators he would have one final argument to make his case. He prayed that could only be one thing. Polybius reached the top of the rock, and then pulled up his horse and turned. 'There is something else you should know,' he said. 'I haven't mentioned it yet so as not to raise false hopes, but here it is. There are early rumblings of war in Spain. There is discontent among the Arevaci of Numantia, who have rebuilt the fortifications around their *oppida*.'

Scipio reined his horse in, his eyes gleaming. 'Tell me more.'

'Unlike Carthage, where they are flouting Roman restrictions by rebuilding, the Roman procurator in Hispania Citerior has allowed the Celtiberians to do so, on the grounds that earthworks are an important symbol of strength and that allowing them to rebuild might boost the martial pride that took a battering when a Roman army defeated them during the first Celtiberian War, when you were a boy. The hope is that the grateful Celtiberians will be persuaded to become our allies rather than hire themselves out to our enemies as in the past. But another view is that the procurator will claim that they fortified too extensively, beyond their allowance, an excuse for war by those in Rome aspiring to the consulship who see the prospect of an easy triumph.'

'There is nothing easy about fighting the Celtiberians,' Scipio said. 'My father said that they were among the most formidable warriors in Hannibal's army.'

'Which brings us back to Carthage,' Polybius said. 'With the city newly rearmed and defiant, she will be seeking mercenaries to bolster her army. A war against the Celtiberians could be a war against those who would confront us on the walls of Carthage. It could be a first step to reclaiming the legacy of Scipio Africanus.'

Fabius watched Scipio squint ahead into the mist, then straighten in his saddle and take a deep breath. There was fire in his eyes. *Polybius had won.* Scipio turned to him. 'Before I tell you my decision, I will finish this hunt. There may be no boar to be found, but I will not be satisfied until I reach the edge of the forest. The weather is closing in. Let's move.'

9

After a final difficult climb the horses broke through the treeline and they were on open ground. Ahead of them the slope lay covered with huge fragments of rock, shattered and jagged, like the weapons of giants from some prodigious battle at the dawn of time. Beyond that, Fabius could see the first patches of snow, and then a bank of cloud far above that obscured the snow-capped peaks he had seen on clear days from the forest clearings below. It was a forbidding place, and he could see why the ancients had thought it the abode of the gods. He remembered the last time he and Scipio had climbed this high, almost ten years ago on the eve of the Battle of Pydna, when they had raced up the slopes of Olympus and stood at the summit like gods themselves, surveying a world that seemed theirs for the taking. Far below them the battleground had appeared laid out like the strategy games that Scipio and the others had played in the academy only months before, as if real war could indeed seem little different from a game, far above the smell of blood and the anguish of the wounded they were to experience when they came down again. But that had been a long time ago, and things now were different. Scipio was no longer a young blood yearning for his first command, but had made himself an outcast, dismissive of the career path laid out for him in Rome and tormented by his love for Julia. And there would be no thought of climbing a mountain peak today. If they were to stand any chance of catching a boar, they were going to have to remain on the edge of the forest, skirting the undergrowth where the great beast was said to lurk, keeping on guard all the time for its frenzied attack.

Scipio saw something on the ground, slid off his horse and

drew his cloak around him. A flurry of snow swept over them like a cold exhalation from the mountains, and Fabius shivered. Soon the temperature would drop below freezing and this place would be under many feet of snow, impassable until spring. Scipio knelt down and pointed to an upturned rock and a patch of a fresh disturbance in the soil, and then looked up at Polybius. 'Boar?'

Polybius leaned forward in his saddle, staring. 'It's just where I'd expect a boar to dig for roots, along the treeline. We need to see if there's a scent trail. Fabius, where's your dog?'

Fabius started, and looked around. He had forgotten about Rufius in the last awkward stretch up the path. He stood up in his stirrups, peering into the mist that was now rolling down and enveloping the fringes of the forest, reducing the visibility to less than fifty feet. He put his fingers to his mouth to whistle, but then thought better of it. Some instinct told him not to give their position away, or reveal that they knew the dog was missing. The feeling of unease he had experienced earlier returned, stronger than before. 'Rufius never goes off by himself,' he said. 'That's why I never bother keeping an eye out for him.'

'Wolves?' Polybius said.

Fabius shook his head, frowning. 'They've been shadowing us in the forest, but if they'd taken Rufius there would have been a fight and we'd have heard it. You can hear Rufius' bark for miles.'

Scipio stared at him, and then at Polybius. 'Could somebody have been following us?'

Fabius felt the blood course through him, and he no longer felt cold. His senses were sharpened, and he suddenly seemed to hear noises more clearly in the forest, branches wavering in the wind, crackles in the undergrowth. He was Scipio's bodyguard again, no longer just his hunting companion. He slipped off his horse, gave the reins to Scipio and pointed up the slope. 'Take the horses into the mist and conceal yourselves among those rocks. When it's safe to come out, I'll blow three times on my horn.'

Polybius dismounted and came alongside. 'What will you do?' he said.

'If there is someone following us, he may have been doing so for some time and will know that Rufius answers to me, that he comes back as soon as I whistle. If he has taken Rufius he may be trying to induce me to go back along the trail to look for him. If he takes me down, then you two are easier picking. I'm going to whistle, but I'm not going back along the trail.'

Polybius offered him the boar spear. 'You'll need a weapon.'

Fabius opened his cloak, revealing the handle of the Celtic dagger his father had given him. 'I have all that I need. But if he's stalking us he may well have a bow, and we're within arrow range of the treeline. You need to get to those rocks. *Now.*'

He put his fingers to his mouth and blew a long, piercing whistle, repeating it three times. He waited in silence for a few minutes, but Rufius still did not appear. Then he slapped the hindquarters of his horse and watched Scipio and Polybius lead the three animals up into the mist. He took off his cloak, dropped it and then crouched down and ran into the treeline to the left of the trail, ducking forward as he pushed his way through the thicket of spruce and fir that skirted the forest. The dense foliage gave way to more widely spaced pine trees, and he made his way more easily towards a marshy plateau they had passed on the way up, a residue of the mountain torrent where it had over-flowed during the spring melt. He worked his way round the edge of the marsh, taking care to keep himself concealed from the trail some five hundred feet to his right.

Midway along the edge of the marsh a small stream cut through and drained the boggy water down the slope, bubbling through the undergrowth below him. It was only about three feet wide, but he knew that the embankments on either side would be less solid than they seemed, saturated with water from the marsh. He spotted a rock in the centre of the stream, leapt over and stood on it, feeling it sink slightly with his weight, and then flung himself towards the far bank, hoping that the sound of the stream would drown out the noise. As he hit the bank it gave way in a cascade of mud and rock, and he scrabbled frantically at the tree roots that had become exposed, grabbing one and hauling himself up onto the bank. He silently cursed the noise. Anyone on the trail would have heard it. He would have to take his chances with an enemy who might now be expecting him to come from this direction, and pick him off with ease if he had a bow.

But suddenly there was another noise, an immense crashing through the undergrowth, a grunting and panting like he had never heard before. A gigantic beast bounded past him, snorting and slavering, its tusks thrust forward and its eyes red like fire. It was gone before he could properly register it, a blur of black, hurtling across the marsh in a spray of mud and crashing into the undergrowth on the opposite side of the trail, intent on some unknown quest. Fabius lay back, trying to control his breathing, and shut his eyes for a moment. *The Macedonian royal boar.* Scipio would be none too pleased that he had seen one and they had not been able to give chase. But he thanked the gods that they had never had the chance. Their spears would have splintered off its sides like twigs, and they would have been gored like prisoners in the circus. He opened his eyes and held his breath, listening hard. The sound of the boar had been swallowed up by the forest. He had been hoping to hear barking. If Rufius had been alive, then the boar would have set him off and his bark would have been audible for miles. But there was nothing, just the discordant cackle and bubbling of the stream and an eerie whistling in the treetops from the wind that was picking up across the mountain slopes.

His heart sank. Rufius had been his link out here to Eudoxia, and he could hardly bear to think of him being gone. He felt an anger stir up inside him, a bloodlust he had not felt since he had stood in the line at Pydna and watched the Macedonians spear his wounded comrades to death. *Whoever had done this would pay.*

He thought hard. The sound of the boar would have covered up the noise of his fall. He might still have a chance. He knelt up, listening for anything unusual, and then resumed his trek around the edge of the marsh, keeping below the level of the bank. The mud that now caked his body would camouflage him, help him meld with the underbrush. He would come out on the trail near the last place where he had seen Rufius trotting beside him as he had ridden up towards the treeline. He reached the dried-up stream bed, looked carefully in both directions, and then clambered over the trunks that criss-crossed the bed where they had been felled by the foresters who had cut timbers for Philip of Macedon's tomb a hundred and fifty years before. The trail followed the line of the stream on the other side, and after making his way over the last trunk, he crouched down beside the marks made by their horses' hooves less than an hour before. The snow had begun to fall more thickly, swirling down the cut from the mountain slope, reducing the visibility to below a hundred feet. If his gamble had worked, their assailant would be somewhere ahead of him looking upslope, his back to Fabius, expecting him to come down the trail from the treeline.

He took the dagger from his belt, its blade gleaming dully but the edge razor-sharp where he had honed it by the fireside the night before. He held it in his left hand, the blade pointing backwards, and walked slowly forward with the marsh on his right, half-expecting at each step to hear the whistle of an arrow. After about twenty feet he saw a large black crow hopping determinedly over the rocky ground of the trail, and then another. They were bustling around something, pecking at it, pulling away flesh. Fabius saw a splash of blood on the rocks, then the familiar black and white fur, the feathered flights of an arrow sticking out. He shut his eyes, trying to control himself. He could not afford to stop now, or to disturb the crows. He crept past, gripping the dagger as hard as he could, his eyes focused ahead, hardly breathing.

And then the snow parted and he saw it. About twenty feet ahead a man was lying on his front behind a rock, facing up the slope, a bow of Scythian shape held in front of him with an arrow strung, ready to pull back. He was wearing a sheepskin coat, but the hood was down and his long black hair lay in braids on his back. Fabius recognized him from the foresters' camp three days before, a burly mountain man who claimed to be from Pamphylia in Asia Minor, whom Fabius had taken to be a simpleton. The man had offered to guide them towards the best boar-hunting grounds but one of the foresters had taken Fabius aside and warned him to stay well clear; the man had only arrived a few days before and had no knowledge of the forest, but had known plenty about Scipio and had been asking about his hunting success even before he and Fabius had arrived in the camp. Fabius had put it from his mind, but now he remembered how discomfited the foresters had been, as if they were afraid of him. The man had even played with Rufius and thrown him a stick, feeding him choice morsels of meat until Fabius had stopped him. Now he knew how the man had coaxed Rufius to within killing range. He had been planning this for days. Fabius felt his body surge with rage, a barely controllable desire to kill.

He crept closer. A crow behind him squawked, and the man shifted. Fabius froze, holding his breath. Then the man pulled up his hood and resumed his position. Fabius leaned forward, head down, just as Rufius would have done, his whole being focused on his prey. Then he sprinted forward, leaping with his dagger poised just as the man realized something was wrong, landing heavily on the man's back and smashing his face into the rock. The man howled in pain, blood gushing from his mouth. Fabius ripped back the hood and grabbed his braids, pulling his head back as far as it would go and holding the dagger against the man's throat. He brought his face near the man's ear, close enough to smell the sweat and the oil in his hair. 'We meet again, Pamphylian,' he snarled in Greek, yanking the man's hair back and seeing the shock in his eyes. 'If you want this to be quick, you will tell me who sent you.'

The man coughed and spat out teeth, his nose streaming blood, then curled his lips and wrenched his head against Fabius' hold, drawing blood as the dagger sliced into the skin of his neck. He struggled again and then went still as Fabius pulled his head back close to the breaking point. 'Go to Hades,' he muttered, his mouth clenched in pain.

Fabius whipped the dagger out from beneath the man's neck and slammed his face into the mud below the rock. He brought the dagger down into the man's outstretched hand, driving it hard and twisting it round so that the bones and sinews cracked and snapped. He felt the man convulse with pain and heave upwards as he tried to breathe in the mud. He pulled out the dagger and thrust it back under the man's neck, pulling his face out of the mud and holding it back again. The man coughed and retched, spewing out blood and mud and saliva, his eyes caked over and his nose broken and contorted.

Fabius came close to his ear again. 'Tell me what I want to hear, and I may decide to spare you long enough for Scipio to question you. Then he can decide your fate. He may be generous.'

The man spat, and said something. Scipio leaned down, listening. 'Say it again,' he snarled. The man did so, and Scipio heard the name. *So that was it.* He kept the knife at the man's neck, and then looked at the mangled hand, noticing the distinctive red graze on the inside of the man's wrist, the mark of an archer using a bow without a leather wrist guard. He remembered how he had got that mark: the tufts of black and white fur on the trail behind, the crows. He let go of the man's head, lifted him up under his midriff until he was half-kneeling and brought the point of the dagger to just below his sternum. The man stiffened, terrified. 'What are you doing?' he mumbled, his face dripping blood. 'You said that you would spare me.'

'I only said maybe. And then I remembered my dog.'

In one swift move he thrust the dagger in up to the hilt, ripping through the man's heart and lungs, twisting for maximum effect. He pulled it out and then grasped his head and twisted it sideways, breaking his neck. He saw the man's eyes glaze over, and his last breath crystallize in the cold air. He got up, wiped the dagger on a grassy knoll and sheathed it, and then took out his horn and blew three short blasts. The snow was coming down harder now, already lying like a ghostly sheen on the man's body and beginning to obscure the hoofprints on the trail ahead. He started to run towards the edge of the forest where he had last seen Scipio and Polybius. They would need to get down off the mountainside before the trails became impassable. They had little time to lose.

Fifteen minutes later, Fabius reached Scipio and Polybius, who had left the rocks when they had heard his horn and brought the horses back to the edge of the forest. He had found a trickle of water from a spring on the way up to wash the mud off his face and hands, but he realized that he had been sweating profusely, and the halt at the spring and then the bitter wind from the mountain had chilled him, making him shiver. He picked up his cloak and wrapped it round himself, and then took the skin proffered by Polybius, gulping the wine down gratefully. He wiped his mouth on the back of his hand, passed back the skin and then took the reins of his horse. 'It was the Pamphylian from the foresters' camp,' he said to Scipio, and then he turned to Polybius. 'He had offered to guide us, but we were wary of him. He'd arrived only a few days before, asking questions about Scipio.'

Polybius grunted. 'Did you give him a chance to say who sent him?

'He killed my dog. But he had his chance. It was Andriscus.'

Polybius looked at Scipio grimly. 'Andriscus may have been

the one who gave this man his instructions, but Metellus would have been behind it.'

Scipio looked pensively up the mountain slope, narrowing his eyes against the snow and the wind. 'It seems that even here in the abode of the gods I cannot escape the vindictiveness of Rome.'

'The only way to better Metellus will be to rise through the *cursus honorum* as he has done, to become a senator and qualify as a legate. You will be safer from him in Rome, where you will show the strength of your personality and the power of your *gens*, and make it less easy for him to undermine you. In places like this, on the edge of the unknown, you are no longer safe. Your death out hunting would arouse no suspicions, only regret among those of your *gens* and supporters who have watched you seemingly throw away your destiny and escape as far as you could towards the very edge of the world.'

Scipio looked down at the imprint of the tracks they had seen earlier, now only shapes in the snow. 'Without Rufius, we have no hope of chasing a royal boar. Perhaps we have strayed too far into the hunting preserve of the gods, and that is one beast beyond the hope of men to see.'

Fabius began to speak, but then stopped, feigning a cough. Scipio's mind was still not made up, and Fabius did not want to be the one to persuade him to stay here any longer. He would tell him about his encounter with the boar at an opportune time later, perhaps when Scipio was at last wearing a legate's helmet and had turned his mind from hunting to war.

'A wise decision, Scipio.' Polybius mounted his horse and drew it round so that it faced down the slope, and he peered over the treetops towards the west. 'Do we have to return by the same route, or is there a way out that avoids going past the foresters' camp? Where there's one in the pay of Andriscus, there may be others. Best for them to believe that we have disappeared and the task is done, or else we will be hunted throughout Macedonia until we escape.'

Scipio nodded. 'About five *stades* back down the trail a narrow track leads off to the west, skirting the edge of the mountains until it reaches the kingdom of Epirus. It is arduous going, but we have our bedding rolls and we can hunt for food. Once we reach the shore of the Adriatic, we can find a ship to take us to Brundisium and safety.'

'Should we leave the body exposed? To conceal it might be to delay others on our trail.'

Scipio mounted his horse and shook his head. 'No. We will use two timbers cut and left here by the foresters, and we will crucify the corpse in the middle of the trail. Anyone coming this way expecting to find our bodies will know never to cross the path of Scipio Aemilianus.'

Polybius gestured at Fabius. 'Or his bodyguard.'

Scipio's horse reared up, smelling something that Fabius knew could have been the boar, and Scipio pulled hard on the reins until it pawed the ground, snorting and whinnying like a cavalry horse about to charge. He brought it under control again, and then looked at Fabius, nodding acknowledgement. 'You have done a deed of valour today, Fabius Petronius Secundus, and I will not forget it. When I lead a Roman army, you will be *primipilus* of the first legion.'

Fabius squinted at him and shook his head. 'Make me a centurion if I earn it, but I'd rather stay your bodyguard. Someone needs to watch your back while you two talk about strategy and the best way to use a boar spear to kill a man.'

Polybius grinned and put his hand on Fabius' shoulder. 'I am sorry about your dog. He will await you in Elysium. And you will remain Scipio's bodyguard, whatever rank he gives you, I will see to that. One day Rome will realize the value of men like you, and she will create a professional army that will conquer the world.' A bitingly cold wind swept down from the mountain slope, ruffling the manes of the horses, and he pushed away from Fabius' horse and pulled up his hood, turning to Scipio. 'Winter is upon us. We need to leave. To Rome?'

Scipio gave him a steely look, watching Fabius mount up, and then kicked his heels into the flanks of his horse. 'We will crucify the man who killed our dog first. Then to Rome.'

PART FOUR

INTERCATIA, SPAIN

151 BC

10

An eagle swooped low over the hills, its cry resounding down the valleys, the beat of its wings harsh and hard in the damp air. Fabius looked up from his work, breathing deeply, tasting the sweat that had been coursing down his face all morning. He eased off his helmet, wiped his stubble with the back of his hand and tilted his face to the sky, for once enjoying the cool wetness of this place. It had begun to drizzle again, the perennial rain that seemed to have shrouded these low hills for the entire three months since he and Scipio had disembarked from Rome, a permanent low cloud in the lee of the towering mountains to the north that divided Spain from Gaul. He had convinced himself that he actually liked it; to feel the sun again would only be to remind him of the last time he had seen Eudoxia and their little boy, born a year ago now, playing beside the sparkling waters of the Mediterranean. He looked up the slope at the walls of the *oppidum*, the enclosed citadel of the Celtiberians. There were women and children in there, too, but he had not yet seen them, only their husbands and fathers when they had sallied forth, wild-haired and screaming, brandishing the double-edged swords that struck fear into all but the most battle-hardened enemies.

The catapult a few yards behind him released its load with a jarring shudder, sending a fireball high over the wall into the *oppidum* beyond. It had been like that for a week now, day and night, one every hour, raining down death and destruction and slowly grinding the enemy into submission. Before that it had been solid stone shot, battering the wall until a breach had been made that had allowed the legionaries in, forcing the enemy back to their secondary line of defence in front of their huts and houses. Taking the wall made the work they were doing now seem redundant, digging a ditch below the outer slope of the *oppidum*. But Ennius knew how to keep his *fabri* happy, men recruited from the building trade in Rome who liked nothing better than to dig ditches and erect palisades, and to work siege machines that reminded them of the great counterpoise cranes beside the river Tiber that were used to swing blocks of marble out of ship's hulls. Fabius had been all too willing to pitch in and help, remembering the hours he had spent as a young recruit building practice fortifications on the Field of Mars, and how the old centurion had told him that building was just as much the job of the soldier as fighting. And, despite his discomfort in the ditch, it still sent a course of satisfaction through him to be wearing the armour of a legionary again, whatever the task at hand. It had been seventeen years since Pydna, and even after weeks of hard slog since they had arrived in Spain, he still felt the novelty and excitement of bearing arms for Rome that he had first experienced as a young recruit in Macedonia all those years ago.

There was a great grunt of satisfaction beside him, and a splash. The two elephants that had worked hard at the wall all morning lay slumped in the mud pool at the bottom of the ditch, cooling off and using their tails to flick away the flies that swarmed around them. Higher up the slope the third elephant was toiling away under the watchful gaze of its Numidian master, using its trunk to tear rocks away from the ragged edge of the breach and clear rubble to make an easier passage for the assaulting troops. After breaching the wall and forcing the defenders back within the *oppidum*, Scipio had consolidated his gains, quickly opening the main entrance to let more men inside; but once he had seen the secondary defensive line, a wooden palisade across the centre of the *oppidum* some five hundred yards ahead, he had decided not to go further, instead withdrawing his troops to the breach and leaving the open space ahead as a killing ground for whenever the enemy should choose to sally forth.

They had been waiting for almost a week now, a week during which the Celtiberians had endured yet more starvation and misery, pelted by the hail and rain that had turned the place into a soggy mire, and by the fireballs that Ennius' artillerymen had been lobbing over the walls into the houses, where even in the rain the burning pitch and oil had ignited the thatched roofs of the houses and forced the people out into the open, unprotected from the elements and the ballista balls. It seemed hardly credible that they had held out for so long, but Fabius had been hearing from the other legionaries of the Celtiberian endurance and how a siege like this could last until every person inside had died of starvation or by their own sword.

He looked across at Scipio, who was hunched over a tactical diorama that he and Ennius had created using mud and stones from the riverbank. Scipio was almost thirty-five years old now, his face craggier than it had been the last time they had gone to war together, his stubble and short-cropped hair flecked with grey. It was six years since they had left Macedonia, six years that Scipio had devoted with reluctance to the law courts and debating chambers of Rome – a burden they had managed to ease by spending months every year hunting in the foothills of the Apennines and on the high slopes of the Cisalpine mountians to the north, and in Rome working out daily with the gladiators to keep themselves fit and battle-ready. Unlike his contemporaries in Rome who had succumbed to self-indulgence, Scipio was as muscular and sinewy as the *fabri* who toiled around them now, as comfortable pitching in with ditch-digging as he was at joining the wrestling matches and swordplay that kept the legionaries in shape while they waited for the siege to wear down the Celt-iberians and force them into battle again.

Scipio's battered breastplate was shaped like the musculature of a human torso, a legacy of the Aemilii Paulli that had once been a splendid example of Etruscan metalwork but was now pocked and dented by war. It had been worn by Scipio's father as a young tribune in the war against Hannibal and by his grandfather in the war before that, the first great clash with Carthage over a hundred years ago. War with Carthage was never far from their thoughts, even out here. They were only fighting now because the Celtiberians had sided with Hannibal in his trek through Spain towards Rome more than sixty years before, and since then had proved an obstacle to Roman attempts to reach the gold-mining districts further to the north-west. War had flared up three years earlier and been put down by the Romans only after an arduous campaign in these desolate foothills, sapping the energy of attacker and defender alike. But then with peace in the offing Lucullus had been elected consul and had decided to raise a new legion and go out to finish the job in Spain in his own terms, reneging on the promises that had been made to the Celtiberians by his predecessors. Everyone knew that the campaign was a way to an easy triumph, the first opportunity in almost two decades for a consul to lead a victory parade through Rome, and that the Celtiberians had been treated with a contempt that angered those who had fought against them and learned to respect their sense of honour as warriors.

Scipio had been privately scornful of Lucullus, a boorish *novus homo* with little military background, and had thought the renewed war in Spain a distraction from the imminent threat of Carthage. But Scipio had just been made a senator and had seen his future trapped in Rome, with no other chance of attaining the military reputation he would need to be appointed to command a legion or an army when the time came for an assault on Carthage. For once Polybius had been absent, away in Greece advising the Achaean League on its military organization, and Scipio had been forced to mull over the question on his own, weighing his own ambition and sense of destiny against his conscience over joining a dishonourable war. Then, a few days before Lucullus and his legion were due to depart from Rome, word had reached him that a group of older senators who opposed Cato and were suspicious of anyone with the name Scipio were engineering an appointment for him as aedile in Macedonia, a post that would have been a welcome break from Rome except for the fact that the new provincial governor was his arch-rival Metellus. He had discussed it with Fabius, and the die was set. They had remembered what had happened in the forest of Macedonia six years before, and had no wish to end their days with a knife-thrust in some back alley of Pella.

Scipio had gone to Lucullus as he was forming up the legion on the Field of Mars and volunteered. He had accepted appointment as a military tribune, not among the young men who led the maniples and cohorts, but as an officer on Lucullus' staff, to act as an emissary when the time came to discuss terms again with the Celtiberians. Lucullus was trading on Scipio's reputation for *fides*, for keeping his word, a role that Fabius knew would batter Scipio's conscience given Lucullus' duplicity towards the Celtiberians. Scipio and Fabius were only here at Intercatia while they waited for the rains to abate and the road to the coast to become passable again, having marched into the camp ten days before with a reduced century from the *oppidum* of Cauca where Lucullus was encamped with his legion. Ennius was already here, commander of the small besieging force, and had deferred to Scipio because he knew how much Scipio yearned to see action, and honouring his seniority in the academy years before. Ennius' main force was a cohort of *fabri* who were meant to complete the fortifications before the arrival of Lucullus' legion, at which point Lucullus expected the *oppidum* to capitulate and another victory to be added to his basket without any need to risk his own skin leading his men into battle.

Fabius watched Scipio stand upright and peer at the walls. He was not wearing the silver *phalera* disc that his father had awarded him for valour at Pydna. Scipio had told Fabius that Pydna had been fought when most of the legionaries here were boys, and would have been an old war story told by their fathers. They all knew that he was the son of the legendary Aemilius Paullus and adoptive grandson of Scipio Africanus; they all knew that princes often wore decorations bestowed on them by kings, even when they had never seen action. He would not rest on past laurels, but would earn their respect before their eyes. And he had done it a week before, storming the walls at the head of the legionaries, the first to stand atop the rubble and see the Celtiberian warriors fall back on their second defensive position, the wall across the centre of the *oppidum* that enclosed the huts and wooden halls of their settlement. The scars that gleamed fresh on Scipio's breast-plate from those few moments of ferocious fighting on the walls had far greater meaning to him than any decoration that Rome might bestow. And out here, where set-piece battles were never going to happen, where war meant tedious days and weeks of sieges punctuated by terrifying moments of violence when the Celtiberians sallied forth, individual combat was the key to a man's reputation. No general was ever going to lead a fully formed legion into battle in this part of Spain, where the terrain of hills and confined river valleys only suited small-unit action by maniples and cohorts led by centurions and tribunes, or where action only took place during sieges in places where the Celtiberians themselves were prepared to give fight, on sloping ground below the *oppida* or in confined spaces within the curtain walls that were more like arenas for gladiatorial duels than battle-grounds for armies.

Fabius knew there was another reason why Scipio was not wearing the *phalera*. He had not worn it since the night of his father's triumph in Rome when he had been jeered at by Metellus, when Julia had been by his side for the last time. It was the night when Scipio knew he had lost Julia, and when he had hardened his resolve not to let the derision of others and the conventions of Rome blur his focus on his destiny. Spain was to be his proving ground, and he would prove himself not as the son of Aemilius Paullus or the grandson of Scipio Africanus but as a soldier, engaging the enemy close-up as the legionaries did, when the fight was for survival and for your comrades and not for any other glory or honour.

Fabius leapt out of the ditch and walked over to Scipio and Ennius. He stared at the diorama, at the marks in the mud that Scipio had made with his stick, and pointed at a long furrow. 'If that's meant to be the river, it's not quite right,' he said. 'It curves around to the south, beyond the camp of the *fabri*.'

Scipio shook his head. 'This isn't Intercatia, but Numantia. If we're ever going to defeat the Celtiberians, we'll need to take Numantia.'

'It is their greatest stronghold,' Ennius said.

Scipio pursed his lips, staring thoughtfully. 'The biggest weakness of the Celtiberians is their clan structure, which means a lack of overall strategic control. They're shepherds, just as we at Rome were cattle-drovers at the time of Romulus, loyal to our families and clans on each of the seven hills, but sharing allegiance with them only when we were attacked by a confederation of the Latin tribes. It's a weakness of the Celtiberians but it's also what makes the war arduous for us, as we have to fight each tribe piecemeal and besiege the *oppida* one at a time with no assurance that the fall of one *oppidum* will make the siege of the next one any less difficult, as the inhabitants may be from different clans and normally hostile to one another.'

'It's as if we're fighting lots of small wars in succession,' Ennius muttered. 'You can finish each war by negotiating peace and keeping your word, giving the chieftain a sense of honourable defeat, even aloofness from the other tribes that remain at war. But if you break your word, it's a different story; the clans might respond by banding together and presenting a more unified opposition. That's what seems to have happened now with the arrival of Lucullus, and his reneging on the deal that pacified the Celtiberians last year.'

Scipio nodded. 'The dynamic of the war against the Celtiberians has changed. The Arevaci are the largest tribe, and their main *oppidum* is Numantia. Take Numantia, and the other *oppida* of that tribe might fall to you without a fight, and the war would be over.'

'Is that Lucullus' plan?' Fabius asked.

Scipio's face was impassive. 'He has only one legion, freshly raised and inexperienced. He intends to win enough sieges for a triumph, and then to leave. But by coming to Spain with no more than personal glory in mind he has set in train a war with Rome that will not be extinguished until Numantia is taken, perhaps years from now. That's what Ennius and I have been war-gaming.'

'What would you do?' Fabius asked.

Ennius pointed with his stick. 'This is the river Durius. I'd build towers on either side of the river, in two places five hundred feet apart. The towers on the near side of the river would be close enough for archers to rain down arrows inside the *oppidum*. I'd circumvallate the *oppidum* with a deep ditch and rampart, and double it outside the main entrances where a strong force sallying forth might overwhelm a single ditch system.'

Scipio grinned at him. 'Spoken like a true engineer. You'd build another set of walls around Rome if you had the chance.'

'That's not a joke. The city is getting too big for the Servian walls. They're over two hundred years old now. And the more wooden tenement houses that are crammed inside the walls, the more likely there is to be a devastating fire.'

'Polybius and one of his scientist friends from Alexandria did a mathematical calculation about city walls,' Scipio said. 'They established that unless you have a population even more densely crowded than the population of Rome, living in tenements that would have to be eight or ten storeys high, you simply wouldn't have enough manpower in a city to defend its outer limits.'

Ennius nodded. 'City walls are only really ever for show.'

'You need defence in depth, a smaller area of fortification to fall back on. That's what the Celtiberians did here at Intercatia a week ago.'

'Do you remember Polybius taking us to Athens and showing us the Acropolis? That's something the Greeks have got right, and we haven't.'

'Because the Roman spirit is offensive, not defensive. But the Celtiberians, like the Greeks, are generally inward looking; it's unusual for them to expand beyond their borders and to take over adjoining *oppida*. Rome, by contrast, has been outward looking for centuries now, devouring surrounding tribes and then the city-states of the Greeks and the Carthaginians, forever expanding.'

Ennius gave him a wry look. 'Yes, and see what happens when invaders do reach Rome: the Gauls two and a half centuries ago, and very nearly Hannibal in our grandfathers' time. The Capitoline Hill where people took refuge from the Gauls was easily overwhelmed, and remains unfortified. One day Rome will reach the limits of its expansion and will suffer from the same weakness revealed by Polybius' calculation, of not having enough manpower to defend the frontiers. Yet great efforts will be expended to fortify the frontiers at the expense of Rome itself, which will remain vulnerable and will fall.'

Scipio grunted. 'The Celtiberians regard their *oppida* as refuges, as do the Gauls,' he said. 'The lower courses of their walls are built of stone, the upper structure of wood with thatched roofs, vulnerable to fire. That is their greatest defensive weakness. They knew nothing of siege engines when their walls were designed.'

Ennius nodded. 'I would bring up batteries of ballistas and catapults, for solid shot and fireballs.'

Scipio pursed his lips. 'The river is still the weak point.'

Ennius stared for a moment, and then traced a line across the furrow between the two stones. 'What about this. You attach a thick cable between the towers, tensed so that it lies on the surface of the water. You twist the cable around sections of tree trunks, so that they form a boom. Then there is no way that boats could be dispatched from the *oppidum* to reach safety.'

Fabius looked at him. 'I have a suggestion.'

'Speak your mind.'

'Have you ever been to the chariot races in the Circus Maximus when they attach blades to the wheels?'

'A great spectacle, total carnage,' Ennius said. 'It's not just what the blades do to the chariots when they lock together, but to the charioteers who fall within them.'

'What's your point, Fabius?' Scipio said. 'Numantia's a long way from the Circus Maximus, and chariots would just bog down in the mud out here.'

'Not chariots, Scipio, but those floating logs. A week after we arrived in Spain I went with a reconnaissance patrol to Numantia, to size up the defences. Now that I know your model is meant to represent the *oppidum*, I recognize the lie of the river. At those points where you've put the towers it flows particularly fast, being narrower, especially when it's bloated with the rains that seem to fall all the time here. Instead of seeing that weather as an impediment, we could turn it to our advantage. Paddles affixed like the spokes of a wheel at either end of those logs would make them spin around with the current.'

'I've got you,' Ennius said enthusiastically. 'Attach blades jutting outwards along the length of the logs, and they would scythe away like the wheels of a chariot. Not only would boats be unable to get through, but neither would swimmers.'

Fabius took the stick from Scipio and traced two lines across the furrow. 'The river is nearly fordable at these points. Place your towers and the log booms there, and the blades would nearly brush the riverbed. Swimmers would be unable to dive beneath.'

Ennius nodded, staring at the mud. 'A brilliant suggestion, Fabius. That's one for Polybius' textbook. If the Intercatians continue to tax our patience and hold out longer, I will keep my *fabri* occupied by having them build an experimental boom on the river here to see how it works.'

Scipio slapped Fabius on the shoulder. 'We'll make a general of you yet.'

'Centurion will do, Scipio. One day, when I've earned it.'

Ennius peered at Scipio. 'So much for our siege works. How would you dispose your men?'

'One third for the assault force, one third in reserve. One third of the reserve to move up and man the enemy walls once the assault force has moved through the breaches made by artillery, including all available archers and slingers. The forward line of the reserve to include *fabri* ready to spring forward and provide scaling ladders and demolition teams if called for. The remaining third of the force to comprise ballista and catapult crews, the heavy cavalry to repel any sally from the enemy and a light cavalry force to hunt down any who would escape from the *oppidum* to seek aid.'

Ennius grinned at him. 'Now *that's* straight out of the textbook.'

'I've had plenty of time to prepare. When I haven't been hunting and training, I've been war-gaming. The law courts and the debating chamber only take up a few mornings every week. They've knocked down the old Gladiator School where we held the academy, but Fabius and I managed to salvage the diorama table where we studied battles. Whenever Polybius and any of the others are around we get together in a room I've had specially added to my house on the Palatine and recreate the great battles of the past, changing the variables to try to alter the outcome, just as we were taught to do. We must have done Zama fifty times, Cannae about the same. But my special fascination has always been sieges.'

'I wonder why,' Ennius said, eyeing Scipio. 'Let me guess. A large city on the southern Mediterranean shore, with enclosed harbours and a high acropolis housing a temple to Ba'al Hammon, and a place where they sacrifice children. Rome's greatest enemy, still unvanquished.'

'It's all I can think about. It's my destiny.'

'Well, Intercatia is not Carthage, and you have only five hundred men here, two thirds of them *fabri*.'

'*Fabri* are legionaries too.'

'Of course. The best.'

'Then they shall form the assault force, and the century I brought with me from Cauca will be held in reserve.'

'That's wise. I've learned in my three years in Spain that a general should always use the men he has deployed as his besieging force to carry out the final assault. To use fresh troops would be to provoke discontent among those who have spent weeks and months before the walls, and would be to throw away the knowledge they have gleaned of the ways of the enemy, of his weaknesses. Even legionaries who seem worn down will find renewed energy with the end in sight and fight more savagely than fresh troops.'

'Then those who were first on the walls with me last week will form the front line of the force I will use to enter the *oppidum*.'

'And there's something else that we didn't learn in the academy. A besieging commander must not let his own troops or the enemy think that he's backed off because of cowardice, or lack of aggression. Your plan for the siege of Numantia is sound because it shows resolve and effort, that you are in for the long haul and intend to see it through to the end. A weaker commander who intends only to put on a show of force might leave the river undefended, relying on its flow as a natural boundary, or place lines of picquets where you would dig ditches and build a *vallum*. You might convince some in Rome that you had tried your utmost against an unassailable enemy, but your soldiers would think less of you for it and so would the enemy. They might think that you don't have the guts for an assault, or that you think your soldiers don't. If your soldiers believe that you have no faith in them, you will never lead them to victory.'

Scipio cracked a smile. 'But what you really like about my plan is that it involves a great deal of ingenious engineering work for you and your *fabri*.'

'Even that has another advantage. It keeps the men occupied. It's what they've been trained to do, not sitting around all day waiting for an enemy. They like nothing more than to see fortifications spring up around them, and it cows the enemy.'

Fabius peered at the breach in the walls a hundred yards up the slope from them, watching the sentries in the rubble who were guarding for any signs of enemy activity. He remembered the old centurion in Rome growl at the boys, taming their enthusiasm for joining battle at the earliest opportunity. *Do not fight desperate men*, he had said. *Let them wear themselves out by starvation and thirst. Only take a besieged city once you are certain of victory.*

Scipio looked at Ennius. 'Do you remember once when we were taken to see the lions, and what the head of the Gladiator School told us about preparing wild animals for the games?'

Ennius nodded. 'He said that an experienced gladiator should refuse to do battle with beasts until he knows they have been reduced by hunger, that invincible enemy.'

'He said that hunger enrages the beast, but also weakens it,' Scipio said. 'A lion who is hungry puts on a greater spectacle, but is easier to kill. He said you must choose the best time for the spectacle, when the beast is enraged by hunger but still strong enough to put up a fight, yet with its guard down and hunger leaving it vulnerable to your death blow.'

'But war is not a gladiatorial contest,' Fabius said.

'Don't be too sure of it,' Ennius replied. 'You have yet to campaign against this enemy for as long as I have. You cannot choose between starving a city out and storming it, one or the other. You must satisfy your own men, who will expect a bloody finale, and also the honour of an enemy, who will only allow themselves to be vanquished once they have been defeated in battle. Only then will they submit.'

'We will let hunger do its worst, and then offer terms,' Scipio said.

'The Intercatians will only submit when they can no longer fight. They will eat boiled hides, and their own clothing. Their wives and children are watching them, and will expect them to fight to the death in front of their own eyes. Those who survive will ask for death rather than submit to slavery.'

'Then they would have their wish,' Scipio said.

Ennius pointed to the diorama. 'So, to the final phase at Numantia. What would you do after it had capitulated?'

'I would not make the mistake that was made at Carthage sixty years ago. I would raze Numantia to the ground. I would divide their territory equally among the surrounding *oppida*, to make friends for us of those who had once been enemies. For the same reason I would take the sons of the surviving warriors to Rome, not to humiliate them but to show them in my triumphal processions as the noble and worthy adversaries that they are. I would educate them as Roman officers like Gulussa and Hippolyta and put them in charge of an auxiliary Celtiberian force to fight alongside Rome as we advance north over the mountains into Gaulish territory, which is where I would go after vanquishing them. The legacy of the siege of Numantia would not be the empty triumph of a foe so beaten down that they could never rise again, but the celebration of a foe turned to fight for Rome.'

Ennius grinned at him. 'You sound fresh out of the academy. Polybius would be proud of you. But I have served three long years against the Celtiberians, and a long campaign wears a commander down, Scipio. Noble intentions get lost in the mud and the squalor. You might be less magnanimous in defeat, less inclined to look to the future. When you see your own men suffering and dying for little gain, the desire to finish the war by whatever means possible closes down your vision of the enemy, and leaves you less merciful. And after a long siege you must accede to the wishes of your men too. A weak general might agree to allow them to plunder and massacre. A stronger general would bar them from the gates of the vanquished citadel, but be a man whom they would follow for no other reason than to draw strength from his virtue and his honour. Would you be such a general?'

Scipio picked up his leather wrist guard and buckled it on, squinting at the walls of the *oppidum*. 'Well, all I can tell you is that Licinius Lucullus is most definitely *not* such a general. What do the centurions say, Fabius?'

Fabius helped Scipio to tie the leather thongs around the wrist guard. 'Those who have served out here as Ennius has say that peace with the Celtiberians was hard won, and that Lucullus has only reignited the conflict in the hope of an easy victory to make it seem as if the war was won during his consulship. They say he has stoked his new legion with promises of plunder that the veterans know is not to be had among the Celtiberians, and can only lead to destruction and carnage by ill-trained legionaries seeking retribution after they find nothing to loot. The veterans respect the Celtiberians as warriors, and would rather they were our allies and comrades-in-arms. They expect much of you, Scipio. Those few who were at Pydna know of your courage in battle, but it is your name that gives them hope. A son of Aemilius Paullus and a grandson of the great Scipio Africanus can only lead them to greater glory. They look not to further campaigning in Spain, but to Africa.'

Scipio lifted the other arm, and Fabius picked up the second leather guard. 'I have to prove myself here first. Pydna was seventeen years ago, and I am twice the age I was then. Few of the centurions here now can have been there.'

Ennius jerked his head towards the rough track leading up to the tent, where a man on horseback had clattered up and dismounted beside the guard post. 'Speaking of Lucullus, that looks like one of his gallopers. Let's hear what he has to say.'

11

The messenger who had dismounted from his horse hurried towards them, putting his right hand on his chest in salute. He was a man Fabius knew and trusted, Quintus Appius Probus, an experienced legionary of the old guard who had been made a messenger because he could ride and had been wounded in the leg. 'I have news from Cauca. The *oppidum* has fallen.'

Ennius looked at him sharply. 'Fallen? But my catapults weren't ready. Without them, they'd never have breached the walls.'

'They didn't have to. It was a negotiated capitulation.'

'*Negotiated?* Lucius Licinius Lucullus? That's one for the books.'

'It wasn't the general who did the talking. It was the senior tribune on his staff, Sextus Julius Caesar.'

'Ah,' Ennius replied. 'Julia's brother.' He turned to Scipio. 'He's a linguist, and can speak their language. One of their household slaves in Rome was an old Celtiberian chieftain, a warrior whom Hannibal brought over to his cause when he marched through here with his elephants on the way to Rome. Do you remember him, Scipio? He taught us how to use the Iberian double-edged sword.'

Scipio nodded, and then peered at the man. 'You look troubled, Quintus Appius. There's more to tell, isn't there? You can speak freely. You have my word.'

Quintus cleared his throat. 'Sextus guaranteed the safety of the people in return for them allowing a Roman garrison to occupy the *oppidum*. Lucullus himself led them in. But it was a maniple from the new legion, the men Lucullus himself had recruited from the fourth district in Rome, promising them plunder and then press-ganging those who refused to volunteer. I grew up on the edge of that quarter, and I know what they're like. They make the best legionaries if trained with an iron hand, the worst if not. The only action these men have ever seen is gang warfare in Rome after the chariot races; the only discipline the lashes from the military proctors when they were herded into the ships for Iberia.'

Scipio's jaw was set grimly. 'So what happened?'

Lucullus allowed them to plunder the *oppidum*. But we all know that the Celtiberians have little to offer. They're shepherds and cattle-herders, not traders. These new recruits have been spoiled by stories of loot from Macedonia, and think every foreign city is heaped high with gold and silver. But when they found nothing in Cauca, Lucullus gave them second best. He is a good enough general to know that men sent to war who have not yet killed will want their bloodlust satiated, and then when they have done so it will occupy their thoughts for days to come, until they want more.'

Scipio stepped back, shutting his eyes for a moment and pinching the top of his nose. 'Don't tell me.'

'All of the male inhabitants. They rounded them up and hacked them to death, and then set fire to the place.'

'Jupiter above,' Ennius muttered.

Scipio took a deep breath, and gritted his teeth. 'How long ago?'

'Six hours. I came as fast as I could. I am to warn you that Lucullus is on his way here, and his men will expect more of the same. They should arrive by nightfall.'

'The entire legion?'

Quintus nodded. 'Including the maniple that went into the *oppidum*. That place has no need of a garrison any more.'

Ennius grunted. 'At least they'll bring the ballistas with them. Then I can begin bombarding Intercatia properly. If they don't capitulate soon, it's the only way we're going to force their surrender. It'll only be a matter of time before they hear what has happened at Cauca. They use runners to pass news between the *oppida*, and sometimes we don't catch them.'

Quintus turned to Scipio. 'There might still be a chance for you to negotiate a surrender before Lucullus arrives. The Celtiberian prisoner who interprets for us at headquarters told me that there are only two Romans they know to be with the army in Spain that they trust, Sextus Julius Caesar and Scipio Aemilianus. Sextus negotiated the peace with them last year before Lucullus arrived to start his own war, but now of course they will have lost all faith in Sextus' ability to make his general keep the Roman side of the bargain. With you, though, it might be different. You were not part of the previous campaign, so they don't know your measure. They only know you as one who shares the name of Scipio Africanus, the great general who defeated Hannibal and was magnanimous to the Celtiberian warriors in Hannibal's vanquished army, keeping only a few as slaves in Rome and executing only the top chieftains. You, they might still listen to, and trust.'

'Only if I show them that I can back my words with force,' Scipio murmured, squinting up through the drizzle at the walls. 'I need to assault the *oppidum*, and bring them to their knees. Only when they see that the legionaries are under my control will they believe my word.'

Ennius looked at him. 'Be careful about taking matters into your own hands, Scipio Aemilianus. Remember that Lucullus is your general, and your patron. Think of where you'd be without him.'

'I know too well,' Scipio said. 'I'd be back in Macedonia, a provincial aedile under the thumb of Metellus, setting up a law court in some town so obscure it would hardly be worth Metellus' while to try to make me disappear for good, with my continuing survival as a dead-end official giving him something to gloat over. I have Lucullus' boorishness to thank for that, the quality that allowed him to ride roughshod over the Senate when I volunteered for Spain and to have my appointment to Macedonia postponed. But I also know how it works in Rome. Lucullus is consul, but that's only for a year. He's a *novus homo*, a new man from an unknown family. He's already been placed under house arrest by the tribunes for his heavy-handedness in recruiting for his legion in Rome, and now he's gone against the express instructions of the Senate by reigniting the war when he was only supposed to come out here to establish a garrison. I have to be thankful to Lucullus and his war for giving me my first field appointment since Pydna. But a Lucullus is no patron for a Scipio. I'd never rise above military tribune, and a year from now I'd be looking back on a military career that would be the envy of nobody, of promise unfulfilled.'

'So what will you do?' Ennius said.

Scipio paused. 'I always remember the words of my father: The only true path to glory is through your own deeds on the battlefield, as a warrior and as a leader of men, and it is only those deeds that will secure your reputation. I will earn the esteem of my men, and the trust of my enemies. If there is to be a future for Scipio Aemilianus it will be won through his reputation and his *fides*, his word of honour.'

Ennius eyed him, and then jerked his head towards the walls. 'Will you take an assault force through the breach?'

'We have five hours until sundown, and then the arrival of the legion. The Celtiberians are always on the alert, but will not be expecting an attack this late in the day. How soon can you be ready?'

Ennius peered intently at him. 'We have five hundred men waiting on your every word. They are itching to go. We can launch an assault within the hour.'

Scipio nodded, and then looked at Quintus. His face was set, and he had fire in his eyes. 'Find a *pilum*, and sharpen your blade. We are going to war.'

Quintus saluted and left. Fabius turned to Scipio. 'You should know that there is discontent among the centurions.'

Scipio peered at him. 'Speak freely.'

Fabius paused. 'It is about Lucullus being a *novus homo*. That's another reason why he needs to offer his men plunder and blood. They know that he has come from nowhere, that he is one of them, that two generations ago his family were butchers in the Cattle Forum. The legionaries expect one of their own to rise to be *primipilus*, but not to be army commander. He is a rabble-rouser, like one of the tribunes of the people in Rome, pandering to these men as if they are still the undisciplined street thugs they were when he rounded them up, and not legionaries. The legionaries expect their officers to be patricians with an honourable lineage of military service in their families, men who will lead from the front. Lucullus is neither of those things. You may feel that you still have to prove yourself worthy of your lineage, Scipio, but the battle-hardened centurions would follow you over Lucullus any day.'

Ennius spoke quietly. 'Keep these thoughts to yourself, Fabius. Scipio is only a tribune and we only have a maniple of five hundred men, most of them *fabri*. It is here before the walls of Intercatia that he must earn his reputation, not as a usurper responding to the discontent of a few centurions. When he is a legate, perhaps, but not now. Rome would destroy him for breaking the rules.'

'I do not fault Lucullus for ordering the draft,' Scipio said pensively. 'He was punished because he conducted it as it should be conducted, without favouritism, and refused to exempt those who had been promised it by the tribunes. He may be boorish and a poor general, but he is not corrupt. The tribunes of the people came down harshly on Lucullus because he was a *novus homo*, one of their own, a man of plebeian origins who had forsaken his roots and aspired to become a patrician. I do not fault him for that either. But I do fault him for inducing men to volunteer by offering them booty, and for bringing them here without basic training. Because there has been no other war since Pydna, most of the existing veterans were already with the army in Spain and this new legion is composed almost entirely of men unversed in war, without discipline or skills or the cynicism of the veteran who takes promises of booty with a pinch of salt.' Scipio put his hand on Fabius' shoulder. 'Our time for bigger things will come, Fabius. Until then I must show my loyalty to my general. And for now, we have an *oppidum* to take.'

Fifteen minutes later, they made their way up a rough path where the larger fragments of fallen stone from the breach had been pushed aside by the elephants. At the top the two sentries beside the wall moved aside, and they peered through the opening. Immediately in front of them was a large area of open ground, denuded of upstanding vegetation and pockmarked with muddy pools, occupying perhaps a third of the area within the outer walls of the *oppidum*. Beyond that was an inner curtain wall, built of rough stone like the wall they were standing on and surmounted by a wooden palisade that still survived in places to its original height, with one partly burned watchtower remaining intact above the entranceway. Through smouldering gaps in the palisade made by Ennius' fireballs, they could see the crude houses of the Celtiberians inside, thatched and circular like the ancient hut of Romulus on the Palatine Hill in Rome. Fabius turned to the optio in charge of the sentry detachment, a grizzled veteran with only one ear, whom he thought he recognized from a draft of young recruits years before at Pydna. 'How many do you reckon are still inside?'

The optio peered at the palisade. 'Maybe two hundred warriors and the same number of civilians, most of them women and children. But the number is falling by the hour. Take a look at that little procession to the left.'

Fabius followed his gaze to a small opening in the inner curtain wall some fifty feet to the left of the entrance below the tower. Out on the open ground in front was a low flickering fire, and he realized that it must be the source of the faint odour of roasting flesh that wafted through the breach in the wall. He could make out several figures through the smoke, dragging something towards the fire, and others around it, seemingly rushing at random and running to and fro. 'Is it some kind of ritual?' Fabius said. 'A sacred ground?'

'It's sacred, all right,' the optio said grimly. 'One of the prisoners says that the open area in front is used for single combat between warriors, to settle scores and select the next chieftain. But what's going on out there is a different kind of ritual.'

Ennius was looking through a long tube with crystal lenses at each end that Fabius remembered seeing him make at the academy. He passed it to Scipio, who balanced it on a rock and aimed it at the smouldering fire and the people, closing one eye and squinting through the lens. 'Jupiter above,' he muttered. He looked down, and then passed the tube to Fabius, who leaned against the shattered edge of the opening and looked through it. The image was wavering, distorted, blurred at the edges with bursts of colour like a rainbow coming in and out of focus, but after a few moments he realized that the centre of the lens was undistorted and he settled his eye on the view, magnified four or five times from the image he could see with the naked eye.

What he saw was a vision of horror. The people going towards the fire were dragging human bodies behind them, mud-caked, emaciated forms barely distinguishable from the living, clothed only in rags and their hair long and knotted. Once there, they threw the bodies into the embers, and waited until they caught fire. But others were there too, circling the pyre like vultures. Fabius saw one of them dash in and pulled out a corpse, chopping frantically at it with an axe and then stumbling away with a severed arm in his grasp, sinking his teeth into the flesh. Those who had brought the corpse then ran after him as he staggered away and brought him down, hacking at him in the mud until he lay still. Surrounding the scene, Fabius could see others who had escaped with their prize, squatting in the mud like dogs and gnawing at hunks of dismembered flesh. Fabius lowered the tube and offered it to the optio, who shook his head. 'Been watching that all day,' he said. 'I don't want to see any more.'

Ennius turned to Scipio. 'We can talk all we like about starving a city into submission, drawing battle lines in the sand and pushing toy soldiers across model landscapes in the academy. But this is the reality. We may let hunger win the war for us, but there is no honour in watching a proud people reduced to this.'

Scipio raised himself on his knees, exposing his body for a moment through the breach. An arrow suddenly whistled in and clanged off his breastplate, cartwheeling away into the distance. They all ducked below the line of the wall, and Scipio looked down at the dent where the arrow would have plunged into his chest. He looked at Fabius, and then at Ennius. 'All right. I've seen enough. With your *fabri* and my century we will have three hundred men to storm through this breach. We will form up on that open ground, and challenge their warriors to come out and meet us.' He turned to the optio. 'What do you say, legionary? Are your men ready?'

'We await your command,' the man growled, half pulling his sword from his scabbard. 'Let's finish it.'

12

Half an hour later, the Roman assault force was drawn up inside the wall, some four hundred strong, arraigned in a line three deep that stretched along a frontage of some five hundred yards. Scipio and Fabius stood a few yards ahead of the line, the *primipilus* of the *fabri* beside them, while Ennius remained with a reserve of one hundred men on the wall where he could also look back down towards their camp and direct the fire of their solitary catapult.

Their plan to mount a pre-emptive assault had been overtaken by the Celtiberians, who had clearly been watching intently and had sallied forth from their palisade as soon as they saw the legionaries begin to form up. They were there now, perhaps three hundred of them, bellowing defiance, solitary piercing yells that joined and rose steadily to a roar, a straggling line about a thousand feet from the Romans in a field that dropped from both lines of soldiers down a slight slope towards a strip of flat ground in the centre, some five hundred feet from where Fabius was standing.

He felt the heft of his sword, weighing it in his hand. He and Scipio had first whetted their blades with Celtiberian blood a week before when they had charged through the breach and taken the wall, and now the battle-lust was coursing through him again, and he was yearning for more. *It was time.*

Scipio turned towards the *primipilus*, and then to him. He raised his sword, and his mouth opened in a snarl. For a few seconds all that Fabius could hear was the pounding of the blood in his ears, and then he was bounding forward, running as fast as he could towards the charging Celtiberians, his sword raised, yelling at the top of his voice.

He could see the centre of the field more clearly now: a strip of level ground about thirty feet across where the two slopes converged. There were pools of standing water left by the recent rains, and patches of mottled ground where the mud showed through. It was a natural feature, an area of boggy ground that would normally have been covered by grass, but something that could have been protected and maintained to give the illusion of continuous firm ground. In that instant Fabius realized that there was something wrong. *It was a trap.* The Celtiberians may have been reduced by hunger and exhaustion, but what had seemed a desperate, disorganized charge had in fact been a ploy, duping the Romans into thinking that they could be met halfway and easily destroyed. They were being drawn into a killing ground, just as he and Scipio had once goaded an enraged water buffalo into a dried-up watercourse that was liquid mud beneath, leaving the beast trapped and wallowing and easy prey to their spears. If they carried on unchecked, the legionaries would become enmired in the same way, thrown into disarray and distracted by the need to stay upright – moments in which they would take their eyes off the enemy and the Celtiberians would have the advantage.

Fabius knew that the Celtiberian chieftain would be watching them with eagle eyes; if Fabius tried to stop the legionaries now, showing that he had spotted the trap, the chieftain would also halt the momentum of his own charge. But Fabius could play them at their own game: he must lead them into thinking that the Romans were going headlong into the morass, ignorant of its dangers. He sprinted further ahead, running as fast as he could, holding his sword high. The Celtiberians were like a foaming floodtide surging down the slope, swords and limbs waving, muddy water spattering above them like spindrift flecking the crest of a raging surf. Fabius was less than a hundred feet away from the mud now, and he counted the seconds. *One. Two. Three.* He suddenly stopped and turned, staggering sideways to regain his balance, and bellowed as loud as he could: *'Halt! Hold the line!'*

The *primipilus* of the *fabri* saw and understood and repeated the command, and it was conveyed down the line by the centurions and optios on either side. In a few seconds the entire Roman force had come to a shuddering halt, on firm ground on the very edge of the mire.

The centurions bawled another order: '*Defensive positions.*' The leading men squatted down and drove the base of the *pila* into the ground, angling them forward towards the enemy and grasping them firmly with both hands. Between them the next line of men held their *pila* at the horizontal, tightening up to present a bristling wall of spears, their legs planted apart and flexed to withstand the coming onslaught. Behind them the third line stood with their *pila* poised to throw and their swords drawn, ready to cut down any who made it through.

Scipio had caught up with Fabius and they both stood ahead of the line, panting hard, every muscle in their bodies tense, swords held hard. Fabius' calculation had worked: it was too late for the Celtiberians to stop. Their chieftain could only stir his men up even further, to increase the momentum of the attack so that they might make it through the mire before it bogged them down.

The centurions bawled again: '*Steady! Hold your positions!*' The lines of *pila* seemed to quiver in unison, shaken by the thunderous approach of the enemy. Individual warriors could be made out more clearly now as they hurtled down the slope, the swifter ones running ahead screaming and waving their shields, then discarding them so that they could sprint even faster. Some were wearing old Corinthian helmets and Roman cuirasses taken in past battles, others nothing more than rough woollen tunics, but all of them held javelins or the curved double-edged Celtiberian sword. The shrieks and screams became a steady roar again, pummelling Fabius' ears, and as they neared the mud he could feel a chill on his face, as if the war god were sweeping in his chariot down across the mire and brushing them with the cold wind of death.

He could barely breathe. He gripped his sword as tight as he could, trying to keep his nerve. Then the first warrior flew into the mud, slipped forward and lunged wildly, running straight into one of the *pila* a few feet to Fabius' left, breaking it as the tip passed through his neck and falling in a spray of blood. Another followed, and then another, each of them speared and then hacked to death by the rear line of legionaries. A javelin narrowly missed Scipio but struck the upper thigh of the *primipilus*, severing the artery and causing blood to gush out in a pulsing fountain, soaking Scipio and Fabius. The *primipilus* fell with a grunt, his hand pressing on the wound, and his place was taken by the second centurion of the cohort, who turned and bellowed at the rear line of legionaries. *'Make ready with your pila.'* He watched for the main mass of Celtiberians to reach the mud, and then bellowed again: *'Let fly.'* The *pila* swished through the air over Fabius like arrows, some of them bouncing off armour, but others finding their mark, bringing down dozens of warriors in a tumbling pile that tripped up many who came behind. The whole mass seemed to slide forward across the mud and crumple against the Roman line, the warriors writhing and shrieking as the legionaries hacked to death any who had not been killed by the *pila* of the front line.

Fabius felt his heart race. The time had come to go forward. Scipio roared, and plunged into the morass. The front two lines of legionaries dropped their *pila* and followed, swords drawn. Then Fabius was in the mire himself, slogging ahead with mud up to his knees, hacking and stabbing. A Celtiberian with braided red hair flew at him just as he was withdrawing his sword from a body, and he slashed upwards with all his might, catching the man under the chin and slicing his entire jaw off through to his forehead, leaving a mass of blood and mucus and brain where his face had been. The man fell with a shriek and Fabius lurched forward, thrusting his sword into another man's head and then slashing the tip across an exposed neck, the jugulars exploding in a sheen of blood that sprayed over his face and into his eyes. He blinked hard, slashing his sword blindly, and as his vision cleared he saw that the legionaries had already moved forward, following Scipio as he ploughed through the slew of mud and blood towards the far slope.

Suddenly a horn blew, a deep, resonating sound, not a Roman trumpet, but from somewhere in the Celtiberian lines. The warrior Fabius had been stalking quickly backed off, and he saw others do the same to his right and left. The legionaries who had surged forward to engage the enemy were left reeling and panting, staring at the retreating Celtiberians, some of them red-faced and spitting and others pale with the shock of combat. It had lasted for only a few minutes, but dozens of bodies lay jumbled in the mud, most of them Celtiberian but the glint of Roman armour visible here and there among them. Fabius felt his left hand, noticing for the first time that it was sliced across with a sword cut, and then looked up again. The centurions were bawling down the line, ordering the men who had gone forward to return to firm ground, and those who had stayed in the line to tighten up and take up their *pila* again, in readiness for another onslaught.

But instead a single warrior came forward, an older man with flowing grey-flecked hair who had not yet taken part in the combat, his armour and weapons still gleaming and clean. He was wearing a muscled cuirass that looked Etruscan, and his helmet was like the Greek ones that Fabius had seen carved on the Parthenon in Athens. He remembered that many of the Celtiberians had served as mercenaries during times of peace at home, fighting for Carthage in the last war, and that battle scars and looted armour were all the pay they wanted. This man was not old enough to have served Carthage, but he could have been among the mercenaries on the Macedonian side at Pydna; his left eye socket was empty and he had a livid weal across his face that must have been caused by a savage blow decades ago, when he was a young man. Behind him an emaciated boy held the great curved cow horn that had signalled the retreat. Fabius realized that the man must be the chieftain. He had stopped at the edge of the mud, resplendent in his armour, his feet planted apart in defiance, looking at the Romans and then focusing his gaze on Scipio, who was standing dripping in the mud a stone's throw away and watching him intently

The man pointed at him. 'You are Scipio,' he bellowed hoarsely, speaking in heavily accented Latin. 'My grandfather fought a Scipio at Cannae, and now I will fight a Scipio at Intercatia.'

'Do you challenge me?' Scipio bellowed back.

'On my command my warriors will return and fight to the death, and many more Romans will die. Or the contest can be finished with a single combat.'

'What are your terms?'

'That my men should be allowed to leave their arms and go free, that the woman and children of Intercatia should be left unmolested with their remaining houses unburned, and that they should be fed. I have heard that the word of a Scipio is a word of honour. Is that so?'

Scipio squinted up at him. 'It is so.'

'Do you give me your word?'

'I give you my word.'

'Then let the contest begin.' He dropped his shield, shoved his sword into the ground and removed his helmet, taking a thong offered to him by the boy and tying his hair back. The boy undid his cuirass and took it from him. He was wearing nothing beneath it except his kilt, revealing a torso that had once been finely muscled but was now showing his age, the scars of many wars standing out as red weals against his pale skin. Scipio stripped off his own armour as the chieftain picked up his sword and limped towards the mud, dragging one leg behind him. Fabius could see why the man had not joined the melee earlier: he would have found it virtually impossible to stand upright. As his warriors closed up in a semi-circle behind him, Fabius sensed that they had done this before, watching duels for honour and women and power in this very place, contests that the chieftain in his younger years had undoubtedly walked away from many times victorious. This time it would be different. The contest with Scipio could only have one outcome, and they all knew it. The terms did not even allow for the chieftain's victory, and if it came to it he could not afford to deal Scipio a death blow; if he did so it could only result in the Roman soldiers going on a rampage and massacring his people, whose future therefore depended on Scipio surviving and keeping his word. The chieftain was sacrificing himself for his women and children, in a time-honoured fashion that would also leave his warriors satisfied that honour had been done and their own rituals observed.

Fabius turned and looked at Scipio, at his hardened torso and his sword held ready by his side, his face grim and emotionless. He could guess the thoughts that were running through his mind. As boys they had dreamed of war as glorious contest, as battles between armies and warriors where the best fights were the most evenly matched, not just for Rome and glory but tests of manhood where the victor could walk away uplifted by killing an opponent who could as easily have won the day. But the reality of war was rarely like that. It was uneven, and messy. There might be honour in Scipio's word, in his *fides*, but there would be no glory for him in this fight. Scipio was doing what he had to do to allow the enemy warriors to walk away with dignity, a decision that might make them more likely to be Rome's allies in future, and to save his legionaries from dying unnecessarily. But this would be little more than an execution, the chieftain's fate as certain as the deaths of the deserters they had watched being mauled by lions at the triumphal games after the Battle of Pydna. After years of yearning to return to war, Scipio was in at the ugly end, and Fabius knew he would be steeling himself to show utter resolve in what he had to do.

He knew that Scipio would not sham a fight, that he would respect the old warrior's pride by fighting him man to man with his full strength for however long it lasted. The chieftain limped into the mud and stood a few feet from Scipio, his legs apart and his sword held in front of him with both hands, the blade down. Scipio nodded, and the man suddenly swung his blade like a scythe in front of Scipio's chest, nicking the skin and making him fall back, staggering slightly. The man still had strength in his arms and a lifetime's skill with the Celtiberian sword, its slashing blade longer than the Roman *gladius* but less versatile at close quarters. His weakness lay in his poor mobility, and Scipio was going to have to get around him and under the arc of the blade, deflecting it and going for a thrust. Scipio edged forward, crouched down this time with his sword held at the ready, just raising it in time to parry another vicious sweep by the chieftain that nearly sent Scipio's *gladius* flying. He backed off again and crouched lower, suddenly springing to the side and catching the chieftain off-balance as he tried to twist his body round to confront him. Scipio darted in and thrust his sword hard into the man's good leg, pulling it out of the calf just in time to avoid another sweeping blow. The man shifted, nearly toppling over, the mud beneath him shiny with fresh blood from the wound, steaming on the cool ground.

The chieftain had shown his skill and courage in front of his warriors, but now they would expect no more. At the next swing Scipio parried the blade, deflecting it, and then leapt forward and this time thrust his own blade into the man's abdomen, running him through to the hilt and then holding him close, swaying together with him in the mud. The chieftain retched, throwing up yellow bile streaked with blood, and then Scipio pushed him back and heaved the sword up and down, slicing open a huge wound from the man's pelvis to his ribcage. He withdrew the sword and the chieftain fell back, staggering and twisting, and as he did so the wound gaped open and his intestines spilled out, blue and red and steaming, dripping with blood. He looked down with his one eye, his face sheet-white, his expression uncomprehending. His intestines had dropped in a loop to the ground and he tripped over them, sprawling forward and then raising himself on his knees, scooping them up with his hands in the mud and trying to put them back inside.

Fabius looked at Scipio. It was time to finish it. Scipio dropped his sword and fell on the chieftain's back, flattening him and holding him there, pushing his head into the liquid mud. The man coughed and spluttered and then suddenly heaved upwards in a last show of strength, tossing Scipio off his back and staggering to his feet, his arms held out and his head high, bellowing something towards the sky. He saw his sword in the mud and staggered towards it, trailing his insides behind him. Scipio leapt back and pushed him down again, this time not trying to drown him but holding his head tightly in an armlock. The man knew what he was trying to do and resisted, his neck and head held rigid against the pressure. Then he gave way, his energy spent. In that instant Scipio twisted the head sharply sideways, and the body suddenly went limp. Scipio pulled up the chieftain's head by his hair, knelt back and then severed it with a single swipe of his sword, holding it high for a moment so that all could see and then dropping it into the mud.

Fabius felt light-headed, as if he had forgotten to breathe. He relaxed, and then inhaled deeply. *It was over.*

Scipio got up on his knees, then to his feet, staggering backwards and almost falling again. He was covered from head to foot in blood. He reached down to a muddy pool beside the chieftain's body and splashed his face, and then caught a cloth tossed to him by one of the *fabri*. He wiped his eyes and then turned to face the Celtiberian warriors, who still stood in a semi-circle, silent and watching. For a few moments nothing happened, and Fabius let his hand drop to the hilt of his sword again. Then the warriors began to drop their weapons and turn back up the hill, where the entrance to the palisade was open and the women and children stood outside, also witness to the fight. Scipio remained where he was standing until the last of them had gone, and then he turned and made his way out of the mud, his feet squelching and slipping until he reached firm ground. The legionary who had given him the cloth gave him a wineskin, and he tipped it up and drank gratefully, and then shut his eyes as he poured the wine over his face and his neck, letting it drip to the ground. He wiped his face again, passed the skin back and looked at Fabius. His eyes were hard, burning with fervour. He scanned the legionaries, and raised his right arm. 'Men, gather round.' The legionaries came closer, forming a circle around him, several hundred exhausted and mud-spattered men. Within the space the second centurion was hunched over the body of the *primipilus*, laying his sword across his chest. Fabius stared at him, his mind blank. It had been less than fifteen minutes since the *primipilus* had taken the javelin thrust to his leg, yet it seemed almost too far back in time to remember.

Scipio raised his hand in salute. 'You have fought hard and with honour today, against a worthy enemy whom we will honour in defeat by allowing the surviving warriors to return unharmed to their families.' He turned towards the body on the ground, and the second centurion. 'To the *primipilus*, *ave atque vale*. To the new *primipilus*, you are a worthy successor. To all who fell here today, we will meet again in Elysium.' He turned to Fabius, and put a bloody hand on his shoulder, his eyes gleaming. 'And to the legionary Fabius Petronius Secundus, you have earned the insignia of a centurion. The promotion is for Ennius to give as commander of our force, but he was watching from the walls and will have seen you in action this day. By spotting the danger and stopping our advance when you did, you won the battle for us and saved many Roman lives.'

There was a ragged cheer of approval from the legionaries. Fabius turned to Scipio. 'You have earned the esteem of your men, Scipio Aemilianus. No legionary forgets a commander who fights an enemy chieftain in single combat.'

Scipio wiped his mouth with the back of his hand, and looked around the assembled legionaries. 'One day, one day soon, I may lead an army. Will you men be my personal guard? I can't promise you booty. But I can promise you glory. And for those of you who are *fabri*, I can promise you plenty of digging and building and siege works.'

The new *primipilus* stood at attention. 'We know your destiny, Scipio Aemilianus. We know where you will lead your army. And we will follow you anywhere, in this world or the next.'

Scipio nodded, and slapped him on the shoulder too. 'Good. And now I think there is a cartload of Falernian wine sitting down below, sent ahead of the legion to be ready for Lucullus' head-quarters staff. I think they might just discover that the cart was in an accident and the amphorae smashed, don't you think? But make sure you dilute it with plenty of water from the river. We need to remain clear-headed for funerary rites for our fallen comrades, and to build a pyre high enough to send them to their rightful place alongside the war god himself. Only then, when the fire is lit, can we let the wine flow freely and let ourselves go.'

13

Twenty minutes later, Scipio stood before Ennius, who had come down from his position on the walls and was addressing him. 'I am the only officer of tribunician rank who saw what you did today. I will recommend you for the *spolia opima*, for defeating an enemy leader in single combat. You must strip the armour of your opponent and affix it to an oak tree, and then take it to Rome and dedicate it at the Temple of Jupiter Feretrius. You will be only the fourth in Rome's history to receive this honour, as Romulus did for defeating Acro after the rape of the Sabine women. You will be the greatest living hero in Rome. Your military reputation will be assured.'

Scipio draped an arm around Ennius' shoulder, leaning against him and breathing heavily. He wiped the mud and spittle from his mouth with his other hand, and then pushed back, turning and looking at the body of the chieftain. 'Do you remember what Achilles did at Troy? He stripped the fallen Hector and dragged the body round the walls, taunting his enemy and distressing Hector's wife and children. And then, just days later, Achilles himself lay dying, felled by an arrow to his heel, the one place where he was mortal. It's an allegory, or so Polybius tells me. Achilles had let pride and exaltation overtake him and had forgotten to protect his vulnerable spot, just as Icarus flew too close to the sun and the wax in his wings melted.' He wiped his face again, and then straightened up, looking at the ring of Roman soldiers who had been watching the combat, and at the Celtiberian dead on the other side. 'I will receive the *corona muralis* for being the first on the walls of Intercatia in the assault on the *oppidum* last week. To receive the *spolia opima* on the same day as Lucullus' triumph in Rome would be to overshadow his glory, and earn me suspicion and envy that might play into the hands of Metellus and his supporters – those who would see me never command a legion. On this day there are many among the legionaries now who have fought their own battles worthy of the *spolia opima*. I care little for the esteem of Rome, but I care everything for the esteem of these legionaries. You and your cohort of *fabri* will form the core of the army that I will one day lead. When your men advance into battle they will always remember this day before the walls of Intercatia. That will be my reward.'

He walked back to the body of the chieftain, picked up the sword and laid it alongside. He went down on one knee in the mud and briefly bowed his head, and then stood up. A wild-haired woman had appeared with two small children at the edge of the mud, and was making her way towards the body. Scipio slogged back and stood beside Ennius again. 'Have the optio sound the withdrawal. We will give them time to honour and burn their dead. Order the commissariat to bring up two cartloads of grain, and leave it at the entrance of their palisade. These people know they are defeated. But if they are to trust my word, they must know that I am magnanimous in victory. I will keep my word to the chieftain.'

'Some of the surviving warriors will kill themselves. We have seen that before among the Celtiberians.'

'So be it. They have fought well and hard, and deserve to part this life with honour. It is better than being put to the sword, as Lucullus will doubtless wish to do to those who refuse to submit, even in captivity. But those are not the ones whom we would take to Rome. We want their sons, those who could be trained and nurtured to be our allies.' He looked across again at the woman and her boys. 'It is their children who must be allowed to live. They will soon hear of the massacre at Cauca, and they must not be allowed to think that Lucullus' legionaries will be let loose in their *oppidum* and that they will suffer the same fate.'

'Speaking of Lucullus, I have had a message that the legion is less than a mile away. By nightfall, they will be in the camp. What would you have me do?'

'Take your *fabri* and repair that breach in the wall. Station men there, and at the entrance to the *oppidum*. They are to keep the men from the legion out, and the Celtiberians in. Once you have seen the fire from the funeral pyres and know that the Celtiberians have completed their rites, march the remainder of your cohort inside to occupy the town. Nobody is to leave their post until the legion has left.'

'What do you know of Lucullus' plans?'

Scipio watched the legionaries make their way off the walls and back through the entrance to the camp, and saw the other Celtiberian women begin to search through the mud for the bodies of their menfolk. There was no sound, no cry of lamentation, only a whisper of wind over the battlements and the distant crackle of fire from the houses that were still burning in the *oppidum*. Over the battlefield the wisps of steam rising from the entrails and abdomen wounds of corpses had mingled with the dampness in the air to form a thin mist, floating a few feet above the ground, as if the souls of the dead were being drawn away in a ghostly miasma. Fabius watched Scipio stare at it, and then turn back to Ennius. 'Lucullus has rekindled a war that will simmer on far into the future, like those burning embers in the *oppidum*, and will only finish when Numantia itself falls. If your *fabri* had not achieved what they have done today, this campaign could have ground on like the other ones, for months, probably years. But now that we have given him Intercatia to add to Cauca, Lucullus will have what he came for. He has enough victories for a triumph.'

'And you?'

Scipio cracked a grin. 'A river to wash off the mud and the blood, and then some wine and food. But not at this place.

Lucullus sent me on a mission, and I don't want him to change his mind when he sees that we've finished the job here for him.'

'A mission? You have not yet told me.'

'To find more elephants for this campaign. He knows of my friendship with Gulussa and his father Masinissa. He thinks the name Scipio is magic in Africa, and that elephants will appear out of the sand dunes of Numidia as soon as I arrive. He wants fifty of them, elephants that will be useless here if he returns home now.'

'You can have them sent directly to Rome, for his triumph. He can pretend that our three elephants were fifty, and that he was at their head.'

'He can take them across the Alps like Hannibal for all I care. With Intercatia fallen and this campaign all but over, I will seek reappointment as a special envoy to Numidia. There are big things afoot in Africa. Polybius hinted at it six years ago in Macedonia, when it was only a rumour. But yesterday I had a message from Gulussa. The Carthaginians are rearming. Their new circular harbour is complete, and galleys have been constructed in the shipsheds. They have recruited mercenaries from Gaul, and sent them out to the very borders of Carthaginian territory. It is only a matter of time before they clash with Masinissa's forces. If Rome provides support and we play our cards right, it could be the beginning of the final showdown with Carthage that Cato has been clamouring for in Rome for two generations now.'

Ennius grasped Scipio's hand, the sinews of his forearms hard and strong. '*Ave atque vale*, Scipio Aemilianus Africanus. May Fortuna smile on you.'

'Perhaps I can earn that *agnomen* now. But it will need Mars Ultor the war god, not just Fortuna.'

'Remember what Polybius taught us. Gods do not win wars, just men.'

Scipio jerked his head towards the camp. 'Not just men. Roman legionaries.'

'When you summon us, we will join you.'

'Perhaps not this year, or even the next. But it will be soon. I can smell it, the smell of the desert sands of Africa blowing north, just as they did in my grandfather's day. There will be war again before you and I are much older, and it is that war that is our destiny.'

'Go now. I can hear the pounding of the approaching legion.'

Scipio released Ennius' hand, slapped him on the shoulder and turned to Fabius. 'A fast galley is waiting for us at Tarraco. If we ride now, we could be there by dawn and with Gulussa in four days. We have no time to lose.'

PART FIVE

AFRICA
148 BC

14

Fabius and Scipio stood on the deck of a small merchant galley off the coast of North Africa, its single square sail billowing above them. They had rowed hard all morning to get as far as they could offshore, taking their turn at the sweeps with the crew, the sail furled and the wind on the starboard beam; but then the captain had decided that they were far enough out into the bay to avoid being blown inshore before their objective had been reached, and had ordered the sail unfurled and the tiller heaved to starboard, causing the twin rudder oars to bring the bow to the south-west and the ship to plough across the waves towards land with the wind on her starboard quarter. Fabius had just finished helping the helmsman to push the tiller hard to the right and lash it to the gunwales, to counteract the tendency of the vessel to run before the wind. They had adjusted the ropes holding the sail to keep it at the best angle to fill with wind without buckling and flapping, and to avoid filling so much that it risked capsizing the ship.

Fabius was sweating in the sun, and took a swig from a water skin. He had enjoyed the rowing, pulling hard as the ship sliced through the waves on an even keel, but now that she was heaving up and down with every peak and trough he felt considerably less comfortable. He could scarcely believe that they were now within sight of Carthage, its whitewashed buildings spread out along the seafront less than a mile away, rising to the Byrsa hill with its temple in the centre. He knew he should have been apprehensive, weighing up their chances of getting in and making it out alive, but with the motion of the ship getting worse rather than better he found himself praying for landfall, anywhere, whatever the dangers. The sooner they arrived, the better.

He looked at Scipio, who was standing with his feet firmly planted on the deck, swaying with the ship and staring ahead. He had let his hair and beard grow for several months in anticipation of this mission, to look more like a merchant and less like a Roman soldier in disguise. In the three years since they had left Spain his features had become more chiselled and his skin dark and lined from the African sun. He was thirty-seven now, old for a tribune, but he still relished the opportunity that the rank gave him to lead men from the front, and he knew that the odds would be stacked in his favour for command of a legion should the Senate finally be persuaded to commit to all-out war. It had been three years of hard grind, of small-unit action supporting Gulussa and his Numidians on the fringes of the desert, violent clashes with the Carthaginian patrols that were constantly probing forward into the scrubland, pushing against the boundaries that had been agreed by treaty with Rome over fifty years before. Six months ago, Scipio and Gulussa had begun to sense that something bigger was afoot, an increasing stream of mercenaries reaching the front from the Carthaginian training camps under the walls of the city, a massing of men large enough to force a breakthrough. They knew that if that happened there would be little they could do to stop it, and Numidia would be overrun. The mission that Scipio had proposed was a last-ditch attempt to provide Polybius with evidence of Carthaginian intentions to take to Rome and present to the Senate. There would be those who would be suspicious of it, knowing Scipio's position and suspecting exaggeration, but his reputation for *fides* might be enough to persuade even the doubters. Their mission was a huge risk, but it was better than dying in the desert. Everything depended on what they found out today.

Fabius swallowed hard, focusing on the horizon as he had been told to do by the captain when he had seen his discomfort, surveying the shoreline to the south. Behind them lay Bou Kornine, the mountain whose twin peaks shaped like a bull's horns had been a navigational waymarker from the time when the Phoenicians had first come this way centuries before. On the shoreline below the slopes lay the Roman encampment, their point of embarkation the previous evening. The beach landing site of a few years before was now a semi-permanent depot, with hundreds of fresh troops passing through it every week on their way to bolster Numidian forces to the south. What had begun as a covert mission of advisers and trainers, of men experienced from Macedonia and Spain, had become an expeditionary force that was having its first major clashes with the vanguard of the enemy field army, with cohorts of mercenaries who had been sent forward to exploit weaknesses along the Numidian lines. Neither side was yet ready for full-blown war; the Carthaginians were merely occupying reclaimed territory that was rightfully theirs, and the Romans were coming to the aid of their Numidian allies with whom they were bound by treaty. But Fabius remembered what Polybius had said in the academy, that ill-defined borders were the most likely flashpoint for war, and the former Carthaginian territory ceded to Masinissa after the defeat of Hannibal was a case in point. Something was bound to crack soon, when Hasdrubal was ready for full-scale battle, and when Rome was willing to commit herself to an endgame that had been predestined all those years before when Scipio Africanus had been obliged by the Senate to spare Hannibal after his defeat at Zama and allow Carthage to escape final destruction.

He thought of Hasdrubal, a man whom few on the Roman side had yet seen, who had grown to power behind the walls of Carthage after the city had shut herself off from unwanted visitors. He was said to be monstrous, a huge bull of a man who wore a lionskin and affected a roar like a beast, yet who showed tenderness to his beautiful young wife and their children, showering them with gifts taken from the spoils of past Carthaginian wars against the rich Greek cities of Sicily. There were some within the Senate, enemies of Cato, who decried Hasdrubal as an empty-headed braggart, but Scipio knew better than to belittle a man he might one day face in battle. Hasdrubal had shown himself to be impetuous, arrogant, a gambler who was willing to take risks that might suggest a bent towards self-destruction, but more often than not in his clashes with Gulussa's cavalry and their Roman advisers he had shown himself to be an able and ruthless tactician. Their friend Terence the playwright who had spent his childhood in Carthage had said that Hasdrubal revelled in being from the same bloodline as the great Hannibal himself, a legacy that Scipio knew he could not afford to ignore; Scipio knew how much strength and sense of purpose he himself gained through his own legacy from Hannibal's arch-rival Scipio Africanus, and how any coming conflict with Hasdrubal could not be taken lightly.

Fabius had felt uneasy enough over the past months, in the shadowland of a war that officially did not exist, but he and Scipio were about to step into an even murkier world, into the byways of espionage and subterfuge that were the domain of Polybius and his agents. They had removed their armour to travel as an Italian wine merchant and his servant, and Fabius felt uncomfortable and exposed without his weapons. Scipio had spent hours that night discussing Carthage with the kybernetes, the ship's captain, an Achaian Greek on Polybius' books who had offered his ship for the mission, and they had run over the topography of the city again and again. Fabius remembered the model of Carthage that had been built for Scipio Africanus in the *tablinum* of his house on the Palatine, and stories from the slaves of how the old man used to retire to the room and brood over it. The young Scipio Aemilianus had gone there too, inviting his friend Terence the playwright to pore over it with him; by the time Scipio had gone to the academy he had known it like the back of his hand. Terence had knocked down the old harbour structure and a ring of housing around the Byrsa, the acropolis of Carthage, saying that as a boy growing up in the city he had seen that secret new building was going on in both places. That was what Fabius and

Scipio were there to find out now, and to discover what they could about Carthaginian intentions. Scipio was convinced that there was more to Carthage rearming herself than Hasdrubal's defiance, that his belligerence was about more than just turning his city into a doomed fortress that would sell its existence dearly when the time came.

Fabius swallowed hard again, feeling seriously nauseous now, hoping that he did not look as bad as he felt. He had never liked sea crossings and this was the smallest ship he had been in on the open sea, swaying and rocking like a cork. At the moment, as far as he was concerned, the Carthaginians could have the sea, for all he cared; the Romans may have bettered them in naval battles in the past but were not seafarers by nature, and the only proper place for a Roman to fight was on land. He closed his eyes, instantly regretted it and then said a little prayer of thanks as the kybernetes ordered the sail furled and the sweeps drawn out and manned. They were now less than a *stade* out, and to keep the sail up would have been to risk being blown onshore. There was going to be some tricky navigation ahead to get them safely past the long quayside and into the harbour entrance.

He stared at the shimmering façade of the city, shielding his eyes against the brilliance of the sun. The entire north-facing seafront was backed by a defensive wall some fifteen feet high, in front of which lay a wide quay backed by a continuous line of offices and warehouses built against the wall. The quay was too exposed to serve as a dock for all but the largest ships, one of which was visible near the western end; instead most vessels would enter a protected complex to the east where goods would be offloaded and then transported to warehouses along the seafront by bullock cart and on the backs of slaves. A further harbour, for ships with high-value cargoes or on commercial expeditions controlled by the state, lay in a landlocked position behind, entered by a channel to the south and leading to a second landlocked harbour that contained the naval shipsheds. The channel to the landlocked harbours was heavily guarded and they knew there was no point in seeking a berth there without attracting unwanted attention. Instead the captain directed the helmsman to steer towards the east end of the quay, ordering the rowers to ship oars as they came close and steering the remainder of the way on the momentum from their efforts. Fabius and Scipio moved to the stern behind the helmsman, keeping well back as he heaved the tiller to angle the steering oars in the direction that the captain was pointing from his position in the bow, bringing the ship expertly into the outer harbour.

As the momentum dropped off, the ship closed with an open section of wharf, bumping against the nets of brushwood that were hung down from the quay to soften the impact. The helmsman quickly pulled the pins that locked the steering oars in place and pushed the tiller forward, raising the oars to the gunwales so that they would not be damaged by the quay or by other vessels. Fabius lent a hand, heaving hard against the tiller until the oars were horizontal, but Scipio remained in his place, knowing that watching officials might look suspiciously at a merchant pitching in alongside his servant to help the crew. The helmsman and the captain heaved lines ashore from bow and stern and then leapt ashore, securing them through looped stone bolsters set into the side of the quay. They left a little leeway in the ropes, enough to take account of the small drop of a foot or two in the tide at this time of the month, and then two of the sailors laid a plank from the gunwales to the quay, ushering Scipio and Fabius off in turn. Fabius landed heavily, glad to be on land again but swaying precariously. He walked a few steps along the quay to get his legs working properly again, and then stopped and looked around. He forgot the sea, and felt himself course with excitement. *They were in Carthage.*

Half an hour later they were still on the quay, waiting for a messenger to return with the merchant's seal that the captain had sent to the port authorities as credentials. Fabius and Scipio were taking in the scene, discreetly absorbing every detail. Hundreds of pottery amphorae lay against each other in the shade under the city wall; slaves picked them up by their necks and spike-shaped bases, heaving them on their shoulders and taking them to the warehouses of merchants along the quay. Fabius could see Carthaginian olive oil amphorae – long, cylindrical shapes with small handles below the shoulders – but by far the largest number were wine amphorae, fat-bellied forms with long necks and handles. He recognized the distinctive high-handled types from Rhodes and Knidos, made to transport the best-quality Greek wines, and further down the quay a large batch of longer-bodied wine amphorae produced in Italy around the Bay of Naples, the old Greek area now controlled by Rome where vines had been cultivated since the first Greek colonists had arrived below Mount Vesuvius centuries earlier, about the time that the Phoenicians were settling Carthage. Scipio had seen the amphorae too and turned to the kybernetes, talking quietly so that he was not over-heard. 'I thought all trade between Rome and Carthage was banned by the treaty that followed the Battle of Zama. It's why my credentials state that I'm an independent merchant, Roman but not representing the state.'

'Trade with Rome, yes, but not with other cities in Italy that still consider themselves to be free agents as far as commerce is concerned,' the kybernetes replied. Where there's profit to be had, merchants can always find a way around a trade treaty.'

'There are clearly big profits to be had here,' Scipio mur-mured. 'Far more so than the Senate in Rome would have believed. This place looks even more prosperous than Ostia. But surely all of this wine is not being imported to be drunk in Carthage itself?'

The captain snorted. 'You forget your history. These people are Phoenicians, the most wily traders the world has ever known. Do you see that ship down the quay?'

He pointed to the one vessel they had seen berthed along the exposed seafront as they came in, a ship whose beam was too wide to get into the enclosed harbour but was large enough to have ridden out even a minor storm without much difficulty. Fabius shaded his eyes against the sun, following his gaze. 'It's huge,' Scipio said. 'It looks like one of the ships that put into Ostia on the way to Massalia in Gaul, carrying Italian wine to trade with the warrior chieftains of the interior.'

'That's exactly what it is,' the captain said ruefully. 'You see my ship here, the *Diana*? She can carry three hundred amphorae, four hundred at a stretch. That ship over there, *Europa*, can carry ten thousand.'

'I can see slaves taking wine amphorae off, and others taking them on,' Scipio said. 'Unless I'm mistaken, the ones going off are Italian, and the ones coming on are Greek, Rhodian and Knidian.'

The kybernetes nodded. '*Europa* should have sailed with her cargo of Italian wine directly from Neapolis to Gaul, but she diverted south to Carthage. Instead of taking Italian wine to Gaul, she'll be taking Greek.'

'I don't understand. Where's the profit?'

'You need to think like a Phoenician. Poseidon knows, if we did we'd all be rich. It goes like this. At the moment, the most profitable venture in all of the Mediterranean is the wine trade to Gaul. It's made a lot of Romans wealthy: the owners of the wine estates in Italy, the shippers, the middlemen in Massalia who deal with the Gauls. But there's been no way that the Carthaginians could get a foothold in it. If they showed up in Ostia or Neapolis or Massalia offering their services as shippers, that *would* raise the ire of Rome. But if you can't join a trading enterprise, you can always undermine it. A consortium of Carthaginian traders supported by the governing council has struck a covert deal with Greek traders in Rhodes. It was quickly done: the Greeks too have come to resent the dominance of Italian wine in the west, pushing aside their own produce.'

Scipio nodded slowly. 'And the Greeks would have known that Carthaginian trading schemes invariably turned a profit for all parties involved.'

'Correct. On that basis, the Greeks have agreed to supply the Carthaginians with as much high-quality wine as they can produce, but without a drachma being required up front. The Carthaginians then replace the Italian wine on these ships with Greek wine, and send it up to Massalia. Before embarking on this venture, they'd researched their market, of course, being true to their Phoenician roots, sending out agents who arrived with wine samples at the *oppida* of the Gauls, discovering that the barbarians have refined taste and are easily able to appreciate the superior Greek wines. So with shiploads of ten thousand *Greek* amphorae reaching Massalia, the Gauls will see that the higher-quality wine can be had in abundance. The Italian wine trade will collapse, and the Carthaginians will reap the profits.'

'Which, if the Carthaginian council has a share in the trade, is ploughed back into the city.'

The kybernetes gestured at the sea walls. 'How do you think these new fortifications were financed? Much of the marble facing is from Greece, and the masons do not come cheap. You'll be amazed by what you see inside. Carthage may not yet again control the overseas territory it did three generations ago, but behind those walls it is a richer city than it ever was before.'

Fabius indicated the amphora ship beside the quay. 'One thing puzzles me. How did the Carthaginians convince that Roman shipper to divert his vessel here? They say that a single amphora of Italian wine trades in Gaul for a slave, and in Rome slaves sell at a high premium these days because there have been too few wars to provide a decent selection. If that cargo of Italian wine was worth ten thousand slaves then the owner would stand to make a fortune in the slave markets in Rome. Why buy into a Carthaginian scheme when such profits are already certain?'

'Because the Carthaginians let it be known that they would

offer twice the profit margin, the equivalent of two slaves per amphora, if the shippers took on Greek wine instead. They have guaranteed them security, even in the event of shipwreck. The more high-quality Greek wine that floods into the Gaulish market, the more certain the Carthaginians will be that the Gauls will reject the inferior Italian vintages. The bottom will fall out of the Italian wine trade, especially if the Carthaginians continue to offer more lucrative contracts to the shippers who had previously taken the Italian wine, persuading them to sail down to Carthage like the *Europa* and load up with wine shipped in from Greece for the trip north to Massalia. Once the Carthaginians have cornered the Gaulish market, they'll be able to up the price from one slave to two and even three, and demand other goods that have always been a Phoenician speciality, particularly copper and tin for bronze, as well as iron.'

Scipio nodded. 'Metals that are in short supply in Africa and are needed so they can make their own armour and weapons.'

'But there's more to it than that,' the kybernetes said quietly, looking around again to make sure that nobody else was listening. 'There's a dark side that you won't like. It's an open secret that many Roman senators of the old *gentes*, men who profess to despise trade and only invest in land, have made enormous profits through allowing middlemen to take wine off their estates and export it to Gaul. But there are other senators, *novi homines*, new men, those with no landed wealth, who are not above dirtying their own hands with trade.'

'I know it,' Scipio said grimly. 'I served under one in Spain, Lucullus. He made his fortune after the Spanish triumph by using the prize money voted to him by his cronies in the Senate to buy up large stocks of excess grain from Sicily at a rock-bottom price, and then to sell it at an extortionate premium the next year to the same people when there was a drought. He has used it to buy land, but the *gentes* will not forget how he made his fortune.'

'Rumour has it that a group of these men banded together

and bought the vessel you see here today, along with her cargo, in a secret deal very profitable to the owner, and that they have done the same with several other shiploads of Italian wine. Rumour also has it that these same senators are the ones who are so strongly opposed to further military action against Carthage, as well as in Greece.'

'Jupiter above,' Scipio murmured. 'This goes to the heart of our problem in persuading Rome to go to war. Now I see what Cato and Polybius are up against.'

'I have another question,' Fabius said. 'With all that Italian wine being offloaded here, what are the Carthaginians going to do with it? They're hardly going to drink it themselves, or sell it back to the Greeks. Better to dump it in the sea.'

The kybernetes raised his eyes. 'Phoenicians? Throw away a trade commodity? Not likely. That wine is part of another scheme, of even greater profitability. Beside the inner harbour, away from prying eyes, they have begun to build huge warehouses, large enough to house a ship as big as that amphora carrier on the quay. Soon these warehouses will fill up not with amphorae of wine but with something even more precious: sacks of an exotic spice called *pipperia*. It comes from India, and will be shipped across the Erythraean Sea to the shore of Egypt, and then transported across the desert to the Nile and Alexandria and to Carthage. The first Greeks to reach the shores of southern India found that the local spice merchants loved their wine, and wanted more; even rough Italian wine is like nectar to them. That's where all of those amphorae are destined.'

'But to transport tens of thousands of heavy amphorae across the Egyptian desert would be an expensive undertaking,' Scipio said. 'I've been there, and the cost would be prohibitive.'

'The Carthaginians are prepared to do so, underwriting the transport cost with the profits from the trade with Gaul. They intend to send only enough to seed the trade, to bring back shiploads of *pipperia* and other spices and luxuries of the east, enough to fire up demand among the wealthy in Rome itself: among the wives of those whose greed they had exploited to set up the trade in the first place, the senators whose ship you see on the quayside now. But then the Carthaginians will move from exporting wine to another commodity that the Indians love, something transported much more easily with profit margins far higher. I mean gold: gold coin, gold bullion, gold specie, gold in any form. The Carthaginians will channel the gold of the Mediterranean to the east, emptying the wealth of nations to create in their own city the richest nation-state the world has ever seen, here where we stand now.'

'How do they get the gold?' Fabius asked. 'Another ingenious trading scheme?'

The kybernetes did not reply, but raised his eyes at Scipio, who turned to Fabius, his expression hard. 'It will come from another source. This time old Phoenician guile takes a back seat, and new Carthaginian strength will be to the fore.'

'What do you mean?'

'I mean war. War not of defence, but of conquest. War against Rome, and war in the east. Wars that may even see Carthage allied with those Romans who, it seems, have already thrown in their lot with her.'

Fabius felt a cold shiver down his spine. They were no longer talking about extinguishing an ancient foe, about finishing business and satisfying honour, about Scipio's own destiny. They were talking about a war that could change everything, a war that could escalate to swallow up the entire known world, from the shore of the Erythraean Sea to the furthest reaches of Gaul and the Albion Isles. The reason for Scipio's presence here now to gather intelligence suddenly seemed so important that it made him feel faint, as if he were standing at one of the pivotal points of history. The stakes could not be higher.

The kybernetes eyed Scipio. 'Perhaps you have now seen all that you need to see. Even Polybius knows little of this, as my knowledge of these plans came since I last saw him in person, and I could not trust others to tell him. But now you have seen enough with your own eyes to trust that what I say is true.'

Scipio paused for a moment, his eyes narrowed, and then shook his head. 'You have told us of the strategic threat. But we came here also to evaluate the tactical challenge of an assault on Carthage. I need to see the soldiers, their equipment, the fortifications, the new war harbour. Without that intelligence, we will be severely hampered. And I cannot yet use the strategic threat as an argument in Rome. If what you say is true, there are too many in the Senate implicated against us, names that I can guess, and to suggest in public that they are treacherous to Rome without clear evidence of Carthaginian military build-up would destroy my case and probably my life. It's the detailed evidence for war preparation that will win the day. After that, I will ponder what you have told me and decide how that will shape my own strategy after the army I lead here is victorious, if they give me the consulship.'

The kybernetes waved at someone, and they could see that the messenger they had sent with their seal was returning from the customs house. 'Good,' the captain said. 'There are no guards returning with him, so we will be let through.' He turned to Scipio, and spoke intensely. 'I'm glad you're confident. But I'll speak my mind. From what I've seen of the Roman forces so far here in Africa, those helping Masinissa's army, I'm not so sure. You've got a lot of work to do, Scipio Aemilianus. Perhaps the name of your father and of the great Scipio Africanus will carry the weight of history forward. Meanwhile, remember that for today you are a mere merchant, and you must play your part with caution. You must be on the alert.'

15

The guards at the entrance from the outer harbour through the city wall were typically Carthaginian in appearance: dark-skinned, swarthy men with curly black hair and beards, the descendants of Phoenician forefathers who had left their homeland in the east Mediterranean centuries before to escape the turmoil that followed the Trojan War, founding Carthage not much before the Trojan prince Aeneas had first alighted on the coast of Italy and set eyes on the site of Rome some six hundred years ago. The two guards closest to Fabius carried long thrusting spears with butt tips of bronze so they would not rust when rammed into damp ground, as well as curved Greek-style *kopis* slashing swords: fearsome-looking weapons with the edged blade on the inside, yet less effective in a close-quarter melee than the straight-bladed Roman thrusting sword. Instead of metal armour they wore the distinctive Carthaginian hardened linen corselet, not thick enough to deflect a determined thrust yet with a white exterior and lighter weight that made it better suited to the African sun than Roman metal armour.

Their most striking equipment was their helmets, made of highly burnished iron with a bulbous crown that rose and extended forward, and detachable cheekpieces; the cheekpieces covered the face entirely, leaving only apertures for the eyes and mouth, and were embossed to represent facial hair. Seeing those helmets made Fabius catch his breath and remember the dreams of his boyhood. They were exactly as his father had described them from the Battle of Zama more than fifty years before, the last time the Romans had encountered the Carthaginians in a set-piece battle. Polybius in his *Histories* had derided the Carthaginians for using too many mercenaries and for fielding an untrained conscript force of their own citizens, but Fabius knew from his father that Polybius' sources had exaggerated to deflect attention from deficiencies in the Roman line, especially the division of forces within each legion according to experience and the quality of their weapons and armour. Seeing these guards here today, confident in their poise and the way they held their weapons, so similar in appearance to his father's description of those supposedly ill-trained levies, Fabius could begin to understand how the infantry battle at Zama had raged for hours before Masinissa's cavalry had arrived and tipped the balance in favour of the Romans. Yet these men today did not look like shadows from the past, a token police force allowed to a vanquished foe, but like highly trained, toughened warriors, men who had probably been blooded in the border clashes of the last three years with Gulussa's cavalry and the Roman expeditionary force. If there were more men like this mustered inside the walls of Carthage, then an assault on the city by the Romans would not be the walkover that some might have predicted.

The kybernetes returned from talking to the customs officer, nodded at Scipio and gestured to the entrance in the city wall beyond the guard tower. 'You are authorized to go through to the merchants' hall, the name they give to the colonnaded space between the outer harbour where we are now and the two inner harbours, the rectangular harbour for state-controlled trade and the circular war harbour. Officially you cannot gain access to those inner harbours or the city beyond. Whether you find a way of doing so is up to your own devices. I will set sail as soon as you return. Your stated purpose here is to conclude a deal with a Carthaginian wine merchant, no more. If you linger any longer than you need to, the port guards will become suspicious. And if I come into the merchants' hall with you I'm liable to be press-ganged into the Carthaginian navy. The only place where sailors have immunity is out here, and I'll busy myself with the chandlers' stores to stock up on supplies for my ship. Whatever happens, you must never reveal your name. For the Carthaginians to have caught the heir of Scipio Africanus on a covert mission within their walls would be to sound the death-knell for any Roman attempt to take this city. They would demand an extortionate ransom, hold you up as a laughing stock that would undermine Roman prestige everywhere, and shatter the morale of the legions. Far better, if you are threatened with capture, to die fighting, or to fall on your own sword. Good luck.'

He scurried off towards a cordage seller beside the quay. Scipio walked confidently past the soldiers, Fabius an appropriate distance behind, and in a few moments they were through the city wall. The colonnaded space they had entered was long and narrow, lined not with warehouses like the quay outside but with small *officinae* fronted by marble tables and seats. The place seemed less like the animated chaos of the merchants' square that Fabius knew well from the port of Rome at Ostia, a favourite haunt of his as a boy, than one of the law courts in the Forum, with clusters of men engaged in solemn discussions. Sitting in the office next to the entrance was a man wearing a robe dyed deep purple, the colour that the Phoenicians extracted from a rare species of seashell; it was the easiest way to spot a Carthaginian state official. On the stone table in front of him was a steelyard weighing scale and a line of balance-pan weights resting in carved-out depressions in the stone, and in the back of the *officina* was a stone strongbox guarded by two burly soldiers. It was evidently an exchange facility, and Fabius could see others interspersed among the colonnades. This place was clearly run by Carthaginian officials, not by free merchants, and their transactions were not the small deals built up piecemeal of a typical shipper's business in Ostia, but instead high-value exchanges, evidenced by a transaction a few offices down, where the pan in the scale was piled high with gold coins.

Scipio walked along the colonnade, looking to the left and

right as if searching for a specific merchant, and then turned casually to Fabius and nodded at the opposite colonnade. 'There's an entrance between the columns,' he said quietly. 'It's a narrow passage guarded by two soldiers about halfway along, out of sight of anyone here unless they were really looking. It must lead to the landlocked harbours. Our disguise as a merchant and his servant is no use to us any more if we want to get in there. Our only chance is to go as Carthaginian soldiers. When I give the signal, you deal with the one on the right.'

Fabius followed Scipio as he turned down the alley and walked up to the soldiers, who wore the same style of armour and equipment as the men at the entrance. They both had their cheekpieces down, obscuring their faces, but by their long beards they looked to be eastern mercenaries, perhaps Assyrian. The man on the left stood forward, slamming his spear butt on the ground. 'You are not allowed through,' he said, his Greek barely comprehensible. 'By order of the high admiral.'

'The high admiral?' Scipio said, pretending ignorance. 'So this is the way to the circular harbour?'

'Yes, but it's not the harbour you want,' the man growled. 'Your harbour is back the way you came. You merchants are even bigger fools than I thought. You have no sense of direction.'

Scipio turned, affecting a puzzled expression, but in reality looking down the alley to make sure they were not being watched. He caught Fabius' eye, and nodded almost impercepibly. In a lightning movement he swivelled round and punched the soldier hard in the throat, catching him as he fell and twisting his head violently to one side until he could hear his neck break. In the same instant Fabius did the same to the other man, keeping hold of his head afterwards and lowering him gently to the ground. There had been no noise, and there was no blood. They dragged the two men out of the alley into a dark space behind a wall, and then quickly stripped them, taking off their own clothes and donning the soldiers' armour, pulling on the helmets and snapping the cheekpieces shut over their faces. The bodies lay with their eyes wide open, caught in the shock of instant death. Scipio kicked their discarded clothes over the corpses so that it looked like a pile of cloth. They picked up the spears, walked out into the alley, turned and moved swiftly along the columns of a portico that extended at right-angles from the merchants' hall for several hundred feet, and then veered right through an opening towards a shimmer of water.

Scipio stopped for a moment, listening for any sign of pursuit, hearing nothing. Fabius took a deep breath, and saw that his hands were shaking. It always happened after he killed, the energy rush, like taking a deep draught of wine at the end of a long run, his heart pumping the nectar through his veins and making him shake. And it was not that he had come to relish killing for its own sake. Taking out those two men had seemed like the first act in the endgame, as if the assault on Carthage was finally in train.

They had come out on the edge of the enclosed rectangular harbour, a basin that led to a fortified entrance at the eastern side, with the twin-peaked mountain of Bou Kornine visible in the background. Fabius realized that the harbour must be parallel to the outer one where the *Diana* had berthed, only completely man-made and landlocked. There were only two ships berthed inside, one a typical Phoenician-style wide-bellied merchantman with eyes painted below the bows, and the other a sleeker design that was neither warship nor merchantman, with gunwales higher and more robust than Fabius was used to seeing. The wharf beside the vessel was lined with baskets filled with fragments of stone, some of it shimmering and metallic. As he and Scipio passed, a slave came down a gangplank and heaved another basket to the ground, sweating and cursing. He glanced ruefully at Fabius, who had stopped to look. 'Feel free to give a hand, if you have nothing better to do,' the slave said in heavily accented Greek. 'I'm just about done in.'

'What is it, in the baskets?' Fabius asked.

'Tin ore, from the Cassiterides, the Tin Isles,' the man said. 'At least, that's what the Punic sailors call the place, after the Greek name, but I know it differently. Some of us from the west of the island call it Albion, and others Britten. You see, it was my home, where I was happily going about my own business until I was snatched during a raid by a neighbouring chieftain, sold to the Gauls, traded by them for an amphora of wine to an Italian shipper, and then given by him as a present to a Carthaginian merchant to oil some deal. So I find myself here, the slave of a Phoenician captain who is about to take me by sea right back again to my home island to help load more of this stuff. I wouldn't mind so much if they shipped it in ingots, which would be easier to carry. They keep it as ore because the weight of the rocks acts as ballast in the rough seas of the Atlantic Ocean.'

'It could be worse,' Fabius said. 'You could be a galley slave.'

'Or mucking out seasick elephants.' The man jerked his head down to the far end of the harbour. 'You see that shipbuilding yard? They're building *elephantegoi*, elephant carriers. They say that not even Hannibal had specialized elephant ships like that.'

Fabius followed his gaze, and then stared at the man. He clearly had no love for the Carthaginians, and was garrulous. Fabius knew that to enquire more might have aroused suspicions had the man not been a slave, but in this case he could take a calculated gamble. He reached into a pouch on his belt and took out one of the Macedonian gold staters that Scipio had given him earlier in case they needed to bribe potential informants, and tossed it to the man. 'Tell me more.'

The man took the coin, eyed Fabius for a moment and quickly concealed the gold. He began to talk animatedly, telling him about the elephant carriers, but after a few minutes a swarthy man appeared on deck, cracking a whip and glaring at him. Fabius shouted at the slave as if telling him off for talking to him, and then marched on. They could not risk suspicious eyes alighting on them, and stopping to talk to the slave had been pushing their luck. Scipio stood waiting at the edge of the channel linking the rectangular harbour to the circular war harbour, and Fabius hurried up to him, talking under his breath. 'It's just as the kybernetes said. The Carthaginians are importing metal not only from Gaul, but also from the Albion Isles. That cargo is worth its weight in gold.'

They walked briskly along the portico beside the channel to the war harbour. As they approached it, an extraordinary structure came into view. The kybernetes had described it to them the night before, but even he had never seen it from the inside. The harbour was built around a circular basin that Fabius estimated at a *stade* and a half in diameter, about a thousand feet, large enough to accommodate the four-banked quadriremes and five-banked quinqueremes – called by the Carthaginians *pentereis*, their Greek name – that had traditionally been the biggest vessels in the Carthaginian fleet. In the centre of the basin was an island perhaps half a *stade* across made up of a circular structure that rose to a watchtower in the centre. The same style of roofed portico had been used around the island and the outer edge of the basin, a uniform design that made the structure more grandiose than anything yet built in Rome. Most remarkable of all, the spaces between the columns served as shipsheds, around the outer edge as well as the island; he could see the prows of warships poking out, galleys that had been drawn up on slipways. There must have been at least two hundred openings, at least half of them occupied. On the far side, a section of sheds was being used as a shipbuilder's yard, with stacks of wood and cordage visible and the partly built shells of vessels propped up on wooden formers. Only one warship was floating in the basin itself, drawn up against the wharf just beyond the entrance, a small, single-banked *lembos* that looked like the vessels that Fabius had seen at the Roman fleet base at Misenum on the Bay of Neapolis, used by crack teams of oarsmen to send people and messages faster than the larger galleys could ever manage.

Fabius remembered Polybius in the Macedonian forest ten years earlier, telling then of rumours that the Carthaginians were rebuilding their war harbour; this structure could not have been much older than that. The marble veneer was still sharp edged and mirror bright, and stacks of it lay in a mason's yard beside the entrance. The marble was a high-quality stone that must have come from Greece, and the columns of the portico were a beautiful honey-coloured stone that Fabius recognized from a stone bowl that Gulussa had shown him, from a newly discovered quarry in Numidian territory south-east of Carthage. This harbour was not some hasty half-measure, built by a people desperate to restore some vestige of their military pride, but was an arsenal far superior to anything of Rome herself or in the Greek world, a structure built by a people who confidently expected to project their power far beyond these shores once again.

He knew that Scipio would be using every moment to size up the tactical implications of a naval encounter with the new Carthaginian warships. Just before the entrance to the circular harbour was another checkpoint, this time one that Fabius knew they could never hope to penetrate, though they might be able to get close enough for a better glimpse of what lay inside. Two guards with spears firmly planted barred their way as they approached. 'No entry without authorization,' one of them said in Greek, guessing that they were mercenaries and not Carthaginians. 'I am the optio of the guard. State your business.'

Scipio stood before the man and saluted, holding his fist to his chest. 'Urgent message from Hasdrubal to Hamilcar, *strategos* of the *pentereis* squadron.'

The man grunted. 'I don't know of a squadron commander with that name, but I'm new to the job. From Hasdrubal himself, you say? I'll need to go to the admiral's island to find out. Wait here.' He clicked his fingers and another guard sauntered out from the guardhouse beside them to take his place. Looking annoyed, the optio stomped off around the edge of the harbour towards a wooden bridge that led to the island in the centre. Scipio yawned, sighed heavily and turned away from the harbour, feigning a lack of interest. He paced slowly back towards the rectangular harbour, stopping and putting his hands on his hips when he knew they were out of earshot of the soldiers. Fabius had followed him and spoke in a low voice. 'Who in Hades is Hamilcar the *strategos*?'

'Every third male in Carthage seems to be called Hamilcar, so the chances are there's someone with that name stationed in the harbour. I guessed that the guard at the entrance wouldn't know the name of all of the captains and squadron commanders, but I spotted a five-banked galley in the sheds opposite us, a *pentereis*. We just have to hope that the *strategos* of that squadron isn't called Hamilcar. Our chance to size this place up is now, before the optio returns, but we must be careful. We don't want to appear too interested.'

Scipio stretched, turned, and then walked back in front of the guards, peering beyond them and drumming his fingers impatiently against his thigh. 'Bide your time, soldier,' one of the guards said. 'It's always difficult finding people in this place. There are two hundred and twenty sheds to check, as well as the head-quarters rooms on the island.'

Scipio pursed his lips. 'You know what it's like. If I don't return to the Byrsa soon with my message delivered, I'll be for it. Anyway, I thought this place was the pride of Carthage. It should be the height of efficiency.'

The man snorted. 'How long have you been in Carthage, soldier?'

'Only a matter of days. We're Italian mercenaries, got into trouble while we were with Demetrius' army in Syria and ended up as galley slaves, but then slipped ship in the harbour here and offered our services to the guard before our captain could reclaim us.'

'Well, if you're skilled oarsmen, I'd keep quiet about it. Otherwise the Carthaginians will recruit you for their war galleys. They've built this harbour and these ships, but they don't have the slaves to man them. Carthage hasn't conducted wars of conquest since the time of Hannibal, and war is the only way you get a good supply of fit men for the galleys. If you ask me, that's why they've started up this war against Masinissa again: not to conquer a few more square miles of wasteland but to capture Numidians to use as galley slaves.'

The other guard joined in. 'They say they'll use Gauls, too, brought back as slaves by the wine traders.' He jerked his head towards the island. The optio was returning, and the two guards stood to attention. After a few minutes the optio rounded the portico and marched up to them, eyeing Scipio suspiciously. 'There's a Hamilcar who's a captain of the triremes, currently seconded to the infantry, but not a squadron commander of the *pentereis*. In fact, there's no such squadron. There's only one of those big ships left, and it's a relic. The largest vessels in the fleet now are triremes. Unless you can explain yourself to me, I'm to take you to the admiral for questioning.'

He nodded curtly to the two guards, who stomped their legs apart and held their spears at the ready. Fabius felt his pulse quicken: this was precisely the kind of encounter that they had wanted to avoid. Scipio affected nonchalance, shrugging. 'It was a new appointment, for one of Hasdrubal's cousins. Maybe it was more of an honorary rank. This place is so cut off that information doesn't pass often enough up to the Bysra, and Hasdrubal's eyes have been elsewhere, on the war with Masinissa. I'll return and tell him that his cousin Hamilcar is nowhere to be seen and that ships are still under construction. Maybe that will make him come here himself for an inspection.'

'Don't do that,' the man said hastily. 'You don't know Hasdrubal yet. If he finds fault and loses his temper, heads will roll.'

Scipio slapped him on the shoulder. 'All we soldiers want is to go off-duty and get to the taverns, right? We were told that if we didn't find Hamilcar here, he might be in the Tophet sanctuary, as he's also a priest. We'll go and look for him there.'

'Your nearest route is directly opposite us. I'll escort you past the guards.' The optio turned and walked to the left, heading along the southern side of the portico around the harbour, and Scipio and Fabius followed. They walked within a few feet of the docked *lembos* and past the first shipsheds, and then they veered right through a gap in the portico. Moments later, the optio had left them at the guard post and they were in the city proper, in a street that ran parallel to the high retaining wall of the harbour complex. They made their way quickly out of sight of the soldiers, and past the busy fish market that lined the street. Scipio turned to Fabius as they walked, speaking urgently. 'Did you see that *lembos*?'

'It looked Roman.'

'It *was* Roman. I saw bundles of *pila* in the stern. No other soldiers carry spears like ours. And the amphorae of wine and olive oil for the crew were Italian.'

'Captured?'

Scipio shook his head. 'That would be an act of war, and they can't risk that until they have the slaves to man their galleys and confront us at sea.'

'This war harbour is an empty threat until then.'

'But it might only take one victory in the field to supply enough slaves. Once that happens, the threat is very real.'

'We'll have to tell Gulussa to redouble his efforts not to let his men get captured.'

'I don't think we need to worry,' Scipio replied. 'His men will fight to the death.'

'There's something else,' Fabius said, navigating his way

around a pair of bullock carts. 'The warships I saw in the sheds were small, most of them *liburnae*, double-bankers at most.'

Scipio nodded. 'There were only a few triremes. That's our most important intelligence for Polybius so far. We know they haven't got the manpower for a fleet of large galleys as in the past. But last night the kybernetes said that many of the Carthaginian merchant captains have been conscripted by the state. Those men would make up a highly experienced cadre of officers for a new fleet of *liburnae*, with the oarsmen of an elite squadron perhaps made up not of slaves but of mercenaries attracted by the promise of higher pay, and a cut of the profits. *Liburnae* are well-suited to break through a blockade and take messages to allies. But they're also suited to another kind of war, perfectly in keeping with a state that prides itself on its prowess and ruthlessness in trade.'

Fabius stopped and stared at him. 'Are you saying what I think you're saying?'

'Some would call it trade war, taken to its logical conclusion.'

'You're talking about state-sponsored piracy.'

'With a fleet of this size, Carthage could sweep the seas clean of rivals, and the *liburnae* could return in safety to their lair. The profits to the state might be less in what they actually plunder than in ensuring that Carthaginian merchant ships and their trade partners have a monopoly of the sea lanes. The cargoes of captured ships could even be split among the *liburnae* crews as an incentive. With her present constitution, Rome would be powerless to stop it. Look how difficult it is getting the consuls to agree to raise the legions for a campaign that might extend beyond their year in office, giving no glory to them. Imagine the problems suppressing organized piracy on this scale. It would be a proxy war with Carthage, but would have to be fought piecemeal over years, even decades. It would require Rome to sanction an admiral with a remit unlike any other given to a war leader, and to authorize the formation of a truly professional navy. The

Senate in Rome is too wrapped up in its own politics and *gens* rivalry to allow that, and Carthage knows it.'

'There's another purpose for those *liburnae*, and that's as escort vessels,' Fabius said. 'It's something else that the slave carrying the tin ore pointed out to me. At the far end of the rectangular harbour is another shipbuilding yard, with huge wooden formers and a vessel being built up from the keel. He said the timbers were cedar of Lebanon supplied by a convoy that came under naval escort from King Demetrius of Syria, with his son leading a special delegation from Syria that was met by Hasdrubal himself at the harbour entrance.'

'*Demetrius?*' Scipio exclaimed. 'So he has finally turned against Rome.'

'That might not be the way he sees it,' Fabius said. 'Perhaps he's just aligned himself to a new Rome, one that sees Carthage as an ally.'

Scipio strode forward grimly. 'Do you have anything else to tell me?

'It gets worse. The vessel under construction was at least the size of the *Europa*, the huge amphora carrier we saw at the quayside. Yet the slave said this was no amphora carrier, but an *elephantegos*, an elephant transporter. He said that it was being built by Egyptian shipwrights who specialized in ships for bringing elephants and other beasts up the coast of the Erythraean Sea from the land they call Punt. He said the shipwrights arrived with a delegation from your other friend, Ptolemy Philometor, King of Egypt, and that his treacherous wife and sister Cleopatra herself accompanied them.'

'Jupiter above,' Scipio muttered. 'Ptolemy too? He never was cut out to be a king. Cleopatra must be behind this.'

'With Demetrius and Ptolemy siding with Carthage, perhaps in secret alliance with Metellus in Macedonia and his supporters in the Senate in Rome, it means that more than half of those who were in the academy are now aligned against you and against the

Rome that you were trained to defend. Demetrius and Ptolemy may have spent their adult lives entangled in the power politics of Syria and of Egypt, but they were both trained in the academy by Polybius and the old centurion; put in charge of an army, they could be formidable strategists and tacticians. If there is to be a world war, the balance of power is swinging dangerously against us.'

'A *world war*,' Scipio exclaimed. 'Could it come to that?'

'Think of that *elephantegos*,' Fabius said. 'What other purpose can such a vessel have for the Carthaginians than to send elephants to war? I saw other formers in the yard beyond, for other hulls under construction. Shipwrights specialized in making large vessels for elephants could easily transfer their skills to making troop transports.'

'I understand now what you mean about the *liburnae* making perfect escort galleys,' Scipio said. 'If the Carthaginians are intent on conquest to increase their gold reserves, they will find little in Africa beyond the Numidian towns, only hundreds of miles of impassable desert. What we've seen here, the harbours and the ships, is not just about increasing trade and controlling the sea lanes. Carthage is building an invasion fleet, a fleet that could land troops anywhere along the Mediterranean shore and besiege the great cities of Greece and the east. With support from Demetrius and Ptolemy as well as Metellus, the entire territory of Alexander's empire could fall before such an alliance.'

'And while Metellus may be focusing on consolidating the east, Hasdrubal may have his eyes set elsewhere. The legacy of history remains as firmly embedded for Carthage as it is for us, the legacy that generations of war and bloodshed have yet to resolve.'

'You mean he will look to conquer Rome.'

Fabius nodded. 'Carthage may be unfinished business for you, for the *gens* Scipiones. But Rome is also unfinished business for Carthage. Just as Scipio Africanus stood before Carthage after the

Battle of Zama and then turned away, so Hannibal stood within sight of the walls of Rome before he too was forced back. Just as you have a legacy from your grandfather, so Hasdrubal has his own legacy from Hannibal.'

'And yet we have no invasion fleet in preparation, only a token force in Africa and a dithering Senate,' Scipio muttered.

Fabius squinted up, seeing the sun low in the western sky. 'Where to next? We don't have much time.'

Scipio took a deep breath. 'Remember Intercatia? The Celtiberians defended their *oppidum* in depth, with that second wall within the main circuit. From what Terence told me, the Carthaginians may have done the same. We've seen evidence of Hasdrubal's offensive strategy, but now we need to see his defensive plans. We'll go past the Tophet sanctuary and up the main street from the harbours towards the Byrsa. We need to see as much as we can. Let's move.'

16

The narrow alleys on either side of the street lay deep in shadow, and Fabius looked ahead to see that the afternoon sun had fallen behind the level of the Byrsa. 'We don't have long,' he said. 'The kybernetes wanted to be out on the open sea by nightfall. If the bodies of those soldiers are found and they suspect us, they'll send out one of those *liburna* galleys to hunt us down. We'll need to use the cover of night to row as fast as we can to get to our own naval cordon, and that's more than ten miles to the east.'

Scipio nodded. 'We'll carry on here for half an hour, no more. Do you remember the model of Carthage that my grandfather Scipio Africanus had made – the one that our playwright friend Terence helped me to modify? He told me about the maze of old Punic houses that he used to play in as a boy, and I want to see whether the Carthaginians have knocked them down during all of this rebuilding to make a final killing zone before the Byrsa hill.'

They hurried up the street, ascending now so that when they turned they could glimpse the distant sea beyond the harbours, shimmering above the rooftops. The buildings on either side were higher, more like fortress walls than a street frontage, and as they neared the end of the street they could see that the rooftops were crenellated and linked by low towers. They marched determinedly ahead as several people passed, and then Scipio stopped and looked along the walls, judging the field of fire for arrows and spears.

'It's just as I thought, coming up,' he said grimly. 'The Carthaginians have planned for defence in depth, deliberately narrowing these streets as they lead towards the Byrsa to funnel an attacking force into them, to this place where a hidden force could appear suddenly on the walls and rain down death. The only way to counter it would be to mount an attack of sufficient speed and ferocity to break through and overwhelm them, with archers in the vanguard to fire up at these walls to keep the defenders back. For an attacking force to hesitate, to be caught up in street fighting, would be to make this place a death trap. The assault on Carthage could end right here.'

Fabius nodded. 'At this stage in an assault, with their final stronghold threatened, they could mount suicide attacks, sending fighters down the street to try to pin down the advance. Even though such defenders might be killed within moments, it would only take a few of them hurtling down one after the other to cause the advance to halt, and then the assault troops would be killed in larger numbers by the men on the walls as they were able to find their targets. It would take the strongest leadership to maintain the determination of the legionaries and keep the assault force driving forward.'

'And imaginative use of shields,' Scipio murmured, squinting up at the walls. 'Ennius and I have discussed a new drill for the *testudo*, for locking shields together to form a continuous protective cover above a marching cohort. We need to practise it, not in the open but in the streets and alleys of a town where the centurions can train the legionaries to raise and lower their shields as the width and direction of a street changes.'

'We would need to find a Punic town with a similar arrangement,' Fabius said. 'One with similar street alignments and house layouts.'

'I know exactly the place,' Scipio replied. 'Kerkouane, on the eastern shore beyond the cape, supposedly the place where the Phoenicians landed when they first came to Africa. The city was abandoned after the war between Rome and Carthage a century ago, and has never been reoccupied. Ennius has already been there to test a new siege engine against the weaknesses in Punic walls. It would be a perfect place to practise urban warfare.'

'We need to remember what we are up against,' Fabius said. 'Hasdrubal is not a reasonable man like Hannibal. He's defiant, and will hold out to the death. If he's infected his fighters with the same spirit, then they will give up this place dearly. The men needed for suicide attacks down those streets would not be mercenaries. You can pay a man to risk his life, but not to face certain death. They could only be Carthaginian citizens.'

Scipio nodded. 'If they've put such thought into building these defences, they will also have trained men for that purpose: men who have a fanatical allegiance to Carthage, perhaps under the sway of the priests. It would be a cohort of suicide warriors with only one objective: to throw themselves at an attacker in these streets.'

They had reached a mass of buildings below the edge of the Byrsa, where the slopes began to angle more steeply towards the temple platform on top of the hill. To their right they could see the processional way that rose up the Byrsa in a westerly direction, a place where the morning sun would cast a brilliant light on the stone steps. But the street they were on came to an end before a dense accumulation of houses, structures joined by ladders and stairways on the rooftops that allowed overhead access between the buildings. Whereas they had passed few others in the street on the way up, the alleyways ahead were teeming with people: slaves carrying amphorae and other goods on their shoulders, women making their way between houses with baskets of food, children running and playing. Fabius planted his spear in the ground and stood as if on guard. 'This looks like an old quarter, like the descriptions of ancient towns in the east that I have heard slaves in Rome talk about,' he said. 'It looks as if the rebuilding programme has not extended this far yet. Perhaps this quarter has special significance, like the house of Romulus on the Palatine Hill, preserved because it was the first settled part of the city.'

Scipio squinted at the houses. 'I think there's more to it than that. I think it's been left like this deliberately. If an attack force managed to push through to this point, the surviving Carthaginians could fall back among these houses, holing themselves up. This is the last-ditch line of defence in depth.'

'If you were to take this quarter without incurring massive casualties, you would need to drive your men without hesitation into the houses, having stoked up their ardour for individual combat. Hasdrubal might hold back his best warriors for this fight.'

Scipio nodded. 'All right. I've seen all I need to see. We've got all the ammunition we need to give Polybius and Cato for their fight with the Senate. We should return now.'

They took one last look at the Punic houses and the Byrsa beyond, the shining white of its marble backlit by the red sheen in the late afternoon sky. Fabius wondered whether they would ever be here again, and whether the street they were standing on would be a river of blood. They turned and walked quickly back down in the direction of the harbours, turning sharply as the street opened out into a wider avenue just beyond the fortified frontage that formed the second line of defence. They heard a clashing of arms and shouted commands to their right. Scipio stopped and turned to Fabius. 'That sounds like a training ground. Let's take a look.'

In front of them was a space where the buildings had been cleared away to create open ground. A low wall had been built across it to maintain a street frontage, linking the fortified houses of the approach to the Byrsa with the buildings below. In the centre of the wall was an open entrance, and two guards. To Fabius they looked like mountain men from northern Macedonia or Thrace, huge men with dark eyes and thick beards. Scipio strode brazenly up to them, speaking in Greek. 'Message from Hasdrubal to the *strategos*,' he said. Fabius tensed, keeping his arm ready beside his sword, watching as the guard to the left eyed them suspiciously.

The man spoke in Greek. 'I haven't seen you two before,' he said. 'You're not Iberian, or Greek. You look Roman.'

Scipio snorted, and spat. 'Roman by birth, but not by allegiance. We fought as legionaries at Pydna, but then deserted. The generals thought we were fighting solely for the honour of Rome, so they took all of the loot for themselves. Can you believe it? I tell you, when the Romans run short of men they're going to come looking for mercenaries, but don't think of joining them. Anyway, we had too much to drink one night in Tyre and woke up chained to the oars in a galley, but managed to escape when the galley put into the harbour here a few weeks ago, and we offered our services.' He had spotted the distinctive shape of the bow slung on the man's back, confirming his nationality. 'It's good to see Thracians again. We spent ten years after Pydna with a band of Thracian mercenaries, drinking and whoring our way around the kingdoms of the east, working wherever the pay was right. They say that one day, when the star of Rome has faded, a Thracian will rise who will put Alexander the Great in the pale, leading an army to conquer all of those lands. From what I've seen of Thracians, I wouldn't doubt it.'

The guard looked Scipio hard in the eyes, and then grunted, cracking a lopsided smile. 'You're all right. When we're off-duty, we go to a tavern by the sea that serves Thracian wine. Just ask for the tavern of Menander. Meet us there this evening. The owner has two Egyptian girls who are always up for fresh meat. You can show us what you're worth.' He jerked his head to the door. 'Take your message inside. Just don't linger too long. If you do, they'll use you for sword practice.'

'Mercenaries?'

The man shook his head. 'Carthaginians. Not much more than boys, and none of them has seen battle. But they've been training like this, day in and day out, for as long as we've been stationed here. It's said that they're the first-born sons of Carthaginian nobility, spared sacrifice in the Tophet so that they could train to be the last-ditch defenders of Carthage, Hasdrubal's personal suicide force for when the Romans finally have the guts to assault this place. I tell you, when that happens, Skylax here and me, we'll be long gone. We'll chain ourselves to a galley to get out. Among the mercenaries, only the bone-headed Celtiberians will stick around, because they fight for honour and not for loot. Staying here when the Romans appear on the horizon will be a one-way ticket to Hades.'

Scipio stared at the man, looked around and then spoke quietly. 'We know a kybernetes who can help you. He's not looking for slaves, but for the best mercenaries he can find, for an elite force to join Andriscus the Macedonian in his attempt to regain the kingdom of Alexander.' He reached into his tunic and pulled out a leather bag, opening it and spilling out gold coins into his hand. 'These are staters of Alexander the Great, made from Thracian gold. There's more gold in this one bag than you'll get for a year serving Carthage, and this is just for starters.' He put the coins back into the bag and pulled out another bag, handing one to each of the men. 'There's another bag for each of you on the ship, and another when you get to Macedonia. Once we're there, the real pay starts. You'll form part of Andriscus' personal bodyguard, a stone's throw from Thrace. You'll be sent there to recruit others to the Macedonian army. You'll arrive home rich men.'

The Thracian looked at his companion, stared at Scipio again and slowly nodded, weighing the bag in his hand and then slipping it under his tunic. 'We've been looking for a way out for months.'

'Wait for us here. When we've delivered our message, we'll go down to the harbour together. There will be others.'

The man jerked his head at the entranceway. 'You still want to go in there?'

'The kybernetes knows a Roman who's willing to pay for intelligence. If I can say that I've seen these Carthaginians with my own eyes, he'll believe it. The Roman pays well, and there will be a cut in it for you.'

'All right. Try not to be spotted.'

Scipio nodded at Fabius, and they both went in. The entrance-way led through a narrow passage towards a wider opening behind some columns. Fabius spoke quietly to Scipio. 'That was a risk. What do you intend to do with these men?'

Scipio replied quickly, his voice low. 'Polybius said that if at all possible, we should coerce one or two soldiers to provide eyewitness descriptions in an attempt to persuade the Senate. They wouldn't believe Carthaginians, doubting their sincerity, but they might believe mercenaries who have no vested loyalty to the place. Once we're on the ship and I tell them who I really am and that I will guarantee their safety and reward, they'll still agree to go along with us, I'm sure of it. They'd have no choice – to return to Carthage after deserting would be to face certain execution. But before that they'll also be useful when we march down to the harbour together, making us into a more credible unit. The Thracian can claim to the customs police that we are on a mission from Hasdrubal himself to inspect the newly arrived ships, and in the darkness with our cheekpieces down we might go unrecognized even if the alarm has been raised. By the time they know that the Thracians are also on the run, the ship should have slipped away.'

'Do you think they have the intelligence we need?'

'Already this man has given us valuable hints about the morale of the mercenary force and how it's likely to be depleted by desertion by the time a Roman army arrives. I believe there may be enough of them to defend the harbour area, putting up a stout resistance, but once we break through the harbour defences the way will be clear through the city until we reach this point, where the final defenders will be Carthaginians prepared to die for their city.'

Fabius pointed ahead. 'Here we are.' They stared into a wide space about the size of a stadium, reminiscent of the training arena in the gladiator school in Rome. Ahead of them was a unit of soldiers in drill formation, about the size of a century, stomping forward and sideways and hollering in unison, slapping their sword blades against their shields. Their armour and weapons were burnished like silver, dazzling even in the fading light. They were equipped like nothing Fabius had seen before, with muscled cuirasses and Corinthian-style helmets, the nose guards and cheekpieces extending below their chins. They looked like a vision from the past, like Greek hoplites, soldiers Fabius had only ever seen before in carvings and paintings.

At a barked command the soldiers turned and faced them directly; Scipio and Fabius quickly pulled back behind the columns before peering out again, cautiously. Their shields were white all over, except for a painted red crescent moon over a truncated triangle on the boss. Fabius recognized it from the entrance to the Tophet sanctuary they had passed on the way up, the symbol of the goddess Tanit. He remembered what the mercenary had said, that these were men who had been given a second lease of life, who had escaped sacrifice at birth only to spend their lives training for another kind of sacrifice, a debt owed to the goddess whose symbol they wore so defiantly on their shields.

'Jupiter above,' Scipio whispered. 'It's the *hieros lockos*, the Sacred Band.'

The soldiers stomped again, turned and marched towards a cluster of men below the walls fronting the Byrsa that Fabius could see included white-robed priests as well as officers in armour. He turned to Scipio. 'But I thought the Sacred Band was ancient history.'

'They were destroyed almost two hundred years ago at the Battle of the Krimissus in Sicily against Timoleon of Syracuse, and then again by Agathocles a generation later outside Carthage,' Scipio replied. 'They were the elite of the Carthaginian citizen army, but since then Carthage has relied on mercenaries.'

'Yet from what the Thracian tells us, the mercenaries will no longer defend Carthage.'

'So the Carthaginians have reformed the Sacred Band,' Scipio said grimly. 'For all these years while Rome has turned a blind eye, Carthage has not only rebuilt her naval might but also her most feared infantry force.'

'If they fought to the death twice, that will be part of their sacred history and they will be prepared to do so again.'

'They are training for war in these streets, in the narrowing alley leading to the Byrsa and the old houses of the Punic quarter. When an assault force reaches this place, they will know that they stand no chance of survival, that war is about selling victory at the highest possible price. These men are being trained to throw themselves into death. They are suicide warriors.'

'Yet if an assault does not come soon and Carthage regains her strength, such a force could swiftly be turned into an offensive unit, a spearhead force or a special guard for Hasdrubal.'

There was a sharp blast from a pair of trumpets and they turned to look at the entrance in the wall where the priests and officers had been standing. The trumpeters moved aside and a figure walked through, followed by several others. The first figure was a huge man, broad shouldered and muscular, wearing a lionskin with the gaping head draped over his own, his beard square-cut and braided. Fabius stared, and reeled. Only one man in Carthage wore a lionskin cloak. *It was Hasdrubal.* He seemed a physical embodiment of everything that made Carthage a place to fear: the hardiness of a Phoenician and the strength of a Numidian. It was extraordinary to think that he was within a stone's throw of Scipio, heir of the Roman who had brought Carthage to her knees, the one whose destiny since childhood had been to stand before these very walls and confront the successor to the great Hannibal.

Hasdrubal came down the steps and stood with his feet planted firmly apart, staring at the ranks of warriors facing him. From another entrance to the south a throng of slaves pulled a bullock towards him, its legs kicking and eyes red with fear. A priest handed Hasdrubal a sword, a huge, curved shape that Fabius had never seen before, and he turned towards the bull. The slaves dragged it to a halt, several of them hanging on each leg and another two at the neck. Two priests pushed a wide metal bowl beneath it and stood back as Hasdrubal himself came forward, standing in front of it. He suddenly lunged at the bull and held its neck with one arm in a lock, twisted it up and pulling it off balance. With his other hand he thrust the sword through the bull's neck from the bottom up, ripping the blade outwards so that its head was nearly severed. The bull emitted a terrible hollow belch as a gush of bile came up from its stomach, and fountains of blood poured into the bowl. After a few seconds the flow of blood abated and Hasdrubal let the carcass fall heavily into the dust, and the priests pulled away the bowl, now brimming. One of them scooped a drinking horn into it and held it high in the direction of Bou Kornine, the twin-peaked mountain just visible in the distance above the rooftops to the east.

One by one, the soldiers came up and drank deeply from the horn, letting the blood flow freely down their faces and breast-plates, the priest replenishing it frequently. As they walked away, each warrior took off his helmet, and Fabius could see that the Thracian had been right. These were mere boys, sixteen or seventeen years old, some of them barely able to grow a beard. Fabius felt a sudden frisson of familiarity. They looked just like the boys in the academy in Rome all those years ago, the age that he and Scipio had been when they first went off to war in Macedonia. If Rome did not attack Carthage, if the trainers of these boys were able to look beyond their suicide, then they could be groomed as the next generation of Carthaginian war leaders, just as Scipio and the others had been for Rome.

He knew what Scipio had to do. He had to harden himself against the innocence of these boys, against their enthusiasm for war and thirst for honour, qualities that Scipio himself rated more highly than anything else. Scipio had to return here before they got much older, at the head of an army that would drive up the streets of this city like a tidal wave. He had to ensure that the darkness for which these boys had been trained came to pass. He had to kill them all.

Fabius peered towards the men who had come out of the entrance with Hasdrubal. Two were priests, and two others were evidently Carthaginian officials, dressed not in armour but in purple-rimmed robes. It was the fifth man who caught his eye, a stocky, muscular man with short grey hair wearing a Greek *chiton*, clothing that seemed incongruous with his physique.

Fabius stared. And then he realized why the clothing seemed odd. It was because the last time he had seen this man he was dressed in armour, not the armour of a Carthaginian or a Greek but the chain mail and helmet of a Roman legionary.

He turned to Scipio. 'On the platform, beside Hasdrubal. I've just recognized him, the one in the *chiton*. That's my old nemesis Porcus Entestius Supinus.'

Scipio stared. 'Are you sure?'

'When someone has fought with you as often as he did when we were boys, you get to know every contour of their face.'

'But Porcus is Metellus' servant. I mean, his soldier companion, as you are to me. And Metellus is in Macedonia.'

'He's also Metellus' version of Polybius. He's something I could never be, a wily emissary. He must be here on some business for Metellus.'

Scipio looked down, thinking hard. 'Of course. That *lembos* by the wharf – just the vessel to bring him here at high speed from Macedonia.'

'Carefully hidden away in the war harbour, with signs of a Roman crew.'

'A mission that the Senate could never have sanctioned,' Scipio said.

'Even though some of its most powerful members might have done so in secret.'

'What do you mean?' Scipio asked.

'Remember what the kybernetes told us. About the involvement of Roman senators in those Carthaginian trading enterprises.'

'You think Metellus could be one of them?'

'I'm just a simple legionary, Scipio. I can't get my head around trade deals, but I have learned a bit about military strategy. I think it's even worse than the kybernetes suggested. To my eyes, seeing a secret embassy here from Metellus smacks of a military alliance in the making.'

Scipio's eyes narrowed. 'An alliance between the Roman governor of Macedonia and Hasdrubal of Carthage.'

'Maybe not just the governor of Macedonia. Maybe he intends to be more than that. We know that Metellus has been a secret supporter of Andriscus, but perhaps it's not Andriscus who had pretentions to the Macedonian throne. It has always seemed only a matter of time before Andriscus ceases to be useful and Metellus finds some excuse to destroy him. Do you remember how fascinated Metellus always was by Alexander the Great? When I used to listen to you in the academy war-gaming past battles, Metellus always brought his name up, in tones of reverence. He said the main thing that the academy had taught him was how if he were Alexander he would have solidified his gains and not overstretched himself.'

'A new Alexander,' Scipio breathed. 'Rome's main enemy has not been Carthage after all. It's been herself, a dark force unleashed because Rome has not been able to provide men like Metellus with satisfaction in their careers, men who would not just be kings, but emperors.'

Fabius was silent for a moment. *Men like you too, Scipio Aemilianus.* He peered at the soldiers. 'They could see us if we move now. But as soon as the last warrior passes, we should go. We need to get to the harbour and then to Polybius. We have no time to lose.'

They watched the final line of men drink their libations. Fabius' mind raced. Their mission to Carthage had uncovered far more than they could have imagined. Carthage was not only rearming, but was on the cusp of becoming the richest state ever known. Worse still, she was conducting negotiations with a Roman whom most in the Senate would believe was one of their most loyal generals, yet who might be on the verge of setting himself up as the successor of Alexander the Great, ruler of a new Rome in the east.

Rome had allowed herself to become complacent. Only one man stood in the way of this new world order, and that was Scipio Aemilianus. Yet Scipio's own future, his ability to lead an army to destroy Carthage and swing the pendulum back towards Rome, hung in the balance. And few in Rome knew as well as Fabius how precarious Scipio's own loyalty was, and what he might do if one day he were to stand on the burning ruins of the temple that towered above them now.

The last Carthaginian walked past them, wiping his mouth and flicking droplets of blood on the ground. Fabius stared Scipio in the eye, and then nodded at him.

His mind flashed back to the men they had killed beside the harbour. They were only two, but they would be the first of many. Scipio would return to this city.

They turned down the alley where the two Thracians were waiting for them, and began to run.

17

Near the Numidian border, five months later

Fabius reined in his horse and came to a halt, watching the solitary rider with the crested helmet framed against the early morning light on the escarpment ahead. In the months since their covert mission to Carthage and return to the Roman head-quarters encampment, he and Scipio had devoted themselves relentlessly to Gulussa's cause, helping to muster and train Numidian cavalry in the plains and semi-desert scrubland far to the south of Carthage. Fabius had relished proper soldiering again, but this morning he was tired and hungry, caked in dust from their ride through the night; he knew that as soon as he lay down with the others in the wadi below he would go out like a snuffed candle, and sleep for hours.

Gulussa reckoned that they still had five days' hard ride ahead before they reached the dried-up marshland below Carthage, their final stretch after weeks spent trawling the outer limits of his father's kingdom for men to join the cavalry force that he and Hippolyta were readying to counter further Carthaginian incursions into the territory of Numidia. They were all here now, over a thousand men with their horses, teeming in the wadi below, their breakfast fires dotting the edge of the shallow stream where they had watered the animals and would sleep through the heat of the day. Coming to the wadi had been a diversion of a few hours to the west of their main route, but Scipio had planned at the outset to visit this place; Fabius himself had been given strict instructions by Polybius to write down everything he saw. Polybius had yearned to come himself, but his return to Rome to report to Cato on their reconnaissance into Carthage had kept him there for months longer than expected, lobbying hard in place of the increasingly ailing Cato, now well over ninety years old. Despite their overwhelming evidence of Carthaginian war preparations, the argument had continued to be an uphill struggle against those who dismissed the importance of Africa in favour of Greece and the east, and who even argued for withdrawing support from Masinissa in his attempt to defend the integrity of his kingdom against the resurgence of Carthage. Fabius knew that Polybius had kept their most potent ammunition until last, the evidence for the complicity of Roman senators at the highest level with Carthaginian plans, fearing that a premature attempt to expose the culprits would be disbelieved and count against them unless they had a majority of the Senate already in their camp. But they also knew that time was running short, that this waiting game could not go on much longer while Carthage continued to rearm. Polybius would have to play his cards soon, risking censure and proscription for himself as well as Scipio, if there was not movement in their favour very soon in the Senate.

Fabius took a swig from his water skin, and then poured water over his horse's mane, leaning back as it shook its head and neighed. Soon they would be back at the watercourse, and the horse would be able to drink its fill. He watched Gulussa ride up the ridge from the wadi to join him, still wearing his cloak against the chill of the night, and together they made their way further up the rocky ground to the figure on the escarpment. For Scipio, coming to Zama was a personal pilgrimage: it was here that his adoptive grandfather Scipio Africanus had won his greatest glory almost sixty years before, when two armies had come to this place on the edge of the unknown to decide whether Carthage or Rome would hold sway as the greatest power the world had ever seen.

They reached the crest of the escarpment and reined in beside Scipio. Ahead of them the ground dropped into a plain like a shallow bowl, bounded to the south and west by further ridges. They knew that the Roman camp had been just below them now, and the Carthaginian one a mile or so away below the opposite ridge to the west. There was little to see – just a wasteland of scrub and rocky ground, a goatherd and his few desultory animals making their way across the centre of the depression in the distance – nothing to suggest that one of the most decisive events of history had taken place here only two generations before. Over the far ridge lay the frontier of Masinissa's realm, not with another kingdom but with the African desert, a vast tract that extended from Egypt to the Atlantic shore and south into the unknown. Fabius remembered riding with Scipio and Polybius ten years before in the Macedonian forest, and Polybius sketching out Eratosthenes' map of the world; they had been close to the northern edge then, and now they were at the south. Whether they reached the other extremities, to west and to east, would depend on what happened here in Africa, on whether Scipio would be able to stand above a vanquished city and see through the haze of war to horizons far beyond the restricted world that the senators in Rome had mapped out for themselves.

Fabius spoke the word under his breath: *Zama*. It was a name the veterans had come to call this place, after a nearby Berber settlement, and it was one that Fabius had grown up hearing on the lips of drunken old men in the taverns and crumpled up begging on the streets around the Forum. It was a place that few in Rome who had not fought here could have envisaged, so far was it removed from the landscapes of Italy. At the academy Polybius had said that North Africa was the perfect terrain for set-piece battles, and Fabius could now see why. There was little human settlement to hamper large-scale army manoeuvres, or high mountain ranges or complex coastlines to hinder transport and communications. Hannibal and Scipio Africanus had chosen this battle site, a place where the terrain would afford neither side a clear tactical advantage and everything would depend on the nature and disposition of the formations: infantry, cavalry, elephants. It was the nearest equivalent he had seen in real life to a war game played out on a flat board, the type of abstract exercise that the boys had started with in the academy before moving on to dioramas representing real battles where terrain and topography were important variables.

Scipio spurred his horse and they followed him towards the centre of the battlefield. Along the way they passed the piled-up rocks and thorny branches that delimited the site of the Roman encampment, still visible after more than sixty years, and then the scorched rock strewn with blackened bone fragments that marked the place where the Carthaginian prisoners had been made to mound up and burn the dead. Further on, over the battlefield itself, Fabius looked among the scrub and dust and saw detritus that had escaped the scavengers of battle, some of it perhaps buried for years and recently uncovered by the desert wind: the rusty heads of spears, a broken Celtiberian sword, a mass of rusty mail with the mummified skin and toenails of an elephant's foot still attached. Gulussa pointed to the bleached leg-bones of a human skeleton, denuded of weapons and armour with the skull crushed, the ribs already pulled apart by the wild dogs and foxes that would undoubtedly finish the job here as they had in the past for any other human remains that emerged from the dusty terrain.

They picked their way forward until they were in the centre of the depression, and then Scipio stopped and turned his horse around so that he was facing the Carthaginian lines, just as his grandfather Africanus must have done. Fabius did the same, and then closed his eyes for a moment, hearing only the breathing of the horses and a faint westerly wind that brushed the low-lying scrub, making the horses turn their heads towards it. He remembered his father, who had fought here as a young legionary and then been one of those old veterans in the taverns, telling the same stories of battle to the few who would listen. Fabius had been one of those, and opened his eyes. His father had told how the Carthaginian war elephants had charged, eighty of them, like nothing the Romans had ever seen. Hannibal and his elephants had gone down in history, but in the years since he had led them over the Alps the Romans had learned their weaknesses, and Africanus had used a technique he had learned from ivory hunters: a herd of elephants will always go for gaps if they can see them, refusing to charge into a dense mass of men. At Zama they had been channelled into spaces that opened up in the Roman line and then been hacked down one by one as they charged into the trap, all of them dying behind the Roman lines. After that, Masinissa's cavalry and the Roman *alae* on the flanks had charged, routing the Carthaginian cavalry and chasing them off the battlefield, leaving the infantry to slog it out. Only with the return of the Roman cavalry was the day finally decided, forcing Hannibal down on a bended knee before Scipio and leaving thousands of dead and dying strewn over the battlefield.

But it was not the tactics and the course of the battle that Fabius found himself trying to envisage. It was the moments of combat that his father had described: periods of a few minutes each of unparalleled savagery, hacking and stabbing, punching and biting. The infantry at Zama had been like two equally matched beasts engaged in mortal combat, clashing and retreating, over and over again, wearing away each other's reserves but never faltering. For his father, those minutes of combat had shaped his life; he had never been able to shake them off. They were memories that had kept him awake and sweating at night, that he had only been able to control with the drink and violence that had destroyed his life and made his family fear him. Fabius had hated him for it, had derided him and walked away when the same old slurred stories were repeated to him, but years after his father's death, when he himself was a soldier, he had bitterly regretted it – after Pydna, when he had experienced the maelstrom and horror of battle and had begun to understand what his father had gone through.

Fabius had learned at Pydna that only those who have experienced battle can ever truly understand what it is like. But here at Zama, even as a combat veteran, he felt an interloper. This place belonged to those who had fought and died here, and its history was locked up with them. Polybius could write all he liked about the grander scheme of the battle, about its tactics and the lie of the land, but the truth of it lay with individual experiences that could never be told, or were only half remembered by those few still alive who had endured the shadow of that day. In the dust and rock of this place were imprinted deeds of valour and desperate last stands that would remain forever here, known only to the gods who presided over this battle just as Scipio and the others had presided over the war games in the academy in Rome.

Gulussa drew up alongside them, and Scipio turned to him. 'Your father Masinissa must have brought you here. Zama was the scene of his greatest triumph, as well as that of Scipio Africanus.'

'We came here after I returned from the academy in Rome, when you and the others were appointed tribunes for the war against Macedon. I told my father how envious I was of you going into battle, and he brought me here to try to show me what it was like. Back then, there was much more to be seen, human bones and the collapsed and desiccated carcasses of elephants that had failed to burn fully in the funeral pyres. It was a bleak scene, and I learned that even the greatest of battles can be forgotten at a whim, and leave little trace. My father told me that battles are only worthwhile if you use them to destroy an enemy, or they are doomed to be repeated. He was right: here we are again, confronting Carthage just as we were before Zama.'

'In the academy it was the other way round, Gulussa. We envied you. We knew that Masinissa was constantly at war with his neighbours, and we thought you had a glorious future in store.'

Gulussa gave him a tired smile. 'Not glorious, Scipio. That's not exactly the right word. Twenty years of raiding, of chasing down marauders and brigands in the desert, of retaliation against desert villages for housing fugitives. I've killed often enough, hundreds of times, but rarely with any glory, and it's only with Carthage now encroaching on our land that I've led my cavalry for the first time against a proper enemy, in skirmishes and chases. I've lived my life planning for it, but I've not yet been in a proper battle.'

'Your time will come, Gulussa. You will follow in your father's footsteps.'

'My father Masinissa gave me an interesting piece of advice that day. It was something he'd been trying to get to grips with through more than sixty years of experience in war, and witnessing numerous battles. He'd been schooled as a boy in Carthage with a Greek mathematician as one of his favourite teachers, and that made him think that there might even have been a formula to his observation.'

'Go on.'

'He had seen enough battles with very similar starting conditions go very differently from each other to observe that one small alteration of a variable at the outset could change the entire course of events, resulting in certain victory becoming resounding defeat. There would sometimes be no apparent logic to it, no obvious sequence of effects from that one change, but instead – at a certain point in the battle – the whole structure would seem to collapse. Because small variables are changed all the time, such as the movement of a century or a cohort in the order of battle, he had become doubtful that battles could ever be forecast at all, that beyond ensuring that your line-up was strong enough to put up a good fight, everything was in the lap of the gods. But then he began to observe a very interesting thing. The more uniform your force – the more homogeneous – the less likely a small change was to produce a catastrophic outcome. The more varied your force, the more heterogeneous, the more likely you are to be in trouble.

He said Scipio Africanus was lucky to win that day at Zama, because his force had precisely that weakness.'

Scipio leapt off his horse, smoothed down an area of ground and unsheathed his sword, using the tip to inscribe three parallel lines in the dust. He glanced at Gulussa, his face flushed with excitement. 'That fits perfectly with what I argued when we simulated Zama at the academy. This is Scipio's order of battle for each legion: *hastati* in the front rank, *principes* in the second, and *triarii* in the third, with *velites* on the flanks. Everyone who's studied that battle knows that the balance was nearly tipped against us when the *hastati* were thrown back after the initial Carthaginian attack. But the weakness that Masinissa identified was in the overall division of forces: in the line of battle, the legions were not homogeneous. Why do we persist in organizing our legions in this way, with divisions that go back to the days of individual citizen warriors, when their weapons and armour and their role in battle were based on their own personal wealth? We claim to have done away with the wealth test, now that all recruits have access to basic arms and equipment, but we still maintain these divisions in training and in battle order based on age and experience. How can it be sensible to put all of the inexperienced men in one division, the *hastati*, and put them up at the front as if they are no more than a human buffer, expendable and practically useless?'

'The centurions have been grumbling about it for years,' Fabius said. 'Like the disbandment of legions after each campaign, it's something that prevents the experience of veterans from filtering down to the new recruits. Unless you mix them up in the same units, the recruits have to learn everything the hard way by themselves and the generals have a much less effective fighting force.'

'Precisely.' Scipio kicked away the lines in the dust and slapped his sword against the palm of his hand, staring out at the battlefield. 'Rome needs a professional army. It is the only solution.'

'You would have a hard time persuading the Senate of it,' Gulussa said. 'Those with no experience of battle, and that's most of the Roman Senate these days, would look at Zama and say that the existing army organization was good enough to beat Hannibal, so why change it? And stronger, more cohesive legions would make stronger armies and produce stronger generals who might return to Rome with their eye on dictatorship, or more. That's what really frightens them.'

Scipio sheathed his sword and mounted his horse, then took up the reins. 'We'll see about that. To take Carthage is either going to require a professional army, or a general who will already be seen as a threat by those in the Senate who oppose change.'

'There's something else my father told me,' Gulussa said. 'Hannibal was an honourable man who accepted defeat. But Hasdrubal is different. In Spain you experienced the resilience of the Celtiberian chieftains, those who would die rather than dishonour themselves by surrender. Hasdrubal is more than that: he has a huge grudge against Rome, and he's obsessively defiant. That's a far more dangerous thing. There will be no honourable way out for him, no single combat as you fought with the chieftain at Intercatia. Hasdrubal will fall only when the city of Carthage falls. That is something else that the Senate in Rome must understand. The surrender of Hannibal does not provide a foretaste of what is to come if Carthage were to be besieged now. This new war, if it happens, can only end in the utter destruction of Carthage and of Hasdrubal.'

'Let's hope that Polybius has luck in his mission,' Scipio said grimly. 'But, for now, we must honour those who fell here that day, whose shades watch us from Elysium. There is one who must join them, whose wishes I must now fulfil. On his deathbed I promised that I would one day return to Zama, and that I would see that their general would rejoin his beloved legionaries for all eternity. I must ride along the lines of battle, and they must see that Scipio Africanus has returned. Leave me now.'

Fabius had seen the sealed alabaster cremation canister in Scipio's saddlebag, something he had rarely let out of his sight. As long as Rome lasted, Scipio Africanus would be honoured by his *gens* in his family *lararium* and at the tomb on the Appian Way, but his spirit would be here, alongside those he honoured the most. Fabius thought of his own father, and of the old centurion Petraeus, both men who had been here on this battlefield alongside Africanus, and both now among those shades too. Fabius swallowed hard, closed his eyes and spoke their two names under his breath, then spurred his horse and followed Gulussa, who was already part-way up the ridge. He could hear Scipio galloping away across the plain behind him, but he did not look back. In a few minutes the sun would break through the haze, and he wanted to return to the watercourse to let his horse drink and then to find a rock to sleep behind. He was dead tired, and they still had a long hard slog ahead of them before they reached the Roman camp on the plain outside Carthage.

Three weeks later they sat drinking wine in Scipio's tent at the cavalry depot that he commanded some ten miles east of Carthage, on the edge of a wide lagoon within sight of the twin-peaked mountain of Bou Kornine. Polybius had arrived back from Rome two days previously, with the news that Cato had died. He and Scipio had conferred together for hours after that, with Fabius always in attendance, running over various possible courses of action. It had become clear to Fabius that the only way forward would be for Scipio himself to return to Rome; for him to stay in Africa any longer as a mere tribune would advance neither their cause nor his career. There were now enough veterans in Rome who had served alongside Scipio in Spain and Africa to bolster his popularity among the plebs, and Cato had died with the satisfaction of bringing the tribunes of the people to their cause. If Scipio could be persuaded to return now, the pendulum might swing in their favour. One thing seemed certain: if he were to return to Africa, it would no longer be as a tribune. If there was to be war, Scipio would accept nothing less than a legion, and as a senator with support from the tribunes of the people he had the chance of an emergency election to the consulship, even though he was still officially too young. Events could now move very fast if Scipio seized the opportunity that Polybius had been presenting him to bolster their case by returning to Rome itself.

One of the legionaries at the entrance to the tent entered and spoke quietly to the centurion in charge of the guard, who turned to Polybius. 'It seems there is a man here to see you. He claims to have come by fast galley from Pella. He's a Macedonian, named Phillipus.'

At the mention of the name, Polybius jumped up and went out of the tent, followed by the legionary. A few minutes later he returned, his face solemn. 'Phillipus is one of my informants. He works on Metellus' staff as an interpreter for the Thracian mercenary commander, who knows little Latin, so he hears everything that goes on in the Roman army headquarters in Macedonia. It seems that four days ago Metellus defeated and killed Andriscus in a big battle, at Pydna.'

'At *Pydna*?' Scipio exclaimed. 'The same place where my father Aemilius Paullus celebrated his victory? The battle where I was first blooded?'

Polybius looked at Scipio grimly. 'My informant tells me that Metellus deliberately chose the battleground to try to overshadow your father's achievement. Andriscus' army was a ragtag force, and the battle was a massacre. But Metellus is presenting it as a great victory, as the final conquest of Macedonia, as if he has finished what your father left undone twenty years ago. He brags to his officers that both the Scipiones and the Aemilii Paulli make a great scene of going to war, but after winning an easy battle or two they run back home with their tails between their legs because they haven't got the guts to finish the job. He's talking about you, of course. And there's more. He's dismantled the monument at Dion, the bronze horsemen by Lysippos representing Alexander the Great's companions who died at the Battle of Graviscus. He's boasting that it will far overshadow anything your father brought to Rome. He says that, unlike the wealth that he claims your father took for his own coffers, he will give the bronzes to the people and set them up in a new temple precinct dedicated to Jupiter and Juno that he will have built on his own expense on the Field of Mars.'

Scipio stood up, his fists bunched, trying to control his rage. 'The Battle of Pydna was one of the greatest Roman feats of arms ever, a battle against the largest Macedonian phalanx ever fielded. And if Metellus is referring to my father leaving without annexing Macedonia as a province, that was because Aemilius Paullus was following the express order of the Senate. It was also his own in-stinct, proved right, that the pacification of Macedonia would take a permanent Roman garrison, one that the Senate would not allow either. He was not coming back with his tail between his legs, nor was my grandfather from Zama. They were both obeying orders from Rome. And as for the Graviscus monument, my father and I visited it after the battle to lay wreaths, to honour Alexander's companions. We would never have dreamed of desecrating their memory by removing it. Metellus has shown his true character by what he has done. He is no soldier of Rome.'

Fabius spoke quietly. 'You are right, but you need to be careful not to sound too defensive. As far as the legionaries out here are concerned, the news means that a few more amphorae of wine will be cracked open tonight, so, whatever you say, this news will be a cause for celebration. Few of the legionaries have reason to despise Metellus as we do.'

'And it's a reason for you to return to Rome,' Polybius said, addressing Scipio. 'You've done all that you can out here. You've

won the *corona civilis* and the *corona obsidionalis*. In Spain and in
Africa you've made up for all those years when there was no war
in the offing. No one doubts your courage or your leadership. But
you are still just a military tribune. You must return to Rome to
take up your seat in the Senate and make your mark. Only then
will you be given a legion or an army to command. And this news
increases the odds against you, again. Metellus will celebrate a
huge triumph and try to overshadow you. You must show yourself as a successor not only to your grandfather and your father
but also to Cato, to the cause that he made his own. And you
must remain on your guard. Metellus may believe he now has no
need to try to arrange for your disappearance as he did ten years
ago, when Andriscus was his ally and you were in the Macedonian
forest. But if he feels threatened again, if he sees you rise up in
the Senate and gain popular support, then you must beware.
Fabius, you must remain with Scipio at all times. I have already
arranged for my informant to make his fast galley available for
your passage to Rome. You will be there before Metellus returns
from Macedonia, and you should seize the chance to make your
mark. Drum those words of Cato into the people. *Carthago
delenda est. Carthage must be destroyed*. If there is going to be a final
conquest of Carthage, it is a Scipio who should be standing in
triumph on the temple platform. The people should know that,
and you are the one to tell them. Go now.'

PART SIX

CARTHAGE
146 BC

18

Fabius stood with his feet apart on the wooden platform high above the harbour, his helmet held against his left side and his right hand grasping the pommel of his sword. The old scar on his cheek was throbbing, as it always did before a battle. He took a deep breath, savouring the few moments he had here alone. The sun had not yet risen above the jagged mountain of Bou Kornine across the bay to the east, its twin peaks etched against the red glow of dawn like a giant bull's horns. To the south, the pastel blue of the sky seemed to merge with the horizon, a smudge of dull red that obscured the arid hills and low plain leading up to the coast. For days now a wind had blown in from the desert that covered everything in a fine red dust, making their eyes smart and their throats burn. Today it had abated, and he was able to take in lungfuls of air without coughing. The tang of dust was still there, a coppery taste, and it made his veins pound as if he had just drunk a draught of wine, quickening his pulse. It tasted like blood. *It tasted like war.*

It had been an extraordinary time since he and Scipio had returned from Africa to Rome, leading to Scipio's election as consul and his return to Africa as a general a little over a year previously. Election to the highest office at his age had been unprecedented, but showed the urgency with which Rome had finally been persuaded to regard the threat of Carthage. Almost fifty years of lobbying by Cato had paid off, aided in his final years by Polybius and then by Scipio. After returning to Rome, Scipio had finally thrown himself into the political fray, having seen that the death of Cato might make his own efforts critical in swinging opinion in favour of war. To Scipio's huge satisfaction, it had not been the power of his *gens* and his political manoeuvring that had won the day, but rather his military reputation; and that had been the reputation not of a patrician who had risen swiftly to high command, of a man such as Metellus, but instead of a soldier who had gained it by hard slog as a tribune in Spain and Africa, an officer who led from the front and whom many veterans in Rome had fought alongside and could vouch for personally.

Those in the Senate whom Scipio despised, those who represented the social order that had caused him such personal anguish, had not been instrumental in his success. It was his standing as a soldier's soldier among the legionaries and the veterans and their families that had forced the Senate behind him, even including his enemies, who had feared that not supporting him might lead to a popular uprising and the installation of Scipio as dictator. They included the senators whom Scipio and Polybius knew were traitors to Rome, who had conducted secret negotiations with Carthage to line their own pockets and who looked to the rise of Metellus in Macedonia and Greece as the driving power of a new Rome in the east. In the event, Scipio and Polybius had not needed to expose these men to get Rome behind their cause, but it was a trump card, should there be any hint of the Senate withdrawing support. For now, he was secure in his power base; his regard for his legionaries had paid off in the support that the plebs had given him, and he in turn would provide those men with the glorious victory and future that would more than repay their trust in him.

Fabius looked back over the vast expanse of the Roman fleet anchored behind him, and the encampment of the legions in the plain to the south. There had been another reason for the emergency election of Scipio to the consulship. War with Carthage had been openly declared more than two years before, ending the period of shady conflict in which Rome had officially only been providing training and advisers for her ally Masinissa in his attempt to counter Carthaginian incursions into Numidian territory. With the arrival of the legions, the Carthaginian stronghold at Utica had been taken, Carthage had been forced to relinquish all territorial gains and there had even been a Roman break-through into the northern suburbs of the city itself, albeit quickly repulsed. But the campaign had not gone as hoped. Carthage had become a city besieged, but the war had quickly become a stale-mate. There had been a danger of Roman resolve plummeting, the support of the people fading and the next elections producing consuls who were appeasers rather than warmongers. That further lobbying by Polybius had made the election go the other way had put the onus on Scipio to bring the siege to a head, a task that he had taken on with huge relish. In six months of extraor-dinary activity he had brought the full might of Rome to bear, mustering the largest assault force ever seen. It was now no more than a matter of days, possibly less then twenty-four hours, before the final signal would be given. No army had ever been better prepared to end a siege, one that could change the course of history.

Fabius glanced at the plume on his helmet. Scipio had been true to his word, given five years ago when he had promoted Fabius to centurion after the siege at Intercatia; on being made consul he had promoted Fabius to *primipilus*, chief centurion, not of a particular legion but on his headquarters staff, meaning that Fabius was the senior centurion of the entire army under Scipio's command. It was a huge responsibility, giving him de facto authority even over the junior tribunes, as the man the legionaries looked up to as much as they did to Scipio. Fabius had remem-bered the old centurion Petraeus on his promotion; he had returned to the farm in the Alban Hills to collect the ashes that had been buried in a jar by Brutus after the terrible night when Petraeus had been murdered, and he had taken them to the tomb of Scipio Africanus in Liternum as he had promised Petraeus that he would do, fulfilling Africanus' own request. Part of him was still in awe of the grizzled old centurions that he saw among the legions before Carthage, and he had to remind himself that he too was now over forty and would have looked just as gnarled to the young legionaries here today. He was one of the dwindling cadre still in the army who had served under Aemilius Paullus at Pydna, the last great set-piece battle fought by a Roman army, but his memories were shared in the mess tents only with other centurions, not with the new recruits. His job as senior *primipilus* was to maintain discipline in the army, and he could no longer commingle with the men and tell stories of past wars by the campfire; that would be for their fathers and uncles in the taverns of Rome, veterans who would tell of Pydna just as their fathers had of Zama, and as those here today who survived would of the final siege in a conflict that had soaked up Roman blood and treasure for over a century now.

He remembered going with Scipio to the cave of the Sibyl on the eve of their departure for war in Macedonia more than twenty years before, when they had been little more than boys. There had been a smell there too, a reek of sulphur rising from the underworld, and the fragrance of leaves she threw on the hearth that made his head reel. He was meant to have stayed outside while Scipio entered, but had secretly run into the cave for a few moments after the others had left. She had touched him, a wizened finger extending from the darkness, and had spoken in riddles that he knew pointed to his destiny, to the destiny of Scipio and Rome, though he still did not know what they meant. All he knew today was that they were near the endgame in a war that had ravaged Rome for generations and bled out the best of her manhood on fields of battle across half the civilized world.

He remembered standing in front of a map of the Mediterranean in the academy in Rome a few days before that visit, while the old centurion Petraeus traced out Hannibal's march over the Alps more than fifty years before, showing where they had fought in Gaul, in Italy, in North Africa, but his pointer always coming back to unfinished business: to the city of Carthage itself. Fabius stared out over the city now, a mass of flat-topped buildings and narrow streets leading up to the great temple on the Byrsa hill, the place where Queen Dido of Tyre had staked her claim almost seven hundred years before, centuries that had seen Carthage rise from a Phoenician trading post to the most powerful city in the west, with colonies in Sicily and Sardinia and Spain and ambitions that had nearly eclipsed Rome itself.

The tower he was standing on had been constructed by Ennius and his engineers on the admiral's island in the centre of the circular harbour, where the Carthaginian fleet had once been housed in shipsheds radiating from the shore. The harbour had been taken after savage fighting a few days earlier, leaving the foreshore drenched with blood and heaped with Carthaginian dead, their bodies still smouldering on the funeral pyres outside. It was only a toehold into the city, but it meant that Carthaginian naval might was smashed for all time. Scipio had ordered his legionaries to go no further, but instead to consolidate their position so that they could exploit the weakness now exposed in the Carthaginian defences behind the harbour, to make sure that when he gave the order the largest amphibious and land assault in history would sweep through the city like a tidal wave.

The enemy killed in the harbour had been soldiers, mostly mercenaries; ahead lay thousands of civilians, men, women and children, terrified and cowering in their homes, counting down their final hours. The night before, on their ship offshore, Polybius had read them passages from Homer's *The Fall of Troy* and the playwright Euripides' *The Trojan Women*, wanting them to remember the cost of war. Looking across from the ship towards Carthage, the moonlight sparkling off the waves as they lapped the shore, they had listened to the story of Astyanax, the brave son of Hector, Prince of Troy, a little boy who had been hurled off the walls of Troy by the victorious Greeks a thousand years ago, his mother weeping as she was led into slavery. For a while Fabius had let the play affect him, and had thought of his own wife Eudoxia in Rome, of their young son. But now, in the cold light of dawn, compassion seemed a weakness. Now, death, all death, whether to soldier or civilian, was just a calculation of war.

The day before, they had looked across at the walls and seen the Carthaginian general Hasdrubal: a great bear of a man, sun-bronzed with a braided beard, his armour draped in a lionskin with jaws that opened over his head. His people may have wanted to surrender, looking in despair at the massed Roman fleet and the legions, but history weighed heavily on Hasdrubal, leader of a city that had lived on borrowed time and might never rise again. Hasdrubal had ordered his soldiers to burn the crops and hack down the olive trees, denying them to the Romans but also taking away the last food source for his own people – a suicidal gesture of defiance. He had executed Roman prisoners in full view of the legions, ensuring that he would be shown no mercy. He was up against a war machine more powerful than any in history, and he was egging them on, taunting them. For Hasdrubal, there was only one way out, and taking as many of his people with him as possible seemed to be his own calculation of war.

Fabius looked back up, and for a few moments, staring at the horizon, it was as if he were suspended in mid-air above the scene; he felt as if he had risen to join the gods and move the affairs of men around like gaming pieces, like the dioramas of battles Scipio and the others had practised on years before in the academy. Then he heard the clatter of Scipio and Polybius climbing the ladder to join him, and he snapped back to reality. They were no gods, but Scipio was consul and general of the largest Roman army ever assembled, and this tower had been built to allow him an eagle's eye view of the battlefield, to prepare the most devastating assault on a city ever seen in history.

'Ave, Fabius Petronius Secundus, *primipilus.*' Polybius had come up first, and cracked a smile. He had changed little in appearance over the years, except for grey streaks in his beard and lines around his eyes, and seeing him in his decorated breastplate and Corinthian helmet took Fabius back to the last time he had seen Polybius in armour, more than twenty years before on the field of Pydna when he had charged single-handedly against the might of the Macedonian phalanx.

Fabius saluted. '*Ave*, Polybius. Any word from Ennius yet?'

'His men are clearing the last mound of rubble from beside the walls. We will be joining him shortly to see the preparations first hand.'

Scipio came up the ladder, wearing the breastplate he had inherited from his grandfather, newly polished but with the dents and scars of war deliberately left unrepaired. 'He'd better hurry up,' he said testily, coming up beside them. 'I intend to order the attack today.'

'He knows it. He will be ready.'

Fabius turned to his general. '*Ave*, Scipio Aemilianus Africanus.'

Scipio put a hand on his shoulder. '*Ave*, Fabius, my old friend. We are close to battle again. Are you ready for the assault?'

'I have been ready for this all my life.'

Fabius glanced at Scipio and Polybius. The two men were very different, one more a man of action and the other by inclination a scholar, but they had been close friends since they had first met when Polybius had been appointed Scipio's teacher in Rome. Polybius sometimes forgot who was general and who was adviser, but he had an encyclopedic knowledge of military history and gave good counsel, even if Scipio sometimes did not heed it. On this of all days, Fabius had deliberately addressed Scipio by his full name: as Africanus, the *cognomen* he had inherited from his adoptive grandfather, the great Scipio Africanus who had confronted Hannibal more than fifty years before, yet whose intention to crush Carthage had been thwarted by the weakness of the Senate in Rome, by men who wanted to appease rather than destroy. They had learned their lesson over the next fifty years, had seen Carthage rise again, had seen her war leaders become defiant, and now Scipio stood before the city walls as his grandfather had done, ready to finish the job.

In those fifty years, a new generation of Roman officers had emerged: ruthless, professional, schooled together in the art of war. They had burned and rampaged their way through Greece, where Scipio's rival Metellus was now poised to take Corinth, and under Scipio they had brought Rome back to the walls of Carthage. The best of them were here now, those who had not died in battle or were not still in Greece: Ennius, chief of the specialist cohort of *fabri* engineers; Brutus, a monster of a man with his curved scimitar, so unlike the Roman *gladius*; and in the plain to the south, the Numidian prince Gulussa and the Scythian princess Hippolyta, both brought under Rome's wing at an early age and now poised to lead their cavalry in the onslaught against the city's southern wall. They were all in their fighting prime, hardened, blooded, experienced, exactly what the old centurion Petraeus who had trained them in Rome had wanted.

Scipio took his hand off the sword pommel and gestured at the scene. 'Tomorrow will be a day for your *Histories*, Polybius.'

'If you ever let me write it. I seem to have traded in my stylus for a *gladius*.'

Scipio cracked a smile. 'Your day will come. In the afterlife, perhaps.'

'We should have a good vantage point to view the battle from here.'

Scipio pointed at the red welt on his thigh, a wound that had never properly healed. 'I didn't get this from staying behind, did I? The only view I will get will be the tunnel of smoke and spattered blood as I follow Brutus into the attack. As soon as the trumpets sound, I will be at the head of my legionaries.'

'You know that's against my advice,' Polybius said. 'This army can fight on without a Brutus, but not without a Scipio. And if you follow Brutus, expecting to kill, you'll be disappointed. The last time I followed him into battle was at Pydna, when he was perfecting the cross-cut with his sword: one cut from the groin to the head, and then, in the same sweep, while the two halves are still standing, another cut across the midriff. One man becomes four pieces. There won't be any left in your path alive.'

'I will ask him as a favour to leave me a few. In one piece.'

Scipio put his hand back on his sword pommel and stared out. He had acquired the scar on his leg more than twenty years ago against the Macedonian phalanx, as a junior tribune who always led his men from the front. Fabius well remembered how the old centurion Petraeus had won his greatest honour, the *corona obsidionalis*, by killing his tribune when he had faltered and by leading his maniple into battle himself, winning the day. He had never let the boys at the school forget it. They may be destined for high rank, to command maniples, legions, armies, but they would always be under the watchful eye of their own centurions, never able to slip up. That was how the Roman army operated. The centurion had taught them well.

A bellowing noise came up from the harbour, and the sound of cursing. They looked down to where a wide-bellied merchant ship had been offloading war supplies onto the wharf. A gang of legionaries with their armour stripped off had been hauling a beast up from the hold, a hoary old elephant covered in welts and scars, its bloodshot eyes flashing up at them each time it swung its head. The optio in charge of the work party yelled and the two lines of men hauled on the ropes again, but the beast refused to budge, and with an angry swoosh of its trunk knocked two men sideways into the water. Then a large Numidian slave in the hold, the elephant-master, cracked a whip against its backside and the beast finally moved, bellowing and hobbling across the planks until it stood tottering on the wharfside, scanning the legionaries balefully as they kept their distance.

Polybius stared. 'Zeus above. I recognize that backside. That's old Hannibal, isn't it? I last saw him at the triumph of your father Aemilius Paullus.'

Scipio nodded. 'Our friend from the academy in Rome. The last surviving prisoner of the war against his namesake.'

Polybius narrowed his eyes. 'Was this your idea?'

'You know what they say about elephants. When they're ready to die, they go to the same graveyard. Well, this is Hannibal's home, and it is about to become a graveyard. It was an act of compassion.'

'Compassion?' Polybius scoffed. 'I don't think the old centurion taught anything about that.'

Scipio grunted. 'Well, if Hasdrubal taunts us, I can taunt him back. There could be nothing more humiliating for him than to see the last survivor of the glorious Hannibal's elephant corps hobble through the ruins of Carthage, to collapse and die on the steps of their temple.'

Polybius cast Scipio a wry look. 'That's more like it.'

'Do you remember at the academy in Rome, how Petraeus punished Ennius once by making him sleep in the dung in the elephant's stable?'

'For a week. He's never got rid of the smell.'

'The centurion has been much on my mind lately, on this of all days. I wish he could have seen us here.'

'He was a hard taskmaster, but a true Roman,' Polybius said.

'He is with my adoptive grandfather now, in Elysium.'

'He knew he could never be here. His time was another war, with your grandfather against Hannibal. And he died an honourable death.'

'Fighting an enemy from within,' Scipio muttered.

'He died for the honour of your grandfather. For the honour of Rome.'

'He will be avenged.'

Fabius stared at the elephant, suddenly remembering the scene all those years before of the old senator Cato following that swishing tail through the Forum during the triumph of Aemilius Paullus, an act of warning about Carthage that had stunned the crowd to silence; Cato had gone now to the fields of Elysium, but the legacy of his warning lived on in the irascible beast now about to lumber its final steps through a city it had last seen more than seventy years before, when Hannibal had mustered his elephant corps for their extraordinary but ill-fated campaign through Spain and over the Alps towards Rome.

Fabius guessed the thoughts that would be running through Scipio's mind. The centurion had made them into professional army officers, the first in Rome's history. Since the Celtiberian War their success in battle had led to more wars, to more conquests; they had not had to return to Rome to endure the tedious succession of civic offices that had been the lot of their fathers and grandfathers. And the men under them, the legionaries, were no longer just civilian levies recruited for one campaign and disbanded when it was over. Those here before the walls of Carthage included men Scipio had fought alongside five, even ten years before: battle-hardened, gnarled, tough. Scipio had seen to that. If the Senate in Rome would not create a professional army, Scipio would do it for them. And he knew that those who had tried to bring Scipio's grandfather down, those who had ordered the death of the centurion, were driven not just by envy. They feared the power of the army, and the rise of a new breed of generals. Above all, they feared the name Scipio Africanus, now born again.

Fabius remembered the inscription on the elder Scipio's tomb at Liternum, more than a hundred miles south of Rome near the Bay of Naples, the tomb of a man who had been forced into exile and lived his final years in bitterness. *Ingrata patria, ne ossa quidem habebis. Ungrateful fatherland, you will not even have my bones.* Fabius watched Scipio's knuckles turn white as he gripped the railing. The centurion Petraeus was not the only one who would be avenged. And there was something else, something that Scipio never spoke of. Fabius could see the amulet on Scipio's chest, a little carved eagle on a leather thong, soaked and hardened with the sweat and blood of war. He remembered who had given it to him all those years ago, and he swallowed hard. To become who he was now, consul, general, he had been forced to sacrifice a love that would have destroyed his military career. He had sworn that he would play the game, do what was needed to rise to the top, and then throw off the shackles that had caused him such anguish. He would not go back to Rome as his grandfather had done. This day would be his vengeance; after this he would no longer be enslaved to Rome. *He would become Rome.*

19

That night, Fabius had stayed up with Scipio and Polybius on the foredeck of the ship, drinking wine and leaning back against the raking *artemon* mast that extended out over the bows. The sea was flat and shimmering in the starlight, the wind having died down during the evening, leaving only a residual swell that lapped against the side of the ship. Hardly a sound came from the fleet anchored in the darkness around them, and Carthage seemed as quiet as a tomb. Fabius remembered the same silence in the night before Pydna, of two armies sleeping before battle. The men were marshalling their strength for the day to come, but also dreaming of themselves in the arms of loved ones, embracing their children and telling them that they would always watch over them, from this world or the next, as if their souls had left the machinery of war to return to their homes for a few precious hours before the day of battle dawned.

It was a moonless night and the heavens shone brilliantly, a thousand pinpricks that reflected like an undulating carpet of light on the water. Arched high above them in vivid folds of light and colour was the Via Lacteal, the Milky Way, its centre the constellation Sagittarius, the stars outlining the shape of the centaur drawing his bow towards the eastern horizon. Scipio took a deep drink from the wine flagon and passed it to Polybius, who took a mouthful and then passed it back. 'I remember you teaching me about the Pythagoreans,' Scipio said, gesturing with the flagon at the sky. 'About how they think the universe is ruled by divine numbers, and by music. About how for them the number seven is sacred, representing the seven celestial orbits of the sun, the moon and the five planets, and the seven gates of the senses: the mouth, the nostrils, the ears, the eyes.' He passed the flagon to Fabius. 'What do you think, Fabius? What does a centurion think when he contemplates the stars?'

Fabius drank deeply, and stared up. 'I'm not a philosopher, but I can count. If each one of those pinpricks is a star or a planet, then there are many more than seven celestial orbits.'

Scipio smiled at him. 'You sound like Polybius.'

'When I was a boy in your household Polybius taught me about astronomy, as well as the world map of Eratosthenes. He said that we needed to know the shape of the world if we were to conquer it, and to know the vastness of the heavens to keep us in our place.'

Polybius looked at the sky. 'I also told you that the Stoics believe the cycle of the universe will last as long as it takes the stars to resume their original place in the heavens, and then all will be consumed by fire and fall into chaos, and it will begin again. And because everything is in a state of movement, there can be no fixed measure of distance, nor likewise of time.'

Scipio raised his arms in mock frustration. 'My dear Polybius, I sometimes forget that you are a Greek, and therefore have a weakness for sophistry. I *will* fix our measure on the walls ahead, and I will *not* have you saying that an anchored ship and those walls are in constant movement in relation to one another, as Ennius will then be unable to aim his weapons with accuracy.'

Polybius gave a look of feigned surprise. 'My point was merely that science allows us to contemplate but not to measure our allotted span, and our place in the universe.'

Scipio took another deep draught of wine, and wiped his mouth. 'In which case I must be a god, for I believe I can measure the allotted span of those in Carthage who dare to confront Scipio Aemilanus, son of Aemilius Paullus and heir of Scipio Africanus.'

'Spoken like a true general, Scipio.'

Scipio was quiet for a moment, and then squinted up at the

sky. 'Three years ago, when I was still a tribune and an assault on Carthage seemed a distant prospect, I went to sleep under the stars in our camp and had a dream. In it, my adoptive grandfather Scipio Africanus came to me, dressed in a ghostly white robe, like the shroud I remember as a child seeing on his body as it was taken to the funeral pyre. In my dream he took me by the hand and we rose high above the earth, higher than the birds and the clouds, until we were in the heavens themselves. I looked down, and I saw that the city of Rome had become a mere pinprick like the stars, and then it became nothing at all. Surrounding the Middle Sea I saw the inhabited lands of the earth, and beyond that the narrow band of Ocean, frozen at each pole and burning hot in the centre where the sun's heat is strongest. I saw the convex plane of the earth, and beyond Ocean the outer edge and the stars beyond.'

He paused, drinking again from the flagon. 'My grandfather pointed down, and showed how the inhabited parts are scattered and small, and how as you move away from the Middle Sea those inhabited places become fewer and more widespread as if separated by the spokes of a wheel, and how few who live in those areas can communicate between themselves or know of each other's existence. He turned to me, and said this: *What places can you name beyond the desert of Africa, or the Ganges in India, or the isles of Albion? Yet you see here that those places exist, and account for the larger part of the world. Who in those places will ever know your name? You see, therefore, the narrow bounds in which your fame will spread.* He pointed to where the boundaries of nations that we fight and die for were no longer visible, where all that could be seen was sea and land. *And how long, even in these inhabited parts where they know you, will they speak your name? The memory of your fame will be broken like that of all men, by devastation and fire and flood, by the ravages of time and war.*'

Scipio took a deep breath. 'I looked up, away from the earth and towards the heavens. There were stars we never see from down below, constellations and galaxies vast beyond our imagining, far surpassing the earth in magnitude. I had observed Sagittarius the night before, as clear as on this night, and when I looked to the stars I suddenly saw my father, Aemilius Paullus, riding across the heavens on a ghostly horse just like the centaur with his bow, as Aemilius Paullus is shown on the monument to the Battle of Pydna that is now in the sacred enclosure at Delphi. I yearned to join him, to ride with him, but as I stretched out my arms he only seemed to recede, galloping forever beyond my reach. I turned to Africanus, and asked him how I could ride alongside my father across the heavens. At first, he asked me a question: *Do you hope for the future of Rome, or are you contemptuous of it? Will you know shadow and decline, or will you rise above Rome as you are now risen above the world, and see your future mapped out before you?'*

'How did you reply?' Polybius asked quietly.

'I told him that I did not know, that I could only know when I stood on the ruins of Carthage. He said that triumphs are hollow if they are only built on the praise of others. To the wise, the mere consciousness of noble deeds is ample reward for virtue. Statues of victors need clamps of lead to hold them to their pedestals, or else they will topple and fall. The greatest triumphs are soon enough graced by mere withering laurels, which dry and crumble to dust, as short-lived as the memory of the people. *If you live your life for the esteem of the people, you will become disappointed, embittered in old age.'*

Scipio paused. 'I asked him again how I might reach my father. This time he answered me directly, that the way was justice and sacred observance, things of greatest value to Rome; that is the way to heaven. He said that everything people will say of me will be confined to the narrow regions they inhabit. Virtue alone can draw a man to true honour, not the opinions of others. Praise in speech is buried with those who die, and lost in oblivion to those who come afterwards.'

'Your legacy of personal honour from your grandfather is a heavy burden for you, Scipio, but a worthy one,' Polybius said solemnly. 'You were dreaming the thoughts that have guided your life. These were the virtues that first drew me to you when I was brought as a captive from Achaia and made to be your teacher.'

'In my dream, my grandfather said that there is music, a special sacred note that can open up a way to heaven,' Scipio said. 'But those who are not yet ready cannot hear it, just as they cannot look at the sun.'

'You were remembering our visit when you were a boy to the Pythagoreans,' Polybius said. 'We joined them outside Corinth, watching the sun rise and feeling its warmth, wondering if we too were feeling the divine spirit enter our bodies.'

'Africanus said that in heaven were all the things that great and excellent men desire; and so, he asked, *Of what worth is earthly glory that across space and time is so limited?* Look up to heaven, and you will no longer be restricted by having your thoughts of well-being based on that which men alone can bestow. From up here, you move about like a god, for that is what the gods are, the souls of those of us who have risen above the world as you are now, who can contemplate men and their battles as the gods did over the plain of Troy, divining the fates of Hector and Achilles and Priam as if they were pieces on a gaming board.'

'And did he say how you were to conduct yourself before you reach heaven?'

'If I keep my soul ready, aloof and contemplating my actions, I will be safe, but if I surrender to the temptations of bloodlust and power I will be no different from those who have surrendered themselves to the vices of drink and women.'

'Those like Metellus whom you despised as a boy in Rome,' Polybius said.

Scipio pointed up to the stars. 'In my dream we were up there above the orb of the earth, and then my grandfather pointed down to a place by the sea and it was as if that place rushed up to me, so fast was our descent, and I saw a city as if from the clouds, dust-shrouded and on fire. He said: *Do you see that city, which I brought to heel for Rome, but which now renews its old hostility and cannot remain quiet? Soon you will return to that place, and have the chance to earn that* agnomen *that you have inherited from me, Africanus.*'

'The soothsayers would call that a prophetic dream,' Polybius murmured.

'And do you?' Scipio asked.

'You know my opinion of soothsayers. A man makes his own life, though if he believes in a prophecy it may shape his destiny.'

Scipio looked away from the stars at the shimmering city walls, his face troubled. 'He brought me back down to earth, but suddenly it was a different place: barren, scorched, shrouded in smoke, reeking of burned flesh like some wasteland of Hades. And through the smoke I saw that it was not Carthage but Rome, all in ruins: the Capitoline Temple, my house on the Palatine, the great walls of Servius Tullus – every building crumbled and blackened. And when I turned to find him, Scipio Africanus was no longer standing beside me but was lying contorted on the ground, grey and naked, fearfully gashed, his mouth open in a grimace and his arms extended towards the smouldering ruins of the city.'

Fabius remembered their last image of the old centurion, mutilated in the dust all those years ago in the Alban Hills, and wondered whether Scipio had melded that memory with the vision of Africanus, both of them men who had reached for glory but had been brought low by the machinations of Rome: the one bowing before those who wished to restrain him from destroying Carthage and living the remainder of his life in shadow and disappointment, the other hacked down ingloriously for training a new generation to take up where Africanus had left off, to add conquest to conquest and go where Africanus had not been allowed to go by the Senate, and by a sense of duty to authority in Rome that he would later come to regret.

Polybius looked penetratingly at Scipio, and then put his hand on his arm. 'You have much on your mind, my friend: a burden that has played in your dreams for years now. It will be lifted tomorrow.'

Scipio continued to stare at the walls of Carthage, his eyes dark and unfathomable. 'You taught me that the Pythagoreans believe in the power of music, just as Africanus told me in my dream, that a single note might purify the soul and prepare it for Elysium. I used to think I heard it, at night alone in the forest, or encamped by the sea when the water was dead calm. But now, when I try to listen for it, all I hear is discordance, clamour, distant howls like the wolves in the Macedonian forest, shrieks and yells, a terrible groaning. Sometimes I can only sleep with other noises around me to drown it out: the crackling of a campfire in the desert, the creaking of a ship's timbers and the slapping of the waves when I am at sea.'

Polybius leaned back. 'Just as we cannot look at the sun, so we cannot truly hear the divine note that would allow us to ascend to the heavens; it is a note that we can only hear when our souls are ready for Elysium. But the sounds that haunt you are the sounds of war, my friend, of war and death in your past, and war that is your future.'

'Then that is my music,' Scipio said quietly. 'When I woke from that dream, night was over, and when I looked towards the sun in the east its rays seemed to encircle the earth, cutting it off from the heavens; when I gazed up I could no longer see the stars, and instead saw only storm clouds rolling in from the south. Tomorrow when we awaken, they will be the clouds of war.' He picked up the flagon, tipped it up so that the last dregs spilled out, and then tossed it into the sea. 'We need clear heads for tomorrow. Dawn is only a few hours away, and before then Ennius and his *fabri* will be cranking up the catapults in readiness for the assault. We should try to sleep now.'

20

Shortly after dawn, Fabius stood with Scipio and Polybius on the quay beside the rectangular harbour. Around them lay all the panoply of war, piles of supplies brought in by ship over the last two days: stacks of amphorae filled with wine and olive oil and fish sauce, crates of iron-tipped ballista bolts, bundles of new *pila* spears and fresh swords. The stores were stacked where there was space among the rubble and collapsed warehouses that still smouldered from the fighting three days before. They picked their way over to a group of legionaries stripped to the waist working on a large pile of masonry that blocked an entrance into the main street of the city. Ennius detached himself from the group and came over to them, his stubble and forearms white with dust from the fallen masonry and his forehead glistening with sweat. Fabius could see the forged war hammer hanging from the left side of his belt, a gift from Scipio on his promotion to command the specialized cohort of *fabri*, the engineers, and on the other side the vicious *makhaira* sword with its curved cutting edge that showed his lineage from the Etruscan warriors of Tarquinia to the north of Rome. He stood before Scipio, and raised his right fist in salute over his chest. '*Ave*, Scipio Aemilianus Africanus.'

Scipio put a hand on his shoulder. '*Ave*, Ennius. You look as if you could do with a week in the baths of Dionysius at Neapolis.'

'When this job is done, Scipio.'

'How go the preparations?'

Ennius swept one hand back in the direction of the harbour and the massive wall dividing it from the open sea. Through gaps smashed in the masonry by Roman ballista balls six months previously they could see the prows and curved stems of war galleys

264

hove-to just offshore, their oars angled forward ready to launch the ships into the quay and disgorge waves of legionaries to scale the walls. Fabius knew there were hundreds of ships now, quinquiremes, triremes, ram-tipped Ligurian galleys, all anchored in rows before the sea wall ready for the final assault. Ennius turned back to Scipio. 'Twenty-five specially built barges with catapults lie two *stades* offshore, beyond the range of the Carthaginian archers,' he said. 'They are anchored at all four quarters, and the quinquiremes to seaward are positioned broadside on to the waves, making a breakwater to keep the barges as stable as possible. As we speak, my men are mixing the final ingredient of the Greek fire. At your command, the catapults will rain fireballs on the city and wreak destruction as you have never seen it before in a siege.'

'And you are able to keep the barrage falling ahead of our advancing legionaries?'

'We have forward observers concealed at the highest points on the sea walls, sharp-eyed Alpine Celts who can spot a deer in the mountains at a hundred *stades*. They will use coded flag signals to direct the ballista crews to adjust their aim. We have Polybius to thank for that, the code that he has given us.'

Scipio looked sceptical. 'Do your men truly know this code?'

'It's brilliant. You've got to hand it to those Greeks. All twenty-four letters of the Greek alphabet are arranged in a square, numbered from one to five vertically and the same horizontally, with one letter fewer in the last division. The signaller raises his left hand to indicate the vertical column, his right hand for the horizontal. He raises a torch in each hand the correct number of times to signify a letter. We've practised it in the desert for weeks now. We even have a short-hand to indicate directional changes to the ballista crews.'

'All right.' Scipio looked from Ennius to the tall Greek beside him, cracking a smile. 'Good to know you've been keeping Polybius' nose out of his books.'

'It was books that taught me the code, Scipio, as you very well know,' Polybius said. 'To be specific, an ancient hieroglyphic scroll in the possession of an old priest in the Temple of Saïs in the Nile Delta. It told how the earliest priests used this technique to signal from pyramid to pyramid.'

'Is there anything else you need to tell me?' Scipio asked Ennius, looking up at the sky and sensing the wind, and then back at the wooden observation tower on the island in the centre of the harbour. 'We have only hours before I intend to order the final assault.'

'Then there is time for a quick look at this. Polybius asked me to watch out for any inscriptions that might help with his history of Carthage. We found this bronze plaque with lettering, which had been used to strengthen a door. We're about to melt it down to make arrowheads for the Numidian auxiliaries, which is why Gulussa is here.'

Polybius took the sheet of bronze from Ennius. It was about two feet across, and the lettering on it had been smoothed by polishing. He glanced over at Gulussa, who had just joined them. 'Can you read this? I believe the script is an old version of Libyo-Phoenician.'

Gulussa knelt down beside the plaque, tracing his hands over the letters. 'Two of these plaques used to be set up outside the Temple of Ba'al Hammon on the acropolis. I saw them there when my father Masinissa allowed me to accompany a Numidian embassy to Carthage when I was a boy. They're an account by a navigator called Hanno of a Carthaginian expedition through the Pillars of Hercules and down the west coast of Africa over three hundred years ago. On the same pillar outside the temple was nailed the desiccated remains of skin, like old camel hide but covered in thick black hair, that Hanno cut from a savage he called a gorilla. The Carthaginians tried to kidnap their women but were no match for them in strength.'

'How far south did the expedition go?' Ennius asked.

Gulussa pointed at the base of the plaque, where the last line of text ended abruptly. 'It is said that the rulers of Carthage ordered the lower part removed because they were fearful of giving away Carthaginian secrets to foreigners who might read this,' he replied. 'But my father was told by a priest that Hanno circumnavigated Africa, and came back through the Erythraean Sea to Egypt.'

Ennius looked at Polybius. 'When I was in Alexandria learning about Greek fire I spoke to a ship's captain who had sailed beyond the Erythraean Sea to the east and claimed to have seen mountains of fire emerging from the sea on the horizon, at the very edge of the world.'

'If the world is a sphere, then there can be no edge,' Polybius said patiently.

Ennius stood up, his hands on his hips. 'How do you know it's a sphere?'

'If you had been attentive in Alexandria, you would have visited the school of Eratosthenes of Cyrene and learned how he had determined the circumference of the earth by observing the difference in the sun's angle from the zenith on the day of the summer solstice at Alexandria and at Syene in upper Egypt, a known distance away.' Polybius picked up a splinter of wood and used it to sketch a rough image in the dust. 'This is Eratosthenes' map of the world. You can see the Mediterranean Sea in the centre, surrounded by Europe and Africa and Asia, and the thin band of Ocean surrounding that. But the edge of the map isn't the edge of the world. It's the edge of our knowledge. What lies beyond that is open to exploration.'

'And conquest,' Ennius said.

Scipio put his sandalled foot on the line representing the coast of North Africa, and then on Greece. 'We are here, in Carthage, and Metellus is there, in Corinth,' he murmured. 'The world is divided between us.'

Gulussa pointed at the map. 'If Hanno the Carthaginian went

south along the coast of Africa, surely others have gone through the Pillars of Hercules to the north?'

'Timaeus writes of it,' Ennius said. 'And Pytheas the Greek navigator in Massalia is said to have gone to the northern tip of the Cassiterides, the Tin Islands, to a place called Ultima Thule. If the Carthaginians had found those routes, they would have kept them secret too.'

Polybius curled his lip in disdain. 'Timaeus claims to be the pre-eminent historian of the west, but he never leaves the comfort of his library in Alexandria. When I decided to write my history of the war against Hannibal, did I not speak *only* to those who had seen the war with their own eyes? And did I not trace the route of Hannibal *with my own two feet*, marching from Spain through the Alps in the path of his elephants?'

'And did you not muck out Hannibal's last elephant with your own hands, when we were young warriors in the academy at Rome?' Gulussa said with gentle mockery. He gestured at the leathery back of the beast tethered on the other side of the harbour. 'And do I not smell that very ordure here with us now?

Polybius cast him a withering glance. 'I write history that I see with my own eyes. I am neither a mythographer like Herodotus, nor a writer of fables like Timaeus. My history is not for entertainment. It is to teach us better tactics and strategy. It is to guide our course of action in the future.'

Fabius put his centurion's staff on the map above Europe, and spoke quietly. 'The Cassiterides exist; my wife's people call it Pritani, land of the painted people, and others call it Albion. She was the daughter of a Gallic chieftain who shipped wine there from Massalia, exchanging it for slaves and tin.'

Polybius eyed Fabius shrewdly, nodding, and then he turned to Scipio. 'It is not to the east that we should be looking, but to the west. And it is not tin or slaves that interest me, but strategy.' He put his pointer on the map beside Fabius' staff. 'We should be seeking a route for our transport ships to sail around Iberia and land our legions in Gaul, to sweep south over the expanse of land occupied by the Celtic tribes. We have already fought them, and know them as formidable enemies. During my travels across the Alps I learned of fearsome tribes to the north of the mountains, in the forest lands of the upper rivers. If we do not conquer these tribes, they will grow ever stronger and in years to come will sweep down on Rome itself, as the Celts of northern Italy did two centuries ago. Once we control the west and vanquish these tribes, then the world is truly open to us.'

Scipio put a hand on his friend's shoulder. 'When we have laid waste to Carthage, I will provide you with a ship to sail west through the Pillars of Hercules to find these fabled isles and a northern sea route to Gaul.'

'I should like that above all things,' Polybius said fervently.

'But now is not the time for future strategy. Now is the time for war.' Scipio looked piercingly at Ennius. 'Do you remember what I told you, when I allowed you to create this special cohort of *fabri*?'

Ennius grasped the head of the war hammer with one hand. 'You said I must be a soldier first, an engineer second. My armour lies to hand, ready to put on when the work on the wall is done. And once the ballistas have unleashed hell, I will lead my cohort of *fabri* through the breach in the wall on the north side. We will fight through the streets and destroy the enemy. We will win more crowns and wreaths and bear more battle scars than any other unit in the army. My hammer and my sword will be steeped in Carthaginian blood.'

'Good.' Scipio slapped him on the upper arm. 'Now, to the preparations for war.'

21

Just as they were turning to go, a huge commotion erupted from the entrance to the circular harbour, and to Fabius' astonishment a small galley came powering through, its oarsmen pulling furiously. Behind it he could just make out a dark opening on the far side of the harbour that had evidently housed the galley, just within the Carthaginian defensive curtain. As the galley crashed through into the rectangular harbour, followed by legionaries shouting and hurling missiles at it from shore, his astonishment doubled. It was the same *lembos* that he and Scipio had seen three years earlier, recognizable by the distinctive rake of the bow. The crew of some twenty oarsmen were bent double to avoid the missiles and he could make out half a dozen men in the stern, cowering under shields. There would be no time to chain off the entrance to the harbour; nobody had expected a hidden shipshed, let alone a fully prepared and manned warship. Fabius ran up to the quay at the harbour entrance for a better view, and managed to catch a glimpse before the *lembos* swept round the corner and into the bay, powering past the anchored warships and heading for the open sea. It had only been a few seconds, but it had been enough for him to be certain. *The crew was Roman.*

He turned and hurried back to tell Scipio. A centurion came running up from the circular harbour, followed by two legionaries, pushing a man ahead of them whose hands had been tied behind his back. The centurion saluted, caught his breath and gestured back. 'This man's a Thracian mercenary, and he's deserted to us because he says he's got information for Scipio Aemilianus.'

Fabius glanced the man over, checking that he had been disarmed. 'He can tell me.'

The centurion shook his head. 'Only the general. It's about that *lembos*.'

Scipio had overheard, and came marching towards them. 'If this man is telling the truth and has good information, I will spare him execution.'

The man stumbled forward and fell on his knees, speaking Greek. 'I know about that *lembos*. I've guarded it for weeks now. The man who's just escaped in it is a Roman, called Porcus.'

Fabius stared at Scipio, astonished. It could only be the Porcus who had been his enemy from the backstreets of Rome, the wily thug who had grown up to be Metellus' right-hand man and adviser. They had last seen Porcus in Carthage during their reconnaissance three years earlier, but had not expected him to be here again. Scipio turned to the man. 'Do you know what he was doing here?'

'That's what I have to tell you. I overheard him talking to Hasdrubal. I want to be spared.'

'If your information is good, you have my word.'

'This man Porcus is going to Metellus in Greece with a message. He is to tell Metellus that Hasdrubal will surrender, but only to Metellus. Metellus is to return by the *lembos* and accept the surrender here beside the harbours.'

Everyone seemed stunned. Scipio stared at the ground for a moment, and then nodded at the centurion, who led the Thracian off to the nearest slave galley. Petraeus turned to him. 'We have no time to spare. We have to cut him off. We have nothing as fast as that *lembos* in short bursts, but one of our *liburnae* could catch them up. The *lembos* is too small to carry a reserve complement of rowers, whereas the *liburnae* are large enough to rest some of the rowers and keep up the pace. But we must order a pursuit now. The captain of the *lembos* will be putting all of his effort into pulling away as fast as he can. Once they're out of sight, then we've lost them.'

Scipio turned to Ennius, who had joined them. 'What do we have?'

'My personal *liburna*. She's docked in the outer harbour on standby for my use so will be ready to go immediately. I use her for getting to the assault ships, and for going offshore to view the Carthaginian defences. She has a crack complement of Illyrian oarsmen, the best in the Mediterranean, and a section of thirty marines trained in ship-to-ship warfare. She's one of the vessels that we had specially designed and equipped under your instructions to counter the threat of Carthaginian privateering. She even has a ram.'

'A *ram*? On a *liburna*?'

Ennius grinned. 'My idea. A ram on a *liburna* wouldn't be much use against triremes and polyremes. But against other *liburnae* and smaller vessels such as the *lembos*, it's a potent weapon. The design of the *lembos* has sacrificed hull thickness for speed, so it would be vulnerable to ramming. When we reviewed the Roman fleet last year, we were no longer thinking of set-piece battle between triremes and polyremes, where vessels of the size of the *liburna* would have little direct role. We were thinking of a new kind of naval warfare involving swifter, smaller vessels, in response to the build-up of such vessels that you and Fabius saw when you got inside the circular harbour three years ago. If the Thracian mercenary is telling the truth, chasing down that *lembos* could make all of our preparations worthwhile.'

'I want you to go to that *liburna* now and put the crew on a war footing. They will need extra water and provisions and be ready to leave in half an hour.'

'By then the *lembos* may be out of sight.'

'What her captain doesn't know is that we know their destination. If your captain lays in a north-easterly course for the Gulf of Corinth then you should catch them. You will not join them as I need you to remain here in charge of your *fabri* and the catapults. I need an officer who can identify the man we are after and who understands the urgency of the mission, but who is unattached to a unit here and can be spared. A man I can trust to terminate this threat.'

He looked to Fabius, and Ennius and Polybius followed his gaze. Fabius stood stiffly to attention. 'I am sworn to remain by your side as your bodyguard, Scipio Aemilianus. I promised Polybius, and your father Aemilius Paullus.'

Scipio put a hand on his shoulder. 'Polybius is here now, and he absolves you. We are no longer alone against the world, as we were in the Macedonian forest. I am now surrounded by an entire army of bodyguards, the best men a general could ever have. There is no more important mission than this one I am sending you on. You know Porcus personally, and you have fought him before. You have unfinished business with him. And if this *liburna* is as good as Ennius says it is, you should be back in time to watch my back when I order the assault on Carthage.'

Fabius remained at attention, and then saluted. '*Ave atque vale*, Scipio Aemilianus. The job will be done.' He turned to Ennius. 'I will not let scum like Porcus deny me a place in the assault on Carthage. Let's move.'

An hour and a half later, Fabius stood in the bows of the *liburna* as she cut through the waves in pursuit of the *lembos*, his clothing drenched with spray and blinking hard to keep the salt from his eyes. It had been an exhilarating chase; with the galley riding the swell rather than wallowing in it, he had felt none of the discomfort that made sailing ships such an unpleasant experience for him. He stood on the starboard side, overlooking the forward sweep of the prow and the great bronze ram that sliced through the troughs a few feet ahead, rearing up and down like the school of dolphins that had accompanied them after they had left the shallow approaches to Carthage and rowed out over deeper water into the open sea.

To begin with, the *lembos* had pulled away at great speed,

nimbler on the waves than the *liburna*, but her smaller crew had quickly tired of the pace and Fabius had gained on her, to the point where she was now almost within hailing distance directly ahead. The captain of the *liburna*, a swarthy Sardinian who had pushed his rowers relentlessly, had no intention of bringing the *lembos* to heel and every intention of trying out the ram, his first opportunity to use the ship in action and see whether the iron reinforcement along the length of the keel would keep it from buckling on impact. Fabius had concurred; he too had no intention of negotiating, and would give no quarter. The men on the *lembos* were Romans, a crew doubtless from Metellus' Aegean fleet, but rather than making him hesitate it strengthened his resolve. Romans who had been secretly harboured by the Carthaginians would be shown no mercy by Scipio, and it was Fabius' duty to carry out the orders he had been given when he had left the harbour.

On the opposite side of the bow platform was the naval centurion who commanded the marines, a unit of thirty shock troops who specialized in ship-to-ship assault, trained during peacetime to counter piracy. They knelt in pairs along the central walkway that ran the length of the galley, their swords drawn, bracing themselves for impact. The rowers were heaving at the oars faster now, the inner of the two men on each oar having been replaced by a fresh rower kept in reserve to help give a final burst of speed. Fabius gripped the rail as he watched the ram break completely free from the waves, the spray bursting back as it dropped down again and cleaved the sea like an arrow. Ahead of them the *lembos* was now less than three lengths away. Her captain was panicking, pushing the helmsman aside and heaving the steering oar himself, bringing the galley to port in a desperate attempt to escape but only leaving her exposed beam-on to the *liburna*, wallowing in the trough of a wave as her oarsmen gave up in terror and jumped from their benches towards the bow and stern, joining the small cluster of marines and other men, Porcus included, who must by now have known that their time was up.

'Brace for impact!' The captain of the *liburna* bellowed at them from the stern, and the oarsmen gave a last mighty effort. Fabius drew his sword and squatted down as he had been shown to do, moving back from the railing so he would not be thrown into it. A second later there was a splintering crash as the ram sliced into the thin planks of the other galley's hull, cutting it nearly in half and driving the broken keel down as the *liburna* settled over it. He felt the galley heave forward in the swell, caught in the wreckage, and watched the expert axemen leap over the side and hack away at the keel to release it. Meanwhile, the marines had thrown out grapples and a *corvus* ladder on each side and were already among the *lembos* oarsmen, thrusting and hacking mercilessly. Fabius had spotted Porcus and jumped into the water over the wreckage, now red with blood, and sloshed his way towards a man standing alone in the stern, staring with disbelief as he recognized the one who was approaching him. The naval centurion saw Fabius' intent and ordered his men to hold back and finish off any others still alive in the wreckage. Fabius came within a few paces of the man, the water now up to his knees, and stood before him, staring with contempt. 'Porcus Entestius Supinus, by order of the consul Lucius Scipio Aemilianus Africanus, you are condemned to death as a traitor.'

'*Africanus.*' The other man smirked, waving his sword. 'Who is this man? The only Africanus I know of died a miserable pauper thirty-five years ago in Liternum, unable to hold his head high in Rome for shame at having failed to take Carthage. Like grandfather, like grandson, only worse. How can Scipio Aemilianus hope to succeed when he is but a pale shadow of a man who himself had failed? You serve the wrong general, Fabius.'

'You can die with dignity, so that I can tell your family that you behaved as a Roman at the end, or you can die a traitor, servant to a man who is no longer a Roman.'

'Metellus is three times the general that Scipio is. Days from now he will stand in Acrocorinth, and Greece will be his for the taking. Once he knows that Carthage has surrendered to him, he will have eclipsed Scipio and be master of the world. A new empire will arise, and a new Rome.'

'You forget that your message from Hasdrubal will never reach him.'

'You forget that there are other ways. Runners were dispatched in the night to make their way through the Numidian lines and reach the port of Kerouane, where another *lembos* awaits to take the message to Metellus. You see, you have failed.'

'It is irrelevant,' Fabius said dismissively. 'Even before your runners reach the coast, the assault on Carthage will have begun. Once Hasdrubal is destroyed, Scipio will stand atop Carthage. Metellus can receive offers of surrender from whoever he likes, if he wishes to be the laughing stock of Rome.'

Porcus faltered, and then sneered at him. 'You always did choose the wrong gang, Fabius, don't you remember? You were always getting beaten up, and then you met Scipio and he protected you. Before we knew it, you were licking his boots. At least we didn't have to hear more stories about your miserable father's military glory. The only heroic exploit I ever saw him undertake was when he managed to stay upright long enough to get into the tavern, day in and day out. We gave him a few knocks about the head when he was lying in the gutter, I can tell you, to help him along to his miserable little corner of Hades.'

Fabius lunged forward, flicking Porcus' sword away into the sea, and then came within inches of his face, snarling at him. 'You never were much of a swordsman, were you, Porcus? You should have fought at Pydna and in Spain and in Africa, instead of toadying up to Metellus. And you won't see my father when you reach Hades, because he is in Elysium with his comrades.' He thrust his sword deep into Porcus' abdomen, twisted it and withdrew it, and then slashed it across his throat, standing back while Porcus staggered forward with his mouth and eyes wide open, his hands pressing against the blood that pulsed from his neck, and then toppled face-first into the sea. Fabius lifted one foot and pushed the body away, watching it slowly sink, and then picked up the dispatch tube that Porcus had been carrying and pulled out the scroll inside, tearing it up and throwing the shreds after the body.

He turned and looked at the *liburna*, which had broken free of the wreckage and was now hove-to alongside, a rope net hanging over the side to allow the last of the marines to climb back on board. The *lembos* was a mass of wreckage and bodies, with none of the crew left alive. The naval centurion was standing a few paces away from Fabius, up to his waist in the water, gesturing for him to come. 'The job is finished, *primipilus*. The captain wants to return before the wind picks up. And I don't know about you, but none of my boys wants to miss the assault.'

22

Two hours later, Fabius was back on the wharfside with Scipio and Polybius. He felt drained, but exhilarated. Had Porcus reached Corinth and the message fire been lit on Bou Kornine, it would have been Metellus on Acrocorinth and not Scipio who would have been celebrating the defeat of Carthage. Fabius had focused solely on the task in hand and was barely conscious of his own role, but he knew that by pursuing and destroying the *lembos*, he had changed history. At the moment all that was important was the added urgency it put on the countdown to the assault; he could see Scipio beginning to look impatient as he watched the preparations at sea. The catapult ships had assembled in a line off the sea wall, with the transport barges containing the legionaries finding their places behind in preparation for heaving forward and landing the first wave of shock troops with grapnels and ladders on the quay, ready to scale the walls. The gamble was that the defenders would be caught off-guard, not expecting a breach of the harbour defences as well as an assault on the sea walls, and that, with Carthaginian attention turned to an attack from the sea, the legionaries assembled at the harbour would be able to pour in to the breach and advance fast towards the upper city and the secondary line of defence around the Byrsa hill to the west.

A young tribune appeared on the platform, took off his helmet and stood to attention. He had startlingly blue eyes, fair hair and angular features – a face that seemed quintessentially Roman, destined to become craggy and hard and one day take its place in the *lararium* of some patrician house alongside the images of his ancestors. Scipio looked up and nodded at the tribune, who saluted. 'I bring word from Gulussa, Scipio Aemilianus. The assault force outside the land walls is now ready. The catapults are all aimed at the same length of wall, already weakened by bombardment over the last weeks, and Gulussa thinks a breach will be made immediately. As soon as you give the word, they will let fly.'

Scipio squinted at the line of catapult ships being drawn up close to the sea wall. 'Then tell him to make it so. By the time you return to him, Ennius will be ready in the ships. The assault will begin in an hour, when you hear my signallers blast the horns.'

'I will lead the first cohort myself.'

Scipio looked him up and down, and then stared into his eyes, his gaze lingering as if he saw something in the boy. 'Do you have a good centurion?'

'The best. Abius Quintus Aberis, *primipilus* of the first legion. He fought at Pydna, and in Spain.'

'Good. The centurions are the backbone of the army. Respect them, and they will respect you. But they will expect you to lead from the front. Have you seen action before?'

'I have spent my whole life preparing for this day. I have studied all of the works of Polybius. I won the sword-fighting competition held for boys in the Circus Maximus, for two years running.'

Scipio glanced at the boy's belt, where Fabius could see the thin line of shimmer along both sides of the blade where it was visible for an inch or so above the scabbard. 'You have a double-edged sword.'

The young tribune nodded enthusiastically, pulling the sword out and holding it forward, his grip strong and unwavering. 'A lot of veterans came back from Spain with Celtiberian swords, and many of us have had the smiths create Roman versions. This one was a present from my uncle.'

'Your uncle?'

'You will know him,' the young man said proudly. 'He served with distinction in Spain. Sextus Julius Caesar.'

Polybius glanced up from the plan, peering over his crystal spectacles. 'Did I hear someone mention my name a while back?' He caught sight of the boy. 'Ah. This is Julia's son. I don't think you've met him before. Gnaeus Metellus Julius Caesar.'

Fabius suddenly realized what had been familiar about the boy: he had Julia's hair and eyes. But there was something more, something that made him stare hard at the boy. Scipio clearly saw it too, and after looking at the boy in silence for a few moments he spoke to him again, his voice strangely taut. 'When were you born?'

'Four days before the Ides of March, in the year of the consulships of Marcus Claudius Marcellus and Gaius Sulpicius Gallus.'

'The year after the triumph of my father Aemilius Paullus.'

'Nine months, to be exact. My mother said that I was conceived on that very night, that it was auspicious. Every year on that day when I was a child we went to the tomb of the Aemilii Paulli on the Appian Way and made offerings.'

Fabius remembered that evening on the day of the triumph almost twenty-two years before, when Scipio had taken up Polybius' offer of his rooms and taken Julia there for an hour, just the two of them, and then later in the theatre when Metellus had come to take her away. But he also knew from Julia's slave girl Dianne that she had resisted Metellus' advances that night, and had gone straight to the Vestals to be with her mother until the marriage a month later. She would have known who the father was, and Metellus too must eventually have guessed. *Gnaeus Metellus Julius Caesar was Scipio's son.*

Scipio suddenly looked sternly at the boy. 'It is unheard of to make offerings at the tomb of another *gens*. You must be wary of offending the social order. Does your father know?'

'We went without his knowledge. But my mother wanted me to tell you that we did it, when I had the chance to speak to you. My father was absent for most of my childhood, on campaign or holding administrative posts in the provinces. My mother never accompanied him. Even in Rome he lives in a separate house. I have lived with the failure of their marriage all my life.'

Polybius turned to Scipio. 'I know that you had no interest in gossip among the *gentes* during your recent time in Rome, but it's become an open secret that Metellus is more at home among the *prostibulae* than he is with his own wife. He has changed little in his habits since you were at the academy. It is said that they have not shared a bed for years.'

'Not since my sister Metella was born,' the young man said, looking at Scipio. 'He tried to beat my mother, and I have no love for him. I was brought up in the household of my uncle Sextus Julius Caesar, and am betrothed to his daughter Octavia. My mother says that her legacy and mine will be in the bloodline of the Julii Caesares not the Metelli.'

Fabius remembered the words of the Sibyl: *The eagle and the sun shall unite, and in their union shall lie the future of Rome*. He looked at the embossed symbols on the breastplates of the two men in front of him now: Scipio with the radiating sun symbol over a solid line of his adoptive grandfather Africanus, representing his ascendancy over Hannibal in the desert, and Gnaeus with the eagle symbol of the Julii Caesares, the same image that was in the pendant that Julia had given Scipio and that he still wore. He suddenly realized what the prophecy had meant: not Scipio and Metellus, a union of generals, but Scipio and Julia, a union of blood lines, of *gentes*. For a moment, Fabius felt dislocated, as if all around him had become a blur and he was seeing only these two men, as if they alone were the strength of history. Somewhere in the future, perhaps many generations hence, this union of *gentes* might create a new world order, not because of some divine prophecy of the Sibyl but because of the power of men to shape their own destinies, a strength of vision that had led Scipio Aemilianus to stand before the walls of Carthage now alongside the future that he had created with Julia, their son.

Gnaeus stood to attention again. 'I will be the first through the breach, just as you were at Intercatia.'

Scipio reached out and put his right hand on the young man's shoulder. '*Ave atque vale*, Gnaeus Metellus Julius Caesar. Keep your sword blade sharp.'

'*Ave atque vale*, Scipio Aemilianus Africanus. May victory this day be yours.'

'Victory is for the legionaries, tribune. For the men of Rome. You must never forget that.'

Gnaeus saluted, turned and strode away, holding the hilt of his sword. Scipio turned to Polybius. 'One evening twenty-two years ago you gave me the keys to your house, so that Julia and I could be alone for a precious hour. Perhaps in that single act you shaped the destiny of Rome, more than all of your books and your advice to me in the field.'

Polybius put a hand on Scipio's shoulder. 'My job is to observe history, not to create it. But even a historian can make a few adjustments here and there, making possible what had previously seemed impossible. Your union with Julia may have ended that night, but it lives on in your son. This day, when you stand victorious over Carthage, you may see your destiny fulfilled and return to the folds of Rome, having brought the highest honour to the *gens* Cornelii Scipiones and the *gens* Aemilii Paulii, your place in history assured. Or you may choose to break away, to see the world unfold before you as Alexander did, only this time with the might of the world's greatest army behind you. Yet, even if you turn from that vision, you now know that your bloodline will carry it forward.'

Scipio said nothing, but stared forward. His face was set and hard, but Fabius knew the emotion within. Rome held only one attraction for Scipio, the possibility that one day he might be with Julia again, that their future together did not lie just in the glades of Elysium. If Scipio turned from Rome, he might never see Julia again; if he passed on the torch to his bloodline, he might. His love for her might shape the future of Rome. But everything would depend on the outcome of this day, on the blood that coursed through Scipio's veins as he saw what his army had achieved, on a vision of the future that Scipio might see before him: a vision fuelled not just by the bloodlust of war, but by the exultation of conquest.

There was a harsh sound from the ships, of torsion being released, and they turned to look. A fireball rose lazily to the sky from one of the catapults, arching over the city walls and slapping into a building near the Byrsa, spraying burning tendrils of naphtha over the city streets below. Ennius was finding his range, and testing the volatility of his substance. Scipio turned to Fabius. 'Take a message to the *strategos* of the fleet. Tell him to issue the men with their ration of wine, and to make their final libations to their ancestors. Before this hour is done they will be at war.'

Twenty minutes later, Fabius watched Scipio stare at the whitewashed walls of the city in front of them, tapping his fingers against his sword pommel. He remembered the last time they had stood before a besieged city, at Intercatia in Spain, when Scipio himself had led the assault and was the first to stand on the walls, sword in hand. Then, he had killed the chieftain but spared the city. Intercatia pacified was no threat to Rome, and its destruction was not part of his destiny. This time it was different. This time he knew that Scipio would show no mercy: Carthage must be destroyed.

A centurion from the guard came striding up from the naval party on the wharfside, where Fabius had noticed a commotion a few minutes earlier beside a transport ship. The centurion slapped his breastplate in salute. '*Ave, primipilus.* I would speak with Scipio Aemilianus.'

'What is it?'

'We have a deserter.'

Fabius pursed his lips, and led him to Scipio. The centurion spoke quickly, and pointed back to the ship's crew, who were assembled on the quay. Two legionaries dragged a man from among them and brought him before Scipio. Fabius looked at the man in astonishment: it was one of the marines who had accompanied him on the *liburna*, who had fought alongside him when they had boarded the *lembos*. The centurion turned to Scipio. 'This man was a marine with the special assault unit, but his true identity was revealed when a veteran of the Macedonian war identified him. He then ran, discarded his armour and weapons and tried to join that transport crew in disguise, but he was recognized. It turns out that he had first deserted at the Battle of Pydna, twenty-two years ago. He changed his name and lived a quiet life as a fisherman near Ostia, but says that he could not bear the remorse and joined up again three years ago, when he saw that the galleys were being fitted out for the assault on Carthage. His optio in the marines says that he has been a brave fighter in several naval actions, killing many of the enemy and putting himself in front of the other men, including the action with Fabius.'

Fabius looked at the man, and at Scipio. They were about the same age: tough, sinewy men with grey-flecked hair, the sailor darker-skinned and more swarthy from years at sea, but both hard-eyed and strong. They were men whose lives had been shaped by the battle they had experienced as teenagers: Scipio to live up to it and the reputation of his father, the other man to make amends for the guilt of desertion that had clouded his life. They stood together now in front of the walls of Carthage as they had stood before the Macedonian phalanx all those years before – one of them resolute and unwavering, the other baulking and abandoning his comrades.

Scipio turned to Fabius. 'What do you have to say for this man?'

'He personally accounted for many of the enemy. On one occasion he put himself over a fallen comrade to protect him.

Had I been of sufficient rank to do so, I would have recommended him for the *ornamentalia*. He fought bravely and with honour.'

'Then he shall be spared being beaten to death by his comrades, and will be yours to deal with as *primipilus*.' Scipio nodded to the trumpeter, who raised his horn and blew three shorts blasts in quick succession, over and over again, a signal bound to provoke dread and fascination in any legionary: the call to witness field punishment. When the final blast died away, Fabius ordered the two legionaries to drag the man back into the centre of the wharf, in full view of several thousand men around the harbour, including his former marine unit who had been mustered to attention to watch. Fabius knew what he had to do: he was *primipilus* now. The legionaries held the man with his arms pinned behind, and Fabius stood before him. 'Do you have anything to say for yourself?'

'I have a wife and child, in Sicily,' the man said hoarsely. He fumbled with a leather pouch at his waist, and pulled out a little lead dog, his hand shaking. 'My son made this for me. It's our dog. It's to bring me luck, so that Neptune will spare me.'

The man's knees gave way, and the two centurions held him up, his head lolling. He dropped the dog, and it hit the stone with a leaden thump. Fabius stood over him, unflinching. *They all had wives and children. It was the lot of soldiers, everywhere. Sometimes they returned to them, sometimes not.* He reached down and picked up the dog, remembering his own dog Rufius, and put it into the man's hand, closing his fist around it. 'Neptune may have spared you death at sea, but Mars will not spare you now that you are on land,' he said. 'Your son's prayers will speed you to Elysium, where you must await him, just as those who fell in battle at Pydna await their loved ones. To those comrades whom you deserted in their hour of need, you must account for yourself.'

He drew his sword and ran one finger along the blade, feeling its sharpness. He stood back and slowly turned around, the sword held high, so that all of the assembled soldiers could see. The man bowed backwards against the two legionaries, who had twisted him round and pinned his legs with their own to stop him from kicking. He was wild eyed, panting and foaming at the mouth, and Fabius saw the brown wetness down the legs that he had so often seen at executions, and smelt the foul odour. For a split second he remembered the boy Gaius Paullus, another casualty of Pydna all those years ago – whether he too had been a coward or a hero, and whether had he survived he might have proved himself as brave as this man had been in battle: the truth could never be known, only that the fortunes of war could break a man as easily as make him. He stood before the man, and spoke quietly. 'Remember your son. Do not dishonour him. Remember who you are. You are a legionary of Rome. Stand to attention. Salute your general.'

Fabius nodded at the two legionaries, who looked at him uncertainly and then released the man, leaving him reeling and staggering backwards, slipping on his own faeces and urine. He fell down heavily on one hand and stayed there, panting and grimacing. Fabius gestured to the two legionaries to keep back, to give the man a chance to stand up without help, to allow those of his comrades who were watching the chance to tell his wife that he faced death with dignity. The man wiped his face with the back of his other hand, and then raised himself slowly up, wobbling back to where he had stood before and bringing his hand up in salute to Scipio, his fingers still bunched around the little model of the dog.

Fabius grasped the back of the man's neck with his left hand and with the other thrust the sword below his ribcage, driving it up through the heart and lungs and windpipe until the tip came out through the back of his neck. The man exhaled once, a moaning gargle, and then died, his eyes wide open and his mouth gushing blood in pulses with the final beating of his heart.

Fabius let him fall, withdrawing the sword as he did so. He

held the blade up, dripping with blood, and looked around. All of the men around the harbour were watching him. He knew what he had to do now. He had shown the man compassion in life; there could be none in death. He gestured to the nearest of the two legionaries. 'Give me his tunic.' The man went over and ripped the clothing off the corpse, leaving it rolling naked in its own blood and faeces, and passed it to Fabius. He wiped his sword on it, carefully and deliberately so that all could see, and then sheathed it and tossed the bloody tunic back on the corpse.

He walked back to Scipio, who turned and spoke to the centurion. 'Get those *navi* of the transport ship, those who helped to conceal him, to clean up this mess and toss his body on that pile of Carthaginian corpses by the harbour entrance. Nail a board to his head saying 'Deserter' and have every cohort march past, close enough to smell it, before sundown today. The *navi* of that ship are to stand down and be replaced, and put on cremation duty. The captain and his officers are to be taken in chains to the outer harbour, stripped naked and given fifty lashes in full view of the fleet. If they survive that, they are to be distributed among the *liburnae* and chained up as galley slaves. That is all.'

The centurion saluted and marched away as the harbour bustled back to life again. A great siege ballista creaked along the shore, drawn by two lines of Nubian slaves, its counterpoised timber tottering precariously on a loose lashing. Ennius saw it, shouted at the slave-driver to stop and ran over to supervise. Fabius put his hand on his sword hilt and stood alongside Scipio. 'How did it feel?' Scipio asked.

Fabius drew his sword again and looked at the blade, its double-edged design copied from the Celtiberian swords they had taken from the battlefield at Intercatia, but retaining the short thrusting shape of the Roman *gladius*. 'It slides in easily, and doesn't bend. It will serve well as a slashing sword too. It felt good.'

'Well, Fabius,' Scipio said, peering up at the defences of Carthage. 'Shall you be first on the walls of Carthage, or shall I?'

'You are the general, Scipio Aemilianus. I am a mere centurion.'

'But I already have the *corona muralis*, for Intercatia. It is time for another to take the glory.'

Fabius thought for a moment, and then reached into a leather pouch on his belt. 'Well then, we should toss a coin for it, soldier to soldier.'

Scipio cracked a smile. 'I should like that.'

Fabius took out a shiny silver denarius, and raised it up. On one side was the head of the goddess Roma, straight-nosed and clear-eyed and wearing a winged helmet, with the name ANTESTIUS along the edge. On the other side was the word ROMA and above it two galloping horsemen with spears, a dog leaping up on its hind legs below them. He handed the coin to Scipio. 'This is fresh from the mint, given to me by my friend the moneyer Antestius just before I embarked at Ostia. He wanted me to throw it into the ruins of Carthage, in memory of his grandfather who fell at Zama. But I reckon if we toss it and leave it here, that'll do the trick.'

Scipio turned the coin in his hand. 'Six hundred and eight years *ab urbe condita*, in the year of the consulship of Lentulus and Mummius,' he murmured. 'I wonder if history will remember this year in that way, or as the year in which Carthage fell?'

Fabius was quiet for a moment, and then pointed to the horsemen on the coin. 'If you were to ask Antestius, he would say that those are the Dioscuri, Castor and Pollux,' he said. 'But Antestius sketched this design in the tavern after I'd come back from Macedonia and told him about our hunting exploits together, and the goods times we'd had before my dog Rufius was killed.'

Scipio peered at it closely, shaking his head and smiling. 'Who needs to conquer cities when a mere moneyer in Rome can give you immortality like this?'

'Antestius told me something else about that coin. He said

that one day when he was a boy he passed the most beautiful girl he had ever seen, walking with you in the Forum. It was Julia, of the *gens* Caesares. When he came to design that image of the goddess Roma, it was really Julia that he was depicting.'

Scipio stared at the coin, his voice hushed. 'That's her?'

'Antestius said that the people no longer want gods and goddesses on their coins, but real men and women, those who are shaping Rome and her future, in our lifetimes and those of our children and grandchildren.'

Scipio swallowed hard, and his lips quivered. He held the coin up against Carthage as a backdrop, and then turned to Fabius, his voice hoarse with emotion. 'I gave her up for this, you know. So that I could stand before the walls of Carthage with an army, about to order its destruction.'

'You gave her up for Rome, and for your destiny. And Julia lives on with you now in your son.'

Scipio looked at the image on the coin again, and held it ready to toss. 'If that's Julia, she's my call, then.'

'And mine's Rufius.'

Scipio flicked the coin on his thumb and it spun high into the air, flashing silver in the sky, then falling and bouncing on the stone pavement of the harbour front, the horsemen and the dog facing up.

Scipio turned and peered at him. 'Rufius it is. You will lead the first maniple through the breach in the wall. You will finally have a chance at that crown.'

Fabius kicked the coin into a crack between the stones, and turned to Scipio, standing to attention. '*Ave atque vale*, Scipio. Until we meet again, in this world or the next.'

Scipio slapped him on the shoulder. '*Ave atque vale*, Fabius. Go now and gird yourself for war.'

23

A quarter of an hour later, Fabius stood with Scipio and Polybius again on the tower. He could feel the tension in the air, the edginess as they knew the time for action was approaching fast. Polybius pointed along the foreshore to the west, where the Roman fleet stood just out of bowshot range from the walls. 'The wind is still coming from the south. Ennius is worried that it will blow the flames back over our own ships. You must give the order before the wind picks up much more.'

'That's exactly why I don't like him messing with fire,' Scipio grumbled. 'I've been telling him that for twenty years. I wish he'd stick to catapults and battering rams.'

'The die is cast, Scipio. And as for battering rams, he's got those in place too. Look, they're already swinging.'

Fabius peered down at the Carthaginian defences just inside the city from the edge of the harbour. Out of sight to the south, beyond the great wall that protected the city from the isthmus, Ennius' cohort had spent several weeks building a battering ram of conventional design, a huge timber made from a single cedar of Lebanon shipped over specially for the purpose, capped with a bronze ram in the shape of a boar's head taken from one of the triremes anchored offshore. It took more than a thousand men to wield it, and it would be the only way they could hope to break through the massive southern gateway.

But here beside the harbour it was a different matter: the walls blocking the streets had been hastily constructed by the Carthaginians in the past few weeks when they knew the Romans were coming. Ennius had spotted the structural weakness of the masonry, built in the Carthaginian manner with tall upright stones a few paces apart, the spaces between filled with courses of smaller blocks. The pillars had strength, but a ram aimed between them could easily break through. The Carthaginians had realized this and placed the walls at angles in the streets where they thought a ram could not be brought to bear, where the open space before the wall was too small for the run-up needed to punch a hole big enough for an assaulting force to break through.

But they had been wrong; they had not counted on Roman engineering genius. Ennius had demonstrated his invention on an abandoned villa with walls built in this fashion just outside the city, and Scipio had been convinced. He could see Ennius' machines now, poking above the flat rooftops, triangular wooden frames that had been pushed on wheels close to the walls, with rams a hundred feet long suspended from ropes like pendulums. Ennius had built them using material his men had salvaged from the ruined warships in the harbour, from masts, ropes and iron rams, turning the last vestiges of Carthaginian naval might against the city, while the Carthaginians themselves had been reduced to using women's hair to make rope for catapults. And these rams did not take thousands of men to operate, only a few dozen each; those men were specialized marines from the galleys, trained to help the slaves row in the final assault on an enemy fleet, and then as they struck home to leap off their benches and surge forward into the attack. Once the men swinging the rams had breached the walls and crashed through, the massed legionaries waiting behind would follow and the city would be open to conquest.

Fabius peered at the rams again. Polybius was right. They were swinging already, marking time, the teams waiting for the order that would see the ropes pulled taut and the rams crash into the walls. It was as if the engine of war were beginning to flex itself, inexorably. He felt his pulse quicken. It was nearly time.

Polybius pointed to an open area just inside the Carthaginian defensive wall about five hundred paces to the south of the harbour. 'There's smoke coming from the Tophet,' he said.

'What of it?' Scipio replied, still looking at the rams.

'Do you know what Tophet means?'

'I don't speak Carthaginian.'

'It means "roasting place".'

'Well?'

'The sanctuary is used to cremate and bury dead children, but in the past was used as a place of sacrifice. It hasn't been used for that purpose for generations now, not since before the war with Hannibal. But rumour has it that in times of great duress, a sacrifice would be offered to the god Ba'al Hammon, who supposedly resides on the twin peaks of the mountain to the east. When the morning sun rises above the mountain it casts a beam of light across the Tophet, and that's when the sacrifice is meant to take place.'

'I don't think sacrifice can save them now. And that first shaft of light is when I will order the assault.'

Polybius took out a bronze tube about a foot long with disc-shaped crystals at either end, and peered through it in the direction of the smoke. 'There are two priests in white robes mounting the stone platform in the centre of the sanctuary, each carrying a coiled chain and wearing what look like large gloves made of leather – elephant hide I shouldn't wonder. And that strange structure that looks like a large kiln behind is the source of the smoke. There are slaves at the bottom working bellows, stoking a fire. If you ever wondered where Hasdrubal put the olive trees he had his men cut down from the surrounding fields, there's your answer. Piles of it behind the kiln, clearly firewood. And there are men with sledge-hammers smashing the kiln, only it's not a kiln at all. It's something else entirely, concealed beneath.'

He passed the eyeglass to Fabius, who squinted down it, saw only a distorted blur and passed it back. They all stared at what was being revealed. It was fire-blackened and mottled on the surface from fire, but clearly made of bronze. As the men knocked away the final sections of clay the shape came into view. It was a gigantic squatting figure, the size of several elephants, human in form but of monstrous proportions. Its huge arms were raised palms upwards, and its bearded head was set back with the mouth open wide, large enough for a man to enter. They could see the smoke issuing from the mouth, and an occasional lick of flame from a fire below.

'Extraordinary,' Polybius muttered. 'It's mentioned by the historians, but nobody really believed it. Unless I'm mistaken, it's meant to represent the Carthaginian god Ba'al Hammon.' He peered through the eyeglass again. 'Hasdrubal has just arrived, and is mounting the steps to the platform where the two priests are waiting. He's got gloves on too.'

Fabius shaded his eyes to get a better view. He remembered the first time he had seen the Carthaginian general, when he and Scipio had made their reconnaissance into the city three years before; Hasdrubal had been wearing the distinctive lionskin over his armour then too. He saw Scipio glancing at the ships and the harbour, waiting for Ennius' signal, then looking back at the Tophet. 'Where's the sacrificial animal? I thought they'd have eaten everything by now, rats and cockroaches included.'

Polybius put down his eyeglass again, and spoke with the detachment of a scholar. 'Unless I'm mistaken, we are about to witness a Carthaginian child sacrifice.'

Scipio was aghast. 'Jupiter above. What?'

'Child sacrifice has a long history among the Semitic peoples of the east Mediterranean, the ancestors of the Carthaginians. The writings of the Israelites tell of how their ancient prophet Abraham offered up a boy called Isaac to their god.'

A drum began to beat, slowly, insistently, from somewhere inside the sanctuary. 'The drumbeat was originally meant to drown out the screams of the victim,' Polybius said. 'But I doubt whether they'll wish to do that this time. I think what we're about to see is mainly for our benefit, so the more screams, the better.'

A boy in a white tunic, perhaps ten years old, came walking out into the sanctuary, then mounted the stone stairs towards the three men standing at the top. As he neared the platform, Hasdrubal beckoned him, and the boy leapt up and embraced him, clinging to the arms of the lionskin. Hasdrubal put him down gently, and held his hand. The boy could not know what was about to happen. Fabius' stomach lurched as he realized the truth. *The boy was Hasdrubal's son.*

The drumbeat slowed. The two priests suddenly pulled the boy off his feet, one taking the arms and the other the legs, quickly wrapping his wrists and ankles together with chains. Down below at the base of the bronze god the slaves hung on to the arms of the bellows, ready to compress them. Hasdrubal took the boy from the priests and held him in front of the gaping maw of the beast; the heat coming from within was already visible, shimmering in the air above. Fabius could see the boy's head on one side of Hasdrubal, looking around frantically, sensing the horror that was about to befall him. For a moment Fabius felt for the man. Somewhere beneath that lionskin, beneath the rage, the cruelty, the self-destruction, was the utter despair of a father who knew that his son loved him, had felt his embrace, and yet he had been driven to carry out the unthinkable, the worst that war could make a man do.

Hasdrubal took a step forward, and tossed the boy into the beast's mouth. There was a tumbling and clanking sound, magnified and echoing, as the priests let out the chains and the boy rolled down. A high pitched scream rent the air, and then a terrible shriek rose from somewhere behind the walls of the Tophet, the cry of his mother, followed by a wail of lamentation that seemed to ripple through the city. The bronze god erupted in a roar of fire, as if the god himself were awakening; a sheet of flame belched out and curled up high above. Down below, the slaves worked the giant bellows, the whips of the priests slashing into their backs. The smell of burned meat began to waft across the harbour. Then the drumbeat changed, faster now, and the slaves ceased their work. The two priests on the platform began to haul on the chains, link by link, keeping to either side of the beast's mouth to avoid the scorching heat. They pulled out their ghastly burden, and Hasdrubal took it.

He turned, and Fabius could see the charred and shrivelled body of the boy, the legs and arms contracted and the mouth stretched open, caught in a scream. Hasdrubal raised the corpse towards the twin peaks of the mountain, towards Bou Kornine. But then he turned towards the harbour, raising the body of his son as high as he could.

Fabius stared in horror. Hasdrubal was not offering his sacrifice to the god. *He was offering it to them.*

Polybius put a hand on his Scipio's arm. 'He's taunting us. He knows that no Roman who loves his son could stand this. He's trying to make you order the attack before we are ready. Keep your nerve.'

'Scipio Aemilianus,' Hasdrubal bellowed, his voice carrying across the harbour, over the ranks of legionaries who had been watching him, transfixed. *'Carthago delenda est.'*

It was the cry of those in the Roman Senate who had sent Scipio here, words now used by a man who could have no purpose left in living. *Carthago delenda est. Carthage must be destroyed.*

A streak of sunlight burst through the twin peaks of the mountain and lit up the Tophet, then seared through the city as if it had been struck by a bolt of lightning. A moment later there was a dull thud from one of Ennius' catapult ships and a ball of fire rose into the air, lingering for a moment over the city like a giant burning star and then crashing down on to the temple platform, spraying gobs of fire into the streets below.

It was the signal.

Scipio turned to Polybius. 'Hasdrubal shall have what he

wants.' He raised his left arm and held it straight out in front of him. Down below, he saw the trumpeters lift their long horns to their lips, watching him. The drumbeat had stopped, and for a moment there was silence. Fabius felt a wisp of wind on his cheek, and looked out to the horizon again, squinting now against the sun. He saw only red.

Scipio let his arm drop.

'Unleash war,' he snarled.

24

Twenty minutes later, Fabius stood beside Scipio in front of the first maniple of the first legion, their swords drawn. They had crashed through the breach made by the ram, Fabius slightly ahead, and had run up the street towards the Byrsa hill, expecting opposition behind every street block. But there had been none, and they had quickly realized that Hasdrubal and his depleted force of mercenaries and Carthaginian troops must have retreated to a defensible position close to the centre of the city, to the place that Fabius and Scipio had seen three years before near the old quarter of houses below the Byrsa. The two men had reached that place now, and stood aside while the legionaries streamed into the open area where they had seen the Sacred Band training, now stripped of its embellishments; it had clearly been used as a storage facility for the troops, with wooden grain bins around the edge that all seemed empty.

Ahead of them lay a wall of rubble hastily built to block the streets on the south side of the city; along the top was the wooden palisade they had seen three years ago above the level of the surrounding houses. As the legionaries in the vanguard surged forward and sought gaps in the barrier, a blare of trumpets sounded from the parapet and Hasdrubal appeared with a group of soldiers, all of them wearing the burnished breastplates and lobed helmets of the Sacred Band. Fabius watched in astonishment as two four-horse chariots came into view beside them, veering round and facing in opposite directions, the horses stomping and whinnying on the narrow ledge. It seemed a baffling spectacle, of no clear purpose, until he saw what was held between them: it was a man in a legionary's armour, his head swollen and unrecognizable, his arms tied to the back of one chariot and his legs to the other. Fabius turned to Scipio, gripping his arm. 'Hasdrubal is taunting you again. That must be one of the Roman prisoners taken during the fight for the harbour. Hasdrubal knows that the traditional way of executing traitors in Rome is to draw them between two *quadrigae*.'

Hasdrubal bellowed; there was a swish of whips and the two chariots leapt forward along the parapet, almost immediately tumbling off the side into a tangled mess at the base of the wall, the horses shrieking and neighing. As they did so the man tied between them was torn in half, his upper torso springing forward like a slingshot, spraying his innards over the legionaries watching in horror below. There was a collective howl of anger, and a surge forward that the centurions struggled to control.

But worse was to come. Four wooden poles were quickly raised where the horses had stood on the parapet, and four more prisoners appeared, shackled and naked except for their helmets. Hasdrubal bellowed again, and they were tied to the poles and dangled over the legionaries below. A giant Nubian slave appeared, wearing only a loincloth, with metal hooks where his hands should have been. He clashed them together, and then tore at the nearest prisoner, ripping a jagged chasm across his midriff and pulling out his intestines. He sauntered over to the next one, jeering at the Romans like a circus clown, and then with both hooks gouged the man's eyes out and ripped his cheeks open. He spun around and slashed his hooks over the third man's groin, ripping off his genitals and flinging them out over the legionaries below. He stood in front of them, beating his chest and howling. Fabius felt sick, and he saw Scipio swallow hard. The other legionaries, the comrades of the men on the platform, looked stunned with horror, unable to move.

'Enough of this,' Scipio said to Fabius. 'However we do it, we need to get onto that parapet.'

'No need.' Fabius had caught sight of someone familiar out of the corner of his eye. There was a swooshing sound over the men, and the Nubian reeled and then fell forward, an arrow in his forehead. Enraged, Hasdrubal drew his sword and chopped the legs off the fourth prisoner, leave him to bleed out copiously over the parapet, and then he hastily moved out of sight. The legionaries in the square parted to make way for Gulussa and Hippolyta, who had been with their cavalry on the plain outside the city but had led a dismounted party up from the breach that had been made in the landward walls. Hippolyta was wearing the skin of a white tiger beneath a Roman cuirass, and her red hair was bound in a tight knot behind her helmet. She held her bow with another arrow ready, and looked over at Scipio. The four prisoners on the poles were groaning, terribly mutilated. The senior centurion of the first maniple turned to her, his voice hoarse with emotion. 'Put them out of their misery,' he said. 'They will thank you for it.' Scipio nodded, and Hippolyta raised her bow and in quick succession shot an arrow into the heart of each man, killing them quickly and mercifully. Fabius closed his eyes for a moment, trying to forget the scene. He could see the legionaries looking restless, uncertain. It was essential that they regain the momentum of their charge up from the harbour, or else they would falter and be cut down as they followed the side alley up towards the Byrsa that he and Fabius had seen on the reconnaissance three years before.

It was his job as *primipilus* to take the initiative in situations like this, to restore discipline. He leapt up on a stone grain bin and turned to address the men. 'Legionaries,' he bellowed. 'Our comrades watch us now from Elysium. They wear full armour and are decked with the *dona militaria* of heroes. Now we go forward. There is a way up the alleyway to the acropolis. Our comrades will be avenged.' He looked at the senior centurion of the first maniple. 'Form the *testudo*,' he bellowed.

The centurion ran out in front of his men, turned to face them and raised his shield above his head. Instantly the first line copied him, locking their shields together to form a solid mass above their heads, and then on down the ranks as the cry of 'Testudo' went up from the other centurions until the entire force formed one continuous mass of shields. The centurions ran to the front and the rear and joined the formation just as the Carthaginians began pouring boiling olive oil down on them from the parapet, causing grunts of pain but no disorder in the line. Ahead of them the alleyway was clear of defenders for at least two hundred paces, but Fabius knew that the mercenaries on the walls and the warriors of the Sacred Band would come down and attack once they realized that the testudo was all but impregnable to anything they could drop on it.

Fabius and Scipio raised their shields above their heads and ran forward. Behind them they could hear Brutus pounding along the stones, and he soon overtook them. After about fifty paces they saw the first of the enemy in the alleyway, a mixed lot of mercenaries with the armour and weapons of half a dozen nations, Latins among them. Brutus charged headlong into them, his huge curved sword slashing to the left and right, slicing men in half and spraying their innards over the walls. The first victim of his fearsome cross-stroke was a Celtiberian who made the mistake of standing his ground. Brutus paused for a moment, eyeing the man up and down, and then with shocking speed swept his sword through the man's exposed midriff, cutting him in half, and then up between the man's legs to quarter him, drawing the sword right up through the neck and head. Fabius had seen it once before in practice on a prisoner but was still horrified by the result, an indescribable mess in the narrow confines of the alley. Ahead of him the mercenaries who had seen Brutus at work turned and retreated, bunching up together and inadvertently making themselves easier for him to kill, while others darted away on either side in a suicidal run towards the advancing legionaries; they would know they had no chance of survival, but could hope for a less gruesome end than the one being experienced by their comrades further up the alley.

A Carthaginian of the Sacred Band appeared suddenly in front of Fabius, breathing heavily, his sword at the ready. There was a sound like a rope snapping in the wind and the soldier lurched forward and swayed, a look of incomprehension on his face. Out of the corner of his eye Fabius saw something like a snake's tail slither back down the stone steps of the alleyway. The Carthaginian dropped his sword with a clatter and his neck erupted with blood, spraying Fabius' breastplate and face, and the man then tumbled and fell, the blood pumping out of his body and streaming down the cracks between the stones. Fabius glanced back and saw Gulussa coiling his whip for another strike. He remembered the day in Rome when King Masinissa had presented Gulussa with the rhino-skin whip, a memento of his time fighting alongside the elder Scipio that he had hoped his son would use once again in war with Carthage. That time had come but, fifty years on, the whip was meaner, more vicious. Gulussa had taken it back to Numidia and had his craftsmen splice razor-sharp steel blades into the tip, and then had honed his skills deep in the desert, fighting on camelback, in dust storms, in places that seemed to Fabius barely imaginable. He had returned to Rome with his skill perfected: the ability to use the whip to ring a man's neck at twenty paces and slice through both jugular veins at once.

The whip flicked out again like a lizard's tongue, uncoiling slowly at first and then lightning quick, this time striking a Carthaginian on the base of his helmet and slicing through his lower jaw. The man screamed in agony, dropped his sword and held his severed jaw to his face, spitting and spraying blood. Scipio leapt forward for the kill, thrusting his sword hard under the man's kilt, pushing up from the groin as far as it would go and then twisting and pulling it out, jumping back while the man vomited blood and fell to the ground, dead. Fabius slipped on the slew of blood and bile that pumped out between the man's legs and then righted himself and ran forward behind Scipio. Hippolyta was beside him now too, pulling arrow after arrow from her quiver, using her double-curved Scythian bow to place shots expertly in the neck where the enemy armour left them most vulnerable. Body piled upon body, yet still the Carthaginians came. Ahead of them Brutus scythed his way forward, leaving mutilated bodies and body parts on either side, bloody hunks of meat that piled against each other in the gutters as if they had been swept down from some butcher's shop in a mighty deluge of blood.

They were coming to the end of the alleyway now; the walls on either side were funnelling them towards the cluster of tightly packed houses, the old quarter of the city at the foot of the acropolis. Word had reached Ennius on the ships to halt the creeping barrage of fireballs ahead of the legionaries while they were advancing so quickly, but now the signallers had instructed him on Scipio's command to renew the barrage and pulverize the old quarter of the city before they reached it. The fireballs landed with renewed ferocity, the first ones so close that they made the ground shudder, others landing further ahead among the houses as the observers signalled back to correct the range. Above them on the walls, the Carthaginians were still flinging down rocks, pottery vessels, burning oil, anything they could get their hands on, but most of the missiles were bouncing harmlessly off the *testudo* formation as the legionaries moved inexorably forward, their shields interlocked over their heads. Behind them Hippolyta's Scythian archers were finding their mark, felling Carthaginians on the wall and adding even further to the mounds of corpses that littered the alleyway. Still the legionaries marched on, relentlessly, the clanging of their armour punctuated by the hoarse shouts of the centurions, the *testudo* narrowing to a width of only four or five shields as they approached the end of the alley, their swords drawn and ready.

Fabius had guessed that as soon as they reached that point the remaining defenders would flee the ramparts and retreat into the old quarter ahead of them, to take refuge among the civilians cowering there and make a last stand. They had seen nothing of Hasdrubal since the grisly mutilation of the Roman prisoners on the walls, but Fabius could guess where he had gone. He squinted up at the temple on the Byrsa, its smoke-wreathed roof visible high above the houses, then looked back down at Brutus as he scythed his way to left and right to clear the last of the Carthaginians from the alley. Scipio held up his arm, halting the legionaries. Polybius made his way through from the rear and came alongside, his sword dripping with blood.

'Ennius has exhausted his ammunition,' he panted. 'The last fireball contained green dye as a signal, and I saw it. That means the way ahead is open for you.'

Scipio wiped the sweat and blood from his face on his tunic sleeve. 'There can be no more than a few hundred of them left.'

'The Sacred Band?'

Scipio nodded. 'The mercenaries are all dead or hiding. There's no escape for those who are left. They'll burn to death or die in the smoke.'

'Hasdrubal?'

Scipio pointed his sword at the temple. 'I'm sure he's gone up there, waiting for me. For now, I'm more concerned about my legionaries. They've seen Brutus kill dozens, seen Hippolyta's archers take down more, seen me kill in that alleyway. But so far most of them have spent this battle huddled under their shields.' He took the cloth that Polybius offered, wiped his face again and jerked his head at the *testudo*. 'This lot are the first legion. Some of them fought with me in Spain. They'll be baying for blood. If I don't give it to them, they might just take it out on us.' He grinned at Polybius, tossing the cloth back. 'And then you really would be writing your history book in the afterlife, wouldn't you?'

'Could you offer Hasdrubal terms of surrender?' Polybius

said. 'There are hundreds, maybe thousands of civilians in that quarter. It's where most of the surviving inhabitants of the city have sought refuge from the fires. If you unleash the legionaries, they won't easily distinguish soldiers from civilians. It will be a massacre.'

Scipio shook his head. 'Surrender? Hasdrubal? Not likely. And wasn't it you who read Homer to me last night, about the fall of Troy? I don't recall Achilles hesitating because of women and children. Rome showed Carthage mercy once before, half a century ago. This time there will be none.'

He turned round, facing his centurions and legionaries, and raised his bloody sword. 'Men,' he bellowed. 'It seems that I have had all the fun. Now that's not fair, is it?'

They bellowed back, a great roar, and Scipio grinned at them. 'Men of the first maniple,' he continued, 'some of you have been with me since Spain. Some of you centurions even taught me how to fight. Old Quintus Pesco over there was once so dismayed with my *pilum* throwing that he promised to give me five of the best on my backside and send me to clean out the latrines. And I was his commanding officer.'

There was a roar of approval, and Scipio slapped the nearest centurion on the back, then put his hand on the man's shoulder, looking back at the legionaries. 'You are all my brothers. And like brothers everywhere, we love a good fight.'

There was another roar, and Scipio pointed his sword up the alleyway. 'Over there, in those houses, are the last remaining Carthaginians, the so-called Sacred Band. Kill them all, and you will have won the greatest victory Rome has ever known. You will go home heroes, and your families will be honoured for all time. But do your job well here, and I won't let you stay at home for long. Where we're going after this, I promise you war and plunder like you've never seen before.'

Another deafening chorus rose from the men. The centurion Quintus Pesco turned to him, his voice hoarse. 'Scipio Africanus, the men of the first legion would follow you to Hades and back. As they would have done for your grandfather.'

Scipio raised his sword and moved back against the wall of the alley, pulling Polybius with him. 'Men, are you ready?' he shouted. There was a huge cry, and he nodded at the centurions, who angled their shields forward from the *testudo* formation and raised their swords, followed by the legionaries. Scipio pointed his sword forward and bellowed. '*Do your worst!*'

Ten minutes later, Fabius and Scipio walked into the cloud of dust that had been left by the advancing legionaries, entering a storm of death like nothing Fabius had seen before. The narrow alleys of the old quarter were strewn with flickering patches of fire, some of it consuming the timbers of houses where the fire-balls had impacted half an hour before. In the dust the glowing naphtha made a nightmarish sight, as if they were walking again into the burning fumeroles of the Phlegraean Fields, only this time the fire was man-made. The air was filled with the an acrid smell of burning, and with the stench from a place where people had lived confined together for months with little food and hardly any water for sanitation; each narrow house had its own rain-water cistern, and they had seen lower down in the city that they were nearly all empty.

For a few minutes after the legionaries had gone on ahead there had been a terrible din of shrieking and yelling, a noise that had come from further away as the soldiers had moved forward; now the place was eerily quiet, punctuated only by the sound of soldiers kicking around inside the houses looking for loot, and the occasional grunt as a wounded Carthaginian was finished off. Corpses lay everywhere: soldiers of the Sacred Band with their polished armour, most of them mere boys; mercenaries who had stripped off theirs in a futile attempt to escape recognition, but been hacked down anyway; old men and women, even children, all caught up in the slaughter. To clear the streets the legionaries were hauling bodies off to either side and dumping them in the cisterns, filling them to the brim so that limbs and torsos were visible poking out, some still twitching. The legionaries had been incensed by the terrible scenes of their comrades being mutilated, and they had spared nobody. Fabius knew the inevitable reckoning of war, but this was beyond any rampage he had seen before.

He followed Scipio as he picked his way through the bodies and headed to the foot of the Byrsa. Silently, the legionaries they passed joined them, their swords dripping with blood, until most of the maniple had rallied again under their centurions. Polybius came up and stood beside him, wiping the blood off his face. 'We're at the temple steps. The city is nearly taken.'

Fabius passed Scipio a skin of water that a legionary had brought up to them. He gulped it down gratefully, then raised the skin above his head to let the water pour over his face. He passed it back, and wiped his forehead against his tunic sleeve. Fabius was conscious for the first time of his own rasping breathing, coming short and fast, and he tried to calm himself. The noise of battle had abated all round the city; he heard only the occasional shriek and cry, the sounds of falling masonry as the fires took hold, the stomping and whinnying of horses, the heavy breathing and marching of a thousand legionaries crammed into the streets behind. Even Brutus had stopped, a few paces away to the right, panting like a bear, the bloody point of his scimitar resting on the lower step that led up to the temple. The whole army was waiting, watching to see what Scipio would do next.

Fabius peered through the smoke towards the top of the steps. The Carthaginian army had been annihilated, but he knew there were still people up there, cowering in the temple precinct. He remembered the little boy he had watched mounting the steps in the Tophet less than an hour before, Hasdrubal's own son. He knew the man himself would be up there now, waiting for them. It was as if the temple were another altar and Hasdrubal was orchestrating the ceremony, forcing Scipio to mount the steps as if he himself were a participant in some final, apocalyptic scene of sacrifice.

Fabius sensed the army behind him, shifting, restless. He took a deep breath, tasting the acrid reek of smoke, the coppery tang of blood, feeling his veins engorge. He remembered what the old centurion had taught them. Scipio must not let his men see him hesitate. Fabius watched him grip his sword and look at Polybius, and then at Brutus. 'Let's finish it,' he growled.

He began to run up the steps, sword in hand, his armour clanking, swerving to avoid the burning patches of naphtha from Ennius' fireballs. Fabius followed, and he could hear Polybius and Brutus behind him, and the mass of legionaries surging forward to the base of the steps. He pounded forward, his teeth bared, every muscle and sinew in his body straining, the sweat spraying off his face. Time seemed to slow down, as if the weight of history were pulling him back, a history that had denied this day to Rome for so long. Then he was over the final step and on the temple platform, crouched in readiness with his sword forward, his chest heaving as he tried to catch his breath, hearing only the pounding of blood in his ears. He was beside Scipio, and could only see eight or ten paces ahead; the temple was obscured by a billowing plume of smoke that rolled off the platform to the north to join the pall that hid the city streets, making the group at the temple seem cut off and on their own, invisible to the thousands of legionaries below as they confronted the final nemesis of Carthage.

Polybius and Brutus came up on either side of him, breathing hard, catching their breath. 'I can feel heat, coming from ahead,' Polybius panted. 'The temple must be on fire.'

'I see nobody,' Brutus growled, looking around.

'He's here,' Scipio said under his breath. 'Trust me. Keep alert.'

The four men stood in a semi-circle, their backs to the stairs, their swords held out as they stared into the smoke. Gulussa and Hippolyta joined them silently on either side, Gulussa with his whip coiled in readiness and Hippolyta with her bow drawn, a barbed arrow pulled back. They waited, hearing nothing, not moving. And then a sudden gust of wind blew the smoke aside and revealed the temple, its great stone columns soaring into the air some fifty paces ahead. Polybius had been right, but it was not the fireballs that had caused the heat. The temple was packed around with bundles of olive branches, just as the Tophet sanctuary had been. Hasdrubal had planned the suicide of his own city down to the last detail. Flames licked at the bundles between the columns, a crackling and hissing that soon became a roar. The doorway to the inner sanctum beyond the columns looked like the entrance to a furnace, an orange-red glow where the fire had already consumed the wood that had been rammed inside. Fabius put his hand up to shield his eyes, feeling the heat scorch his arm. He remembered being shown the place in the Phlegraean Fields where Aeneas had descended into the underworld. That had required imagination to envisage, but this needed none. This looked like the entrance to Hades.

The wind gusted again and he saw Hasdrubal, no more than twenty paces away to the left of the temple, a torch burning in a metal holder beside him. He was still wearing his lionskin, but it was smeared with blood; he stood with his feet planted firmly apart. Beside him was a woman with crudely cropped hair, her scalp blotched and bleeding and her clothing in rags, stooping over two small children. Hasdrubal held her by the nape of her neck and pushed her forward, his face contorted with rage and grief.

'Scipio Aemilianus,' he bellowed, his voice hoarse. '*Look what you have done.*' He pulled the woman's head up with his other hand to reveal her face. Fabius stared, and reeled. Even on this day of bloodletting, when he had watched their own legionaries being horribly mutilated on the parapet, he was not prepared to see a woman like this. Her eyes were gone, the sockets empty and red, the blood dripping down her face and spattering on the stone slabs in front of her. Fabius remembered the piercing shriek he had heard after the little boy had been sacrificed. This was the boy's mother, Hasdrubal's wife, and those were her other children. In her anguish she had not only ripped her clothes, and cut her scalp. *She had torn out her own eyes.*

Hasdrubal leaned forward, saying something to her, and then steered her between the two children, placing their hands in hers. He turned them towards the burning entrance to the temple. He pushed, and she stumbled, and then she started to run, dragging the children along. She shrieked as she passed through the columns with her children still beside her, their little bodies erupting like torches as they disappeared in the flames, and then they were gone.

Hasdrubal crouched forward, his huge arms bent in front of him, his fists clenched, and roared like a beast. He stayed there for a few moments, panting, staring at Scipio. Then he reached back and picked up a pottery amphora that had been lying behind him, smashed its neck and raised it up, his biceps bulging as he poured oil over his head, over the lion's mane, until it was dripping and glistening. He tossed the pot aside, and then grasped the burning torch from the holder beside him. With both hands outstretched, he turned towards the mountain of Bou Kornine to the east, its twin peaks just visible over the pall of smoke, and closed his eyes. Then he turned back towards Scipio, roared again and dipped his head into the flaming torch, igniting his beard and the lion skin in a blast of burning oil.

Fabius again seemed to see movements happening slowly, as if in a dream. Hasdrubal crouched down, the flames sizzling over his head, his mouth wide open, the torch held out. He turned towards the temple and began to run, his huge legs pounding the stones, the flames from his head rising high above him as he picked up speed, a human torch rushing to join his wife and children in the underworld. At the last moment the torch tumbled from his hand and he disappeared into the burning temple, fire joining fire, and was gone from sight.

They all stood transfixed for a moment, staring.

'It is finished,' Brutus growled.

Polybius put a grimy hand on Scipio's shoulder. 'Thus ends Carthage.'

Scipio wiped the sweat from his eyes, blinking hard, still staring at the temple that had become a funeral pyre. Gulussa came up beside him, put one foot on the tip of his whip and shook the handle, lowering it as the whip coiled round into a tight bundle. He picked it up, stowed it into a pouch on his belt and sniffed the air, shading his eyes and peering to the south. 'I can taste the desert in the wind,' he said. 'We should be wary of staying here too long. The wind is picking up and will carry with it much dust, and will fan the flames below.'

Polybius walked a few steps over to the north edge of the platform, and came back with a look of concern on his face. 'It's worse than that,' he said. 'Ennius warned me that the substance in his fireballs burns with such intensity that when the fires join together they create their own wind, and that in turn feeds the flames. The houses are mostly built of stone and mud brick, but the frames are timber and the fires are already leaping from house to house. When they reach the old quarter below us with all those bodies for fuel, the fire will burn even more ferociously. Ennius calls it a firestorm, and that's what's happening now. Our soldiers will have to be content with looting what they can find as they leave. We don't have much time.'

Fabius glanced beyond the blackened façade of the temple and saw what he meant. It was a different kind of wind, a sucking, swirling motion in the smoke that seemed to tumble down the side of the platform like a whirlpool. Where it disappeared he could see a red glow in the city street as intense as the glow inside the temple; the leading edge of the fire was advancing along the street at frightening speed, engulfing more and more buildings as it went. Scipio turned to Gulussa and Hippolyta. 'Go down and order the trumpeters to sound the retreat. The legions must evacuate the city immediately, marching back to the harbours. Send messages to Ennius and the naval commander to draw all ships further offshore. Brutus, join them.'

'There are horses from my cavalry without riders after the fighting,' Hippolyta said. 'I will find mounts for us.'

'Go now,' Scipio said. Fabius watched them rush down the steps, leaving only Polybius and Scipio by his side. He looked at the firestorm. Carthage would destroy itself, just as its leader had destroyed himself and his people. He turned to Polybius. 'I remember what you once read to me from Homer's *Iliad*, the words of the goddess Athena. *The day shall come when sacred Troy will fall, and king and people shall perish all.*'

Polybius looked at the scene of devastation in front of them, and then at Scipio. 'But the fall of Carthage owes nothing to the utterances of a god. It was a Roman feat of arms, and the feat of not just one Scipio, but two. Today, your grandfather can rest easy in Elysium. When I come to write my history of this war, people will forget about Achilles and Troy and will instead read about the two generals named Scipio Africanus, and the fall of Carthage.'

Scipio raised an eyebrow at his friend. 'If I ever give you time to write it.'

'The war is over, my friend.'

Scipio said nothing, but looked across the sea to the north-east. Fabius followed his gaze, trying to read his thoughts. *This war is over.* Some day soon, perhaps already, another city would fall, the final Greek stronghold of Corinth, and Metellus would stand on that acropolis too, scanning the devastation and feeling the same rush in his veins as he stared into the future.

Fabius remembered the words of the Sibyl, words that she had told him when he had seen her alone, words that he had never uttered to Scipio: she had told him that both Scipio and

Metellus would stand over fallen cities, as Achilles had done at Troy. It was their destiny, and the destiny of Rome. But then Fabius remembered what else she had said, to him alone, when she had beckoned him back into the cave and touched him with her wizened finger, her breath caressing his ear like an exhalation from all of history.

He mouthed the words to himself now.

One of them will rule, and one will fall.

Polybius had been watching him, but they both looked down as Hippolyta came bounding back up the steps. Halfway to the top she stopped. 'I have horses waiting below, Scipio,' she shouted. 'We must ride.'

She turned to go back down. Polybius gestured for Scipio to move, pointing to the fire rushing towards the temple platform from the north, and then began to clatter down the steps after Hippolyta. Fabius lingered for a moment with Scipio, staring one last time. He took a deep breath, tasting the dust from the desert again, the acrid reek of burning, the smell of blood.

He felt exhilarated.

Carthage was not the end. It was the beginning.

He knew what was to come.

Total War.

Author's Note

My fascination with Scipio Aemilianus and the siege of Carthage began when I was an undergraduate at the University of Bristol and was fortunate to be taught Roman Republican history by Brian Warmington, author of one of the seminal scholarly books on the subject (*Carthage*, Penguin, 1964); it was then greatly spurred when I was a PhD student and postdoctoral research fellow at Cambridge University and took part in the UNESCO 'Save Carthage' project, an international effort to excavate and record as much of ancient Carthage as possible in the face of modern development.

The main focus of the British mission was the ancient harbours, where the most astonishing discovery was the Punic shipsheds surrounding the circular harbour – sheds that proved to date not to the heyday of Carthage in the third century BC but to the years leading up to 146 BC, showing that she was rebuilding her navy and proof that Cato had been right all along to warn Rome of the threat. Teams of underwater archaeologists, including an expedition under my direction, revealed much about the outer harbour, so that my description of the wharf where Scipio and Fabius secretly dock in the *Diana* is based on my own extensive study of the submerged foundations. One of the most exciting discoveries made during my time at Carthage was the channel that linked the landlocked harbours to the sea. While our digger was excavating many metres down into the black anoxic layer at the bottom of the ancient harbour, showing that we had found the gap between the outer quays that marked the entrance, I stood at the very spot where I have imagined Fabius seeing the *lembos* making its breakout during the siege.

Close by the harbours, at the 'Tophet', excavations revealed numerous child cremation burials, some of them very probably the victims of child sacrifice as recounted by the Roman sources. The first-century BC historian Diodorus Siculus (20.14) describes a great bronze god in which children were rolled down while still alive to a roasting place beneath. Further up, on the Byrsa hill, in the 'Punic quarter' that I describe in the novel, I have been literally arm-deep in destruction debris from the siege, excavating through charred building material, smashed pottery, human bone and Roman ballista balls dating from those catastrophic final days in 146 BC. It is rare in archaeology to make discoveries that can be linked so clearly to historic events, even ones as momentous as the siege of 146 BC, and my experiences at Carthage led me to many years of thinking about the relationship between historical and archaeological evidence as well as giving me a vivid personal backdrop to the story in this novel.

The Nature of Roman Historical Evidence

No eyewitness accounts survive of any of the historical events described in this novel. The Battle of Pydna in 168 BC and the triumph that followed are chiefly known from an account written some two hundred and fifty years later, Plutarch's life of Lucius Aemilius Paullus, father of Scipio Aemilianus; yet those few hundred lines make Pydna one of the best-documented battles of the second century BC (*Aemilius Paullus*, 16–23). Although Plutarch was writing so long after the event, similar details, such as the account of the riderless horse galloping between the lines, are found in the surviving references to the battle by the first-century BC historian Livy (44.40–42), who probably had access to a contemporary account by Polybius.

The siege of Intercatia in Spain and Scipio Aemilianus' role in it are known from a few lines by Appian, who is also our main source for the siege of Carthage; he was writing almost three hundred years after the events he describes. Plutarch and Appian relied on contemporary accounts that are now lost – notably the volumes of Polybius' *Histories* for this period – but there can be no certainty of how reliably or impartially those earlier sources were used, at a time when historical scholarship as we know it did not yet exist. Moreover, the works of Plutarch, Appian and the other ancient historians survive only through medieval copies, adding a further layer of uncertainty to their use as source material. The manuscripts often contained errors of transcription, as well as omissions, 'interpretations' and embellishments that reflect the agenda of the monks who carried out the copying.

In studying ancient military history at the level of battle plans and tactics, these limitations of the source material cannot be stressed too strongly. The siege and destruction of Carthage, the culmination of the Punic Wars, was one of the pivotal events of history, as important as the Napoleonic Wars and the Battle of Waterloo in our times. Having to rely almost exclusively on Appian is as if Waterloo were known solely from one account, about ten pages long, with no footnotes, no source references and no illustrations, written by one amateur historian two hundred years after the event (in fact, of course, Appian was writing even longer than that after the siege of Carthage).

The comparison is even more stark in the case of our knowledge of Roman military commanders. Any biography of Napoleon or Wellington represents the distillation of a small library's worth of source material, including autobiographical writings and personal correspondence, eyewitness accounts, military records, maps and plans. Even so, uncertainties remain about their characters, their motivations and the backdrop to their strategic and tactical thinking. In the case of Scipio Aemilianus, a figure of similar historical significance, the sum total of 'facts' about him would fill little more than one page, and a modern biography is therefore not a distillation but rather an analysis of those few pieces of information, including expert translation of the original Greek and Latin texts, an evaluation of the reliability of that source material and an attempt to put it into a wider historical context.

These limitations show just how much scope there is for historical fiction, and how the credibility of any reconstruction – whether historical or fictional – is less about replicating the apparent 'facts' than about understanding the uncertainties of that information and the necessity of a critical approach to it. The line between historical speculation and historical fiction is easily crossed, with archaeology increasingly allowing a fresh evaluation of the written sources as well as an independent basis for new pictures of the past.

The Ancient Historical Sources

The great historian of the second century BC was Polybius, friend and mentor of Scipio Aemilianus and an important character in this novel. His work provided a unique eyewitness account of many of the events of this period, and his treatise on the army was the first detailed account of the Roman military at a time when it was not yet professional. Unfortunately, only about half of his *Histories* survive, none for the main events of this novel and all of them as medieval copies of ancient texts, although some later Greek and Latin historians cited passages of Polybius or wrote accounts that were probably heavily reliant on works of his that are now lost. As well as Livy, writing in the first century BC, the most important of these 'secondary' sources is the second-century AD Greek historian Appian, whose *Libyca* contains a detailed description of the siege of Carthage that is probably a reliable paraphrasing of Polybius' original account. Without Appian, the mute stones of Carthage might tell a very different story, and an account of the final assault such as the one in this novel could no longer be based on a framework of probable historical reality.

Most ancient historians if pressed would have subscribed to what has been called the 'big man' view of history, in which powerful individuals, rather than sweeping tides of change, were primarily responsible for altering the course of events and the world that the historian saw around him, for better or for worse. Admired individuals such as Scipio Aemilianus were not only extolled for their place in history – in his case, for what he achieved, but equally importantly for what he chose not to do – but were also held up as moral exemplars, sometimes even fictionally. An example of the latter is the first-century BC author Cicero's eulogy of Scipio in his fictional dialogue *De Oratore* and also in the *Somnium Scipionis*, the 'Dream of Scipio', a work that may have been a piece of moralizing fiction on Cicero's part but could also have been based on a lost account of a real dream experience, perhaps recounted by Polybius. Another moralizer – but more of a historian than Cicero – was the late first to early second-century AD Greek writer Plutarch, whose life of Scipio's father Aemilius Paullus provides snippets of information about Scipio's early life and his first battle experience at Pydna in 168 BC, as well as a vivid picture of the triumph celebrated after Aemilius Paullus returned to Rome the following year.

In addition to these sources, epigraphical research – the study of inscriptions on tombs and other monuments – helps us to reconstruct the genealogy of the great patrician families of this period, often meaning that we know their names and something of their interrelationships but very little else about them. The lives of common soldiers such as the fictional Fabius are hardly known at all, except from rare tomb inscriptions and occasional mentions by the ancient authors when they had performed a particular feat of valour, or some other notable act.

Where there is enough material to build up the outlines of a biography, we have to be careful not always to take what is written at face value. For Cicero, an avid republican, Scipio Aemilianus was admirable for his restraint, for not leading a coup in Rome after his victory at Carthage and not going for world domination; for Polybius, Scipio was a friend but also an exemplar of the Roman virtues that Polybius so admired, leading him perhaps to emphasize some character traits over others. As with Victorian accounts of top generals of the day – men such as Lord Kitchener – we have to be wary of eulogy and hagiography. By far the best modern collation and critical analysis of the source material on Scipio Aemilianus is by the late Professor Alan Astin, of Queen's University, Belfast, who memorably described Scipio as 'a quasi-autocrat who, but for his own reluctance, could have been a *Princeps* a century before Augustus' (*Scipio Aemilianus*, Oxford University Press, 1967, p. vii).

It is worth stressing how little we know with certainty from written evidence for this period. Almost all of our 'facts' come from authors living several centuries after the events they describe, and much of that in anecdotes, sayings and phrases of a few sentences or less. There are yawning gaps in our knowledge; for example, the years between Aemilius Paullus' triumph in 167 BC and the start of the second Celtiberian war in 154 BC are hardly documented at all, and almost a complete blank in the life of Scipio Aemilianus. This does not necessarily mean that nothing of much interest happened in those years, but instead represents the vagaries of documentary survival. Even an author as important as Polybius, who maintained a high reputation throughout antiquity and was still being read in the Byzantine court of Constantinople, only survives in partial manuscripts that represent less than half of his known works. Other historians could come in and out of fashion and be lost in obscurity, their works discarded and only known through anecdote and quotes by later authors, often of dubious reliability. Since every book in antiquity had to be painstakingly copied by hand, even popular authors might be represented by only a few dozen extant copies of their books, stored in the private libraries of their patrons or in the public libraries of the main cities; most of those were destroyed in time, most notoriously through the burning of the great library at Alexandria in late antiquity.

A huge future excitement may be the discovery of lost original writings from this period, perhaps in fragments of papyrus reused as mummy wrapping in Egypt or in the remains of ancient libraries themselves. One of the most remarkable discoveries in Roman archaeology has been the 'Villa of the Papyri' at Herculaneum in Italy, containing a room full of scrolls that were carbonized after Vesuvius erupted and buried the town in pyroclastic flow in AD 79. The scrolls mainly contained the writings of an obscure Greek philosopher, but they suggest what may lie undiscovered in one of the other wealthy patrician houses still buried beneath the slopes of the volcano. Such a find could revolutionize our knowledge of ancient history and flesh out the reality of those lost years in the second century BC, but meanwhile we have enough surviving material to allow well-informed speculation consistent with everything else we know about this period, including the increasing body of archaeological evidence.

Scipio Aemilianus Africanus

The sum total of knowledge about Scipio prior to his appointment to the Senate in 152 BC would fill perhaps half a page, yet even so provides more detail about his early life than is available for most other Romans of this period. We know something of Scipio's education and character from the few surviving fragments about him by his teacher and friend Polybius, and from references in later authors who relied on Polybius and other contemporary accounts now lost. Plutarch, for example, tells us how Aemilius Paullus sought to educate his sons 'not only in the native and ancestral discipline in which he himself had been trained, but also, and in greater ardour, in that of the Greeks. For not only the grammarians and philosophers and rhetoricians, but also the modellers and painters, the overseers of horses and dogs, and the teachers of the art of hunting, by whom the young men were surrounded, were Greeks' (*Aemilius Paullus*, 6.8). After the Battle of Pydna, Scipio was allowed to take what he liked from the Macedonian Royal Library, and Cicero tells us that Scipio 'always had in his hands' Xenophon's *Cyropaedia*, an account of the life of Cyrus the Great of Persia and his rise to power. Cicero also tells us how as a young man Scipio was eager to hear the discourses of several Athenian philosophers who had come to Rome (*De Oratore*, 2.154).

Scipio's absorption of Greek culture was undoubtedly shaped and restrained by Polybius – himself, of course, a Greek but by no means an uncritical philhellene. Polybius' admiration for the Roman character is revealed in his account of Scipio's reputation for temperance, at that time something that marked him out in Rome, owing to 'the moral deterioration of most of the youths. For some had abandoned themselves to amours with boys, others to prostitutes and musical pleasures and drinking bouts . . . Scipio, however, setting himself to pursue the opposite course of conduct . . . established a universal reputation for self-discipline and temperance' (Polybius, 31.25). Polybius' attitude towards history was of a practical bent, seeing how it could be used to further present-day campaigns and strategies, and Scipio's passion for the *Cyropaedia* suggests that his interest in Greek literature was driven by the same imperative. It is possible, therefore, to see a young man strongly schooled in the *mos maiorum*, the Roman ways of the ancestors, and open to new influences from Greece, yet with those influences mediated by Polybius in such a way that they reinforced the Roman virtues of honour and fidelity that Polybius himself so admired.

The image of a serious and somewhat austere young man is offset by his passion for hunting, something that Scipio shared with Polybius, and by his exceptional prowess as a warrior. Following the Battle of Pydna, he spent time hunting in the Macedonian Royal Forest, given to him by his father as a victory present. At Pydna he had distinguished himself in battle, fighting deep into the Macedonian phalanx and then returning from the pursuit 'with two or three companions, covered with the blood of the enemies he had slain, having been, like a young hound of noble breed, carried away by the uncontrollable pleasure of the victory' (Plutarch, *Aemilius Paullus*, 22.7–8). When he is next heard of in battle, some seventeen years later in Spain, we are told that he killed an enemy chieftain who had challenged him to single combat, and earned the *corona muralis* for being the first on the wall in the assault on the fortress of Intercatia; some two years later in Africa, still only a military tribune, he earned the even more coveted *corona obsidionalis* for rescuing some Roman troops from near-certain annihilation by a Carthaginian force (Appian, *Iberica* 53 and *Libyca* 102–104; Livy, *Periocha* 48-9 31.28.12–29).

It seems likely that Scipio and his contemporaries would have learned basic fighting skills together while they were still boys in Rome, under the guidance of veterans entrusted with their training in weapons. Whether or not such an 'academy' would have provided instruction in the higher arts of war – in strategy and tactics – is unknown, but the concerns of some of the older generation about the military preparedness of future officers, as well as the availability of Greek professors who could teach military history – some of them, like Polybius, former soldiers with combat experience – suggests the possibility. Polybius would certainly have been well suited to the task, not only because of his background but also because of his fascination with all things military, including the 'Polybius square' and telescope for battlefield signalling (Polybius, 10.45–6). Others in the Senate, possibly the majority, would probably have opposed such training, fearing the professionalization of an officer corps, so I have imagined the academy operating discreetly behind the walls of the Gladiator School, a place where weapons training and practice on live victims could have been conducted. In Rome today, the visible ruins of the Gladiator School beside the Colosseum date to a later period, but the archaeological evidence suggests that there may have been an earlier training ground on this site to the south of the Forum in the second century BC.

The relationship between Scipio and Polybius was one of the great friendships of antiquity, one that nevertheless was complicated by the fact that Polybius was, strictly speaking, a prisoner of the Romans, a Greek nobleman obliged by circumstances to accept a request to be mentor to the younger Scipio in Rome. Scipio had an elder brother, Fabius (a name resulting from his adoption into the *gens* Fabii), also a pupil of Polybius; I have used his *praenomen* and his relationship with Polybius in the creation of my fictional legionary Fabius Petronius Secundus, the bodyguard and companion of Scipio whose relationship with him in the novel is in some ways akin to that of brothers.

I have speculated that Polybius was in Rome by 168 BC and was present on the Roman side at the Battle of Pydna, so had surrendered himself as a captive somewhat earlier than most of his contemporaries, consistent perhaps with his admiration for Rome. He certainly became a great proponent of Rome, and found in Scipio a young man who fell outside the usual parameters, sensitized by the opprobrium that may have been heaped on him by his adoptive family in the *gens* Scipiones for his failure to show due interest in the law courts and social niceties of Rome. Like Polybius, he was bookish and intellectual but also a passionate hunter and warrior, one who above all relished the idea of war and a destiny that was to lead him in 146 BC to stand astride the walls of Carthage and contemplate the momentous possibilities that lay ahead of him and of Rome.

Much of the account in this novel of the final hours of Punic Carthage draws on Appian, particularly the fighting and slaughter in the old quarter of the city beneath the Byrsa. As for the fate of Hasdrubal, Appian tells us that he surrendered to Scipio, but that his wife slew her children and flung them and herself into the fire of the temple, 'as Hasdrubal should have died himself' (Appian, *Libyca*, 131); I have taken this cue from Appian as the basis for the final apocalyptic scene in the novel.

The coin used as an illustration in this novel is a beautiful example of the only Roman issue known to date from 146 BC, as contemplated by Scipio in chapter 22; you can see a film of me handling this actual coin at www.davidgibbins.com, where you can also find more facts behind the fiction and imagery related to my archaeological work at Carthage and other sites mentioned in the novel.

About the Author

David Gibbins is a *New York Times* and *Sunday Times* bestselling author whose novels have sold almost three million copies and are published in thirty languages. He is an academic archaeologist by training, and his novels reflect his extensive experience investigating ancient sites around the world, both on land and underwater.

He was born in Canada to English parents and grew up there, in New Zealand and in England. After taking a first-class honours degree in Ancient Mediterranean Studies from the University of Bristol he completed a PhD in archaeology at the University of Cambridge, where he was a research scholar of Corpus Christi College and a postdoctoral fellow in the Faculty of Classics. Before becoming a full-time author he worked for eight years as a university lecturer, teaching Roman archaeology and art, ancient history and maritime archaeology. As well as fiction, he is the author of more than fifty scholarly publications, including articles in *Antiquity*, *World Archaeology*, *International Journal of Nautical Archaeology*, *New Scientist* and other journals, in addition to monographs and edited volumes, including *Shipwrecks* (Routledge, 2001).

He has researched and excavated extensively in the Mediterranean region, from Turkey and Israel to Greece and Crete, Italy and Sicily, Spain and North Africa, as well as in the British Isles and North America. Over the years his work has been supported among others by the British Academy, the British Schools of Archaeology in Rome and Jerusalem, the British Institute at Ankara and the Society of Antiquaries of London, and by a Fellowship from the Winston Churchill Memorial Trust. For two seasons he worked at the ancient site of Carthage, leading an expedition to investigate offshore harbour remains. He learned to dive at the age of fifteen in Canada, and underwater archaeology has been one of his main passions; he has led expeditions to investigate shipwreck sites all over the world, including Roman wrecks off Sicily and elsewhere in the Mediterranean, as well as off the British Isles. He was an adjunct professor of the American Institute of Nautical Archaeology while he worked for two seasons on an ancient Greek shipwreck off the coast of Turkey.

He has a long-standing fascination with military history, partly stemming from an extensive military background in his own family. His wide-ranging interest in arms and armour has focused in recent years on collecting and shooting nineteenth-century British and East India Company firearms, as well as making and shooting reproduction American flintlock longrifles on the wilderness tract in Canada where he does most of his writing. His military interests are reflected in his previous novels, including Roman campaigning in the east (*The Tiger Warrior*), Victorian warfare in India and the Sudan (*The Tiger Warrior, Pharaoh*), and the Second World War (*The Mask of Troy*).

More biographical material is found on his website: www.davidgibbins.com.

Antestius coin

Photographs of the obverse and reverse of a denarius by the moneyer Antestius, minted in 146 BC, have been used on the title pages of each Part of the novel. The obverse shows the goddess Roma in a helmet, and the reverse shows two armed horsemen and a dog with the inscription ROMA beneath.

TOTAL WAR
ROME II

IF YOU WOULD LIKE TO WAGE YOUR OWN
WAR AGAINST CARTHAGE, BUILD AN EMPIRE
AND COMMAND THE MOST INCREDIBLE WAR
MACHINE OF THE ANCIENT WORLD, VISIT
WWW.TOTALWAR.COM FOR MORE INFORMATION
ON THE AWARD-WINNING GAME.